Between Two Suns
The Berean Experience

Omavi & Asali Publishing
P.O. Box 143
Piqua, OH 45356
www.omaviasalipublishing.com

Book cover layout by Lawrence E. Hamilton Jr., Nikki J. DeLaet, and Drew J. Rochotte at Eagle Printing & Graphics, LLC.

Painting on front and back cover by Linda S. Hamilton.

Graphic designer Nikki J. DeLaet.

Photo on back of Loveland Predestinarian Baptist Church, 1926, supplied by Annabelle Smith Rickman.

Thanks to Mr. Shannon H. Wilson for his help in research at the Special Collections & Archives at Berea College.

Supplied picture of Cynthia Ross by Cynthia McNeil.

Supplied picture of Henry Allen Laine by William Holland.

ISBN: 978-0-9824721-1-8

Writer's Note

In writing Lucy's life story, **Between Two Suns,** we have tried to follow the actual sequence of events as truely as possible, with a few minor exceptions that might hinder the flow of the story.

Most of the names are factual, as well as places and locations.

Henry Allen Laine's work is presented here as it appears in his book **Footprints**, which is a culmination of his life's work. It is thought-provoking poetry, reflecting the time period in which he lived as well as his insightful view of human nature.

Each chapter of **Between Two Suns** begins with a verse and autograph entry written by friends and fellow students of Cynthia Ross while at Berea College. All of these are authentic, as well as the newspaper excerpts.

The title of the book came from the explanation given to the author, Mr. Larry Hamilton, by his grandmother about the flight of a relative, John Hamilton. He fled Virginia, fearful for his life, because he had retaliated when something offensive was said or done to his mother. Because of this hasty departure, in which he had little time to ready his affairs, it was said he was forced to leave Virginia *between two suns.*

This can also be applied as the hope connected to a rising sun, a new day. In a sense, a setting sun brings on darkness, which is what settled upon Berea with the passage of the Day Law. It was not until 1950 that the light shone again upon the campus.

When writing of these people who lived long ago, we can only imagine their personalities, and their hopes and dreams, but we do know, in reality, they were no different than we are. In that same respect, we all have hearts and souls that crave that inexpressible inner peace, love, and joy given to creation by our God.

This work is dedicated to:

Our merciful Father and our sovereign Redeemer

My mon cheri of twenty years!

*Mom and Dad B: Happy 50th! That's inspiration
in itself! Thank you for your interest and enthusiasm
always, and our tribe of 47!*

*Mr. Larry Hamilton: A thank you toast for number II!
You have left a life-long impact on me.*

*Mrs. Peggy Thoma: A thank you for all your editing
skills. We appreciate all the time you gave to us.*

*To my own Nar"Sis": Thanks for all your help.
We eagerly await your little angel!*

C. D.

Onyx waves sparkled along a swath of moonlight. They cradled effortlessly a form, now still and shrouded, and rocked it to a watery lullaby. Although dark as night, the river's water had no more a malignant nature than the moon, which strove to uncover the hidden secret of the river. Its inhabitants–crusty barnacles clinging stubbornly to piers and surly fish that dwelt beneath–permeated the air with their incense. The Ohio River's dark and dank waters seemed a natural camouflage.

Docked to the nearby land, The Virginia–a steamer from the Pittsburg-Cincinnati packet line–gave no notice to the "floater" which lolled beside her. Majestic and beautiful, she bobbed serenely as if unaware of what evil occurred within a moon's span. The neutral waves that surrounded her were natured to voice no transgressions.

The diamond path that the moon revealed made the buoyant form appear at relative peace, gently carried on the swells, hoisted from its watery grave, and warped toward an Eternity.

And yet…the inky waters of the Ohio, a faithful scape - goat, were not dark enough to hide the color of the drifting body, nor the unholy deed which had deposited it there.

Prologue
1920

"Mammy, drink your tea. It's getting cold." Esther motioned toward the cup and saucer on the table beside her grandmother's rocking chair. It took persuasion to get her grandmother to take nourishment.

"Harrumph. Why didn't you get me coffee? Always have liked coffee better than tea. Think you'd know that." Mammy's mouth relaxed into a droop, her aged wrinkles coming to rest upon it, giving her eyes an owlish look.

"Coffee's no good for you at naptime, Mammy." Esther bit off the thread to the button she had just sewn on. Now maybe Mammy would realize she had other suitable dresses besides the old gray one she was always attired in.

"There, Mammy, you're ready to hit the town now." She laid the dress on the back of the sofa and studied the old woman. "You want to nap?" She knew what to expect with that question.

It seemed to old Mammy that she was always being ordered around, though in a sugar-coated way. "They did right calling you Esther. You know what your name is in Hebrew? Hadassy! That's what it is! Rhymes with sassy! That's you," Mammy grumbled.

Esther strove to keep her smile in check. "I think it's *Hadassah* in the Bible." She moved near her grandmother. Mammy was all "spit and sputter". "Really, Mammy, I'm sorry I bother you so. But I want to take care of you. Haven't you taken care of six children in your lifetime? And think of all you've done for us grandchildren! It's our turn to look after you, which means no coffee at naptime!"

"I weren't gonna nap, girl. I was gonna tell you a story but–" As Mammy paused and fingered the gray worn house-dress, she suddenly couldn't remember what she wanted to say.

It had all been there seconds before–like a beautiful painting in her mind but with a smudge in the landscape. More and more often her brain failed her, just like her limbs had; she was not sure which was more disconcerting. Old age was becoming an exacting mistress.

Esther brightened, "But what? I'd love to hear a story." Mammy frowned at her. Of all her offspring, Esther had always shown an interest. She probably bored all the others, which explained why they didn't come around more often. She trained her focus on Esther's patient face and softened. The girl looked like her mother but acted a lot like Narciss. *Oh, Narciss, I miss you.*

Esther wondered at the workings in the old woman's mind. What did Mammy think about so often? What hurts did her curt manner hide? Now Mammy's eyes trailed Esther's hairline and dropped to her chin. Her voice broke forth, more a croak than a fluid sound, "You happy, Granddaughter?"

Esther was taken aback. Mammy rarely touched on the present or did so as intensely as she did now. "'Course I'm happy, Mammy. What's not to be happy about?" She smiled to appear more honest than her words were.

Mammy snorted. "You don't fool me, child." With a shaky hand, she gripped her lukewarm teacup and sipped. Wiping the dribble that quivered on the end of her chin, she spoke. "You children all got freedom. But it's the same freedom I had fifty-sumpin' years ago. Twentieth century and Jim Crow laws everywhere, even in the North." She was disgusted and let it show. "My mama would have said, 'Be glad, Lucy-girl, for what you got. Stop wantin' more!' But I always, deep inside this creaky heart, wanted more, Esther. Not for myself, but for my children and their babies."

A strong light sprung forth in the watery black depths of Lucy's old eyes. They gave her a strange look, alarming Esther, so that she leaned back on the heels of her feet, allowing her knees to rest on the cheap rag rug. "Mammy, maybe you should–"

"Esther, child, you look at me and listen. You know

what I never stopped wanting? Not just freedom. I've had that in different ways, 'cept the way my soul's gonna have it when I get to the River Jordan." Her voice had an urgent quality now. "I wanted charity to be on this earth. I'm not talkin' about givin' goods to help poor souls, but charity like the Bible speaks of–the kind that gives us worth. You know what I'm saying?"

Old Lucy closed her tired eyes, and quoted rather imperfectly: "Charity suffers long and is kind, charity envieth not, charity vaunteth not, isn't puffed up. Does not behave unseemly, seeketh not her own, is not provoked, thinketh no evil. Rejoiceth not in iniquity, but rejoiceth in the truth." She creaked open first one eyelid, then the other, to peer at her granddaughter.

Esther was surprised. Her grandmother was sharper than she had realized. "Mammy, you can still recite scripture! That's a blessing." She studied her mammy's form. "What can I do for you, to make you feel better?"

Lucy was fading, but not so much that she couldn't realize how the younger set wanted to fix an old one's discomforts, thinking somehow this made everything better. That maybe a cushion or a shawl here, or a rub and a cup of tea there, made all things well in their sight! As if material things could mend the heart! But she meant well, that granddaughter of hers.

"What can you do for me?" Lucy pondered her thoughts but could not give form to the words that floated like a haunting melody from yesterday across her mind.

And then, the reason and core of her unrest, rose and she grasped the memory and wrestled it from its musty cedar chest of mothballs. Pulling herself up to the edge of the rocker by its rounded, worn maple arms, Lucy rested there on the cane bottom chair. Her voice rasped out, a slight bitterness detectable. "My boy, Henry, never was afforded such charity. He wasn't given the respect a human is worth, you know. That's what I long for. Just for humankind to share a little charity with one another. My boy would have lived then." Lucy sighed, a sound like a dove cooing out over a darkening twilight.

Esther touched her grandmother's knee. "Mammy, your

boy, my Uncle Henry, died a long time ago. They say he worked on one of those old fancy steamers, never getting boat sick or anything. Then one night he disappeared, and they found him floating in the river. He had sleep-walked off the edge and plumb drowned. My, you must have had a hard time dealing with that. What a burden for you, Mammy." She enfolded the old woman with both arms. When she pulled back, Mammy sat dry-eyed and calm.

"Esther, I know what you've been told. When you're older, you think on it a spell. A bird with wings, it's gonna fly, ain't it? But you break those wings, and that's the end of that bird. Ain't that so?"

Esther watched as a hazy kind of gloom descended upon her grandmother. It came like a cloud blocking sunshine and first settled in her eyes. Her features slowly relaxed and the soft wrinkles lay gently, one atop the other, like gentle feathers in a bed of down.

Lucy was tired from the trail of thoughts that straggled back across the years. She was exhausted from the emotions that had twisted through her rickety heart, and weary of the hard, unyielding seat of her rocker. "I'll nap now, Esther." Her spunk had evaporated, tunneling back through time where it had originated. Seemingly, only a feeble worn-out shell of an old woman remained. Lucy rose unsteadily as she reached for her cane lying atop the table. Once secured, she looked at her granddaughter, who had risen to assist her.

"Tell me what the rest of the verse is, Esther. You know, my favorite part."

Esther raked her mind for her grandmother's meaning and, as it surfaced, recited much like a schoolchild, "Beareth all things, believeth all things, hopeth all things, endureth all things. Charity never faileth–"

"No more," Lucy said, one hand upheld to ward off the words. She hobbled off to rest, the last of her granddaughter's words ringing in her ears. *Never faileth?* Not in her lifetime, not *here.* Lucy sank onto the bed. Curling up like a limp ragdoll, Lucy would do what she had done for seven decades–endure that which she must endure–until the last trump was sounded. If only it would come quickly, and sooner rather than later. And just maybe, she earnestly hoped, it would come swiftly like a whirlwind, between the rising of two suns.

> "A few more suns shall set
>   O'er these dark hills of time,
> And we shall be where suns are not,
>   A far serener clime."

Chapter One

Miss Ross,
Save thy toiling, spare thy treasure,
All I ask is friendship's pleasure.
Let the shining orb lie darkling,
Bring no gem in lustre sparkling.
Your classmate,
Maggie S. Cooksery
Berea, Ky 3-9-1888

Magnificent. That was the exclamation that broke the surface of Cynthia's mind. Each brick upon rubicund brick of the massive building rose magnificently before her and Cousin Henry.

"Oh, Henry Allen! Can you believe we're really here? Finally! Our dream come true." Cynthia said it, her hands outswept, with such gushing satisfaction that she failed to observe Cousin Henry's negligence toward her enthusiasm.

Henry Allen tugged at the collar of his tight shirt and forced a swallow downward. "Yeah, we're finally here." His gaze omitted the architecture but was instead riveted on a young coed who swept by.

Cynthia happened to notice. "Henry Allen!" she scolded. "You're here to learn, remember? Think how hard you had to work just to get here! You can gawk at females somewhere else!"

Henry patted Cynthia's arm. "Now cousin, don't fret yourself over me. I'm going to learn plenty. I've got all the time in the world for learning stuff."

"*Stuff?* That's what you think! You've only got two semesters to get serious."

"I do my best work after making observations. I've been

1

told I'm scientifically-minded." He was anything but the sort.

Cynthia raised her delicate eyebrows on her lady-like face. "Uh-huh. So you think. Come on. We'll be late." Cynthia Anne Ross entered the revered building with her cousin, Henry Allan Laine, in tow.

The *magnificent* Berea College, in 1880, was a rising sun in summer's bloom to its students. Scholars of crossed heritage and mixed gender studied together in a contemporary harmony. This was Reverend John G. Fee's vision, when, in 1855, he created Berea College. Rising from unholy ground, a little wooden one-room schoolhouse adorned the 10-acre lot given to John Fee by Cassius M. Clay. On Sabbaths, it converted into a church from which Rev. Fee preached gospel truths. And here, where truth was prevalent, the story of Rev. Fee was obscured until, in time, his legacy prevailed and was brought to light.

Cynthia had heard of John G. Fee since a babe on her mother's lap. He had been an "angel" to her mama and grandmother, Angelina, on their escape from slavery as well as being their benefactor, and Mama's shepherd during her youth. No wonder Cynthia Anne Ross was destined to attend the college that he strove to create and maintain in Berea, Kentucky. Cynthia's five brothers would not go. It was like a parable in the Bible Cynthia had read of. One brother had married a wife and could not come, one brother had bought a piece of ground and must see to it, and one had yokes of oxen to prove. *"I pray have me excused."* Well, not really, but imaginative Cynthia did not mind that the lot had fallen to her. She had once bested her brothers at tree climbing; hence she was perfectly able to be schooled as well as they were. With a teacher's certificate in mind, she was able to forego the snare of an undesirable prospect, who had, in his eager way, singled her out for matrimony.

John G. Fee's history was not lost to Berea's students. Eventually his autobiography would further educate outside regions. Here is what Cynthia and Cousin Henry had learned:

In Kentucky, in 1809 (the same year and state Abraham Lincoln was born), a gentlemen farmer and slave-owner, wel - comed a son, John G., into his colossal antebellum home. As the boy grew, he disappointed his father by choosing a different path. He attended a theological seminary whose teachings led him to believe his upbringing was in danger of the Judgment. From this realization, John took the gospel of "impartial love" to mean that the Almighty was no respecter of persons and had made "one blood all peoples of the earth", which became Berea's ardent slogan.

His slave-owning daddy, dismayed with his son, dis - owned him, severing his name from the family tree. As a black sheep, John G. was further persecuted by his native homeland. Neighboring mobs physically escorted John from the state, where he would return periodically to his commission, a hare among hounds. There was a work to do and John courageously attended to it, bringing Berea to a Kentucky where social prej - udice and moral corruption had attempted with its darkness to smother the flame of righteousness.

Cynthia always felt small when she heard the story. How many others had valiantly labored to chisel the narrow bands into wider paths for their descendents? In Cynthia's own family, her parents, Aunt Narciss, and Grandma Angelina were such ones who had bravely forged a way, a first step for her people since coming to America.

Cynthia had come to the end of the hallway. She turned toward the admissions office, releasing Henry to his own two feet. He settled his suit on his shoulders where Cynthia had accosted it while towing him along. That girl appeared a slender mite, but she was unaccustomedly strong. *Headstrong*, mused Henry. Every time he sang the hymn, "A Mighty Fortress," it conjured images of a capable Annie (as he affectionately called Cynthia Anne), forcing him to ask the Lord's pardon. She had his good at heart, *but really*, he was a *man* now, and if he had wanted a mama, he would have stayed at home.

Cynthia was talking to the lady behind the counter,

pulling out her reticule and paying her fees. She finished and smoothed her dress of gray cotton lawn. "Your turn, Henry Allen."

Henry stepped forward and listened to the woman. "This is a list of the fees you must pay before classes start. It includes your textbooks. You did want a college preparatory course, correct?"

Henry nodded and stuffed the papers in his suit coat. "Thanks. I'll look these over and get back to you." He turned away, grateful to find Cynthia studying the official-looking wall plaques adorning the hallway. This time it was he who grabbed a startled Cynthia's arm, propelling her away from the scowling admission's lady. "Come on, Annie. Let's go see what there is to do for a little fun around here."

Dear Mama and Daddy,

School is all I hoped it would be. I am adjusting well to the curriculum; so far it is not too hard. My teachers are all nice–well nearly all of them. Mr. Beeson, the math teacher, is very demanding and strict. (No Daddy–that is not to his credit. He's never even been in the army!)

The students are all kind, and I've made fast friends with several girls. My housekeeper, Miss Leona Riddler, is efficient and dedicated. (You would approve, Mama.)

I am dismayed Cousin Henry cannot attend with me this semester. It has left me bereft! Henry must secure the funds and join me in the New Year. He simply must!

Give my regards to Willie, Henry, James, and John. Tell Dee he can have my place at the table by the stove, but only until I come home.

> *Love to you all.*
> *Your devoted daughter,*
> *Cynthia Anne*

Chapter Two

Dear Annie,
Little minds are tamed and subdued by
misfortunes, but great minds rise above it.
Yours respectfully,
James D. Walker
Berea, Ky 5-17-1888

Allen Ross trudged home from the sawmill, an invisible mantle of gloom wrapped about him. His feet met the road with considerable thuds, like he was pounding out his frustration. Allen himself did not even notice that his body language tattled on him.

Once he would have been enthused that he wore hard-sole work boots. And that he had a good job where he earned wages for his hourly work, allowing him to be his own man. Not so many years ago, he had struggled to possess both of those things.

After the war, the heady feelings of youth and freedom had created a resilience fueled by hope. Then, in the beginning of their lives after the end of "war and slavery," they had mastered everything that had come their way. But all that exultation had worn thin. Like material, slowly the wear had frayed it until holes began. Holes too large to be patched.

Now Allen and Lucy lived in Warsaw, Kentucky, away from Jessamine and Garrard Counties that were like nests of adders, where poisonous infestations cropped up everywhere. Any false step and a black man's foot was down the hole, in the nest, and viciously bitten.

To say that Jessamine County was unscathed by wartime attitudes was to say that the South had possessed a holy cause. The last time he had lived in that region, he had been forced to walk the thin precarious line where on each side viperous snakes were waiting to pierce his flesh and sink deep the fangs of hatred.

No matter he had minded his own business. Allen had worked the ground, a humble enough occupation. He had used his army pay–sufficient for a mule and plow–to get started. By only borrowing small amounts to get by, he was able to make a go of it for the first few years. Their little house was a shack where Lucy created a home. They had tenant farmed on Thomas Jenkins' property. He had been a decent landlord, and Allen would have stayed on except for the sentiment that began to permeat Lucy's whole being. She insisted it was no place to raise a family when there were other places on the map that could prove fairer.

One lone day was the beginning of a spiral that had led to their leaving. That and Lucy's constant barrage of tears and fears. It wore on him. He refused to admit defeat by leaving.

Even now, the thoughts stealing to that fateful day brought on such a radiating anger it rivaled a branding iron. Though the cold crept into his work coat, Allan felt the perspiration flow. None of it had lost its savor for him.

It had been a hot one, back in '76. A scorching Kentucky summer with a humidity that swallowed a man until it felt as if he were the one relinquishing the heat into the atmosphere. Allen had walked to the general store, one of the few, rare times he had. All to retrieve a bag of sugar the children had left. He had told Lucy to forget it, but she had insisted the money not be wasted. He had known then and he still knew now, no bag of sugar was worth haggling with the Hardin brothers.

This had been when he was a tenant farmer and Cayden and Mel Hardin hated that worse than a black that sharecropped. Allen's mule and plow, all the farming implements he had owned, were enough to earn him the hostility of those secesh whites. The War's end had brought on a more overt form of racial malice, differing from when Allen's people had been their personal property. When things changed, many folks didn't mind letting their grievance over the South's loss out of the gunnysack.

On that stifling day, Allen had unwillingly walked down the two-mile dusty road to Hardins' store. Earlier when Lucy had sent Willie and Cynthia to fetch a few supplies, the children had come back, each with a stub of peppermint between their teeth. The excitement of having such a rare treat had robbed them of their reasoning. Lucy fussed–there was nothing to do but go back for the sugar. She would not send the children, and Allen would not send her.

Allen had stridden across the creaky porch steps of the store, making his usual observations. The smell of the place–like hambones and smoke, pine and sulphur–was stronger and more intensified by the day's heat. He entered the doorway, his frame cutting into the light, causing the brothers to look up. Allen let his eyes adjust to the dim interior before he approached the counter. Somehow he felt his presence goaded the Hardin brothers into an irritable mood.

He was not wrong. He stood and waited an eternity until the Hardins chose to acknowledge him, even though he was the only one in the store. Busily scanning the shelves filled the wait, although he mustn't look *too* hard and disrespect the merchandise. While he waited, indignation built. It was the swift, hot kind that tended to affect a man's reasoning, and he could little afford that.

Mel and Cayden Hardin looked like their daddy and granddaddy before them. Typical southern grassroots reflected in their smooth faces where skin showed. The distinguishing trait that separated the men was the hair on their faces–one favored a mustache and the other a beard. They both had eyes of light blue–not easily forgotten.

"Well, what you need there, boy?" Mel directed his question at Allen, granting him the opportunity to speak. So Allan spoke.

"My children left a bag of sugar here this morning."

Mel's thin sandy eyebrows drew together. "Here? This morning?"

"Yes, sir." Allen nodded. He steeled himself for the encounter.

7

Mel turned to Cayden. "You seen any bag of sugar?"

Cayden came over and shook his head. "You sure, boy?" He tucked his hands in his shopkeeper's apron, looking like the cat that had cornered the canary. "Don't recall no sugar bein' left around here."

Allan knew the matter of the sugar bag was closed. He turned to leave.

"Hey, boy."

Allen paused, his broad back to the men. In that brief instant, he wondered if his tense muscles and stiff frame gave him away. Inside he felt like a coiled snake, yet he would not be the one to strike. How often had he been called "boy" and yet it never failed to unnerve him. The irony of such a term–"boy"–when he stood a good head taller and could whip both men blindfolded. There were those invisible and involuntary bands encircling him, stronger than if they were physically tangible. He would always be "boy" and he knew his place–just as when he was a slave. It was the lot of dark skin–war or no war.

He turned reluctantly around until he faced the two brothers. He kept his eyes on the grained wood counter where sat the peppermint sticks, the faulty demise of his children's memory. "Yes, sir?"

"You do your own farmin'?" Cayden asked, a gleam in his eye that made Allen wary.

Allen nodded in mock patience and politeness. Cayden continued, "Well, me and my brother here got us a need for a good mule. You got one?"

They knew Allen had an animal. He let his shoulders droop, as if in a shrug. "Not worth much, that mule."

"Well, no matter. We got us a need, and if we get our job done, we'll return the critter."

Over my dead body. "Well, sir, I'll just bring him by and help you out." Allen let his brain handle the situation. He could not risk letting his acidic feelings leak out to devour him.

"No need, boy." Mel took up the farce. "We'll do our own work. We want it done right. You just bring that animal around for us next week, now, y'hear?"

Allen nodded and then walked as light-footed as an Indian across those creaky wooden floorboards, out into the blinding sunlight. The heat outside wasn't anywhere near the same degree as his internal body temperature. If he had been more of a man, he would have kept calm and simply walked home, realizing and accepting defeat. Been a good sport about it all. A black man never won against a white one, not while the law and society were against him.

Instead, he picked up his pace, as if his back modeled a target and rounded the dirt road, out of sight of the wooden mercantile. Home came closer, and Allen knew the true bull's-eye, his livelihood, had just been struck.

That momentous day, though twelve years ago, still brought on feelings that very nearly resembled a festered hatred and yet Allen knew better. He understood what hatred did to a man, so he avoided thinking about it. It lay tucked deep within those regions where no one could touch it—not even himself—only God. And Allen had not yet offered it up to Him.

As he walked home from the sawmill, his muscles protested. He took several deep breaths to let the past go and pictured Lucy on their wedding day. How beautiful a woman she had been to him! So full of hopeful plans, so true and undaunted. She had changed, and Allen knew life did that to people. It pushed you along, it pushed you away, and it stole from you. Lucy's youthful vitality had shriveled year by year, tarnished by serious duty. Motherhood had robbed her of that carefree spontaneity. Now she cared more about a worthless pair of clean socks than his feelings. Of course, him being a workingman and all, he should have appreciated it. He should have had little time to dwell on these things, yet he found himself doing so more often.

Why had the lean years—days of scarce food and patched clothes—been so pleasant? Now those needs were met and Allen could not understand how the quality of their life had deteriorated. Maybe only he felt this and Lucy did not notice. She was

9

still raising the children, their youngest being only six. She took her duties seriously, but hadn't he once been the same, back in the army? He wanted to peel away those years of demanding toil, but he was powerless. He woke up and went to work, then came home. In the evenings, he helped little Dee with his homework or went out to the little shed and fixed whatever was broken at the time. Sometimes it was as simple as a cracked ego or just steam from his internal boiler.

That's why he had started going to the pub on Thursday evenings after work. It was someplace that didn't exist in his average life–a life filled entirely with the sawmill and home. Where the feelings of discontentment had cropped up, he wasn't sure. Maybe back in that store, back in the '70's, when he realized what a plumb line life was always to be there. The feeling had come and seemed to infest his very being like ringworm. Except no one noticed the ring, not even Lucy, who saw to his physical comforts and forgot the threads that fabricated a man. Maybe life was just too comfortable anymore.

The city park came into his view. He paused and then walked up behind a bench where a typical fall scene presented itself. Some strode along on a walk or mission, some merely cut through on their way to someplace else. There was a mother pushing a tram and little children shrieking as they skipped along a stone wall. His attention was drawn to an old woman feeding the pigeons. How greedily the birds attacked the morsels! How much like men those birds were.

Past the old woman, Allen saw a pathetic sight. It was a female, he surmised, though she was dressed in a man's overcoat and her hair defied description other than to say it needed a good combing. She stood several yards away, intently standing watching the birds devour the bread. There was no discerning her age. Poor waif of some sort, Allen figured. Then having seen enough, he turned wearily away, disconsolate, to trudge homeward for another night.

*   *   *   *

The door was open and yet Lucy hesitated. She heard the raspy sound of a saw biting into a board, telling her Allen was doing some project. Funny she should feel reluctant to enter, but anymore she wasn't sure in which direction their conversations might go. Lately, they weren't on the same page, not even in the same book. She moved to the doorway and peered in. Little Dee was helping by holding onto one end of a board, trying to steady it, while his daddy labored to divide the wood. With a crash, the board separated and fell. Allen noticed Lucy. He had a smile for her as he bent to retrieve the piece. "Dinner ready?"

Lucy felt encouraged. She nodded and tapped Dee. "Run wash up, Dee. We're ready to eat." As she directed, the boy scampered off, eager for the supper hour. Lucy came into the little shop. She looked around the tight space at the glass jars and tins storing stray nails or bolts. A few meager tools hung on the wall, and an array of dusty boards, different lengths, lay stacked in the corner. A little yellow pile of sawdust, in a mound, sat by the makeshift table.

Lucy inhaled and found this to be male terrain. Somewhere she smelled tar and oil, besides the woodsy smell. Maybe this was a good place to broach the subject she wanted to talk over, right here where Allen was most comfortable.

"Allen, I've been wanting to talk to you about something." She watched as this made him suddenly uncomfortable, a familiar happening anymore. He picked up scraps and slightly turned his back on her. This was the reaction she had come to expect.

"What about?" came his muffled reply. He stacked wood into a neat pile.

Lucy hesitated. Watching his back, she realized how well she knew each muscle, the contour of his shoulders and his arms. She felt a small ache inside, one of love for this man who had used that back and arms to build an army camp, fight for freedom, and wrestle a living from Kentucky's soil. Now in sequence, they handled lumber all day to provide a living for his

11

family. How she hated to speak up, to see that back go tense as though she was suddenly the enemy. She rushed through her carefully constructed mental monologue, giving voice to her concerns.

"Tomorrow is Thursday. I don't want you to go to the Pub. It's no place for a man like you."

"A man like me?" Allen questioned, pausing only for a moment before turning to hang up a hammer.

"Yes. You're too good to go to such a place. That's for drunks and no-good trash."

Allen clanged the saw blade down flat upon the table. It always irritated him when Lucy tended to make him into some good person he felt he wasn't. He was human. She believed some fabricated image she had created and her expectations annoyed him. "What do you know about no-good trash?"

Lucy knew the conversation would follow this course like a meandering river. The die was cast and it had been Allen's throw. She sputtered, "I know plenty. Those places are full of that Irish riff-raff. For a family man–"

"That's prejudice, Lucy. You don't know any Irish." Allen finally stopped moving around and faced her.

Lucy did know some Irish, and they were good people, but she wasn't going to tell Allen that. He knew public sentiment as well as her. She tried another tactic. "Allan, it doesn't look right. You have a family. You're no drinker. Why do you go to such a place?"

Allen didn't answer, mainly because he didn't fully understand it himself. The anonymity that existed there had its appeal, and there was no forced segregation at that little pub. Maybe because there were no demands made on him there. "Lucy, I bring home the paycheck. You're fed and clothed. The children aren't neglected. You have a nice home. I want you to stop nagging and let me be. What I do in my spare time is my concern. I am a grown man and have been for some time. I'm not one of the children."

Lucy stood still, so unlike her it nearly hurt, but Allen was not in the mood to reconcile. He spoke, "I'm going in to

12

wash up." He considered the matter closed. Lucy felt the wind stir as he strode past her on his way towards the house. She felt it fan her cheeks, and in it she sensed a personal dismissal, one that stung deeper than she had ever experienced. She went to the doorway and leaned on the doorpost. The sun was going down. Somehow she wanted to still that orb, beg it not to leave the sky. Not yet, not while an upheaval of emotions surged within Lucy's being. In closing her eyes, she held back the tears that filled the reservoir of her heart.

Chapter Three

The matron of the girls' ward paused before pushing open the door. Sometimes she wondered why she ever took on such a job. She liked young people, or at least she used to. What had changed, the young people or her? They were noisier now–no–rowdier was the word. Just like the commotion coming from behind the door at this moment.

Leona Riddler pushed the door open to reveal four girls in various stages of dress who were shrieking and throwing pillows. As all eyes turned toward the doorway, their activity ceased, except for a pillow in flight. It landed with a thud at Miss Riddler's feet. She stared at it, as though it was the body of the goose whose feathers resided within. She opened her mouth to speak and one errant white feather floated before her face. Her eyes nearly crossed watching its descent until it came to rest on the front of her dress. The girls slowly seemed to melt in their positions: Bertha sank to the floor, Cynthia slumped onto the desk, and Carrie and Adelaide resorted to their beds.

Miss Riddler's scowl was a preface of the reckoning. She plucked the feather from the front of her and held it tightly, as if wringing the bird's neck once more.

"Girls! What is the meaning of this...this bedlam?!"

Miss Riddler was very formidable in her black bombazine with a gold chatelaine hanging from jet buttons. Her expression commanded the girl's attention and it meant discord. No one spoke. Miss Riddler continued. "I am simply shocked! Look at yourselves! Raising your voices and throwing the bed linens around! What has possessed you?" Her voice's caliber mesmerized the girls. "You are supposed to be fine, educated, upstanding ladies of good deportment."

She singled the girls out. "Miss Ross, what would your parents think of your actions? Miss Turner, can you explain yourself?" Her accusations swept to include Adelaide and Bertha too.

"Sorry, Miss Riddler." Cynthia said. "We were just getting ready for the day and well–um–I'm not sure how it all started but–um–we lost control."

"*Lost control*? Well-bred ladies, who I assume you all are, do not 'lose control' as you put it. I expect all of you dressed and down at my office in fifteen minutes, after you right this room into some semblance of order." Eyes blazing, Miss Riddler left the scene.

"Uh-oh." Carrie smoothed back a lock of hair. "Ol' Rhino Riddler is going to get to horn someone yet." She donned a ghastly smile and pretended to gore Cynthia.

Laughing, Cynthia shook her head. "Old Rhino? What's that about?"

Carrie spoke flippantly, "Oh, haven't you noticed how her nose hooks up, like a horn? And she's got that tough hide! Don't you know that's what bombazine really is?"

Cynthia looked at Adelaide and Bertha. "Seriously, she's right about us. My mama told me I was supposed to act like a lady here."

Bertha grabbed a pillowcase and stuffed a down form into it. "Maybe we did get carried away, but all work and no play make Jill a dull girl."

"You said it, sister!" Carrie laughed merrily. "Miss Rhino is just mad. She hates to see anyone having fun, since *her* fun got spoiled."

16

"What do you mean?" Cynthia questioned as the girls moved around the room straightening up things.

"Well, the way I hear it–" Carrie began. Bertha rolled her eyes. "...is Miss Riddler set her cap for Mr. Beeson, the math teacher! Of all men! The administrators got wind of it and told her to "remove that cap" or *move on.* Anyhow, Mr. Beeson valued his job more than Miss Riddler's love and broke off any romantic notions she had toward him."

"How did he do that?" Cynthia looked perturbed. "You can't just order someone to stop caring about you."

Bertha broke in, "What did she possibly see in ol' Beeson anyhow? He's disagreeable, rude–"

"Don't you see?" Carrie demanded, working on pulling her shirtwaist down, ignoring the buttons. "They were like magnets–their common qualities attracting them."

"Well," Cynthia concluded, "I think it sounds a lot like gossip, something my mama is dead set against."

"Quit worrying about your mama, Annie. She's not here to hound you." Carrie instructed.

Fully attired, Cynthia surveyed the room. She enjoyed the quips and fun, but her more serious nature was ingrained. She couldn't shake her upbringing or just ignore any unkindness. "Come on, girls. We'll be late." The other three seemed in no hurry. Finally Cynthia, tired of waiting in the doorway, spoke, "I'm going on down."

"Go on." Bertha said. "Maybe you can get her in a good mood before we appear. Lessen our judgment somewhat, Annie."

Cynthia made to leave, not sure if the girls were making light of her or not.

"Hey, Annie," Carrie called. Cynthia turned, her eyebrows inquiring. "What do you get when you cross a rhino with a bee?"

Cynthia spun on her heel, their peals of laughter trailing after her.

17

Cynthia slid into her seat, hoping Mr. Beeson wouldn't notice her desk had been absent minutes earlier. His back was to her, his arms upraised as he wrote a math problem on the chalkboard. His dull pea-green coat flapped as he wrote, reminding her of a green crow who would soon be interested in and inquisitive about her tardiness.

Cynthia slid her textbook out from the stack now cradled in her lap. Once open, she tried to focus on the equation on the page. But her mind kept going to Miss Riddler's speech and her threat to contact the girls' parents if such an episode occurred again. Cynthia was ashamed, but at the same time, she felt a surge of excitement. It was foreign to her, and it had something to do with being on her own, free to make her own choices. Of course, she had just made a wrong one. Chagrined, she decided to follow Miss Riddler's rules from now on.

Bertha's aversion to being a dull "Jill" had just earned the girls cleanup duty for their floor. Emptying wastebaskets for two weeks would deter any further playful uprisings.

"Miss Ross." Cynthia jumped. The blurred page came into view as her eyes swept up to Mr. Beeson. He had walked to her desk and stood, his arms crossed before his chest in a no-nonsense stance. "You're late for class. Do you have an excuse?"

Cynthia felt her face coloring. She had no desire to tell about that morning's installment in the Ladies' Dormitory Hall. Her embarrassment deepened when she pictured Mr. Beeson as the object of Miss Riddler's affection.

"Yes, sir. I was attending to some business this morning for the house matron. Sorry I'm late, sir."

"See me after class."

The girls surrounded Cynthia at dinnertime. As Adelaide unwrapped a sandwich, she comforted the others. "Emptying trash isn't so bad. It's not like it's an alley in a New York slum or anything."

Carrie spoke around mouthfuls. "Yeah, it's okey-dokey. Who cares? If it makes Rhino feel better, so be it. I'm more worried about the demerits I'm racking up for being tardy."

Cynthia felt sympathetic. Carrie's daddy was one of the first black judges in their county up in Pennsylvania. He made good on his threats. She had more at stake than the others.

Cynthia scraped her plate. She was thankful they hadn't gotten dishwashing detail. "I'm worried about my math. My math grade hasn't exactly graced the dean's list yet, and Mr. Beeson doesn't exactly think of me as one of his favorite students or anything." She looked around anxiously, hoping the math teacher wasn't in the lunch hall.

Bertha shrugged. "Don't fret, Annie. I doubt he even has such a list. Beeson's Best are probably all bores–"

Carrie poked Bertha and motioned. A hush fell over the girls. Mr. Beeson walked by, his eyes regarding the group with disapproval. His eyes settled on Cynthia. She gulped. After his shadow passed by, the four girls found they had held their breath. And this time, Cynthia noted, there were no peals of laughter as the group departed.

"This poetry is very good, Miss Ross." Cynthia felt like beaming. Miss Dyerson was applauding her work, and she was encouraged. After all the trouble she had been in, it was pleasant to hear. "Keep it up. It's very important for a teacher to be able to express her thoughts clearly."

Cynthia took her paper and smiled shyly, "Thank you, Miss Dyerson." She was leaving the room in a dreamy state when she bumped into someone. "Oh, excuse me," Cynthia blurted. She looked down on the girl scooping up books off the floor. She bent to help her. "I'm so sorry."

"Oh, it's alright. I'm the one who got in your way," the girl said. Once all the books were retrieved, Cynthia got a good look at her. *Spectacular.* Not so much her looks as her whole persona, which definitely labeled her as *different.* She was a white girl with strange pale hair and brown eyes fringed with lashes that resembled lace. She looked soulful to Cynthia. She liked her immediately. "Where you off to?"

"I'm being tutored in language by one of the literature

students. I'm on my way there now."

Cynthia peered at the hall clock. "I've got time. Can I walk with you?"

"Sure." The slight blond was pleased. She juggled her books to get a better hold on her belongings.

"Here, let me help you." Cynthia took three books from the girl's overloaded arm. She wondered how the slight frame, less than five feet, could be burdened with so much. "My name's Cynthia Ross, Warsaw, Kentucky. Everyone calls me Annie."

"Pleased to make your acquaintance. I'm Nellie Mason, Franklin, Tennessee. Where you boarding at?"

"The Ladies' Hall, floor C. How about you?"

"I'm off campus at Mrs. Meriwether's boardinghouse. Papa wanted to make sure I didn't room–. Oh well, never mind. What are you working on here?"

"A teacher's certificate. You?"

"Oh, just a comprehensive learning experience. The whole cherry pie, pits included, so to speak. Papa wants his daughter to know it all." Her tone was tinged with bitterness.

Cynthia spoke, "I didn't know there were any poppas who would allow such a thing. My daddy's indulging me until I get this out of my system and settle down and marry." Allen Ross had never said that in so many words, but Cynthia knew. Didn't all daddies want to see their daughters married and in the care of another man once they relinquished their own hold? It was the common nineteenth century's barometer of decorum, and it lay mainly unchallenged.

"My Papa's not the average man." Nellie smiled as though in apology. "He thinks–. Well, anyhow, I don't have to worry about being married. Any would-be suitor would tuck tail and run once they've met Papa." She said it so matter-of-factly that Cynthia felt sudden empathy. Nellie paused in front of Literature Hall. "We're here. Maybe we can meet again, Annie. It'd be fun to talk some more." She looked wistful.

"Sure. I'd like it too, Nellie." Cynthia watched the pale girl disappear into the building. Cynthia smiled at the thought of her new friendship. There was no end to the wonders of Berea.

One fall afternoon, Cynthia stepped briskly along between classes. She was reciting Tennyson for English class when her mind paused and noticed the leaves. There were a lot of trees at Berea and most of them were shedding. Piles of leaves littered the sidewalks and small paths, yet the trees seemed as heavy laden as before. They had traded their dresses of green for splashy reds and yellows, and blends of orange.

Cynthia let her mind wander over the campus. She had yet to see the famed Rev. John G. Fee. This man was the icon of freedom, of all that was pure and good, to Mama and Aunt Narciss. Nearly all of Cynthia's life, she had heard how Rev. Fee had rescued her mother, grandmother, and Aunt Narciss when they had been hindered by soldiers and by the Kentucky River, unable to cross on to Camp Nelson.

Then the Rev. had found them a place within the camp's circuitry, through the aid of an angel named Miss Fair. Mama said she learned just what good men were at that camp and the meaning of true independence. The knowledge Rev. Fee had imparted to Mama had been priceless. It had enabled her to journey through her life thus far, unencumbered by the social and spiritual ignorance that had been a plague to their people since the first dark-skinned man had been brought to the shores of America.

Cynthia could hardly wait to catch a glimpse of this father figure, this hero from the pathos of war time who reshaped attitudes and gave so much hope to a dispirited people who suffered a multitude of afflictions caused by the manacles of oppression.

A slight movement caught in Cynthia's peripheral vision, and she headed for the gazebo that graced a quiet corner of the college yard. There sat Nellie, surrounded by books. On her lap, she held a notepad. She hastily dipped her pen into her inkwell, writing as if her hand were on fire.

"Nellie," Cynthia said, surprised. She hesitated to interrupt her. Nellie looked harried, but smiled when she saw it was her friend.

"Oh, Annie! Come sit here a spell. I'm trying to record my progress in school. I have to keep Papa updated each week. This is Friday, right?" She looked scattered, her hairpins tumbling out of a figure-eight knot on the back of her head and a smudge of ink staining her chin.

Cynthia sat down unceremoniously on the wooden plank floor of the little outbuilding. "Yes it is. You mean you have to do this every week?"

Nellie nodded. "Papa wants to be sure he's not wasting any of his money."

"What do you write?" Cynthia asked curiously.

Nellie shrugged. "Lots of facts mainly. Anything to sound smart."

Cynthia smiled, "Do you write him in any of the languages you're learning?"

Nellie frowned. "I would if I could. I'm not too great at French. But I can read Latin decently."

"Tell me something in French." Cynthia prompted.

Nellie hesitated. "*Bonjour* means hello and *mon ami* means my friend."

Cynthia nodded encouragingly. Nellie swallowed and shook her head miserably. "It's really no use. I can't speak or write it well enough to escape the guillotine."

"Oh, well. I don't see why your poppa should care. When will you ever use other languages? You're not going to be a world traveler, are you?"

Nellie snorted, "My Papa is a stickler for old aristocratic things. I'm surprised I'm not forced to play the spinet or do fancy piecework. Not yet anyhow."

"Your daddy a bear or what?" Cynthia demanded.

"He's just very wealthy and influential and has his own opinions. He doesn't take kindly to opposition. Besides being stuck in the 1860's." Nellie added.

Poor girl! Cynthia thought. He sounded heartless.

"In fact, Annie–" Nellie looked miserable. "I'm doing an experiment here. Papa wants the college closed due to its–well, policies. He's working on it. I hate to see such a place like Berea shut down, not after all the hardships there have been. 'Course Papa doesn't see any of that. I begged him to be allowed to attend, to prove how good an environment it can be. He agreed to give me one semester to change his mind or rather, my mind. That's why I feel I must learn so much and include it all in my letters to Papa."

"Oh, Nellie. That's so good of you, but your daddy is only one man. He couldn't really shut down such a college as this, could he?"

Nellie's eyes were wide with earnestness. "Annie, my papa is head of a very large organization, and he is very persuasive. Nothing has ever stood in his way. I'm so torn over him. I love him, because he's my papa. But deep down, I don't understand what motivates him. He's cruel, and I hope I'm nothing like him. My mother–" Nellie paused, and then shook her head. "Please don't tell a soul about this. I'm worried enough for the future. If people started rumors–" She looked over her shoulder and around the gazebo.

Cynthia took her hand in her own. "Don't worry, Nellie. I won't say a word. I wish you didn't feel so burdened, that you could just enjoy your studies."

Nellie squeezed Cynthia's hand and smiled wanly. "I will try harder to enjoy myself. I'm to be here for such a short time."

"Listen, you ought to come to my room and visit. My three other roommates would love to meet you. Say you will?" Cynthia pleaded.

Nellie's smile broadened. "Sure. I will sometime. Maybe next Friday. Mrs. Meriwether's curfew is later that night."

As Cynthia left her friend, she found it hard to cast aside the serious uncertainty which Nellie had voiced.

Interminable! That was the word to describe the minutes ticking (or seemingly, not ticking) by on the face of "little Ben"

23

adjacent to Cynthia, on the wall. Mr. Beeson took his time looking over her paper, as if he had never seen it before. An *inter - minable* amount of time in his examination of it.

"Is there something wrong, Mr. Beeson?" Cynthia's nerves were taut. She wondered a little fearfully why she was asked to remain after class. Mr. Beeson had no call to. She had finished the test with a 97%.

"Curious, Miss Ross. Just curious. You did considerably better on this test than usual. Are you being tutored by chance?" her teacher questioned. His expression reminded Cynthia of a thundercloud ready to shake a house's foundations.

"No, sir. I studied real hard for that one." Cynthia nodded toward the paper on his desk. Her mouth felt like chalk.

"You're aware you received a 73% last time, on these very same problems?"

"Yes, sir. My textbook gave examples and it finally came to me–"

"Miss Ross, could it have come to you by looking on Louella Speer's paper during test time? Because she got the same score. She also missed the one problem that you did. And–" he tapped a wooden ruler on the desktop, "you two sit right next to each other."

Cynthia froze. A flare of ire, like a spark to gunpowder, began to warm Cynthia inside. Indignation blazed. Could Mr. Beeson really be accusing her of...*cheating*?

"Mr. Beeson, sir, what are you suggesting?" But Cynthia knew what he was suggesting. Her sweat glands began to work as her mind crackled like kindling.

"I'm not suggesting anything, Miss Ross. Merely curious. So I'm asking you, honestly, if you used Miss Speer's work in place of your own?"

"Cheating! That's what you mean!" Cynthia calmed herself with a deep breath and looked into Mr. Beeson's eyes. "I've never cheated in my life!"

Mr. Beeson was quiet. He continued to look at Cynthia, and she continued to meet his gaze.

"You're dismissed, Miss Ross."

24

Cynthia turned to leave when a thought struck her. She faced Mr. Beeson again and found her voice, "Have you questioned Louella Speer on *her* grade?"

Mr. Beeson's stare fell to his desktop. He took Cynthia's paper and shuffled it into the pile existing there. It seemed a protracted amount of time passed before he answered. "I'll look into it."

Cynthia's weak legs carried her to the student study room, where she found an empty chair and sank into it. She took a book off the shelves within her reach, *Fauna in Native Regions.* And for the next hour, Cynthia absorbed herself in reading an exacting account of the plant life existing in Kentucky's hollows to compose herself and keep from weeping miserably.

The evenings at Berea were most often spent in educational pursuits. Literature and debate club meetings were scheduled each week. Cynthia sat in on several of these sessions but had yet to join any groups. She was still fitting into the atmosphere of college life.

The college, though structured, was "radical" for its day. Cynthia liked how everyone seemed linked together by a common bond to pursue higher learning. There was no male or female status quo, lending a comfort to the college environment. Therefore, Cynthia had no fear of some "prospect" urging her toward the altar, like she had back home. Mama had had her anxious moments over the "coed" factor of Berea. Cynthia loved being a part of such an impartial school.

On Wednesday evening, she sat listening to the debate on whether the Native American had a greater impact upon the European or had the Europeans influenced the Indians more? Back and forth the dialogue went. Cynthia followed carefully until Albert Shultz turned to her and asked, "What is your opinion, Miss Ross?"

Cynthia's mind went blank and would not yield a coherent thought. Bertha poked her. "Uh, well–I would have to say–that's a very hard question. Uh, I guess, uh, probably the Europeans. They had all the guns and liquor, a very unfair factor, when it comes to men. My mama says…"

Everyone was staring at her. Albert Schultz coughed. Charles Johnson averted his face. Manuel Welles raised his brows. Politely the group turned to Teacher Nickols, who redirected the debate.

Needless to say, Cynthia made the decision to not ever attend another one of the Hall's controversial conversations. Bertha looped her arm through Cynthia's as the girls exited the building.

"Hey, Annie, don't get your bloomers in a bunch. So what if you're not debatable material? It's more important to be *dateable* material anyhow."

Cynthia stopped short so that Bertha bounced off her. "Don't be upset, Annie."

"I'm not. And I have no interest in dating, nor do I ever want to be asked such a lame question worthy of such an absurd answer again!" Bertha, ever the friend, wisely said no more.

On Thursday evening, all four girls were gathered in their room engaged in various pursuits. Adelaide scribbled on an essay, crossing out and adding words randomly. Cynthia labored to read a science text, her eyes following the words while her mind omitted them just as hastily. Bertha sat on the floorboards; her legs outstretched attempting some gymnastic pose. She grunted. Meanwhile Carrie, in her first layer of garments only, lay haphazardly across the bed. She was reading a dime novel, all the while humming tunelessly "*A Traveling Man.*"

A knock sounded at the door. Eight eyes riveted on the wooden panels, which hid the owner of the knuckles that had interrupted their leisurely evening. Carrie mouthed "Miss Riddler" and pretended to strangle herself, then promptly hid her novel under her pillow while covering her form for a more modest appearance. Bertha motioned for Cynthia to go to the door as she clambered up off the floor to perch on a bed.

Cynthia hastily opened the door. Surprise lit her face.

"Nellie! Come in!" she exclaimed. Cynthia ushered the girl into the room and turned to the others. "This is the Nellie Mason I've told you about from Franklin, Tennessee." Pulling the desk chair around, she offered it to Nellie and said, "I thought you would come on Friday. What a surprise!" As Cynthia settled on a bed, she noticed how quiet the room had become. A sense of awkwardness had descended which perplexed Cynthia.

She continued, hoping to ease it, "Nellie is doing an experiment here at the college. She is proving to her family what a fine learning place Berea is." Silence met the statement. Cynthia expected someone to say something. When no one did, she pressed on, "Nellie's studying language too. She's learning French and Latin so far. You would enjoy that, wouldn't you, Adelaide?"

Adelaide nodded and then offered, "But that's not part of a teacher's certificate course." She looked questioningly at Nellie.

Nellie looked uncomfortable. "Well, my father's wishes were for me to pursue language, as an extra."

Bertha spoke and her words had a nip to them. "Most of us can only afford a teacher's curriculum. None of those little "extras". Of course if you're a *Mason* from Franklin…"

Nellie looked down at her hands in her lap. They looked paler than Cynthia remembered, like two lost white doves on her fawn taffeta dress.

As the stale atmosphere hung in place, Cynthia looked at Nellie through her friends' eyes. Her white skin was luminescent in the room amid their darker coloring. Her blonde hair, the color of fresh-made butter, along with her mellow brown eyes, created a distance between them like a river receding against its banks. Her dress emanated quality the way a yellow flake of fool's gold did in a piece of dark rock. It radiated wealth, just the material alone, not to mention the style. She obviously didn't do her own laundry.

None of these things had been apparent to Cynthia

before. She had not noticed the differences when it had just been the two of them. Now she wished she were still as ignorant as she had been yesterday.

Nellie stayed for ten minutes, which was six hundred seconds of discomfort. She stood and attempted the social niceties. She nodded at the girls and thanked Cynthia, then took her leave. Cynthia watched her recede down the hallway, wanting to call her back, yet unsure what she could possibly say to soften the minutes before.

She shut the door and looked around the room. No one met her eyes. Carrie was once more engrossed in her book, Adelaide scratched laboriously on her essay. Only Bertha spoke, "Annie, you're a sap for stray cats, huh?"

Cynthia's hands went to her hips. "What's that supposed to mean?"

"Picking up that girl for a friend. You desperate or what? Aren't we good enough for you?"

Cynthia took a huffy breath. "You should all be ashamed of your unfriendliness." No one spoke for a space of a moment until Bertha continued, "Maybe so. But I happen to come from Spring Hill, near Franklin. Everyone knows about the Masons. You'd do yourself a favor to stay away from that girl."

"Meaning?" Cynthia demanded again. Adelaide paused and looked up as Carrie tossed her book on the floor and shrugged. Bertha began to undress for the night.

"If you don't understand, I'm not going to enlighten you. But Annie, don't say I didn't warn you."

"Just what are you warning me about?" But Cynthia's voice had lost its sharpness. She wasn't sure she wanted to hear what was wrong with her new friend.

"You ever seen fire in the night? Wicked shadows in the darkness? You ever had them come call for your daddy?" Bertha's face was drawn tight. "I don't 'spect you ever have, but if you ever had, then you would stay away from any Mason!" She said each word slowly, like a knife sinking into its prey.

Cynthia didn't answer. There was no need. She gathered her science book up and shut it, her hand rubbing the binding, gently smoothing out the spine. Bertha was wrong. Cynthia had seen the flames at night and she knew. Because at one time, in a distant memory barely discernable, the "Masons" *had* come calling. And it was *her* daddy they had wanted.

Chapter Four

Dear Miss Ross,
While in this world you meet with
cares and disappointments, always
remember that the "virtue" lies in
the struggle—not the Prize.
Your sincere friend,
James S. Estill
Berea, Ky 5-27-1888

A train whistled in the distance, and John Hannon found himself pausing. He consulted his pocket watch. Right on time, Warsaw's S & E 4:35 from Cincinnati had just arrived. It was one of two matters John found himself meticulously intent on keeping track of. The other—dinnertime. His mother should be calling him before the sun dropped much lower in the western sky.

He gazed over the buggy he had just finished washing and threw out the tub of dirty water. Gathering up his rags, he felt satisfaction in his labor. It had been a nice fall day to accomplish the job, as the roads were hard on conveyances. It wasn't very often he found time to wash the buggy, but Mama would be thankful and Dad would be pleased. His father worked at the sawmill and wasn't home days. He was getting on in years and had a bad back, which he often described as feeling like a bear-mauled tree.

But his dad was a strong, determined man. He had laid track in his youth, all the way up out of North Carolina to Kentucky. He had been a fugitive, a slave on the run. John enjoyed hearing the stories of how his daddy had accomplished his escape and worked his way north even as the Fugitive Slave

31

Law was in effect. Then there were the war tales. John's life felt so tame in comparison, he often nearly felt ashamed. What things would he be called to do?

But just now, he had no need to worry over it. Mama was calling, "Din-ner-time, John-ny!"

"Mama, you make the best biscuits and gravy ever! Where'd you learn this good stuff?" John spoke around mouthfuls.

Betty Hannon's eyes twinkled. "Son, you haven't ever eaten anyone else's gravy and biscuits, have you?"

John swallowed and put his fork down. "Mama, 'course I have. I've had Aunt Dolly's and Liza's and Miss June Rose's. And yours got them beat by a mile!"

Betty watched her son with pride. He had a healthy appetite and was sound in the mind. He also knew his scriptures, memorized in his handsome head. Growing up, she had seen and lived with young boys who weren't blessed like her John was. She had to resist the urge to go around the table and smooth the wayward hair back from his forehead or squeeze his frame of goodly-sized shoulders. Twenty-year-old young men did not think much of such doting motherisms. A mama could not tell the next generation how glad she was for the way they lived now. They just didn't appreciate it.

"So, tell me, what are you going to do tomorrow?" Betty inquired as she stacked their plates and scraped the gravy into an enamel pot.

John thought. "Well, I need to see if Dad has any jobs for me. But I did tell Mr. Hopkins I would come by sometime and stack his merchandise and gather up crates to return to Cincinnati on the S & E trains. He wanted me to do some hauling too, to the junction depot."

Betty nodded. "You like the grocer business?" She wondered what vocation her son might decide upon. Wonder of wonders, she marveled, he had a choice. He would not have to work as hard as his daddy had before him. Railroading was tough drudgery. So was the sawmill.

John stood up, "I'm going to walk down and meet Dad. Alright?"

Betty smiled. "He would like that."

Betty stood back from the table and let her mind wander, only to start and shake herself. *A little old woman,* she thought, *that's what I am.* She was barely a third of a century old, not hardly much over two score years as a sage likes to count time, and here she stood, seeing her life in retrospect. Just like an older person, she mused. Maybe it was because she *was* older than her years. Maybe slavery did that to a being.

Sometimes she felt like two people. One, like an aged soul who always reminded herself to be aware of the blessings she came into or one–so wrapped up in life–like a youthful, thoughtless creature that forgot her humble origins. It proved vexing to her sometimes, this co-existing nature; this dual personality she possessed. Dear silly Samuel told her he loved her for it, or else she would have long given up and sought an asylum.

She carried the dishes to the washbasin and put them in the dishpan. She pumped water on them to set and stared out the kitchen windows at the descending sun. The reddish-gold light fell across the sill in a shadowy effect, losing its warmth. Fall sunshine had its own-jeweled quality. No one could argue it. Betty loved dusk, always had, even on the two farms she had been raised on. Here in town, it wasn't the same, but she *knew* the beauty as it was happening. How the light-ball would slip away, leaving a painting in its wake. Abstract or neatly plaid, it would be inspiring. Another day finished and another to be begun, chores finished, and Sam–yes, Sam was coming home.

Betty stood in the doorway and watched her husband, Samuel and her son talking. One slapped his knee and the other was holding his stomach. She was used to these chuckling discussions they held, evidence of their male camaraderie.

"Men, I can see you are too busy to notice, but I'm

going to bed." She clutched her worn robe, or what she still called a dressing grown (to which John couldn't help make fun of–it was such an old fashioned term!) about her and smiled at them.

Samuel Hannon rose hastily, shoving his paper aside, and came to her. He placed his hands on her shoulders and smiled, "So soon, Betty?"

"Sam, it's nigh ten o'clock. You know that? What of your day tomorrow? John, you too!"

Samuel agreed, "I'm coming right along, honey. John's going to read me a Bible chapter, and I'll be in. You get your rest." He tenderly kissed her forehead, and she smiled as she left for the bedroom.

John watched his parents and checked the urge to laugh. It seemed preposterous that old folks would act like that, but even at his age, John realized they had been young once. It seemed they would have used it all up.

Sam noticed his son's amused expression. "What's funny?"

"Nothing, sir." John sobered.

His father eyed him sternly and settled down in his favorite worn chair. "You think we're too old to show our love?"

"Well, sir, I think you must have been powerful in love in the beginning to still have that much left." John looked to see if he had irked his dad.

Now Samuel Hannon chuckled. "In the beginning?" He laughed outright. "As I recollect, your mama and I didn't even much like each other–in the beginning."

"Didn't like each other at first?" John, surprised, leaned his elbows on his knees, intent on his father's next words. "How come?"

"Oh, your mother thought she couldn't take a liking to a rough fellow like me, and I thought she was a mite too stuffy."

"Stuffy? Rough fellow?" John guffawed.

"Yes. She was, a tad bit. She knows that now. And I know I was a man who needed all my sharp edges polished round. But you'll find it all out soon enough."

John looked down, suddenly serious. "I'm starting to doubt that."

Sam leaned forward. "Well don't. All things in their own good time. You find the right woman, and she'll be worth waiting on."

John looked as doubtful as he felt. "Maybe there's no 'right woman'. Anyhow," he brightened, "I'm in no hurry. There's things I want to do."

"Good. I hope you get to do them. But," his father cautioned, "don't have your eyes closed or your ears shut too tightly. You don't want to miss the Lord's blessing when it comes."

Blessing? John tried to look agreeable. "What do you want to read, Dad?" He rose. "Besides your paper?"

"Fetch the Bible there, John. Never mind that fish wrapper. Let's read about Samson and Delilah. There's a lesson in there it don't hurt learning." He relegated the newspaper to the back of the table. "And you and I aren't getting any younger!"

John pulled the rig into the alley behind the grocery store and set the brake. He jumped down nimbly and patted the horse nearest him. Mr. Hopkins, the grocer, appeared from the back of the store. Dropping the crate in his hand, he smiled up at John. "Back already?" He wiped his hands on his stained grocer's apron covering his rotund form and passed a hand over his bald pate in pleasure. John heard children's laughter filtering from the store.

He nodded. "Easy job, Mr. Hopkins. I'll just take this wagon and the horses back to the livery now. Here's your train receipt."

Mr. Hopkins stuffed it in his pocket and fished out two bills, which he pressed into John's hand. "Here. Thanks for the delivery, son. Don't know how I would have worked it in without you."

John shrugged and noticed the bills. "Here, Mr. Hopkins. You take some of this back. That's way too much for just a delivery." He knew the grocery man's income was modest. He had the support of half the colored folks of Warsaw, as one of the two stores open to them. John also knew Mr. Hopkins didn't charge enough for his merchandise. That's why John didn't mind helping him out. He felt for the family. The Hopkins had five children, and the youngest sat in a little chair, unable to move on his own. They would take him here or there, and inquire of his comfort. And the seven-year-old boy, who saw only a continual darkness in the world around him, would smile. It would rend even a toughened outlaw's heart tender.

"Well, thanks, John." Mr. Hopkins accepted back a bill and stood rocking on his heels. "Now I have another favor to ask of you. But maybe–just maybe–I'll be doin' you the favor."

John looked questioningly at the older man. Mr. Hopkins continued, "I've got a piece of meat I'd like delivered to the parsonage. Might be the parson's daughter is home to receive it." He winked.

John raised his eyebrows, then felt himself sputter. Quickly he coughed to cover up his reaction. "Ah–sure–Mr. Hopkins." He waited while the grocer hurried to fetch the meat. He observed the patient team and stroked the two velvety noses. "You boys are lucky. No one trying to pair you up with some mare," he whispered. June Rose Hughes' pert face hovered before John, and he swallowed. There was nothing wrong with her but there was nothing *right* about her either ...

"Here you are John. Thanks so much for your help. You tell your folks I said 'hello', alright?"

John assured him he would and turned the horses around in the snug alley in two attempts. Pleased, he climbed in the buckboard and drove to the livery. After paying his bill, he pocketed the change. A little rueful, he realized his whole savings wouldn't even keep a cigar box from closing. It would all fit snugly inside, a pitiful pile. He had to make some decisions soon.

Suddenly loud shouts woke him from his reverie. A buggy came towards him, careening wildly, its springs tossing the carriage's body from side to side. In front of the black box, a brown standardbred horse ran, panicked by some unseen concern.

John had little time to think the situation over. He reacted with what consisted of a form of bravery; he must stop the runaway horse or it would stop him. He dropped the brown-papered package of meat into the road without a thought. Rushing quickly, he reached the animal, loping beside it as it tried to veer away from him. Grabbing hold of the bridle, he pulled, causing the animal to rear up. It brought him down heavily on his feet, with a jolt he felt all the way to his crown. *Dumb beast!* Using his weight as an anchor, he clung, hoping the horse would give out before *he* did. Dust rose up in John's face until he choked, all the while mindful he must keep his feet out from under the hooves as he was dragged along. The horse began to slow, and John was encouraged. Fully aware the clinging appendage could not be thrown off, the animal dropped to a walk, ending its jaunt with a sudden halt. Relieved, John worked at catching his breath.

He led the animal and carriage to a tie post near the boardwalk, safely out of the thoroughfare of the street. It had all occurred within a block's range, yet people gathered around, arriving to congratulate John on his quick thinking. John tried to be polite but he was busy taking inventory of his personal stock. He dusted his clothes off, slapping his hat repeatedly. One sore shoulder and one torn spot on the knee of his trousers. Now he was left with only one pair of un-patched pants and those were Sunday go-to-meeting ones. *Rats!*

The buggy door opened, the window slipped up and was secured by a pair of ivory silk gloves. The group milling around the buggy left off any notion to stare. A feminine face appeared. "What a welcome to Warsaw!"

John stepped around to better see the visage inside the dark interior. More of her appeared as she leaned out the opening. She wore a lavender wool traveling suit, trimmed with frilly, ivory lace. On her head, she carried a perched hat, adorned with feathers matching the ensemble.

She was light-skinned, but an exotic mixture. Her eyes

and hair whispered of some black blood. John had never seen a woman quite like her in Warsaw. There was paint on her face, making her eyes darker and her cheeks and lips were rosier and redder than God had intended. The Bible image of Delilah rose to mind.

"Ma'am? Are you alright in there?" His voice cracked with an incredulous note.

A shaky laugh filtered out. "Yes. I guess so." She seemed to be taking her own person into account. "Yes, definitely I am not harmed. Only frightened a little. But much calmer now." She smiled and held out a hand. "And to whom do I owe my gratitude, my knight in shining armor?"

Embarrassed, John could only give his name, wishing the crowd would disperse. "John W. Hannon, ma'am."

"Well, dear Mr. Hannon. You have saved me for a surety." She pressed a gloved hand over her heart. "I'm visiting Warsaw from Cincinnati. I'm staying at my uncle's house, Mr. William Elmer Alton. My cousin went into the post office to mail something for me and the horse spooked …oh, there he is."

An eleven-year-old boy came trotting up, his eyes wide. "Angel, you alright?"

"Of course. I'm glad you found me. I'm not where you left me, am I?"

The boy swallowed and looked at John. "He don't normally spook."

"Did you tie him?" John asked. The boy shook his head. John raised his eyebrows. "I suggest you do so the next time."

The boy nodded but lost no time climbing up beside "Angel". She leaned out. "Here's my calling card. I would like very much if you looked me up." She gave him a curved smile that somehow momentarily bewildered him, making him feel like a poor peasant who had just received an unexpected parcel of food.

Off they drove and the crowd broke apart, with old Mrs. Warner giving him a scrutiny that matched her name–the look of warning dripping off her face. A few men passed him grins, bespeaking of their envy and desire to be in his shoes.

John ignored them. *Old coots! Shoot, that woman was just that–a woman!* When John thought of his dream girl, she was someone he would be more equated with. He knew nothing whatsoever about women, only girls who fussed about their hair or a mussed up apron. That he could handle.

John trudged back the block to see if Mr. Hopkin's package of meat had survived the ordeal and was still edible. He dusted off the brown paper and was satisfied. The Parson Hughes wasn't usually too picky–he hoped Mrs. Parson wasn't either. He hurried toward the church.

Arriving at the little white house which sat near the church, John knocked firmly. He was eager to drop off Mr. Hopkin's gift and be on his way. Mama was fixing sauerkraut with mashed potatoes tonight.

"Yes?" June Rose, the preacher's daughter, stood there, her surprised expression giving way to one of pleasure, much to John's dismay. She ran a hand over her hair and tucked a strand behind her ear. She deftly untied her work apron and flung it behind her in one fluid motion, hoping John wouldn't notice.

"John?" Her voice trilled at his unexpected visit. She had been baking and she looked a sight! "I didn't expect to see you today! Do come in. No, better yet–would you like to sit on the side-porch? I'll bring us some tea–"

John held up the package. "Thanks, Miss June Rose, but I have to get on home. I just wanted to drop this off from Mr. Hopkins first." He handed it over.

"Well, thank you, John. Are you sure you can't stay and visit? I just baked a batch of cookies."

"I'm sorry, June Rose, I really can't." *Liar!* John tried to look contrite as possible. She smiled sweetly and said, "Just wait. I'll send some home with you. Your folks would like that, wouldn't they?"

He need not answer, she had flitted away to retrieve them. She returned momentarily, a folded towel containing her offering. "You can just return the towel and stay to visit next time, you hear?"

John nodded and made a mental note to let Mama do

that chore. "Thank you. Have a nice day, Miss June Rose."

"Oh, you too, John W. You have a real nice one yourself." John waved. *Oh, I will, now that I'm on my way home!*

When John arrived home, he cleaned up around outside, then went in to read the paper. When Dad had worked his way north, out of slavery, he had learned to read. It was important to him that everyone know how. So he subscribed to the *Warsaw Independent.* John skimmed over the front, listening to his mother hum in the kitchen. He enjoyed the sound, it meant all was well in their world. He hadn't told her about his day, she would just be concerned, and really, it was no big deal.

He pulled the little cream-colored card out of his shirt pocket and studied the name printed there. **Angelique M. Dubois, Cincinnati, Ohio.** There on the flip side, was written with flourishing penmanship, her name, along with her uncle's name and address: *314 Cherry Street, Warsaw, Ohio.*

Hmm. Cherry Street was a prosperous street, shared by both a wealthy black population and affluent whites. John decided to ask Dad what he knew of the uncle–William E. Alton.

Laying his head back on his chair, John thought of the preacher's daughter. June Rose was a nice girl, a neat little homebody, but he didn't feel the connection there that one surely ought to feel. Maybe he resisted because everyone seemed to gravitate the two toward one another. It didn't help the matter any that she fawned over him so much. It gave him the feeling of a watchful mama, and he had one of those already. As far as he was concerned, there was no probable chance he would meet June Rose at the altar. This would not be a problem except for the idea that kept cropping up in his head. He thought he might want to study under Preacher Hughes. The notion kept persisting in his mind. Comforting and feeding people with God's Word seemed a lofty occupation. But anything would be good at this point. John sighed. That cigar box still had a lot of empty room in it, lacking more than just cigars.

Chapter Five

Dear Miss Ross,
Remember well and bear in mind,
That a constant friend is hard to find.
And when you have one good and true,
Never forsake the old for the new.
Yours respectively,
W.B. Arnold
Warsaw, Ky 2-6-1888

Cynthia was troubled. Her world was tumbling like an earthquake and shaking loose the moorings of her mind, because the reasoning of her childhood was being threatened. She had always believed people should *like* people, however feeble the attempt. In a major attempt, they should really follow the Golden Rule. She realized that often took more effort than most people wanted to utilize. Still, why were humans natured so contrary to doing the *right* thing?

It was unsettling, so she behaved as any young girl on her own would do. She skipped meals, slept little, dreamed a lot, rearranged her hairstyle, and nearly flunked math. This all resulted in a haggard-looking Cynthia (which Carrie tried to remedy with a little paint, something she called "rouge"), and more stinging encounters with "The Bee". Cynthia felt her back was against the wall and a charging brigade before her. Her only course of action was to affix bayonet.

She pulled out the stationary she had brought from home (a gift from brother Henry) and the ink well and pen and proceeded to pour out her frustrations to her dear and trusted aunt.

Aunt Narciss was wise, yet not stuffy like a lot of older people turned out. She knew things, collected in her calm, gentle nature, things that gave reason to life. Mama said Aunt Narciss had more common sense than God should have allowed a human to have and not made them an angel. Mama loved her sister.

Cynthia felt the same. Aunt Narciss was the one who pulled her out of the "miry clay" and "set her feet upon a rock" in this life, while encouraging Cynthia to let the Higher One do the very same for her. And Cynthia listened. There were some things that young people knew they must do to navigate this channel of existence. This was one of them.

Dear Aunt Narciss,

I hope this correspondence finds you and Uncle Henry well. I also hope cousin Elizabeth is coming along with her wedding plans as expected. Christmas will be here soon and I can hardly wait to see all of the family. Tell Elizabeth to store it all up to tell me when I get home.

I have things I need to figure out before Christmas comes, so this brings me to write you, Aunt Narciss. One of my friends may have to leave on the Holiday break and I'll probably never see her again, so I must straighten out the quagmire in my mind.

I've recently met up with feelings not foreign to me, but in a different capacity. That contemptible kind of prejudice has crept in among my friends. One set of friends doesn't care for my friend, Nellie. They don't like her family name, saying she's associated with the white robed cross-burners—the new "paddy rollers". I can hardly believe it; she's so kind and nice. I am confused. How can they dislike her because of these things, without knowing the real person inside? Isn't it unfair to judge? Shouldn't we all learn the inside of a person before we let circumstances around them color our feelings? Who is right here, my friends or me? I'm torn between opinions.

My math teacher continues to present math as a mun - dane chore although I'm not sure there is any other way to address it. He gets an "A" in torment.

My love to all of you,
Your affectionate niece,
Cynthia Anne

    *   *   *   *

Bertha and Cynthia walked along the campus path, sharing a laugh over Adelaide's composition on the fine points of conversation when the girl hardly ever spoke. Cynthia was en route to literature class and Bertha must tackle geometry. She was in no hurry to encounter polygons that she was sure Mr. Beeson had invented during the night in his wildest dreams. "Can you tell me what shares the shape of a rhombus? Have you actually ever *seen* one, Annie?"

As the girls talked, they noticed Nellie Mason approaching. Bertha told Cynthia she would see her at lunch and hastily sidled away, suddenly eager to embark upon the dreaded geometry.

"Hello, Nellie. How's things going for you?" The girls fell into step, and Nellie juggled her book load before answering.

"I'm fine, Annie. I haven't ran into you lately and I missed you, so when I saw you …"

Cynthia felt her face redden. She had purposely avoided Nellie until she could sort out her feelings and the guilt surfaced. It had been unfair to treat Nellie that way.

"I've been so busy lately, Nellie. But I'm glad you found me." She gave her friend a sincere smile. "Let's go sit down over there and talk."

The girls settled on an iron bench and pulled their outer garments about them. Cynthia wore a shawl of Mama's and Nellie wore a stylish baby blue cape with an ermine collar. Fall was beginning to turn into an early winter.

"Papa wrote that I'm to come home at Christmas. For good." Nellie's face looked glum. "I never persuaded Papa that Berea was worthwhile, that we can all live in harmony, learning

43

together. He's intent on pursuing his plans."

"Plans? What plans?" Cynthia asked. She was puzzled.

Nellie looked miserable. "His demolition plans I told you about. He's determined that this school shouldn't last and he ...well, he doesn't believe it will last, given Kentucky's mindset."

Cynthia shook her head. "Don't worry so, Nellie. Things will work out. Berea is going strong. Maybe your daddy is just a pessimist. But I can't believe that I might not ever see you again." Cynthia was troubled at the thought. She studied Nellie's fine features and pale buttery-color hair. Nellie's eyes were deep and shining. "I've never had a real true friend, Annie. Someone who liked me for me. My papa's money has always bought the others. And bought friends are cheap ones, I'll tell you."

Both girls could not bring themselves to laugh. They felt heavy with the sorrow of parting and the unknown future. "We could write, Nellie." Cynthia offered.

Nellie brightened. "Annie, I would like that so much. Let's plan on it." She looked at the timepiece pinned to her bodice "I've got to run, Annie, or I'll be late for Latin. Can we meet again?"

"Sure, Nellie, tomorrow at 4:00 in the Study Hall." Cynthia laced her arm through Nellie's and spoke quietly. "Friends can't be bought or sold for money. They are loyal, you know, until the end."

Nellie's gazed deepened "Honest Annie? That's the way it is?" She squeezed Cynthia's arm when Cynthia nodded. Teardrops juggled on her sooty lashes until they toppled and made a glistening print down her cheeks. Her voice left her in a whisper, while her braided ashen head dipped to her chest. "Unto the end," she repeated. Then Nellie Mason fled *rapidus*, on foot, to Latin class.

*   *   *   *

Lucy welcomed her sister in, a warmth tingling within

her that she had not felt in a long time. "Narciss, I'm so glad you've come. We have so much to talk about."

Indeed they did. If they were apart a week, there were things to tell. They each picked up their handwork–Narciss had a pillowcase on which she was embroidering a bird upon a tree for her daughter Elizabeth's trousseau, while Lucy sewed on buttons. They talked best when their hands were busy, their minds seeming to think clearer. It made bearing one's heart a little easier. Mama had taught them that clever little feature in life during their early years.

Narciss pulled her thread through, and then commenced to satin stitch the little brown bird. "You haven't mentioned Cynthia. Are you getting along without her?"

Lucy paused, then stuck her needle into the jean material. "I'm managing my house duties, but it would be so much easier with her home. I miss her. I can't help worry about her. She's never been on her own before and, well…she's my only daughter."

Narcissa Wallace understood that. "You know all the growing up we did at Camp Nelson. Well, maybe some before that, but it's a necessary thing. Everyone needs to do it, Lucy. Cynthia's levelheaded. She'll do fine. There's no better place to do it than Berea. Right?"

Lucy nodded but she looked like the persuasion had minimal effect. "Has she written you, about her studies?"

Narciss could have shaken her head "no" because Cynthia hadn't really written about her schoolwork, but Narciss knew Lucy's real meaning. "Cynthia wrote me last week. She'll make a good teacher, won't she?"

Lucy prodded her sister. "So what did she really write you about?"

Narciss smiled at her sister. "Doesn't Cynthia write you?"

Lucy shot Narciss a frustrated look. "Narciss! Don't tease me! You know she wouldn't write me about what's really going on!"

Narciss got serious. "I don't want you burdened, Lucy.

45

She just wrote for some advice. It seems she has ran into that age-old tumult between black and white. Only it's her friends and it has her confused. She also has a teacher who seems to enjoy making things difficult for her."

Lucy was quiet. She could not fight her daughter's battles. She snipped off her thread and laid the pants aside. *But had she prepared her for them?* "You know, Narciss, we have a difficult job as parents." She sighed. "We try to shelter our children growing up, give them a life free of degradation, like we were forced to live through. At the same time, it does them no good to sugarcoat the world. There's a certain amount they have to experience to get through their adult years."

"Yes, we haven't had it easy. But no one ever said raisin' children was an easy job. We've tackled hard things all our life. Don't forget, Lucy."

Lucy stared off, away from the room where the two sisters sat. She saw an escape from bondage and a struggle to learn to think and live like a "normal" individual–a free, independent person. And she recalled the daunting task of enduring the hardships of segregation, the taunts and racial slurs demoting their existence to that of a lower life form. Then, one of the greatest accomplishments in a life's history–in any one's short lifetime–to learn to love. Both man and beast–"beastly men" especially. Lucy would kid no one. Learning to love and trust a man and humankind was no easy job. That love came in the form of true charity, so much more than just pure simple love. It was where one must endure and bear with and believe, coupled with love. But hadn't the Maker commanded it? So she labored at it, as she had had especially good teachers: her mama, Rev. Fee, and a dear angel named Miss Fair.

"Narciss, I'm tired, all this thinking. How about some tea to perk us up?"

Her sister laid her handwork in her lap. She stretched and agreed with Lucy. "Sounds great. But put lots of sugar in mine. I need to stay awake so I don't stick that needle into my finger. 'Course that would wake me up in a hurry, but I'd rather stay awake with a more pleasant approach."

They shared a laugh, remembering how Mama, often in her last years, had stuck herself so often by falling asleep; she was nearly convinced it was the girls that prodded her.

As Lucy readied the tea and put on water to heat, she spoke of Allan. "Narciss, Allan's been going to the pub on Whittaker Street. It's just on Thursday, but it's so unlike him. I've tried to talk to him about it, but there's something between us, and I can't reach him."

Narciss studied Lucy's grave face. She had noticed the small drawn place between her brows. She would not tell Lucy she already knew this. Her husband, Henry Wallace, had heard. Warsaw was small enough that word got around. Any kind of news was material for the designated "grapevine" of Warsaw–namely Mary Hutchins, the Know-It-All; Lottie Wetzel, the postmistress; and Tommy Drake, the town drunk. Among these three town criers, word reached all horizons. Narciss spoke softly to encourage Lucy. "What's between you?"

Lucy looked baffled. "Yes, what? A brick wall couldn't be any more accurate a description. There's something keeping us apart, we're not on common ground. I feel like he's changing, and I'm not sure how and why."

Narciss digested this and tried to reason through it. "Do you think you could be honest and just tell him what you've told me?"

Lucy considered it. "I've tried to explain things to him but he's always thinking about something and seems so far away. He hears but he doesn't respond. It's like I'm water running over the rocks and he's the stones that lie there and take it. I need a new approach."

Narciss smiled, "You could meet him at the pub. See what's so wonderful about it."

Lucy was shocked. Narciss laughed, "Isn't that about giving someone 'a taste of their own medicine'?" She took over pouring the hot water while Lucy sank in a chair and put her elbows up on the table. She brushed her hair back from her temples, her mind working. "I ask myself, 'what would Mama do?'"

Narciss nodded. "No doubt she wouldn't take any nonsense, but you're not on terms to treat your husband like he's one of your daughters. I think you need to pray for an opening and no doubt, there will be one. You just have to wait."

Lucy snorted. "Alright, sis. I'll continue to pray, but 'pray tell me,'" she looked pointedly at her sister, "how do I remain patient?"

Narciss sighed. She absently tapped her cup with her spoon before answering. "You do it by God's grace, Lucy. 'My grace is sufficient for thee,' remember?"

Lucy remembered. She felt like her insides were chewed up meat held between some mongrel dog's paws. She took a gulp of tea and breathed deeply. Looking at her sister's face, each familiar feature and contour, she instinctively felt comforted. Lucy always seemed to draw strength from Narciss' calm gentle eyes and the set of her mouth.

Narciss continued, "One day after church I heard Frieda Hollis and her cousin, Lilly, talking. Lilly says, 'Frieda, when are you going to get that husband of yours to fix your porch door so callers can visit proper-like?' You know Frieda and Willie are newlyweds, only been married a year. Considering young Frieda's background, she's never had a daddy to stay sober and go to work to support her family. What Frieda answered has stuck with me. She, very patient and respectful, said, 'My husband goes to work each day, Lilly, and I can ask no more.'

"She had a true contentment, and she was counting her blessings. Frieda was focusing on what she had, the one important thing, rather than the ten undone things she didn't have, that matter little. I witnessed a real lesson there, out of the 'mouth of babes', so to speak." Narciss felt quiet.

Lucy spoke sharply, "So you're saying I should be content and ask no more of Allan?" Narciss shrugged. Lucy softened, "I've gained a lot from you, Narciss. I'll study on it. It was almost like having Mama here with us today."

48

Narcissa could not have agreed more. Sometimes it was like your loved ones never really had left you, when they had left you their very real remembered presence.

*   *   *   *

"So Narciss spent the day?" Allan asked Lucy as he unlaced his work boots. He heaved one off and tossed it towards the rug beside the door. It landed two inches shy of the rug. He looked to see if Lucy noticed.

Of course she had, but she feigned ignorance of it as she set the table. She was all cheerful, like a little chickadee pleased with its perch. She filled the kitchen with her twitter.

"Narciss said Henry is going to saw wood in Roy Ebbitts' woods Saturday. He wondered if you would want to go along. I told her I didn't know, that sometimes the mill calls you in Saturdays." She looked at Allan, not expecting him to answer. It was like him to want to think on it. He surprised her.

"I'd like to go. Did she mention what rig he would take for hauling?"

Lucy shook her head. "Why, no. But that would be so nice. We don't want to run out this winter."

Allan looked at his wife closely, to see if she had meant any barb by that, because they had run out of wood the last two winters, and she had voiced her displeasure soundly. He stood up and carried his other boot to the rug, placing the pair side by side. "So you had a good day? Talked everything over, got it all out, re-hashed it once more and now you're plumb winded and tonight will be quiet?" He smiled.

Lucy did not. She stopped stirring the potatoes, her chipper mood vanishing. She gave him such a concentrated look, he flushed. He hadn't meant to spoil the mood of the kitchen, but there it was again. He had made a harmless remark, in teasing, and it had been received as if he had physically thrown a rock at Lucy. She looked down at the skillet and then placed a lid over it. When she looked up, her eyes were no longer shining and her mouth had gone slack.

49

"We'll eat in ten minutes. I'll go call the children."

Allan watched her leave the room and felt his emotions rankle. Why did she take everything wrong he uttered? Why did he say things that actually held a note of truth in them? How was it she could always decipher it?

He left the kitchen, too, to seek out his backyard shop, where he might just spend the evening since he wasn't saying another misinterpreted word tonight.

Chapter Six

Dear Cynthia,
Love many, Trust few,
And always paddle
your own canoe.
Adda Higgins

"Now get out! Once and for all, I'm not hiring the Irish likes of you!"

Fiona stumbled and sat down heavily in the dirt alley where she had just been heaved. She should have been surprised at such treatment, but over the course of the last few weeks, she was no longer shocked. She had come to expect it. These United States of America were no kinder in their treatment of her heritage than their British counterparts had ever been.

Fiona watched the burly dishwasher slam the door of the restaurant. She wanted to tell his Polish-self that he was no better; his family had crossed the ocean too, but the words died in her brain. There was no use vocalizing her frustration because the contempt showered on her was consistant everywhere she went. No one cared.

Securing a job had become an obsession with her out of necessity from hunger, but her persistence had not served her very well this time. It had only annoyed the man when she kept insisting she could work there, and she had tried her hand at the bread. What she really wanted to do was eat that raw dough. She was that hungry and more.

Fiona stood up and dusted herself off and looked over her garments. They were not clean; she was not clean. She needed a good bath but she could not take one until she found a place to do so. And that she could not do until she found a job, which was proving very hard in her state of disrepair.

But Fiona O'Hugh was not one to give up. Hadn't her ancestors been of such material, courageous Celts and strong Vikings? She would simply steer her ship to another port.

Fiona's ship had been beached again, as though dashed upon the rocks. She was ready to pronounce it unseaworthy–to do the unthinkable and admit defeat. This colleen of the Emerald Isle was nearly ready to give up. She was down on her Irish luck and there seemed no lower place she could be relegated to. Fiona sank down against a brick building along the alleyway. She almost welcomed the rough feel of the bricks behind her, biting into her frayed coat. It nearly gave her a physical reason to cry, and she knew she had many reasons that could allow her to. Yet she would not. She had cried an ocean of tears when Da had died, and before that, when Mum had slipped away. No, she would not cry. It had never changed things.

She buried her face in the old smelly coat she wore, a castaway thing she had found along the riverfront. How had a daughter of Coleman O'Hugh sunk so low and so far from home? In a country where the people were cold and hard-hearted and so full of themselves, she felt alone and helpless.

Fiona's hunger made her midsection growl. Now it was full of sharp cramps that she must wait to pass. When they had, she would venture out again, although her body wanted to curl up and go to sleep, and her mind felt as if it was stuffed full of Grandda's prize wool from his precious sheep. Hadn't her brother, Daniel, told her she was always woolgathering?

What a mercy it would be if she could stop thinking and worrying! *Could it be I might have to turn to begging? It would be a disgrace, but there is no one to care.* Since her arrival on these shores, she had been treated uncaringly, like a common tramp. No one had warned her that the American country was not partial to the Irish, that this "melting pot" would not accept the refinery of her country's donation.

When she thought back to the beginning of her journey, how long ago it seemed! Almost another lifetime, in which an apricot-haired, blue-eyed lassie had possessed hopes. How sure she had been when she boarded the smelly ship in Galway and begun her voyage to America. She just knew the patron saints of her homeland were blessing her, bidding her to come to Cincinnati, where Uncle Liam lived. It had seemed the natural thing to do since she had been left all alone.

Now Fiona O'Hugh was confused. She had traveled to Cincinnati, in the state called Ohio, and found no Uncle Liam, for he had passed away, and she was once again alone, this time in a strange, big city. She was frightened of the bustle and noise here. Once, as a small girl, she had been to Limerick, and she had been scared then, just the same. Where she had lived in County Claire, it was quiet and peaceful. *The beauty made your heart ache*, Fiona thought. The city of Cincinnati was dirty and malodorous. Horse droppings littered the streets profusely, and pigs ran wild through the streets eating the garbage that lay thrown out in it. There were meatpacking plants, mainly pork, that smelled heavily of blood. The wharves along the Ohio River stunk as well. Noisy ships blew stack horns, and the sailors' voices assaulted the air in wild curses nearly as deafening. She would not go to the riverfront again. It was no place for a female, Da would have said.

The thought of Da made her heart crack clean in two once again, even after all these months. His dear face swam before her mind's eye, and she could nearly reach out and touch the weatherworn cheeks and bristly chin. His ginger-colored hair was always tousled under his cap, and his blue eyes held a gleam of inner light that always gave Fiona the strength to carry on. After Mum's death, Fiona had felt she had lost something of herself. A part that gave her security and comfort. Suddenly many things were in her hands, and she was bewildered by all of the duties. Then her brother, Daniel, had up and left, and they had not heard from him since.

Da had encouraged her and told her O'Hughs did not give up. They had not faltered when Norman invaders had landed upon their shores, not when Henry VIII imposed Protestantism on the people, not through all the persecutions that ravaged the land or even when the hated Penal Laws which deprived her people from their basic rights and their religious freedom, even then they clung to their beliefs and held fast like a clam to its pearl. And Ireland, her homeland, was indeed a pearl. Of many things anymore, Fiona wondered about, but of that she had no doubt. Then the famine years, when whole clans were starved into extinction, her people had held on. A line of descendants had survived; her grandfather alone, and now these personal trials seemed her undoing.

Fiona pulled herself together and gazed out at the endless buildings and brick streets. She must make plans and get herself out of these back alleys. So far her luck had held in that respect; she had remained unaccosted by the unsavory people who huddled there. The miserable individuals were too wretched to bother with her. But luck was known to run out, just as it had with her efforts to secure work. There was something wrong with a world that turned away a person who would work for their way and keep.

Fiona went to the end of the alley and racked her brain for an idea. The absence of food made it hard to sort through the foggy muddle that resided there. It clung like the mists had over Ireland, yet underneath that grew the greenest sod on this earth. That was how Fiona felt about herself. Surely if she persisted, like Da said their Celtic ancestors had, she would come into her own. Some luck would strike her into a favored existence.

Fiona set off, wandering around the city blocks, hopeful she would find something or someone who would be kind. Out of breath, several hours later, she stopped to rest against a tree. She was in a part of the city she had never been in before. A figure moved on the street away from her, where the path was only of dirt. She peered at the dark shape, almost disbelieving when her eyes told her that it was a robed man, a priest. Here was a man of God, of the mother church of her childhood.

Pushing off from the tree, Fiona hurried to catch the

man, a vision welling up before her. It was one of kneeling at the border of this man's robe and being called "Daughter", as once long ago, a woman had done before her, who had pressed among the throng, and beheld her Savior.

*   *   *   *

Fiona smiled to herself for the first time in weeks. She was at the train depot, looking like any other respectable passenger. As long as she kept her hair covered. It seemed to give away her nationality like it was a beacon upon a lighthouse. She was clean and dressed in new apparel. It was hard for her to resist the urge not to continually smooth her hands over her dress, feeling the clean fabric. The rags she had once worn were rightly reduced to ashes now.

Fiona had spent a week with a dear old woman the priest had taken her to for lodging. Here she had bathed and combed the snarls from her hair, which were so plenteous the woman had trimmed many of them out. Eating from a table in a civilized manner had brought tears to her eyes. Fiona would never forget the lady and her kindness.

The priest had come for her on Friday and given her a blanket and a change of clothes. He had secured her money for train fare.

"You should go south, dear. The city only brings a bad end to so many unfortunate colleens. You go south and get off where it seems good for you. You will surely find work among the homes there." Father Doughty had told her the big, old homes of the south would need servants and housekeepers. It would be a good place for her to make an honest living.

Now, amid the jostle of the station, Fiona was slightly intimidated, but strove to keep her head above the current. She had not yet purchased her ticket. A little idea swam in her mind and she wondered if she could actually follow through with the fledgling plan she dwelt on.

It left a sour taste in her mouth to deceive the kindly Father Doughty, but she fiercely refused to part with the fare

55

money. She listened to the schedule calls. It was near departure time. Fiona slipped out the side door to the track and looked about. There was lots of movement up ahead. The baggage cars were being finished with the last of the luggage. Fiona said her prayers as she made for the last boxcars. The huge doors were still open and there appeared to be no one around. She peered into one and met the surprised look of two men. They were tramps according to their clothing, men down on their luck.

"Hello there, sister." The one said, revealing rotting teeth in a smile of welcome. The other one leered at her and patted the car's bed as to assure her there was room for her too. Fiona backed away and raced to another car, flinging her bag up into it, along with herself. She crouched on the edge, balancing, letting her eyes adjust and praying no one else was in there with her. She listened for shouts of being discovered, but heard nothing, to her relief. She resumed breathing. The car was empty, save for her.

Well, almost empty. Now she noticed the odor and sighed. It had been a livestock car and the smell lingered. Droppings littered the bed, along with straw. It was close enough time to departing, Fiona doubted they would clean it out. She would emerge smelling like pigs or cattle, but she still had the money wrapped up in a handkerchief in her parcel. Without inspecting the animal evidence to see which had been the previous occupants, Fiona settled herself in an unsoiled spot and pulled her blanket about her. She topped that with what she hoped was fairly clean straw and rested her head on her parcel to wait. She hoped if anyone looked in, she would appear a lump of straw in the dark corner.

Before long she heard the train whistle, and then she felt the motion. Her spirit hummed within her. The chugging noise gathered momentum, and the rails began to *clickety-clack* under the steel wheels. Fiona offered up thanksgiving and let the lull of the train soothe her to sleep. When she awoke, perhaps she would meet the new town destined to be her surrogate home, since the shores of her own home, like Irish mist, had receded beyond her grasp.

Chapter Seven

Betty Hannon dusted the flour off her hands and grabbed the dishtowel to brush off the front of herself. "Coming," she hollered toward the door. She hoped her voice carried to the person knocking on the porch.

Smoothing her hair back, she hurried, glancing down at her splotchy apron. *Urrgh*, Betty thought as she heaved the door open. *Well, there is nothing ...* her thoughts died away as her eyes lit on the creature standing on her porch. Betty knew her eyes went wide at the fancy woman, who in Betty's book was often termed a *painted lady*. What was she doing in this part of town and in broad daylight? Betty's brows arched into perplexed question marks.

"Excuse me, ma'am, but I'm looking for John W. Hannon. Is this his place of residence?" The woman offered a red smile as she adjusted her opulent hat.

Betty swallowed in shock. "Uh, excuse me for just a moment." She slammed the door closed and leaned against it. A feeling of desperation welled up within her stomach. *What did that kind of woman want with John? Could her son really be acquainted with her?* Betty's heart was reacting like a woodpecker on an elm tree. *Rat-a-tat-tat, rat-a-tat-tat! Calm down, Betty, there has to be a logical explanation for her presence here. Maybe she is a customer at Mr. Hopkins grocery and needs an order.* Betty paused. *What kind of order would she need? Lipstick and talc? Hair tonic or au de parfum?*

Betty shivered with worry. She was letting her imagination take charge over her senses. The thing on the porch was just a woman, not a monster. Betty could handle it. She turned and opened the door. "I'm sorry. Can I help you with something?" she asked, her voice honing a matronly timbre.

"I'm here to see Mr. John Hannon, as I stated earlier. Is this his residence?" The beautiful creature was a trifle miffed.

"Uh, well, yes it is, but he's not home now." Betty attempted a smile and pressed on, "May I say who called?"

The figure in pink wool handed an embossed card to Betty. "Oh, he'll know." She smiled. "Few men forget me. I'm not called Angel for nothing."

I'll bet, Betty breathed, glowering as if Angel were a flower and her look meant to frost her in mid-bloom. "Look here, Miss ...Miss Angel. My son is not just one of those "few men". I'd like to know your business with him."

Angel had dealt with over-protective mamas before. She held up a gloved hand and answered politely, "You may. I came to thank him for saving my life." She watched Betty's jaw drop. "Indeed, ma'am. Didn't you know?" She observed the reaction she had caused, pleased. "I see your son has modesty among his other admirable traits. Well, you have one fine son." She emphasized the word "fine". Angel looked over her shoulder at the waiting hack. "I'll go on, my man's waiting. Do let John tell you about it. And," she moistened her rosy lips, "I'll be back."

Likely story. Betty could only nod and let her eyes follow the elegant showpiece as she descended to her carriage. *John, you better feel like some storytelling tonight!*

Over the supper meal, Betty brought up "Angel". She pulled the little card out of her apron pocket and held it up.

"You had a visitor today, John."

John looked up from his plate and glanced at the embossed card. He choked on his corn.

"Hmm, that's about how I felt seeing her." His mother gave him a you-have-some-explaining-to-do look.

Sam Hannon was curious. "Who was it?" John attacked his plate, suddenly favoring his onioned liver. Betty answered for him. "Angel came, that's who. Guess you know her, son?"

John nodded and took a glug of water. Betty made her voice high and light sounding, like a bird that was welcoming spring. "I'm not called Angel for nothing." She looked at her husband. He looked amused. Betty frowned at him. "You wouldn't be sitting there smiling if you'd seen her." At her husband's interest, she snapped, "Well, maybe you would! John, how do you know such a woman?"

"Mama, I don't think it's necessary to call her "such a woman". She could very well be a Christian lady from a wealthy background. She probably can't help it she's ...she looks ..."

Betty's snort gave her husband a voice. "Are you two going to tell me what this is all about?"

Betty nodded and waited on her son's explanation. John waited on his mother's tirade. Sam decided not to wait on either of them. He took the card and examined it. "So this lady hails from Cincinnati? How did you meet her, John?"

"Well, it's kind of a–"

"Not at church, I can tell you that. She looked like a dressmaker's dummy that lost control with a paintbrush. Son, have you been to a bar?"

"Mama! Calm yourself! You're putting the cart before the horse. No, I haven't been to any bars. She's not the type to hang around those cheap places, I know that much. Just because she's fixed up a little–"

Betty shook her head, "John, you don't know about those type of women. She's a walking snare, bait included. You need to stay away from her."

John felt his chin lifting. A streak of stubbornness promised to rear its head momentarily. He couldn't decide why he suddenly felt like he did. He had no desire to become entangled with Angel, but Mama's quick judgment pushed John into contemplation. Maybe Mama would or could be proved wrong. It wasn't fair to label a book by its binding. The same went for people. His parents had taught him that.

"Mama, you're going back on your teachings. You know, judging someone before you know the person on the inside?"

Betty grabbed the table's edge. She leaned forward over her plate of now cold liver. "John, you know what the Bible says about where your treasure is, there's where the heart is also. Does June Rose dress that way?"

John brought a fist down on the table in frustration. "Not her again!"

Sam Hannon looked at his wife and son. He held up a palm. "You two need to call a truce. Betty, let the boy talk. Maybe he can tell us how he came to know this Angel."

Betty remained quiet but her lips represented an edged ruler. John studied his plate as he told the story of rescuing Angelique Dubois' runaway horse. "She gave me her card and that was it. I didn't expect her to come calling."

"She probably wanted to thank you for what you did. No harm in that. I'd say that's what decent folks do. Betty, you mustn't let your imagination *runaway* with *you*. Maybe we can all be introduced properly if she visits again." He turned to his wife and covered her hand with his own. "Now, where is that pecan pie you've been promising me?"

Betty moved to the counter to fetch it, and John stood up and excused himself. Betty stared after him, stunned, as he left the kitchen.

"He doesn't want pie? Oh my! Sam, that woman has turned his head. No pie!" Betty came to the table and sat down heavily.

"Betty, he doesn't want pie because he's cross, and it don't take no guessin' as to why." He gave her an even stare. "I doubt Angel has 'turned his head'. He's only seen her once.

62

You've got to give John some room. He's twenty now, a man. You can't be telling him things and ordering him around anymore."

"But Sam, he's my boy. I can't let him fall intentionally into a trap as old as Potiphar's wife!"

"Yes, you can. He's not a child, and he's got to live his life, mistakes and all. You don't have control anymore."

"Sam, it scares me–"

"I know, baby. Me too. But this happens to all parents eventually. And you know what? He may just make us proud. He may make the right choices, but we'll never know if we smother him."

"And if he doesn't? What if he doesn't?"

"Well," Sam drawled out, "we'll always have thought he should have." He gave Betty a suave smile that grew gently as he sought to allay his wife's fears. Sometimes a nonsensical answer worked best.

Betty gazed at her husband thoughtfully with a hint of a smile on her face. "If he doesn't, then you and him will be on the same wagon and," her smile tightened, "it'll be headed down the road, if you get my meaning!"

*   *   *   *

John had no intention of letting Angelique Dubois come calling again. He decided he would go to the Cherry Street address and tell her she had no need to thank him and wish her a good day and a pleasant visit in Warsaw. That way Mama wouldn't get her dander up and any disaster could be avoided.

On Saturday night, after a day of stacking wooden crates at the rail yard, John washed up and put on his Sunday clothes. He slapped on a cheap imitation of Bay Rum cologne and left the house. John left a note on the table, while Mama chatted outside with Neighbor Lettie over the wash lines. This way Mama could ask no questions, yet she knew he would be gone for the evening. *I am twenty years old*, he reasoned.

The walk to Cherry Street was a nervous affair. John

quizzed his own sanity and wondered if he should just go see Rev. Hughes. No, June Rose would appear from out of the woodwork. He wished he had asked Dad to check out the uncle. Then he would have some background information to aid him in conversation. He mourned the fact he hadn't practiced more of it in Sunday school, but being a little shy, all he had done there was memorize scripture. He doubted Mr. William Elmer Alton would appreciate a recital of the Beatitudes.

As he neared the block where he supposed the Alton's lived, the houses grew grander. Gabled roofs, porticos, and iron fences adorned the properties, which sported three stone or brick stories. John knew he had entered a foreign domain and it did nothing to ease the tension over the impending visit.

> *What do you do for a living?*–Mr. W.E. Alton
> *Oh, I'm a jack of all trades...*
> *unload freight, make deliveries*–John
> *Well, Jack, nice to meet you...*
> *now what is it you trade in?*–Mr. W.E. Alton

When John reached the massive stone steps, he gazed up at the even more enormous porch and gargantuan front doors made of cherry wood with beveled glass. *Here goes nothing.* John took a deep breath.

At his knock on the door, a butler in uniform answered. "Yes, suh?" He spoke through his nose, and then peered down it to where John stood. His gaze made John feel like a trapped coon, naked without his mask. Swanky music poured out the door, a mixture produced by a hired band.

"Uh, I'm here to see Miss Angelique Dubois." John felt his Adam's apple tremble.

"Indeed? Did you know Mr. Alton is hosting a party this evening? Have you an invitation? A calling card?" This butler took his role seriously, John gathered.

Then, coming from the west end of the huge wrap-around porch, was a woman and man. Their laughter was high and sharp. The man was clearly drunk. As they approached John and the butler, he could see the fellow's eyes were glassy

64

and unfocused. The woman, who was draped on one of his arms, wore a startling red off-the-shoulder evening gown. John watched them speculatively. It was too early in the evening to be drunk and too late in the year to be bare-shouldered. John knew before the woman raised her face–it was Angel.

If she was surprised to see him, she did not reveal it. "Why, John, how good of you to come." She turned to the man beside her, disengaged her arm and pushed him towards the butler. "Here, Jupiter, take Myron back in. He needs a chair." Having dismissed the two other men, she took John's arm and led him to a low loveseat rocker of wicker that John hadn't yet noticed on the porch.

She sat them both down and proceeded to guide the conversation. "What have you been doing lately? Catching anymore run-away horses?"

"Naw, I only do that on the second Wednesday of each month." John joked nervously.

Angel laughed, "And do you have lots of girls lined up to thank you? Am I at the front of the line?"

Embarrassed, John spoke, "I handle freight mostly. I'm still trying to decide where I belong."

"Belong? How about on the arm of a beautiful woman?" Her peal of laughter rang across the porch. She could see his blush and she grew serious. "Oh, I'm just teasing you, John. So tell me what you mean by that?"

John let down his guard. "Well, I need to figure out what I'm going to do with my life. There's not a lot of opportunities, but my Dad didn't want me slaving away like he's always had to do."

Angel tapped her cheek with slender fingers. "Opportunities? I know of lots of them, right here and in Cincinnati. You just have to look in the right places. Tell me, what do you want to do?"

John found himself sharing his uncertainty with her. "I need to make up my mind. It's about time for another preacher in the family." John mused, "Maybe that's my calling."

Angel shrieked, "Oh, no, John. Don't go and do that. I'll

never get you to talk to me again!"

"Now why do you say that?" John demanded.

"Because I'm such a sinner!" She gave a laugh, like it was really of no consequence. She curled her arm around his. "Oh, don't go and be a preacher! They're horribly stuffy and condemning. Why, the biggest hypocrites I know are preachers!"

John was uncomfortable. "Well, if that's the case, they must not be sincere." The fast companionship of a moment ago rapidly began to deteriorate. John sought to loosen his arm without offense. He continued talking, putting some distance between them. "Anyhow, how could anyone named Angel be a sinner?"

When she didn't answer, he asked, "So what do you do? Go to school in Cincinnati?"

Angel's sulky look disappeared. She smiled, "I'm too old for schooling and I've worked most of my life. Now, I work for my uncle. He's very influential. You should see the white people gawk. He buys real estate and has a few nightclubs on the side. I help him run things. I set my own hours. You could say I'm up and coming. Do you like girls like that?"

John felt a rush of color scald his face. He was thankful that dusk had settled in, covering the porch like a hen with her wings.

"Uh, well, Angel. I'm, uh, well, glad you're making it." He looked around and stood. "I'd better go."

"John." Angel stood too, a pout surfacing. "Please don't go. You're so nice and refreshing. Come on in to the party. I'll introduce you to–"

"Angelique!"

Both John and Angel turned. A well-dressed man also stood on the porch, frowning at them. He had eyes that reminded John of a hawk, and his stance belonged to that of the cultivated wealthy. He beckoned to Angel. She shot John a look, and then went obediently to him. He spoke in low undertones. Angel nodded and turned back to John. "Goodnight, Mr. Hannon. Thank you for coming." She moved past the man and disappeared into the blaze of light coming from the doorway.

"Good evening." The man's deep voice cut across the dark porch as a dismissal. John watched him follow Angel and the door shut. Then all was dark and quiet except for the faint vibrations of the party going on within the house.

John left the porch and trotted down the steps, moving briskly to escape the disturbed feelings that now followed him like a moonlit shadow.

Chapter Eight

It was that special time of the year, Christmas, and there was snow. Cynthia came home from school and all the family was together. Yes, Lucy was almost content except for the distance between her and Allen. Even the holiday spirit had not drawn them together. She prayed having the family at home would work some small miracle. Lucy wanted for Allen to turn his head and look at her, to see his eyes light up. *It was just a small dream, wasn't it?* She reasoned. There needn't be any words between them, just a peace, and she would consider God had answered her prayers.

One afternoon, enjoying Cynthia's presence at home, Lucy suggested they set to work on making gifts for each family member. Money was not the issue so much anymore, but this was what Christmas meant to the Rosses. Cynthia's enthusiasm was contagious, and Lucy marveled over her daughter's grown-up attitude. They had a lot of catching up to do.

"Cynthia, do you have many friends at college?" Lucy asked as she cut out a tool belt of canvas for little Dee.

"Oh, yes, Mama. It's the easiest place to make friends. Everyone is so nice." Cynthia's face clouded over.

"What? Why are you looking like that?" Lucy was concerned over the departure of her daughter's smile.

"I have this friend, named Nellie. I'll probably never see her again. Her daddy won't let her come back next semester."

"Oh, I'm sorry, honey. That will be hard, won't it?"

"Yes," Cynthia admitted, "but in a way, it'll be easier for me."

"How so?" Lucy sat down, the unstitched piece of canvas in her hands.

Cynthia let her knitting lie idle in her lap. Lucy noticed how irregular the square was on its way to becoming a potholder. Ignoring the amusement she felt, she listened as Cynthia confided in her. "Nellie is white. My roommates didn't care for her. They said her father was with the Klan." Lucy stiffened. Cynthia didn't seem to notice as she went on. "Nellie told me her daddy didn't like Berea. But she was so nice. I didn't like how they judged her by something she couldn't control."

Lucy spoke carefully, "I know you've been raised to look upon the inner man, or girl I should say, but Cynthia, the Klan is serious. You wouldn't want to get involved."

Cynthia held up her oblong potholder and studied it. "Nellie has nothing to do with it, I'm sure."

Lucy took the potholder and began to unravel the offending stitches. "Why was Nellie at Berea if her daddy is with the Klan?"

"That's the strange part. He let her come so she could prove to him that we can all get along. It doesn't make sense, him letting her try to prove something he's against." Cynthia was puzzled.

"Maybe she wheedled him into it, tears and such," Lucy suggested.

"No," Cynthia watched her mother's deft fingers at work, "She's not spoiled. If anything, she's a little afraid of him."

Both women worked in silence for a while until Lucy

70

spoke, "I know this sounds contradictory of me but your daddy would say the same. Not a lot of good has ever come of a friendship between black and white. Sometimes I wonder if there could be such a thing. Maybe in a different place and time. What we had at Camp Nelson was special, but it ceased to exist because we all scattered. Yet Berea is a step in the right direction. Maybe Rev. Fee's vision will prevail, in time."

Cynthia laid a hand on her mother's arm. "Mama, why not? Nellie and I got along perfectly well. She would be as loyal and true as–"

"Cynthia, sometimes it's not the person, it's the circumstances–things people can't always control. Black and white have always had a strained relationship."

Cynthia's face was grave. "Mama, we all get along fine at school. Why is the world so stupid?"

Lucy smiled, "You get a bunch of enlightened people together and see the harmony? I'm afraid the rest of the world is just behind times."

Cynthia took her yarn piece back from her mother and started again. "Mama, do you think things will ever be like it is at school? Where people get along like God intended?"

Lucy grew sober. She had a far-away look in her eyes. "Oh, Cynthia, I would like to think it could be so. If things are going to change, well, minds will have to. And that doesn't happen very easily. Ignorance breeds ignorance and there's a lot of that in this world.

"You know, after the war, down in Garrard and Madison Counties, I would never have believed it's possible. And I'm sure it's still that way. One daddy raises his son and teaches him to hate, then he in turn raises his the same way. It seems a pattern that can't be broken. That's why we left there thirteen years ago. We wanted you children to be away from that atmosphere. Besides, lots of our people were moving here to Warsaw, where sentiment is better."

"Mama, tell me about it. Tell me about what made you leave so suddenly."

Lucy sighed, "Well, it's a story that I wish weren't true,

but it is. I guess it's time you heard it." She eyed Cynthia's potholder and smiled. "Maybe you should let your fingers rest while you listen. You don't want to end up making a blanket instead." Lucy got comfortable and began to tell her daughter the story about the fire in the night.

*   *   *   *

1875

Back then, you, Willie, and Henry were the oldest. James was just a baby and John and Dee weren't born yet. We were living on Mr. Jenkins' property, in a little shack, too small to be much of a home, but I did my best. Same as your daddy, doing his best to make the worn-out ground yield something.

Allen had used his army pay to buy a mule and plow. He bought seeds too, the first year, but sometimes we had to use credit to get by. Allen planted cotton and corn. Mr. Jenkins was fair to us, but it was the usual situation where he ended out a little ahead of us and the same with the store, no matter how frugal we were. The Hardin brothers owned the store and how your daddy despised them! But he couldn't let it show, or we would have nowhere to buy staples. Allen claimed he could walk the seven miles to Reedsboro but that would have taken all day, and a farmer hasn't got that kind of time to spare. Work's too pressing.

One day the Hardin brothers wanted to borrow your daddy's mule. He was determined not to let the animal out of his sight. He wouldn't take the mule to them and they threatened him by saying they were going to pay him a visit. Now a visit from white men is never a good thing, and I was scared for your daddy. So, one afternoon, I took the mule to the store. When Allen found out, he was furious with me. But I thought I could live with that. After all, I reasoned, I was probably saving his life. Allen didn't see it that way. He was sure they were up to something and he wasn't about to play their game. It may have had something to do with our credit. We did not owe them a cent that year.

72

And he was right; those brothers had it in for him. When a week was up, Allen went back to Mel and Cayden to get his animal, and they told him it had dropped dead while they were working it. Allen was livid and called the men liars. Well, that was not a wise thing to do. They told your daddy he had better watch his mouth or they would fix it for him.

So as he's walking home, he takes the long way around to cool off his anger and think what to do next, when he passes Mr. Harris' pasture, and there is his beloved mule grazing, come back from the dead. Allen knows it's his by its tail and ears; they were stunted in its youth by its first owner. So he calls to it and it responds. That mule always did like your daddy. He goes to the gate at the end of the pasture and takes him out and goes on his way. When he gets home, I see the animal and tell him, see, they gave it back all right and there was nothing to fear. Your daddy just lets me think it's so, and we go on like before.

Well, one day, Mr. Harris shows up and tells me his mule is missing. He's looking for it and he wants to take a look in our barn. We only had a little shed for it, but I can't tell him no. So he looks at him and tells me it's his lost mule, and if I give her up friendly-like, he won't call the law. I was home alone, so what could I do? After much hand wringing and trying to reason with him, I can only watch our mule being led away.

When Allen gets home, he is furious all over again. He knew there was little I could do, but he is mad at everybody. He waits a day and goes to talk to Mr. Harris. But it doesn't make any difference. So he goes and steals the mule back. Everything is quiet for a while. Then things start going wrong.

One morning, there's a dead coon at the end of our lane. It has a noose around its neck. The next day we wake to find drowned birds in the rain barrel. At the store, the Hardin brothers tell us prices have doubled for our kind. Later a bucket of tar is smeared all around our place. Allen got a dog to alert us to these night intruders we could never hear, but after a week, we found him with a rag tied over his muzzle, stiff and cold.

I was scared by now, I can tell you. I told your daddy to go give that mule back to Mr. Harris. But he wouldn't. He said they were trying to break him, and he was not about to give up, his will or his mule, over a few pranks. You see, it wasn't about the mule really. So I worried day and night and watched over you children like a prairie hen afraid of a hawk. It was tedious living. The times became fewer and fewer when I could forget my fear and take any pleasure in living.

The cotton crop got ready, and we worked at picking it. You three children helped, and James lay on a blanket or I carried him on my back while we worked. We had only a quarter of the field left and it was usually what we considered our share once we paid our rent and Mr. Jenkins' his haul. We were getting ready for bed one evening, and we saw a strange glow out the window. We rushed outside, and there was our cotton, burning an orange light in the darkening sky.

There was little we could do to save it. You children stayed up at the house, and Allen and I filled buckets and got wet feed bags. We hauled it out toward the acreage and fought that fire. Mr. Jenkins arrived and some neighbors, but it was over and done before any of us could save the crop.

Mr. Jenkins wasn't any too happy about it. He suspected foul play but had no evidence. He told Allen he couldn't harbor us on his land if Allen was in trouble. Allen told him he wasn't in no trouble at all, because he hadn't done anything wrong, you see. Mr. Jenkins seemed willing to let it rest.

Well, that burnt crop hurt us. Your daddy became very embittered towards the Hardin brothers, but it was many others of the neighboring whites too. They didn't need any excuse to harass us. They had lost the war and their old way of life, and refused to accept our freedom.

*　　　　*　　　　*　　　　*

Lucy stopped and studied her daughter. She could see she was thinking deeply and waited on her to reply.

74

"So you left after that. You know, in my memory, I remember something more than just the cotton on fire. Something hard for me to define. It's hazy in my mind, but I can recall light and darkness, a certain smell and fire. Wonder why that is?"

Lucy nodded. Her daughter knew that night. Should she put words to what Cynthia's senses had harbored through these years?

"We didn't leave then, Cynthia. Your daddy was a fighting man, although he thought he had left that with the end of the war. There was more yet to come before he would leave."

Cynthia's hands were squeezing her potholder, almost as if in apprehension over her mother's next words. "Go on, Mama. Tell me the rest."

Lucy read in Cynthia's eyes that she was of age. Truth was truth, whether it was hard or easy to accept. Lucy looked back into the past and made her daughter's recollections a reality.

*   *   *   *

The day your daddy went for the gun, I knew things were sweeping along at gale-like proportions. He knew violence was wrong, but he wanted one on our place. Just that day he had been walking along home from Mr. Jenkins' house, and two horsemen accosted him. They were Alvin Turner's boys, and they poked fun at your daddy, pretending to trip him and run their horses real close. It was all your daddy could do not to send them sailing right off their horses. They threatened him that next time they would have a little roping fun.

When Allen got home, he told me he was going for Lee Jake's gun. He was a neighbor, a black man, who lived by the woods, all alone. He was one of the few black men who owned a gun, and nobody much knew it, except your daddy. See, he had kept his arms when he was mustered out, on account they

75

refused him his back pay after the war because he was injured. They claimed he wasn't there when they disbanded and pretended he had deserted. Which wasn't so, he said. So Allen borrows his gun and tells me it's just for his family's protection. We were both a little short on faith, I'm ashamed to say, and we owe the Lord over it.

By this time, I'm afraid to let you children go very far. Allen won't let me go away either. I start to think we should leave Garrard county. Narciss is leaving, along with many others. It seemed like a good idea–before something terrible happened.

And that something bad came before long. Things were ugly for lots of our people. There was unrest among the landowners. They were unhappy with their reduced portions of land. They weren't about to treat us Negroes as a free people, and they couldn't quite work us how they would have liked to. Here and there we heard of lynching and battery. Stories circulated of tar and featherings and burnings.

Allen thought it was time to move away from all of this, but he wanted to leave on his own–not be forced out. I pleaded with him to hurry and make plans.

It was on a Sunday when things forced your daddy's decision. We had been at church and visited around most of the afternoon. In the evening, we sat on chairs outside the house and watched the stars appear while you little children played. I put Baby James to bed and got you all into your nightclothes and heard your prayers. Then you snuggled in your beds. Your daddy and I sat out a little longer and talked over our day, then we retired too.

After only a few hours, Allen woke me. I was groggy but snapped to quickly when I saw lights, bobbing and winding their way along the road, coming out of the trees in the distance. I sucked in my breath. I knew what it was, before I really knew, just because this had happened in my imagination, like a nightmare, countless times before. Now it was no dream. The white men were coming for us. Somehow, as I stumbled out of bed and watched Allen move around the room, I thought back to slavery times. My feelings echoed the fright as if my old master was coming to get me.

I got down on the floor and crawled to the window. I watched the lights draw closer while I cried out in my head–"God, please, slavery is over! Please, no more!" I thought of my little babies, all asleep, and prayed for their sake, that the chains that severed our flesh would no more squeeze the life from them, that enough blood had been spilt in this travesty of mankind.

Allen was then beside me. He had barred the door and gripped Lee Jake's gun. The feeble starlight made shiny patches on the cold metal, and as the column of horsemen approached ever closer, their torches threw odd colors on the barrel. It gleamed, giving it a malicious visage that was nearly as frightening as the assemblage in the yard. I looked into Allen's eyes, which mirrored the flames that were dancing wildly. But he was calm. He gripped my hand, but did not speak. Neither did I. We could not trust ourselves. You children slept on.

The men wore white robes and masks robbing them of human characteristics. Even the horses appeared as insane objects outside the window, the smell of the pine torches making their nostrils flare and their eyes toss about wildly. They minded the fire as the white robes had planted a wooden cross and torched it.

The flames licked at it greedily, causing the light within our room to paint the walls in angry colors. Even this was not as frightening as the silence in which this was all done. No one spoke, no horse neighed. It was inhuman, as if it were the skeleton part of a body, absent of flesh and blood.

I shivered uncontrollably, although my nightdress was soaked in sweat. Allen sat there, crouched on his heels, reminding me as if he had forgotten they were there for him. He appeared unnerved, as if he were watching a play unfold. I wondered if the horror of war had tamed many things that would have made him quake at before.

Then the figure that torched the cross, the leader, spoke to the men on horseback, and they chanted something I couldn't decipher. Then they appeared to pray. I was torn, watching them. How could we both be praying to the same God? But then I knew. They were praying to the enemy of Christ. I found it hard to contain my fright, yet it did not contain me. I can't explain it any clearer except to say I knew the meaning of the Bible verse:

"For we wrestle not against flesh and blood, but against principalities, against powers, against the rulers of the darkness of this world, against spiritual wickedness in high places."

The leader turned and above the noise of the crackling flames, told your daddy to come out. I looked at Allen and saw what I dreaded. His face was resolute, fear had been cast aside, and he was going out there. I could read it in his eyes. The bravery there was age-old, when men throw away uncertainty and exchange it for their mortality.

I clung to him, in an attempt to beg him to stay put, to stay in the house, which offered some measure of safety in my mind. Allen pushed me aside and pulled on his trousers and carefully laced up his boots. He laid the gun down on our bed, among the crumpled blankets, having made his decision. Then your daddy took me in his arms and gave me a fierce hug before he went towards the door. Once there, he pulled off his white nightshirt. It made him black as the night was, before the torches had illuminated it. Unbarring the door, he gave me a last look and went out.

Distraught, I stared out the window into the yard, until I heard the baby whimper. I saw you, Cynthia, put your little head up from your pillow. I put my finger to my lips and you lay back down. Willie wriggled under his cover, a small mound on the bed.

I slipped to the door and crawled out in the dirt, to hunker down beside the weathered boards of the house. Your daddy was standing in front of the house, his back glistening with sweat. I willed God to protect him, but shamefully I kept thinking of the gun in there on the bed.

The white robes chanted some more and began to move in circles around the leader, widening out to pass your daddy. It resembled some grotesque maze of swirling whiteness, like a serpent coiling and uncoiling. Their firelight played upon your daddy's tense muscles. As the riders passed him, many threw their pine torches at him. They missed, evidence of God's Hand, and landed in the dirt at his feet to flare and snuff out. Some of the horsemen hurled ropes around in the air, in the shape of a noose. Every time they neared Allen, I flinched and clung to the boards behind me, unmindful of the splinters.

Deliberately, your daddy's boot heel ground out the remaining torches near him. It seemed this drama went on endlessly, all the while the smell of manure and horses wafted in the air, along with the burning aroma of pine. Sweat filled the whole front yard as strongly as the damp smell after a spring rain.

I sunk to my knees in intense prayer. My nightdress was soaked, and I felt my face wet, too. I wasn't even aware I'd been crying. The forces of evil present were over-whelming, and yet I made the decision to trust God to overcome this devilment. These white-robed men were what Jesus spoke of when he told of those whitened sepulchres that "are within full of dead men's bones". On the outside, these men were covered in white, the color of purity, and in life they represented model businessmen and landowners, but beneath it all, resided black hearts reeking of all that's vile.

At long last, it began to come to an end, as if the hour-glass had run out of sand. The horsemen grazed your daddy, some striking out. The column rode away, winding down the road, towards the woods. The very last rider paused before Allen and locked his gaze on him. I saw your daddy's back bend away in revulsion. The figure threw down something at his feet and tore off, dust swirling in his wake. I stumbled over to Allen. He never took his eyes off the trail of them until they disappeared. Finally, he slowly bent down and retrieved the object thrown at his feet. He held it for a moment, then handed it to me. It was dark and warm and sticky. Blood. It was a stunted mule's tail.

I dropped it, my hand scorched as if by fire. I shook and

my knees went weak. Dropping to the dirt, I swallowed the strong urge to relieve my stomach of its contents. Because now, I knew the truth for certain. This was just the beginning of their night rides against us. The only thing finished entirely, this night, was the wooden cross. Charred fragments sputtered to an end–having burnt itself out.

*   *   *   *

The story ended. Cynthia's silent tears coursed down her face as she raised it to her mother's stony one. The day was spoiled, neither had the heart to continue their Christmas preparations. But that was not all that was spoiled.

Lucy knew how the story continued and suddenly understood now why things were unfolding as they were. Today she and Allen were more or less estranged, and it had never been so clear to her before. The past did not lie at rest, but it continued to slither its harmful vestiges and entangle itself in their lives.

"That's why," Lucy whispered, her fierceness misunderstood by her daughter, "That's why things are the way they are now." The cross, that day long ago, was not the only thing that had been charred. Lucy and Allen's feelings had become separated that night, like the splinter in the yard, dividing her and Allen's future. A wedge had been driven between them. And now, unlike the Cross of Calvary, the injury wrought by that blackened fragment of their past suffered from a lacking forgiveness.

Chapter Nine

Dear Annie,
Think of me when we are apart,
and think of me when you
have no other thought.
From a true friend,
Sarah Makle
Berea, Ky 2-10-1888

The holiday season was nearly past and it was time to welcome in a new year, 1889. Cynthia wanted to do it with *her* cousin. "Henry, tell me, please, you're ready to join me at Berea!" They were holed up in the kitchen during a family affair while the adults congregated in the living room.

Henry Allen Laine frowned and studied *his* cousin. Cynthia's hair had a little scroll on each side of her head and was secured in a knot on top. Her clothing, a white shirtwaist and navy skirt, was all "serviceable quality" as Aunt Lucy was fond of saying. The kind of clothing that did nothing to parade the girl yet her warmth and vitality glowed around her like a sort of halo. This was why Henry Allen could rarely be cross with her. Yes, Henry loved his cousin. "I feel bad disappointing you, Annie, but I'm a little shy on funds."

"But, Henry, you've worked all fall! Weren't you able to save most of it?" Cynthia knew her own parents had discreetly contributed to the account. What a disappointment for him! For her!

"I tried, Annie, really, but money doesn't grow on trees. There were a few things that came up I didn't foresee." He didn't tell her that a few of those "few things" maybe weren't quite necessary. The image of the new dandy high top shoes he had

81

purchased surfaced. *Well*, he reasoned, *I could wear them to school.* Although they pinched his feet unmercifully. Then there was the theatre once a week. *But a fellow needed sound enter - tainment, didn't he?* Not to mention Friend Jack, who had talked him into a few "friendly" card games that brought about an uncongenial losing streak.

He turned his attention to Cynthia. "I've worked so hard in my studies, to be able to go to Berea. I've needed a little breather. The money just doesn't add up very fast."

Cynthia poked at the table setting, a scowl dominating her face. "Henry Allen, I've been putting all my spare change into the effort. You just have to join me this semester. We could be a study team. I'll even introduce you to my roommates," she watched his reaction, "if you work diligently."

Henry Allen looked disinterested. "Oh, Annie, I'm going to try real hard to save this year and be there in the fall of 1889."

Cynthia wasn't impressed with his resolution. "You sound like you're being impressed into the chain gang." Henry didn't answer.

Cynthia's four brothers–Henry, 19, James, 14, John, 9, and little Dee, 6–filed into the kitchen. Behind them trailed Cousin Elizabeth–Aunt Narciss' girl–and Brother Willie and his wife, Laura Belle. The family group clustered around the table, their talk centered on their plans for 1889. Cynthia would hope to have her two semesters completed by spring's end, ready for a teaching certificate. Brother Henry wanted to work in Cincinnati, on one of the steamship packet lines, but he had yet to ask Mama and Daddy. Little brothers James and John could only hope the school year flew by and that Teacher Blythe Oiler would retire. Cousin Elizabeth had a wedding to plan and execute, emerging as a "Mrs." by the year's end. Then Willie and Laura Belle wished to further the family tree and make grandparents of Lucy and Allen.

And Henry Allen–well, he too had his hopes for the year 1889–to hear, see, and speak no evil and to ignore Cynthia Anne's ardent beseeching.

Henry Allen Laine shoved his hands deep in his pockets and buried his head down into the muffler he wore wrapped around his neck in a representation of a turtle. Henry was on his way home from work to the boarding house. Often on walks like this he fancied little thoughts, stolen moments from reality. He had lots of goals, and the one he hoped would actually bear fruition was creating written work in some form. Something other people could pick up and read and think about. His own thoughts encased in neat black type.

Just now the turtle image came back and he pictured a deep dark pond, full of water lilies. There he was, a black turtle, rare of species, and strongest in the pond. As a turtle he was able to float with the best of them, related of course to the deep sea green turtle if one really were into family trees. He began to contemplate a story:

The black turtle was one fine turtle in his day. His shell always looked suave, splendid enough that many thought him a politician or at least a lawyer. When he floated among them, everyone took notice–the lady shells and the albinos, too.

One day, one of those albino turtles slipped into the water. He was not near as gifted as the black turtle, but he boast - ed he could best a black turtle any day. He pulled out a wad of lily pads with Ben Franklin's face on them...

Henry's story image vanished when he bumped into a real live albino "turtle". "Watch where you're going, darkie," growled the heavy-set, bearded white fellow.

Henry Allen dropped his eyes, and used the customary tone of voice he was expected to have. "Sorry, suh, real sorry 'bout that." Unlike a terrapin, he shuffled his feet quickly away from the annoyed man. His mental stories usually landed him in some kind of trouble, but he could not seem to break the habit. He loved words and had strove to feast his eyes on them since a tyke. But it always seemed like he was a bird with a broken wing, which only viewed the cherries on the bough overhead, dangling beyond his reach. Henry Allen craved the dream of education he wanted to pursue; yet reality was his master. He had had to work out to help his folks pay off the family farm and now, he must labor for tuition to Berea.

If he could afford to realize the truth, it would be that he was burned out. Weary of the crushing weight that poverty had placed on him. And very nearly drained by the energetic persistence his dream demanded of him. But as it was, he could not give place to the thoughts. He must carry on and be a black turtle with a hard shell.

As Henry came to the boarding house's porch, he unwound the muffler from off his neck. He stepped inside and smelled supper. Mrs. Lawson would soon serve the evening meal. He went to the water closet on the second floor to wash up before entering his tiny quarters and pulling off his coat. He laid his hat beside the bed and sank down on the corn shuck mattress. Henry Allen had to hold up until he ate, and then he could retire and sink into oblivion.

Suddenly, he recalled his conversation with Cynthia Anne at Christmas time. He hated to disappoint the ones who loved him, but he needed a little room to explore and live. He may have been slightly frivolous a time or two, but he needed an outlet. Didn't everyone?

All Henry Allen's life he had worked for Pa, to help him pay off his home. Now he had a life of his own and he intended to be his own man a little, before he bent his shoulder to the wheel or carried the yoke of education and his future on both shoulders. Henry Allen was twenty-one years old but felt like he was forty. He needed time, something he hadn't had much of. Henry was not like Cynthia, who had brothers to handle the rough stuff. He hadn't had parents like Aunt Lucy or Uncle Allen either.

Thinking back, Henry Allen saw himself learning his schooling in a rustic old slave cabin, taught by teachers who had made-do. His eight-year education had been hard won, broken up by farm work and such. Henry Allen's job at the sawmill had helped secure his folks' place, and he was free to start saving for himself. Uncle Allen had seen him on, helped land him work in the de-barking room. Cousin Henry worked there too, but no longer oiled parts of machinery like he once had. Since a little accident in his younger years, he was now part of the clean-up crew.

The dinner bell rang. Henry Allen rose from his bed with stiff muscles, mocking his age. He hoped Mrs. Lawson had fixed a feast since he felt he paid a stiff room and board fee, but at least he did not have to rely on relatives. Now, very much unlike a turtle, Henry Allen hurried toward his supper. He was starved.

*   *   *   *

Fiona had always considered herself tough. She was like a Viking warship, one that her own people had withstood hundreds of years ago. She was feisty and could do a fair imitation of a wailing banshee when the need arose. So when the two arms encircled her in the park at this early morning hour, she expected she should scream or tussle about. But no, she froze, silent and still as stone. Before she could rationalize what was happening, she found herself released and twirled about as if she were–*dancing*! Her "partner" was a scarecrow of a man, dressed in rags and reeking of spirits. He was humming a lullaby and smiling, his eyes just faint slits in a long whiskery face.

Fiona's fear evaporated. The man was floating on two feet in a stupor. No danger there–she exhaled with relief. All the same, she turned and was startled by a man's deep voice coming from behind her shoulder. "All well here, ma'am?"

Fiona came face to face with the speaker, a black man, who stood back from the spectacle of the drunk. Again, she found herself dumb, like an opossum playing dead. The only time she had ever seen an honest-to-goodness black man was on the wharves, unloading cargo. She watched him eye the drunken man, who turned in circles, singing a refrain of "la-de-da" before he deposited himself on a convenient park bench.

"Ma'am?" The question came at her again.

85

"Yes, sure I am." Fiona found her voice and laughed nervously. "I think the old laddie just had a few too many. He's harmless." To this, the drunken scarecrow snored. Both of the observers smiled. "Well, I'd better be on my way to work. Have a pleasant day." He touched his hat's brim in a show of propriety as he turned away.

Fiona watched his form, clothed in clean work clothes, as he strode off. *Pleasant day?* Sure, she could try, but more likely it would be the usual. She had a place at the boarding house, in which she paid for her room and board with housekeeping. She was on her way to the market, to buy a few cuts of meat for the dinner hour. How fortunate she was to secure honorable work. The window signs she had seen at certain establishments still rankled, just as it had in Cincinnati–"No Negroes wanted" and "No Irish need apply". Was this land of the free only free of bias if you were of Anglo-Saxon descent? She felt the need to remind these Americans that her fair country was only a wee jot from England, just across the Channel. She had noticed that it was the Irish who were building the bridges and roadways and laying the train tracks. Beside them also labored dark skin. Didn't the builders of this America count for anything?

Now as she watched the black man disappearing from view, she shook herself and called out "thank you", but he was too far away to hear. Fiona roused her feet, casting one more glance at the poor man asleep on the bench, and hurried toward the market place. She had a job to do, and she wasn't about to lose it over any lollygagging! Even if she had just perceived an amazing realization–that black man was the first gentleman who had tipped his hat to her in this new country.

*   *   *   *

Allen loitered at the park, studying the goldfish pond as twilight stretched itself across the landscape. He had left the pub and paused to kill some more time, before going home. He hoped Lucy would be in bed asleep when he got there. He could hardly deal with her accusing cold eyes. He wanted to find everything peaceful and quiet. The mill was so loud, that when he left there, he wanted complete solitude. Rarely at home did he find it. Son Henry, who went to the mill later than him and left earlier, was rarely around, but James, John, and Dee were bent on bowling over the house and spilling through the rooms at every turn. Lucy needed to give them more to do. That was the downside to living in town, not enough chores for the boys. The bitter feelings of the past flavored his mouth, and he strove to swallow away the pangs of failure that would eventually curdle in his stomach. He longed for the wise old man and woman from his past, Aaron and Bessie, to visit him and assure him he had done the right thing by leaving Garrard County. He couldn't shake the unsettled feeling of defeat and the despondency that clung to him like a shadow.

At times like this he fought a battle–one within his mind. It was like an ocean where the tide went in and out, sparring against the sand. Reckless waves–his thoughts–dashed upon the rocks of his conscience, and a wind bantered about, heaving the water back toward its depths.

Allen was the man and the breadwinner responsible for his family. Like when in the army, he had a duty. But along the way, he had fallen short of this goal. He had turned tail and ran away from a few hard-core bigots. Allen had always felt the racial tension, he had been a slave, so why had he let Lucy coax him into leaving? He should have let her go to Narciss, and he should have stayed and fought for his right to live and farm there. By leaving, Allen had let one more white man have dominion over his race. It was just another tread in a backwards trail his people trod.

Orange fish came up to the surface of the water once more before they would descend to the depths of the pool for the night. Their open mouths worked, back and forth, blowing bubbles upon the facial rim of the water. Wide eyes registered surprise at Allen's face hovering above them, before they darted quickly into the darkness. Allen straightened and stood, wishing strongly for a similar veiled basin in which to conceal all the despair he felt. If only he could follow the fish and plummet to the bottom of the pool and remain hidden.

*   *   *   *

Fiona watched the park for the coming and going of the dark-skinned man whenever she wasn't working. He had been the only man who had taken kindly to her, certainly the only one who had shown any concern over her welfare, besides Father Doughty. The dark eyes of the man had visited her mind frequently in the days that followed. She longed to see them again. Since she had been in Warsaw she had not made a single friend, and she craved the opportunity to make one, no matter the age, gender, or even color. Fiona believed in special connections–like the one the patron St. Bridget fostered between her people. And Fiona had felt a link to that man when he had asked if she was all right days ago. One she wanted to explore further.

Chapter Ten

Dear Annie,
I write in this book
when days have rolled away.
And evening shades appear,
that you may never forget.
Yours truly,
C. W. Rasor
Berea, Ky 3-15-1888

Courage. Lucy willed strength into the face reflected before her. It was rare for her to pause before a mirror, but now her whole being concentrated on her image. *You've got to go through with it, Lucy.*

She looked ferociously at herself. She would have laughed but any humor had dried up as if in a desert. Why should courage elude her now after forty-four years? *Because I'm more afraid than ever. I've got so much to lose!*

She frowned and shook her head. *You always have, girl! Where do you think you've lived your life? In a candy store?* No, certainly not. She could do this thing. Why? Because the jewel of her heart, the daddy of her children, was slipping away. Not like a leaf floating on a current, further from its escaped limb–but a bough, torn asunder and sent downriver by a turbulent flood.

Lucy stared at the face she had always known; only now it flaunted a mist of wrinkles and was surrounded by a gentle frost of silver hairs. Traitor! She was losing her youthful beauty–how quickly it fled–and she was about to lose much more. How shallow, she thought, but were the two intertwined? Did it have any bearing?

But no, she would never accuse Allen of such vanity. He was firm, loyal and true, a man of his vows. She was just feeling frightened, and it conjured up unbridled thoughts to keep pace with it.

"Shore up yourself, Lucy," Mama would have said. The dark eyes blinked back from her reflection, and Lucy drew a deep breath. Mirrors could not tell the truth any more than a disquieted soul.

"I'm going because I love you, Allen Ross." Lucy said it aloud to the quiet room, hoping to still her roaring heart. But her chaotic thoughts rumbled onward, a locomotive accelerating. She grabbed an umbrella from the stand in the front room, whether for the disgruntled weather or an apparition of security, Lucy hardly knew, but many a meek woman had veiled vices. After all, Lucy Ross was about to enter foreign domain. She was going to Allen's pub.

*   *   *   *

Narciss' notion had crept its way into Lucy's mind through the holiday season. Like a wily appendage of poison ivy, it wrapped the unthinkable idea within the crevices of her brain, until Lucy was not sure of how she came to the decision–an utterly preposterous resolution (it was a new year–1889)–to storm the citadel of Allen's pub.

Lucy stood before the building and swallowed her fear. Here it was–a haven for refuse and a destroyer of marriages. The establishment lacked any refinement, evident in the drab, brown decaying wood of the structure. No windows opened out on the first floor, just a squat metal door, uninviting to anyone except those of the slinking reptile genus. The upper story sported two cracked windows, bare with gray shutters hanging limp, looking for the entire world like two vacant eyes crying. Lucy shuddered. Here was a prison by consent. Could anything be more depressing? She cringed at what she would find behind that iron door if the occupants tumbling out of the joint were

90

any testimony to the ones inside. It would not be a pretty sight. Lucy steeled herself.

Just as she was ready to storm the bastion, a bedraggled individual knocked into her. "Uh, sorry, m'lassie. Mine eyesight's not wud it used to be." His laugh revealed mouldering teeth that weren't either.

Lucy gulped, a frightened shiver giving her the shakedown. Fortunately the tipsy man yanked open the door of the bar and was swallowed up by its dark interior.

A cold rain had begun to fall. Lucy hardly noticed it, and when she did, it was too late for the umbrella she had brought. Large drops lapsed over her hat, down upon her shoe tops. She realized she was near to soaked; it was time to go in.

She took hold of the grimy handle, and opening the offending door, stepped inside. Peering around, she let her eyes adjust. The whole place reeked of sour spirits and–vomit? The musty odor of the barroom would make a damp basement smell like a French boudoir in comparison. Lucy's senses, visual and olfactory, were assaulted. She must not breathe too deep.

A massive hand grabbed her arm, appearing out of nowhere. Its grip held her like a hawk's talons would, squeezing off her blood flow until her arm tingled. Lucy froze. The huge giant glared at her, "Whad you want in here, lady?" *Lady?* The bully must have seen the light of day at some point in his life. All coherent thought fled Lucy like hens out of the coop. She was visited by that squeamish feeling she always had when she felt trapped and was reminded of the past.

"Come on, lady. We don't want to hear none of that temperance trash, and if you're lookin' for yer man–better luck next time." The Goliath pulled her effortlessly toward the door. "We got a policy here–no women allowed."

Lucy panicked. She hadn't even seen Allen. Suddenly the gears in her brain kicked in. The burly bouncer had turned the crank. An idea came to mind.

Here goes! Lucy's desperation got the better of her. She planted her feet and let out a rendition of:

"Oh, turn ye poor sinners, for why will you die?"

It came out louder than Lucy had ever sang in church. The bar quieted. Lucy had never had such rapt attention before. All eyes sought the source of the vocal strains. Lucy plunged on—

"Now Jesus invites and the spirit says come".

The bouncer gave her a jerk as if she were a rag doll and pushed open the door. Lucy realized she was going to be tossed out on the walkway like a sack of meal. Her song died. If Allen were in there, he would intercept this giant before she got herself cracked like an egg on the boardwalk. *Or maybe not!*

Lucy felt herself fly through the air, much like throwing slop to the pigs. Then *Whump!* She was on very solid ground, wooden planks to be exact. Afraid to move, yet more afraid not to, Lucy sat up. She was in one piece, but the impact had efficiently jarred her teeth. She rubbed her jaw line.

Suddenly she had an audience—leering, jeering drunks who hung out of the two story windows above, along with the men who cropped up on the street like weeds pushing themselves up through the boardwalk.

"Take that, you temperance ninny!"

"Yeah, wench, get out of here!"

"Go back home to your kitchen, mama!"

Lucy hurried to her feet, still clutching her umbrella. She felt humiliated, her face scarlet. She wanted to just melt away like lard on a hot skillet. Yet another part of her felt an intense urge to rail on the lowlife around her and set them straight. Break all those glass bottles of booze and restore the true "Spirit" on these erroneous husbands. Fainthearted, she wisely decided to leave *that* work to God.

And then Allen burst out the door, like a charging bull. The dark scowl he possessed made Lucy want to quake. Before she could open her mouth—if she had known what to say—Allen gripped her arm like the barroom bouncer had and pulled her away from the gathered crowd of drunken patrons, whose parting farewells followed them:

"Better steer clear of that woman!"

"Hey, Allen, don't let her tie ya to her apron strings!"

"Tell that–"

By the time Allen drew to a stop, Lucy was winded. She could not have spoken if she had wanted to. It turned out there was no need. Allen did all the talking. Chest heaving and dark eyes glittering, he demanded of her, "What do you think you were doing?"

Lucy's face overheated. One humiliation on the street was quite enough. She didn't need Allen drawing attention to them by bellowing.

"Answer me!" He was furious. "What in the world made you walk in there like that? What were you trying to prove? Don't you know women aren't allowed? I'm embarrassed, Lucy–". He was too angry to finish.

You're embarrassed? Lucy worked on catching her breath. She wasn't sure when or what to answer. Allen looked like a heart attack was on the horizon, same as the dark clouds looming overhead. Really, what kind of notion had she just carried through with? A pretty lame one, Lucy decided remorsefully. She had no wish to anger Allen further.

Allen was on a diatribe about her actions. "What kind of woman do you want people to think you are? There's nothing worse than a brazen woman! Your place is at home! You hear me? Minding your own business. What about the children? Did you leave the boys?

"This is the most idiotic thing...what were you thinking–NO–you weren't thinking, were you?"

Lucy watched his face as the shades of anger ruled over it. She studied the vein above his left brow. It pulsed like a wiggling caterpillar. Listening, she wasn't sure of the correct response. Should she cry or lash out in anger? She did neither, to her surprise. Instead, she laughed–bitterly. Yes, she had thought about what she had just done. And why was he suddenly worried about the boys?

Clutching her neglected umbrella like it was her only friend, she mustered, "How can you go on like that? In case you've forgotten, I'm your wife, not your slave."

With a glowering look, he started towards her. "Don't

ever say that again." His tone was threatening, but it was hardly a match for his countenance.

"Why? You afraid that's what's happening to us? You crack the whip and I'm supposed to jump?" Lucy felt the words slip effortlessly off her tongue. An ugly shroud enfolded them. The air was charged with particles of fury.

A headache began its tempo, pounding unmercifully on Lucy's skull. It was urged on by the heat that rose within her. She must hold herself in restraint. *Slow to anger, slow to wrath,* the Bible said.

Allen fumed, "You had no right coming to check up on me. You knew where I was. You think I'd lie to you, Lucy?" His stance told Lucy many things, the least of which to come would be a slow forgiveness. Allen's hands were clenched and resting on his hips, while his shoulders were hunched forward, revealing how provoked he really was.

"Allen. I want you to come home, so I came after you. I've asked you not to go to that gin mill anymore. If you loved me, you would listen."

"Don't parade that line of swill to me, Lucy! You did that to me fourteen years ago, and look where it's gotten me. I'm not listening to your senseless worries anymore. You are not the boss of our household. You're going to abide by my decisions whether you like them or not."

Lucy felt her restraining threads snap. They unraveled at a rapid speed, giving vent to her hurt. "You haven't once been concerned about me today! That overgrown lout *threw* me on the boardwalk! He could have broken my bones! You haven't even asked if I'm all right. I could have easily been hauled off on these dirty, foul streets by any boozing simpleton, and you don't even care!

"You're only worried about how it looks to those low-down drunks you associate with. How do you think it looks to respectable folks that you go to some gin mill?

"Do you want people talking about you–about us–all because you would rather spend your free time wallowing in liquor like a common–"

"That's enough, Lucy." The cold finality of Allen's tone struck Lucy like a slap to the cheek. But what hurt worse were his eyes–devoid of warmth and looking like they belonged to a stranger.

"Allen?" Disturbed, Lucy could not tear hers away from the animosity she saw there.

"What?" His demeanor did not waver. She should just say she was sorry, try to resolve the conflict between them. But the iron will in the dark eyes revealed something–unyielding and rock solid. Lucy was suddenly more scared than when she had entered the pub.

Backing away, she knew her cheeks were wet. The skies had opened, and it was raining again, upon her being and in her heart. Any affection in her life had hid behind an immovable cloud. There was not even left to her any device of rescue–even in the form of an umbrella. Unaware, it had been smashed, its ribs of delicate bone snapped in two. Lucy threw the useless thing down at Allen's feet.

Disconsolate, her feet took her away from the source of her pain. She listened for the call of her name between the pounding of the drops, but there was only silence among the continual sound of the heavens as it released its deluge. Allen grew further from her, and the distance did nothing to ease the grief. Lucy lifted her face upward, and the showers washed clean her cheeks of their tears and her heart free of all sunshine.

*   *   *   *

Dearest Rev. Fee,

I write to you after so many years, wondering how you are faring. Though we are separated by many miles and for a space of time, you have never been far from my thoughts.

I know you still carry on your great work and are a very busy man, but our daughter, Cynthia Anne, is now at Berea, and it would relieve my mind greatly if you could visit her when you are there. She is young and tender, much like another girl you helped to mold during turbulent times. Does not youth fall prey to such times regardless of the bearing that surrounds them?

If you could look her up, I would greatly appreciate it. She would be delighted, and she will know you. I am certain of it.

We are all physically well here, including Narciss and family. Please give my greetings to your dear wife, Mrs. Fee. Until we meet again.

In Christian love,
Lucy Ross

Chapter Eleven

Dear Miss Ross,
Be earnest in thy calling,
Whatever it may be.
Time's sands are ever falling
And will not wait for thee.
Yours truly,
J.T. Owens
Elizabethtown, Ky 6-5-1888

Miss Lottie Wetzel sorted the mail stack before her. She adjusted her eyeglasses to peer at the message on a lavender card. (*Hmm.*) Her long, thin face grew a frown, which steadily reached for her chin. As she read the words written in even script, she emitted an excited clucking noise. Ruffled eyebrows shot towards her hairline. (*My word!*)

Expressions came naturally to Miss Lottie. The position of postmistress of Warsaw was a job she took seriously. She often knew others' business even before they did. Why, she remembered when Joe Roy ordered his new harness–she knew of it before his wife. (*cluck*). When Anne Marie's mama passed on, Miss Lottie had to deliver the sad news (*sigh*). And when Lydia Tyler finally had her baby (*about time*) and named it Dewey George (*ughh!*), Miss Wetzel eagerly got to inform Myra and Bob they had become grandparents. Such were the joys and sorrows of postmistress.

Now the rest of the stack lay neglected. Miss Lottie held the card up to the light. No postmark. Highly suspicious, she looked to the workers back in the mail room. Someone had been bribed to place this card in today's mailbag with no stamp. And

97

just look at whom it was to–

Unsuspecting, John Hannon pushed open the post office door. The little bell attached to the top of the door gave a jingle, announcing his presence. Miss Wetzel looked up, her surprise evident. Hastily she dropped the lavender card on top of the table in front of her. "John," she croaked.

John was used to Miss Lottie's faces, but he was politely concerned anyway. Just now she reminded him of someone who had eaten a sour persimmon. Her puckered mouth reached new heights, and her ears appeared to quiver, creating a tremor which extended to the metal rims on her nose.

"Excuse me, Miss Lottie, but are you all right?" John came towards her, unsure as to whether she was sound or not. She coughed and nodded. The postmistress adjusted her glasses. Regaining her composure, she gripped the partition between them with small thin hands and appeared normal. "Just a touch of my old quinsy. Nothing to worry over." She picked up a stack of mail and pulled out three envelopes. "Here's your folks' mail, John, ready and waiting."

"Thank you, Miss Lottie." John took the mail from her and glanced at it. A letter from Aunt Dolly, one from a cousin, and a bill tallied up from the hardware. "See you later, Miss Lottie." John turned away, headed for the door, as he pocketed the letters. "Have a good day." He tried not to linger with the postmistress. Sometimes she picked your brain.

"John."

John paused at the door. "Yes, Miss Lottie?"

"Come here." Her voice had dropped to a confidential tone. "You have a message. It's from *that woman* who is new in town, you know, the one visiting her uncle." She held up the fancy card. "Do your folks know you're getting notes from her?" Her eyes pinned his brown ones captive.

Now it was John's turn to feel like he had sucked on a sour persimmon. "Well, ma'am," he could reply truthfully, "this is the first one I've received."

Lottie nodded. John had never told a lie that she knew of. With a whisper that bespoke conspiracy, she said, "Just between you and me, I'd steer clear of her. Frankly, I'm a little suspicious, if you get my meaning. Better share this with your folks." She handed him the card. "They'll likely find out about it anyway. You know how things spread."

John took the message in his sweaty hand without a glance at it. He nodded at her satisfied face. *I don't doubt it, you ol' –.* He cut off the unchristian thought as he peevishly stuffed it in his coat pocket with the other letters. The door banged shut behind him, the little bell a protest to his abrupt departure. Once outside, he strode away from the post office and leaned against the side of the mercantile in privacy to peruse the lavender card.

> *John,*
> *Can you meet me at 2:30 tomorrow*
> *afternoon? Please come to the park,*
> *beside the fish pool. I'll be waiting,*
> > *Yours,*
> > *Angel*

*   *   *   *

When John arrived at the goldfish pool, Angel Dubois was already there. She was seated on a park bench, the persona of calm and poise. John felt neither as he hastily swept off his hat. Angel stood and pulled off her ivory gloves and placed her hands within his, as though it was the natural thing to do. "John, you came. I knew you would." She was pleased. "Here, let's sit down." At his pensive look, she giggled, "Don't worry, I won't steal you or anything. My driver is right over there." She pointed to a man in a chauffeur's uniform, complete with a scowl.

John eyed the massive man. "Is he a twin to Myron, your butler?"

Angel gave a merry laugh. "Now what good would a featherweight do me? He's got to handle the roustabouts and the horse, you know."

John raised his brows, "Here in Warsaw?"

Angel fluffed a hand at him. "No. Other places–big

places. Which is why I asked you to meet me here."

John felt a stab of uneasiness, a feeling he was becoming accustomed to around Angel. "Oh?"

Angel beamed at him. "I have a 'purely' business proposition for you, John." She winked. "My uncle needs someone to learn the books of a new business venture he's undertaking. You need a job. When I told him I knew someone who was reliable and honest, he was interested. We're going to ride the rails to Cincinnati, and he wants you to come along. It's a free trip for you. All you have to do is show up next Wednesday morning at 8:00 at the depot. Say you will, John."

John was stunned. He tried to make sense of it. "What kind of job is your uncle wanting to train me for? I mean, he doesn't even know me–"

Angel gripped John's arm. Her hat sparkled in the afternoon sun. Everything about her shimmered. John's head swam, confused at this startling proposition. "Oh, John, it's a manager's position, and I'll be along to help you get the feel for it." At his look, she pressed on, "Don't fret. There will be plenty of others also, my two cousins–Uncle Will's boys–and my maid. It's only for three days, until Saturday. Say you will, please, John? Your mama hasn't got you tied to her apron strings at your age, does she? It'll be a ball! Live a little, John."

Her pleas did not fall on deaf ears. John envisioned the glitzy life Angel lived. Money seemed to adorn her with fancy outfits, a butler and a driver. William E. Alton's home was nothing to snort at either.

An image of Mama, hands on hips, came hurtling through his mind. It was a windbreaker to his rampaging thoughts. She was a barrier against which his pleasant musings broke upon. So was his training. *"For the lips of a strange woman drop as an honeycomb, and her mouth is smoother than oil".*

John stood abruptly, fumbling to replace his hat. "Angel, I'll have to get back to you. I need to…to check out my schedule with Mr. Hopkins."

"Alright, John. But don't wait too long. Leave me something at Uncle Will's box in town. Until then–". She leaned on tiptoe, to kiss his cheek.

John felt his nerve endings jumpstart. With a hasty motion, he grabbed her hand and worked it up and down as if he had ahold of a pump handle and was dying for a drink of water. "See you, Angel," he said as he made his escape.

All the way home, John debated within himself. He wouldn't–he shouldn't–he couldn't–but he just might. Why not? What did he have to lose? "*Live a little*." John heard Angel's smooth voice urge. He made his decision. He would check out this job offer.

John felt a little like Christopher Columbus must have, ready to embark on a New World venture–a bit excited, a little nervous, and extremely worried over the native exchange–with Mama.

*   *   *   *

John's ears were still ringing. He sank down on the porch step beside his father. Both sat quietly, battle-weary, until John spoke, "That was the National Panic thrown together with the Fourth of July." He had just informed Mama of his decision to check out W. E. Alton's job offer.

Sam Hannon smiled, "What did you expect?"

"Well, a little less resistance. I am twenty. I'm just glad Mama saved me the big guns. I can't handle her tears." John, disturbed, placed both hands on his knees.

His father motioned upwards. "She's probably in the bedroom crying now."

"Dad," John said, exasperation taking hold. "I feel bad I've upset Mama. But didn't she know I was going to grow up sometime and need my freedom? She needs to let go."

Sam studied the tree line in the distance. "That may be, but seems to me it's your mama's right to have a vested interest in you. She's been caring for you since before you joined this world."

"You ever felt like I do, Dad?" John questioned, throw-

101

ing his father off track.

Sam's answer came out gruffer than he intended. "Boy, I never had a mama to fuss over me. She was sold south before I could drink cow's milk out of a cup. And I made my own freedom." Funny how the memories brought on a tremor of emotions.

John said nothing. What could he say to Dad? He was right, as usual, but so was John. There was a time for everything, it said so in Ecclesiastes.

"You know, John, there are reasons for the things we sometimes don't understand. Your mama holds on tight for two reasons. One is you're her only living child. And the other...well, I hate to say too much, but slavery times were hard, no doubt about that. We lost people we loved and not always to death. You need to spread your wings, but the things you learn while doing just that sometimes makes you sorry."

John followed his father's line of vision to a hawk soaring above the treetops outfitted in fall's colors. "Sorry?"

Sam Hannon nodded. "There's lots of sorrow out there, caused by evilness. It would be nice if you didn't have to get acquainted with all of it."

John sighed. "I need to go apologize to Mama."

Sam held up his hand. "That would be good, son, but make it easy on her. Don't do anything you'll regret on this trip before the sun rises the next morning. Live by your teachings and you can't go wrong."

"I will, Dad." John meant it. He noticed the gray twining its way into his father's hair. "I'll be careful."

Now it was Sam Hannon's turn to sigh. "If it's a good job offer, you'll have some decisions to make. But if it's anything shady or illegal, get away from there as fast as you can, John. The law is and always has been a white man's law–don't go forgetting."

"No, sir," John replied, but his heart beat in anticipation.

"Till a dart strike through his liver; as a bird hasteth to the snare, and knoweth not that it is for his life." Prov. 7:23

The bright lights aboard the packet liner shimmered on the river like fluorescent jellyfish, sporadic in its floating pattern, sending tendrils of brightness across the crests of water.

The boat rocked to the rhythm of the big band sounds as it spilled out into the night. The stars twinkled and by the standards of the gods of pleasure, all mirrored a perfect setting in which to "live a little".

Angel, adorned in yellow satin, curled an arm around the starboard side of the steamer's railing and let her hand rest on John's arm. "Isn't the night perfect?"

"Uh-huh," John replied and the crease between his eyes, reminiscent of Mama's, widened in affirmation. He turned to Angel. "I'm sorry, Angel, I'm just new to all of this. Things are moving fast, but I'm trying to soak it all up. I know I'm pretty dull by your standards."

"Oh, John, that's not true. You just have to get your sea legs, that's all. Soon it'll be second nature, the lights and noise and action. No more hauling freight. You'll get to use your brains instead of your hands. Life will be easier!"

Yes, John thought, *but how easy?* He had not been raised to pursue a carefree life of leisure. The train ride to Cincinnati proved that. He had fought the urge to hop down onto the platforms and start unloading cars along with the draymen.

On the trip Angel had filled John in on her family history. Uncle William Alton had two brothers and a sister. The sister was Angel's mother, Leticia. All four children had been born on a plantation in Kentucky in Madison County called Alcorn Hill. The eldest son, Emmitt, (a half brother to Uncle William), was followed by another brother named Thad. Uncle William was born three days behind Thad. A lot like twins, they shared a father, but Uncle William's mother (and Angel's) was a slave. "Uncle Thad and Uncle Will were close, being born around the same time. They were best friends. It didn't matter they never

103

shared a mother, the one being black and the other white. But Uncle Emmitt was different. He wanted nothing to do with Uncle Will or my mama. He moved to Tennessee, near his mother's people, after her death. A place called Ridge Top. He's as rich as Solomon and thinks he's some king, too.

"Uncle Thad isn't afraid to own up to his blood. He's a businessman, deals in properties and all sorts of ventures. Since he's white, he helps Uncle William out and they're partners. A black man can't own much, even in Cincinnati. And Uncle Thad has always stood by Uncle Will.

"My mother left for New Orleans at sixteen, where she met my papa, who was Creole. When I turned sixteen, I moved up here to be near Uncle Will. I can't abide the South. It's too hot and just full of old white men remembering their grand rebellion days."

John found her family quite interesting. Angel shook her head. "Interesting? Don't you have a mixed-up mess of family history too? Seems all our folks have a tale of so-and-so being related to this white man or wondering whose slave you were during those hard years, or stories of not finding family since they were sold south."

John was quiet, thinking of how little he really knew about his folks' families. "Well, I guess you're right."

A black waiter appeared, glasses of champagne on a tray. He offered it to Angel. She took one. John refused the glass offered him. Angel pouted. "Are you going to relax or win the prize for being a tight laced boot all night?"

John mumbled, "I don't drink."

Angel frowned. "John, if you call a little champagne drinking, then hymn singing is a sin on Sunday."

John's eyebrows rose. Angel's boldness was swept away with her merry laughter. "Never mind. Come on, let's go see what the dance floor holds. Or is that taboo too?"

John swallowed and raked a hand through his hair. He smiled weakly and followed her. Maybe he would break a leg while going down the stairs before they reached the ballroom.

*　　　*　　　*　　　*

　　The music filled the ballroom from the corners of the inlaid black and white marble floor to the heights where the ceiling chandelier's gaslights twinkled like diamonds.

　　John's ears pulsed with the sound. Angel was gripping his arm, her eyes shining. She tilted her head toward the floor, an invitation, to where other couples promenaded. Ornate dresses and pricey suits whirled by. John's own suit was outdated and worn. Likely these people figured Angel had dug him out of the mothballs. He was plain dowdy, but Angel, for strange reasons, appeared not to notice.

　　When a gentleman approached them and squired Angel away to the dance floor, John ignored the look she cast him under her lashes. *Shoot, she's not my girl. Help yourself, mis-ter.* One of Angel's cousins, Bernard, moved to stand beside him. Bernard favored his daddy, W.E. Alton, except that his expression was like chiseled stone, and John felt his swallow go down hard.

　　Bernard spoke begrudgingly to him, as if out of a sense of duty, his eyes fixed on the swirling dancers who flashed by. "You want a job with Alton Properties, you got to mix a little."

　　John tried to sound causal. "Mix a little?"

　　"Yeah, you know, a few drinks with the ladies and business associates. Mingle. Where you from anyway?"

　　"Warsaw, Kentucky."

　　"Huh. That a hayseed town?"

　　John felt a twinge of annoyance. "Guess you could say that. But that doesn't make me one."

　　Grunt. "No? Well then, you need to hike it up a notch. We've got a reputation to uphold. 'Course, Angel gets whatever she wants, so you better make it work. You don't, you won't just walk away. No one ever has, especially from Angel."

　　John let a silence stand between them. He fidgeted with a coat button waiting on Bernard to leave. Then a woman, sandwiched between pink flounces and a fashionable bustle, came and led Bernard out to the floor. John let out a slow breath.

He had a lot of questions over this job offer and had yet to know what it all detailed. Right now, he had to get through this night and act like the shoe fit the foot.

He motioned to a waiter whose skin was the same color as his and asked for a glass of water. The waiter raised his brows and cast John a disdainful look but glided off to obey.

Once John had his water, he drifted between guests (*mingling*), brandishing the glass like the other partygoers. He slipped between people and cut in on Angel's partner. A sheen of nervous perspiration covered his forehead but he continued his "act". He had no idea how to dance but decided he would have to bluff his way through it.

Angel's partner, a suave-looking guy pushing fifty, glowered at John, but John ignored him. Angel smiled as he cut in and took her hand. They moved around the floor, John following Angel's lead.

"I'm not much for waltzing," he told her.

Angel laughed, "Neither was the codger before you. My toes bear testimony to that." She peered down to the flimsy slippers gracing her feet. "Thanks for another rescue."

John nodded. "No problem. You seem to need rescued regularly. I'll be happy to oblige you on that if you can make me appear a sophisticated buffoon to Bernard."

Angel enjoyed his comment. Her eyes sparkled as she replied, "My pleasure, John. But as for taking the oddness out of you, that may be the part of you I enjoy the most." John's laugh accompanied her silvery peal, but his eyes searched diligently for a clock. Surely the night had to end sometime, didn't it?

*   *   *   *

After three days of rich people, fancy food, and playacting, John lay awake in the cabin he shared with Angel's two cousins. His thoughts sloshed around like the waves that slapped the hull beneath the porthole above his berth. What was he doing here and whom was he fooling? He had the answers now to his questions. A myriad of truths that made him feel as rotten as the pale fish that floated along the bank where they were docked.

A clock chimed once and still the partygoers carried on, oblivious to a new day. *This is the day which the Lord hath made; we will rejoice and be glad in it.* All the people aboard the steamer were celebrating obediently, but not to the Lord. And that, John had put his finger upon, was the main problem. This was a reckless, godless life the people were living–a floating city akin to Sodom and Gomorrah. It troubled John greatly. He twined his fingers together and circled his head. Staring up at the plastered ceiling, he realized he had known it before he had set foot on the train–that it would be this way. Honest work did not make black men rich. He knew Angel's occupation–late night card dealing–was meant to draw in the money and keep it in. John was out of his league and the truth was a mercy. He would be going home tomorrow.

This very evening, John had talked with William Alton. With enticing detail, the man had explained his offer and watched John's reaction. "You have a head for book learning. I saw you tally up the accounts Bernard gave you. I never saw anyone quicker with figures. You're honest and your integrity cannot be questioned, I hear. Besides, Angel has taken a shine to you, and we, men folk, have learned to acquiesce her." Mr. Alton's smile was sharp, his manner professional as he proceeded to explain his business. John listened to the many ventures they ran.

"There's a lot of money to be made out there. My brother, Thad, figured if we had boats and casinos open for the wealthy black population, as well as the whites, we could double our money. I oversee two colored boats, and Thad has three to manage. Pleasure boats are the up and coming thing for the '80's and we want to cash in on it. People need to travel, why not make it fun? You know, our people are coming into their own. They have the brains to make it happen. Of course it's still a small percentage of blacks who have the money to spend, but it's there."

John listened, his mind like an hourglass where the sands leak through a skinny neck. He felt his throat close off. Rich black people were taking other black people's money. Wealthy colored people were wasting this money on pleasure. Black people waiting on other black people as servants. Where did W.E. Alton think John thought this money came from? *Not hauling freight*, John would guarantee. John was not totally ignorant. The money came from the sweat of someone and it didn't belong to anyone rich.

All of *his* people and kindred lived simple lives–sometimes meager lives–but they clung to moral and upright conduct. They were all only a generation away from slavery, for mercy's sake! The contrast bothered him.

He lifted his eyes to the diamond stickpin on the pinstripe suit belonging to Mr. Alton. The gray fabric cost more than half a year's wages, John estimated. This was the kind of lifestyle John could embrace if he kept the record books for Alton Properties. He would never know need in this life. Yet he also knew, he could never walk away, not with the knowledge he would be privy to. It would be there in eternity, where he would suddenly be very needy indeed.

Dad's warning was like a train signal blazing through his mind. The words of Job–"Wherefore I abhor myself, and repent in dust and ashes"–were a message of dots and dashes like a mental telegraph within his thoughts. It was spelled out very clearly.

Mr. William Alton had paused. He waited patiently for John to meet his eyes. And he saw there the mien he was fearfully certain he would see if he could at all judge character. It was the sorry expression a puppy produced when he had disappointed you.

Abruptly Mr. Alton stood. His own eyes mirrored a rueful cast. He gazed down to where John sat in his cheap suit. His voice was not unkind. "John, I see you are not the man I had in mind for the job. Angel made a mistake. When we dock tomorrow, you need to go home." A grave and somber expression smoothed the age lines that weathered the prosperous man's face.

"John, you remind me of myself many years ago, except I was very impressionable. I see you are not. A steadfast character is one thing I greatly admire but unfortunately, it will ruin many a business proposition, at least in my business. I'll explain things to Angel. She'll get over it."

John rose and opened his mouth. The words he wished to say refused to divulge themselves. He knew he was pardoned for being a milksop. "Mr. Alton–"

"You can thank me later, boy. Now go on home." The businessman sat down and scratched his pen on the paperwork before him. John was dismissed. He made his way to the door. Once there, he hesitated, his hand resting on the brass knob. Remorse flooded through him for the current of raw sentiment he had stirred up, like silt in a creek bed.

"Thank you, Mr. Alton, for the chance and…everything."

The only recognition John received from Mr. Alton was the sight of the man's uncalloused, husky hands–shaking–as he wrote in his ledgers.

Chapter Twelve

Dear Miss Annie Ross,
Dear Schoolmate,
In the golden chain of friendship,
Consider me a link.
Your friend,
Narcissus Bain
Berea, Ky 2-12-1888

Out her dormitory window of the Ladies Hall, Cynthia watched the evening shades fall across the land. A giant navy curtain from the northwest crept stealthily upon the sky, swallowing up the great red ball of sun, permitting darkness to overtake the light. Celestrial rays shone out over the snow-dressed ground, and pink and salmon hues kissed "purple majesties" in a mighty panorama. The rare beauty of mid-winter dusk made Cynthia nearly shiver.

Tiny wafts of crisp air stole through the window frame, tingling her fingertips with invisible caresses. The whole campus and surrounding woods looked peaceful in the twilight. *Well, Lord, if any scene should give me peace, this would be it.* Yet Cynthia remained burdened.

The door opened and closed behind Bertha as she burst into the small room. "Brrr! Annie! What are you doing standing here in the dark?"

Cynthia suddenly noticed how the overcast shadows brushed the walls of the room. "It's just now gotten dark," she said to excuse herself. "I'll light the lamp."

Bertha pulled off her wraps and deposited them on her bed. "Why aren't you down for dinner?"

Cynthia shrugged. "I'm not hungry. I was going to work on my literature paper." She sat at the well-worn desk and lit the lamp. The flame winked, then grew stronger, hungrily lapping at the wick, making up for Cynthia's loss of appetite. Bertha's shadow filled the opposite wall. She watched as Cynthia put on the globe. "You know, Annie, you've been despondent for days. It's like your trip home depressed you. What's the feed in your wagon?" She sat down on the bed, her oval face resting in her palm, and she was serious–an unusual occurrence.

Cynthia studied the intense brown eyes. Should she voice her concerns over her visit home? Somewhere inside her a stout wall of loyalty quickly erected itself and a firm resolve forbade her to disclose such secrets. "Bertha, I'm fine really. The holidays are so tiring, you know, the rich foods, all the visiting, less sleep." Cynthia turned her attention to her literature paper. "Help me define the poetry of Percy Bysshe Shelley."

Bertha tossed a blank look at Cynthia. "Whoever heard of him? He's probably some medieval monk left alone in the dark too much. Listen, Annie, you want to talk, I'm all ears. You want a poetry critic, you'll have to go find Adelaide!"

Cynthia ignored her. "Listen to this, Bertha. It's called *To A Skylark.*

> In the golden lightening
> Of the sunken sun,
> O'er which clouds are brightening,
> Thou dost float and run,
> Like an unbodied joy whose race is just begun.

What do you think of that? It reminds me of Berea. The race is just beginning for us, like some land rush. We're just gaining ground. It's something to think about it."

Bertha frowned. "You sure you're all right?"

Cynthia's brow wrinkled. "Why?"

"Because you're getting a little deep there with that bird poem."

"Yes," Cynthia said, her annoyance contained under a thin layer of patience. "I can't help reflecting on the sacrifices my parents have made for me to be here, not just financially, but with all the things they have had to face in life. Our parents have brightened the clouds for us. Don't you agree, Bertha?"

Bertha studied Cynthia skeptically. "Sure, Annie, it's a regular Utopia here." She stood and clutched her stomach. "Come on, let's go eat. We're going to be last in line and have to forage at just crumbs like that skylark you're reading about."

Cynthia shook her head. "You go on, Bertha. I'm really not hungry."

"Suit yourself," Bertha said, jumping up and breezing out. Cynthia watched her leave and turned her attention to the poem before her. Her troubled thoughts ranged freely, like little feathered creatures scattering in all directions before a whirlwind of field stubble.

Why were Mama and Daddy so cold and distant with each other? The strain existing between them was as clear as if a frost had scoured the windows of their hearts. Where had it come from? Her brothers seemed to sense nothing amiss, but Henry and James were absorbed in their own lives and the other two–John and Dee–were too young yet to be concerned.

Cynthia pulled the literature book closer and thumbed the pages absently. The lamp had dimmed. She turned it up and read the poem over again.

> "Higher still and higher
> From the earth thou springest,
> Like a cloud of fire;
> The blue deep thou wingest,
> And singing still dost soar, and soaring
> ever singest."

Cynthia rested her tired eyes, letting the picture of a graceful bird stretching its wings up toward the sun occupy her mind in place of her disturbed thoughts. Instantly she felt warmed. Oh, how she wanted to learn all she could at Berea! She ached to feel as a worthy soul who could change the long-endured falsehoods that exist in life. She hoped to instruct the youthful minds of future students with the principles of equality based on merit, along with the other fundamental studies.

She did not want Mama and Daddy to falter. They were her rock. *No, Cynthia Anne*, she reasoned, *God is your rock and sure foundation.* Mama had told her that a million times. Mama said people will disappoint you, but God will not, nor forsake you. *Be as a lark and soar upward, toward a rising sun,* Cynthia chided herself. She lay her head down on the desk, her thoughts heavy upon her. *While thou soars–ever singest.*

The door opened and Cynthia's roommates clattered in like a noisy troop, merry in their normal routine. The accompanying chatter ran rampant until one by one, they noticed Cynthia, resembling a prosaic statuette, seated at the desk. The three girls instantly ceased their prattle to stare at their friend.

"Annie?"

"What now, girl?

"I knew we shouldn't have left her alone."

Their words prompted an inward smile. The concern on their faces touched Cynthia, sending a surge of warmth and happiness through her that had been absent for the last while. A giggle escaped while she slowly rose and balanced herself on the rickety desk chair. She held out her textbook the way Mr. Beeson did when he introduced a new math concept and was sure the class would not be able to follow.

"'Hail to thee, blithe spirits'!" she intoned. "Doth thou find math troublesome? Be of good cheer. Once ye have borne Beeson, ye can survive any of life's problems, mathematical or otherwise. Let neither beast nor 'Bee' discourage ye...Hail, I say, 'hail to thee, blithe spirits'!" Then executing a dramatic fall, she gave the book a toss and landed gracefully on the bed, outstretched as if ready for the parlor, with eyes closed and her hands clasped together atop her abdomen.

Carrie, Adelaide, and Bertha gazed at Cynthia, their eyes mesmerized by the scene. They were once more rendered totally speechless.

As if a honing magnet, Leona Riddler's knock suddenly sounded upon the door. "Girls!"

Cynthia lifted her head and spoke in a stage whisper. "Fie! Dear Rhino, charge ye not!"

When Miss Riddler entered the room, she was greeted by girls whose faces twitched with suppressed mirth. Sighing, she fulfilled her matron's obligation by giving them the customary discourse on proper etiquette expected by the Institution. Once that duty was discharged, Miss Riddler returned to her own quarters, barely able to contain her disgust at their adolescent behavior. *Would today's youth **ever** grow up*?

$$* \qquad * \qquad * \qquad *$$

It was lunch hour in Warsaw at the sawmill. Men poured out of the brick building like ants from their nests. Soon the courtyard area alongside the building had men occupying every inch of space, rattling tin pails or lard cans or opening knapsacks with similar foods of the working man's variety. No roast beef or filet mignon.

Henry Ross and his cousin, Henry Allen Laine, settled together at the edge of a few flagstones, away from the older men. It seemed the younger set found the company of their peers more enjoyable than that of their elders.

Henry pulled out his mama's three day old bread spread with lard. Besides that, the bucket contained a hard boiled egg and two biscuits. Henry Allen perused his odd-shaped box to see nearly the same fare as his cousin, only his sandwich had bacon on it and there was a slice of cake. At the boardinghouse, Mrs. Lawson sent lunches for those who paid another dollar and quarter a month. It was a steep deal for a man who worked at the sawmill, but Henry decided it was worth it. A fellow had to eat, and Mrs. Lawson was a better than average cook.

Henry looked at Henry Allen's box. "You win today. Look at your spread. Mama hasn't baked anything since I don't know when. Wonder what she does all day."

Henry Allen smiled, "Bet your mama could fill you in on it. Anyhow, remember yours is free and mine isn't."

"Yeah, I know." Henry Ross finished off his sandwich in fifteen seconds. "How is your savings coming?"

"Oh, pretty good, I guess. Your sister is sure fussy about me not attending Berea with her, but she doesn't know how it is."

"'Course not. She's the typical female. Don't let it both-

115

er you. She's never had to work and save. Besides," Henry plopped his egg in his mouth "all girls try to make you feel bad. It's in their nature."

Henry Allen laughed, "Henry, old boy, you sound like a twelve year old! What makes you so grouchy at the fairer side of the Homo Sapiens?"

Henry raised his brows, "Say what? I thought you had limited schooling!"

"Aha, you've been judging a book by its cover. There's more to me than you realize, cousin."

"Yeah, you sure had me fooled. What have you been reading? A dictionary?" Henry had finished his lunch and took a drink of warm water from his daddy's old canteen.

"Exactly. You should try it. Now answer my question. Why are you so down on women?" Henry Allen paused on his lunch.

Henry Ross eyed his cousin's piece of cake. "You gonna eat that?"

Henry Allen looked down at the vanilla cake with smudged chocolate frosting. "Huh, this?" He poked the confection.

"Yes, that! What are you saving it for?"

Henry Allen pulled out his pocket knife and cut down through it. He gave half of it to his drooling cousin. "Now you'll be able to concentrate better. Tell me about it."

After Henry Ross had inhaled the treat, he spoke, "You know Marianne Schaffer?" Henry Allen nodded.

"Well, she's decided she likes that Williams fellow better than me. Dropped me like a hot potato. That's women for you. Friendly one minute, mad at you the next. Mama and Cynthia Anne are the same way. So I've decided to steer clear of them all for a while, maybe forever. Which is why I want to go to Cincinnati."

"I'm pretty sure there's women in Cincinnati, Henry." Henry Allen ignored his cousin's grouchy look. He continued on, "And do what?" He started in on his cake.

"I want to work on one of those fancy new steamboats.

They're beautiful. Imagine traveling from Cincinnati to Pittsburgh and getting paid. It'd be great!" Henry's enthusiasm flowed from him the same as a river did leaving its point of origin–its mouth.

"What kind of job would you get aboard one?" Henry Allen asked, now interested.

"Oh, I don't know. I'd like to be a purser, but I'll take whatever I can get. Problem is, I don't know if I'll be allowed." Henry gathered up his lunch pail and canteen and frowned.

Henry Allen shook his head. "Well, you're of age to make your own decisions, but I guess I was too, and that didn't happen for me until now. Family means obligations, doesn't it? Maybe you've got the right idea. Maybe it's best to avoid the whole female gender if you have plans."

"Sure," Henry agreed. "Why don't you join me, Henry Allen? We would make quite a team aboard some steamboat! What do you say?"

Henry Allen thought for a few moments until the lunch whistle blew. Their thirty minutes had ended; time to return to work. As the men rose, Henry Allen shook his head. "I'm going to Berea. It's what I really want, and I can't afford to get side-tracked."

"Suit yourself. I haven't asked anyhow, but if you change your mind and quit reading the dictionary, we could forego it together." The two cousins walked back into the warm mill, their thoughts on the future.

*　　　　*　　　　*　　　　*

Fiona's blue pinstriped dress swung smartly around her ankles, and she couldn't resist peering down at the new leather boots encasing her feet. Fiona was in her work dress but she thought it was very pretty. The boots were the first purchase she had made with the money she had earned.

Although the agreement between Mrs. Ferguson, who owned the boardinghouse, and herself had been that she would work for her keep, she had worked on her days off as well and received wages. Mrs. Ferguson was firm but fair. Soon Fiona would have a good savings.

She had her eye on a warm wool cloak at the clothier's for her next purchase. It felt good to be working and no longer down on her luck. Throughout her day, Fiona would often give prayers of thanks. The weeks spent living as a tramp had been the worst of her young life–all twenty-four years of it.

Today, she was on her way to the market. Every other day she went for fresh meat at the butcher's. Usually not quite this early but she had her hopes. Maybe she would see that black man, her friend, once more at the park.

She cut her way across the center, and down a tree-lined walkway when she spotted him ahead of her, on his way to work. Elation soared within her. Before she could even contemplate how to gain his notice, she found herself dashing toward him, calling out, " Hallo there. Hallo, remember me?"

Allen paused, and looked over his shoulder, startled to see an apricot-haired girl running towards him. He stopped and turned, a quizzical look on his face. "Miss?"

"There you are!" She arrived in front of him, her hat askew, precariously tipping to one side. Her cheeks were flushed and her lungs heaving. "I didn't think I'd catch you." She smiled, her pleasure evident.

Allen frowned. "Well, it looks like you need to catch your breath instead. Everything alright?"

"Oh, yes, but you see, I've waited and watched for you for weeks, and now I've found you." Her expression conveyed the finding of him was like a miner who had discovered an emerald.

Allen was uneasy. No emotion flickered on his face though as he demanded, "Why? Why are you looking for me?"

For the first time, the girl faltered. Her brow puckered and she straightened her hat in confusion. "Well, I think of you as my friend. Remember the drunk you saved me from?" Her face brightened. "No one has been so nice to me as you, except Mrs. Ferguson, but I do work my green clovers off for her." She held up her hands, wriggling her fingertips, which were red and chapped. "But you know all about work, don't you? I can tell you are a good worker." Her intense eyes made him uncomfortable, along with her smile. Embarrassed, Allen glanced around the park, knowing he wouldn't want to be caught talking to a white girl, no matter if she was only a scullery maid.

"Well, you've seen me, so you can go merrily on your way now. Glad you're getting along." Allen turned towards the sawmill. He had little time to be squandering.

"Wait." Her lilted voice rang out. "Please, can't you visit a spell? Tell me your name?"

Allen scowled at her. *Crazy girl! What was her prob - lem?* "I'm going to be late." He turned once more, and she hurried after him.

"Sir, really, you're my only friend. Can you meet me here next Tuesday? I can be here in the early morning." Her eyes were imploring, but Allen chose to ignore the plea. He moved off to the left of her and picked up his pace. *Fool girl!* She was certainly addled, and he had no intention of becoming entangled as a "friend". He put her out of his mind, hoping he would beat the clock. Excuses never made the grade with the foreman.

Allen gave the incident little thought afterwards, once he had sorted it out in his mind. There was no such thing as a black man and a white girl being friends. Period! *How naïve!* Besides, that was the last thing he needed to capsize his already frail bark. Surely the girl could find someone else to latch on to. The waif was definitely foreign, Irish he guessed, and most likely just arrived in America not to know social propriety.

Allen avoided the park for two weeks and was relieved to see no sign of her. He had his knapsack full of trouble with Lucy. They were barely able to face one another, could not meet one another's eyes, and all words had fled within their presence.

Sometimes Allen thought back to the Garrard County days. It brought a warmth of sunlight to his being. The memories were always of happier times. Lucy's smile and tender eyes were there in those images. There was the absence of any sharp words or any of the disappointed expressions Allen had come to expect.

"Hallo!" The call came whimsically out of the air, but with the deadly accuracy of an arrow in flight. Allen immediately doubted his ears, but there it was again. This time with the cry there appeared the issuer of it.

Allen moaned. He had cut across the park on his way home and would have detoured had he known this possibility would occur.

There was the Irish girl, in a warm cloak, blocking his path. Allen hastily scanned the tree-lined walkways for other pedestrians. He didn't intend to tarry but he could not afford to be the subject of ill-fated gossip.

The girl was delighted, and Allen's sober countenance did nothing to dissuade her. "Can you sit a spell and talk? I've done so much since you've seen me last."

Allen's expression was guarded. "Listen, girl, you need to leave me alone. We can't be friends."

Fiona's smile wavered. "But why not? This is America, right? Anything is possible here, my Da always said." She spoke like that belonged with the Ten Commandments.

Allen shook his head. "Well, your Da was misinformed. That's not so. Since it appears you just got off the boat, I'll enlighten you, black and white don't mix." He stirred impatiently.

Fiona faltered for a moment but then, like a banty hen, stood her ground. "Just so ya know, I don't care what people say. Color counts none with me. It's the person who matters." She bravely carried on. "You needn't be afraid. I'll not take your money. I'm only wanting your friendship."

A laugh escaped Allen before he could suppress it. She was plucky, he had to give her that. "Oh, I'm not scared of you, miss. But if you were wise, you would be worried about what you're suggesting. I don't need a friend, all right? I've got a wife and kids and they're friends enough, believe me. You need to turn your head to other things, like your work and you'll get along. Now goodbye."

Allen was determined to end their conversation, and he pushed past her rather brusquely. This time she offered no resistance.

Later in the day, Allen's conscience tugged at him like an annoying child who begged for a sweet. But he hardened his resolve. The girl was annoying, like a door whose hinges hung crooked. He would hold fast as sap to its pine bark, before and after the saw blade severed it. Because, after all, he was in the right on this one.

Chapter Thirteen

Dear Miss Annie Ross,
In this token of my friendship,
Left for you to think of me,
When these pages you are turning
And shall chance these lines to see.
Your friend,
Rowena Roberson

The murmuring voices distracted Cynthia. Someone was breaking the rules. Her curiosity piqued, she pulled her head out of the book she was engrossed in and peered towards Miss Walsh's desk. Aha! The transgressor was the librarian herself! Cynthia leaned over the table to catch a better view of the other erring one. Meeting her eyes was an aged gentleman, adorned with gray hair and beard. A professor?

Cynthia watched him intently as he stroked his tidy beard methodically in the manner of an educator. Pulling a silver watch from his vest pocket, he whispered once more to Miss Walsh.

Why were the two fraternizing in the library, a place religiously maintained by "Warden Walsh"? The occasional crackle of turning pages was the only acceptable caliber of noise permitted within the confines of the study room by the librarian. Talking, even whispering, was a serious offense.

Whatever the two spoke of, Miss Walsh nodded in admiration, a smile materializing. The man must possess magic to draw that luxury out of the "Warden". Cynthia's eyebrows rose a notch and she squinted to catch more of this spectacle.

The man was departing. He stopped and inspected the book shelves, almost reverently, a pleased expression upon his face. Cynthia was intrigued. Something radiated from the distinguished gentleman. It was more than the gentility of a southern man—it was an aura.

Now he walked by in close proximity to where Cynthia sat camped out with her various textbooks and pen and ink. Something urged Cynthia to make his acquaintance, a drawing force she could not have explained to her friends. Yet Mama and Aunt Narcissa would understand and think it natural, given their life's experiences.

She rose quickly, maneuvering around the table's edge, jarring it in her hurry. "Sir?" she called out, her voice barely above a whisper, yet willing it to reach him. He continued on, with Cynthia scurrying after him. In her rush, she ignored the pointed look shot at her by Miss Walsh.

Then suddenly, Cynthia was directly behind the man, skidding to a halt. Embarrassed over her unladylike display, she debated whether to simply slink away, but the man sensed her presence and turned to face her.

"Sir?" Cynthia's voice wavered, unsure of itself. "Do I know you?" Of course she did not! What lunacy had possessed her to chase the man down, like a miner seeking a vein of ore?

He paused and peered at her where they stood, in the foyer of the great Study Hall's entrance, its glass paneled doors kindly bathing them in a warm saffron light.

"Why, child, are you...Lucy's daughter?" His brows rose as he studied the face before him. A smile dimpled one bearded cheek.

"Yes, sir, and I can guess who you are!" She felt as if she had indeed struck gold.

"And?" He waited, amused.

"You're Mr. Reverend Fee, the Moses-man and dear friend of Mama's!" Cynthia rattled this off, forgetting her earlier reticence.

"Indeed. That is who I am, and you are Cynthia." Rev. Fee's eyes twinkled. "Your mother mentioned you were here at Berea. I intended to look you up. Come, let's sit down over there, and you can tell me about your studies."

They settled in the lobby on faded blue brocade cushions atop a bench which had reached its sunset years. Their conversation flowed in earnest.

"Your folks are well?" Rev. Fee inquired.

"Yes, they…well, they appear to be." Cynthia plucked at her skirt. She slowly raised her eyes to him.

"Hmm." John Fee was interested. "Allen and Lucy were very much in love when I married them. Time measures a marriage, I fear, as well as distance. My own dear Matilda has put up with my gallivanting around for years." He rubbed his beard. "They are not in bad health?"

"Oh no, sir." Cynthia smiled. "All is fine, I'm sure." She changed the subject. "There are six of us children. Dee is the youngest, at seven. Daddy is at the sawmill. I'm the only one who wanted to come to Berea. I'm working on a teacher's certificate."

Rev. Fee's pleasure was evident. His eyes twinkled, and his smile broadened. "A most notable occupation, Cynthia. You won't regret it. We need more teachers in the field. I remember trying to convince your mother to be a teacher once. Then she went and fell in love." He chuckled and queried of her, "Perhaps you will have this little interference, my dear?"

"Oh, no. Nothing can get in my way of being a teacher. It's what I've always wanted to do. Love is for those without direction or purpose. Besides, I'm too young yet."

"A nice sentiment, Miss Ross." Rev. Fee held out his hand for hers. "It would be good if we all viewed life with your vigor." He enfolded her brown hand, like a small wren, within his own white one and squeezed. "But love does have its place. It can be a warm fire during the winters of life." John Fee released her hand and stood. "We will talk more, Cynthia. Now I must attend a lecture. You will hear from me."

"Thank you, Rev. Fee." As Cynthia watched him depart from the Hall, she hugged herself in satisfaction. *You, Mosesman, are all that Mama said you were–a true parter of seas.* Cynthia was left with the impression of having seen a burning bush.

＊　　　＊　　　＊　　　＊

Lucy moved sluggishly around the room, lighting the lamp, chasing the darkness back into the corners. She straightened the doily on back of Allen's chair and stowed a stray book to its rightful place on the shelf of the bookcase.

Lucy was troubled, which cast a sort of stupor over her. There were the children to feed and care for, but as far as a husband to welcome home, that had been an absent part of the evening routine ever since Lucy had visited the bar on Whittaker Street.

She was almost sorry she had done it and yet...what choices did she have to persuade Allen to stay home? Obviously that attempt had not been the answer to halt his weekly transgression.

The door to the kitchen creaked on its hinges, then banged, and Lucy decided it was Henry. The youngest three were upstairs and by the sounds coming from the kitchen, it would not be Allen.

When Henry made his appearance, he was swallowing a cookie and whacking the newspaper against his palm. "Mama?" He stopped and gave her an odd look. "Why are you sitting here all alone?" He plunked down in his dad's chair, crossing his legs carelessly.

Lucy smiled. "And you're concerned?"

"Mama! You know I am. You never just sit alone in the living room. You feel alright?"

No, Henry, I'm sick at heart. "Well, of course, I'm alright. Just relaxing a spell." Lucy strove to don a pleasant look for the sake of her son. "How was your day?"

"The same." A glumness settled over his features. "Every single day it's the same old thing."

"What would you rather be doing? You know, you could have gone to Berea." Lucy, with raised brows, stressed the point.

"Now, Mama, I've had enough book learning. I'd like to be somewhere besides the sawmill, maybe some place a little

126

more action-packed." Henry leaned forward in his chair, an animation suddenly present. "I'd really like to work aboard one of those steamships on the Ohio. The fancy ones that embark from Cincinnati." His eyes lit up at the thoughts he was expressing. "I hear they pay pretty well too."

"Hmm. I'm not sure it would be all that glamorous," Lucy said skeptically. "Your job would probably be stoking the coal furnace, don't you think?"

Henry shrugged. "No matter. Anything would be better than cleaning up sawdust everyday."

Lucy shook her head and stood. She covered the annoyance in her voice. "Well, you've heard about greener pastures over the next fence? It just isn't so, Henry."

"Mama," Henry rose to plead with her. "It's what I want to do. Will you talk to Dad for me? I'm eighteen, Mama. Please."

Lucy bit her lower lip. If only the boy knew what he was asking of her. She was not a bird who could shove her offspring from the nest. She doubted, too, that Allen would listen to her, let alone stay in the same room with her. *He is still so terribly mad at me!*

"Tell you what, Henry, if it's in your heart, I'll stand behind you. But I think it's best if you talk to Dad yourself." Lucy's gaze was frank.

Henry studied his mother, and then nodded in assent. "Alright, Mama." He understood. Lucy reached out and laid a hand on her son's shoulder which rose well above her own. "Good boy, Henry. We'll see how it all works out." And Lucy meant that in more ways than one.

*　　　　*　　　　*　　　　*

There was no lamp light on the street, only the moon to escort the drunks homeward to their various makeshift hovels among Warsaw's alleys. The most coveted spots between the buildings were settled first, and squatters had equal rights, a known alley amendment. The early fox gets the box.

Allen strode out of the bar, pulling his collar up snug around his neck. Somewhere in town a church clock tolled the time, its bell remotely out of place here on the darkened streets of the city's south end.

He rubbed his hands together briskly as he rounded the corner. There on the curb resided a drunk, curled on his side. Only a worn, smelly blanket encased the poor soul. Allen paused, but only for a moment. The old codger was imperturbable, and there was no place Allen could take him. Certainly not home. He picked his way through the refuse that littered the curb. The inebriated man lay upon it as if it were a down comforter, placed there as an amenity for his pleasure. Allen grimaced over the black man's plight. He had been freed from one bondage just to embrace another—in liquid form.

It made Allen thankful he had a warm home to go to instead of a crate behind some building. It would be peaceful too; Lucy no longer spoke to him on Thursday nights. Or any other night, for that matter. She carried a grudge like an officer's badge and did not tire in the wearing of it. He was coming to accept it. They were no longer young folks, full of unrealistic delusions. Allen's heart hammered at the memory of farming warm Kentucky soil and its unjust demise.

Where would he be now if he had stayed, undaunted by the Klan's contemptible efforts to dislodge him? His own manly self-respect would be intact and Lucy...well, Lucy would still be governable and in love with him, instead of some false image she had ascribed to him.

Allen tore his stewing thoughts away from the past and battened down his hat brim against the searing raw air that swept along the brick storefronts, whipping mercilessly through his attire.

Up ahead, a cloaked figure crossed the sidewalk and paused at the intersection. It looked fleetingly both ways, ready to dart across the street, suddenly pausing when it noticed Allen. Beneath a shrouded hood, the face was pale and the eyes wide, like a creature alarmed. Somehow the silhouette looked familiar to Allen. As he drew closer, he knew it was the

Irish girl.

This time it was he who hurried towards her bereft figure. "What are you doing out in this part of town, miss?" His words were neutral, controlled as his expression, but beneath it all, he was concerned for her welfare, the same as he would be for any woman.

Her hands shook, evidently more than from just cold. Her voice quivered. "I took some soup to Mrs. Ferguson's son. His family is ill. Somehow I got lost."

"You alright?" Allen peered at her bleached face where her teeth rattled as if an invisible hand shook her frame.

"Yes, I think so." Fiona swallowed in an effort to gain control of herself. "Now." She did not meet his eyes. "This is not a very nice part of town."

Allen scowled. The waif had obviously run into trouble. "Let me escort you home."

"No," Fiona resisted, but seeing his unwavering countenance like that of a fierce sheep dog, she relented and said, "Thirteen West Cricket Street." She followed Allen's lead, trusting like a lamb to be led aright.

It wasn't until they were near her boarding house that Allen spoke reprovingly to her. "Your employer really should not have sent you out at night. That section of town is no place for a girl."

"I'm not a girl." Fiona's stout demeanor had returned, much like a Viking to his ship. "I'm a grown woman, nearly twenty-four years old. And I know a few things too, mister. You're not the only scholar in Warsaw."

Allen took a step backward, his surprise evident. Fiona continued, her voice fuller in timbre than before. "My name is Fiona O'Hugh. Now this is twice you have seen to my safekeeping. You owe me your name, or I'll not go another step with you." She made a formidable opponent.

"Allen Ross, ma'am." He complied like he had when he was in the army.

"Good. See, that wasn't so hard. Only a formality of acquaintance. Now, what were *you* doing in that part of town?

You aren't drunk, are you?"

"Me?" Allen laughed. "I don't have the money to buy enough drinks to get drunk. I was just heaving off a little steam, you know?"

"Well, sure, my Da did the same. Menfolks got to get it out one way or another. It's a heap better than strapping the wife or beating the little ones." She looked as pleasant as an angel. Her hood lay back now, in folds against her neck, exposing tangerine curls.

Allen said abruptly, "You're young enough to be my daughter. How did you come to understand such things?"

Fiona laughed, a tinkling sound that reminded him of a crystal wind chime. "One doesn't have to live long to know things the way they be. My da was a good parent, bless his soul."

"He must have done right by you." Allen's stiff composure was beginning to crumble.

Their pace slowed while Fiona chatted as though it were a balmy summer day instead of night in the dead of winter. "You see, friends are helpful in this life. They can be in any form, white or black, male or female, and any age. Except, of course, unless they are drunken." She halted on the brick-lined street and shivered. Allen nodded in agreement and watched her face suddenly brighten, as if the whole spectrum of a rainbow had burst forth. "Well, here we are. Thank you, friend, Allen Ross. You must not fret. You'll be seeing me again."

Allen stood still, an odd sensation sweeping over him–one likened to the warmth of brilliant sunshine, in contrast to the winter's chill. And all available in the form of a green wool cloak and vibrant blue eyes. Acceptance and understanding coming from a warm heart. Allen shrugged off the illusion and released a slow smile. The words seeped out before he could ponder them. "I expect I will, Miss Fiona."

Chapter Fourteen

Dear Miss Ross,
When the name that I write here is dim on the page
And the leaves of your album are yellow with age.
Still think of me kindly and do not forget,
That wherever I am, I remember you yet.
Your friend,
G. W. Greene Jr.

John lifted his eyes from the Bible before him to gaze unseeing across the room. Captured within the confines of his mind was the long ago story of twin brothers, Jacob and Esau. The past month had revealed the parallel between his own life and the Bible story.

After his return from Cincinnati, he felt trapped by guilt, like a beaten-down coyote who had encroached upon "Farmer Brown's" livestock. He had had no real true reason for seeking a job with Mr. Alton. It was more the lure of a good time that had drawn him. Yet what he had experienced was far from a merry time. The pleasures of life he had witnessed sickened him. He never would get used to such wantonness. His stomach recoiled over Angel's displeasure when she learned of his refusal. There had been a real unladylike display in her dismissal of him, a revelation unto John. He would beware of how easily the tide of a woman's fickleness could turn hereafter.

John's mind drifted back to the Book in front of him. The story of Jacob and Esau was about two brothers who pursued separate lives. Esau, the mighty hunter, and Jacob, the herdsman, were both the sons of Isaac. Esau, being the elder brother, held the birthright, which was a very precious thing.

131

One day he had been out hunting and returned famished. Esau came upon Jacob, the younger brother, as he was cooking a mess of pottage. So weary and faint, Esau begged of his brother, "Feed me, I pray thee." Jacob agreed, "Sell me this day thy birthright." At this point in the story, man's fleshly nature is revealed for what it truly is as Esau replied, "Behold, I am at the point to die: and what profit shall this birthright do to me?"

John heard the refrain speaking to his heart. *Indeed, what profit is a birthright?* John knew that answer now, as Jacob had known four thousand years ago. Jacob had sought that inheritance because he knew its full worth. It was a holy thing, something precious and priceless, to the man who knew its measure.

Poor Esau did not fully comprehend that his birthright was more than just a few camels and bleating goats. It was a blessing from God.

And the reason John Hannon knew? His own bowl of lentils had come to him in the form of an alluring lifestyle, laced with ease; a temptation to a hunting man, as John had recently been. He had been stalking a life's occupation, wanting an arrow to pin down a profession for him.

John had nearly thrown away his birthright. He had been searching, when right under the soles of his feet was all that he had been seeking. Being born to a Bible-learning mama and daddy had been for a reason. John Hannon enjoyed the Lord's work probably more than the next fellow, maybe that's why scripture clung to his brain cavities so easily. But whatever the reason, one thing had crystallized; John would not be an Esau. He would not sell his birthright for a mess of pottage, no matter how enticing the dish.

*   *   *   *

"So, Rev. Hughes, if you would have me, I would really like to study under you. Whatever you could impart to me, so I could follow my calling, I'd surely appreciate." John finished, forcing a swallow down, as his hands laced together fitfully.

The kind reverend smiled. His fingertips met and he pressed them together as he briefly considered. Then slowly he nodded. "John, I appreciate your earnestness. I'm no master of theology, but I'll be glad to share what insights I can. It's commendable you feel it's your calling."

John's eyes fell to his shoe tops. "Well, I *think* it is, Rev. Hughes. I want to fulfill the Lord's will for me, if this is what He has in mind."

"Excellent, John. Why don't you come by on Tuesday and Thursday evenings to study?"

John agreed and took his leave. He trotted over to Mr. Hopkin's grocery to check on his next delivery. Once his schedule was secured, he turned homeward, relieved the morning was nearly spent. And there had been no Miss June Rose to navigate around, she had been at piano practice.

He slipped in the front door and crossed the living room. Opening his mouth to call out to Mama, he heard voices in the kitchen. Curious, he went to peer in the doorway and was immediately concerned. Dad sat at the table, his back to John. Mama was across from him, a little worried wrinkle squashed between her eyes. Neither was aware he stood there. When he overheard what his father was saying, the air rapidly left his lungs.

$*$ $*$ $*$ $*$

"It's a shock, Betty, but we know things are always changing. Nothing good lasts forever." Samuel Hannon sighed, his large hands fiddling with the salt shaker that sat in the center of the table.

Betty wasn't sure she trusted her voice. "You... you're sure, Sam? But what will we do now?"

Sam shook his head and attempted a smile. "Oh, I'll find something, Betty. There's always a job if a man wants to work. And I'm still able to rise and shine each morning."

"That's what worries me, Sam. I don't want you doing work that's meant for a man half your age. Your back won't

133

stand for it. Neither will I." Betty had a determined look in her eye.

Sam didn't tell his wife that the work he did at the sawmill hadn't exactly been delicate soil for daisies. He leaned over and squeezed her fisted hand. "It'll be all right, honey. If we've learned anything at all by now, it's things are what you make them."

Out of the corner of her eye, Betty suddenly noticed her son in the doorway, hanging back, unsure whether to make his presence known.

"John," she said, indicating for him to come into the kitchen, "Dad's home with some important news for us." She looked at Sam, who released her hand and turned to push a chair out for John.

"The sawmill's cutting down on production and closing their doors eventually. They are letting a lot of men go and I'm one of them. We heard the rumors before now, but I didn't consider any truth to them until I heard it from the boss."

John sat soaking the news in. He thought of the plans he had just made with Rev. Hughes. "Hmm," he said slowly, while his mind resembled a box of Mexican jumping beans. The suddenness required some mulling over. The hasty turn of events became cogs in a wheel, as John's thoughts locked with the next until it had made a complete circle. How would this affect things for all of them? If only he could support both of his parents, his dad wouldn't need to work out again.

Betty opened her palm. She studied the lines in her hand, then let her eyes raise to meet the expectant sets of both father and son. "Well," her sigh was resigned, " I know you've got the will, Sam. We'll manage just fine." Her loyalty was stalwart, refusing to let fear of the future crowd her into a corner.

"Sure, honey," Sam agreed, "I can always work for the railroad. I've done masonry in my time, too. I used to be a jack-of-all-trades. I can be one again, if necessary."

"All except shining shoes, Sam. You won't be kneeling down at no white man's feet anymore. We'll starve first." Betty was adamant.

John was surprised by his mother's resolute attitude. His father was shaking his head. "Now, Betty, an honest day's work is—"

"Sam, those days are gone, no more to return, for you and for me." She looked at her son. "John, that goes for you, too. No matter what the Lord may send, we go forward. I'll say Amen, for all of us!" She cast a look at her menfolk, who were unsure whether she had any further words for them, but very sure if she did, that the context of them would be something decidedly maternal. Meaning, in other words, non-negotiable.

Betty smiled graciously with a nod. "You're both welcome."

* * * *

Allen had not laughed or felt so carefree in such a long time. It was an abandonment that freed him of the weighted millstone he carried around his neck.

This all came about when he met Fiona before work in the park. If a patron saint of Ireland had come right to Warsaw to lighten his load, he could not have been more favored. Fiona had fed him tales of her homeland with its fairies and folklore. Her stout nature had introduced him to the Irish merit. And she was acquainting him with the colorful and courageous Celtic history.

Allen escaped his moody existence for a few brief hours when he was with Fiona O'Hugh. It was not long before he began to spend more time meeting with her. He grew to appreciate how thoughtful she was of his moods. Fiona never seemed to make any assumptions. Before Allen knew it, he had bared some of his innermost frustrations about his failures in the past and how Lucy wanted to make him into someone he wasn't.

Fiona had honed her listening skills since she was a bairn. It seemed she was the one who must listen to all the others. She remembered when her dear Mum had whispered the remnants of her unshed tears into Fiona's wee ears. Next, her

135

brother Danny made her listen to his schemes or she would get her ears boxed. Later, after Mum was in her bury hole, Da flooded her ears with his present sorrows and grief, along with any useless poppycock over his cup of brew. Fiona patiently bore her father's mutterings in his drunken state. She had little choice. It was all part of the row a woman must hoe when she loved someone.

But sometimes, Fiona closed her ears to Da's blathering while she worked peeling the potatoes or stoking the fire with peat. When she kneaded the sour bread, her mind drowned out his voice and concentrated on her own thoughts wherever they might lead her. And it was most certainly away from what kept her da a prisoner. Life was about giving and taking, and she knew there were many modes of survival. Da had his, and she had hers. There was no need to question the rationality of it.

Fiona brought herself back to the present. She had been woolgathering, just when she prided herself on her ability to heed another's words. Allen had been talking to her, and she had been visiting the past. Swinging her gaze from the brick-lined walkway, Fiona looked up to Allen's smooth face. The man may have been in the country's War of Separation and worked hard besides, but he had a youthful demeanor among the fine lines that gracefully surrounded his eyes and mouth. While she admired his features, her ears were open to the explanation of how the sawmill operated.

"Then," Allen concluded, his shoulders rounded in his relaxed state, "the raw boards are ready for transport aboard the S & E rail line and shipped all over the country." He looked pleased with his narrative and glanced at Fiona's rapt face. Her tangerine curls were subdued under a mob cap encircled with a navy ribbon. Even if it was a little outdated, it was still attractive. She wore her hooded cloak over her work uniform, where trim brown boots peeked out beneath the wool hem. He could barely see in the pre-morning darkness, but he knew it was there. A working class wardrobe did nothing to diminish Fiona's vitality. She was like an oasis amid a dry stretch or a renewed season following one that had been wrought with ruin.

Allen missed the interaction he and Lucy once had. Now he felt there was not much hope of attaining this camaraderie with his wife. She was not up in the mornings when he left the house, so she did not know the early hours he was keeping. Nor did she realize his keeping of past grievances, but they pushed upward until they broke the sod of his mind like tombstones that shifted with time. The betrayal he felt over her push to emigrate north still lingered. She had robbed him of his role as provider. Lucy had not trusted him to see to their future, and she had cajoled him until he had turn tail and run. Forgiveness sat hard with him, unaided by her disillusionment of the man he had become. It came down to his resentment that had grown over the years like a worm which fed on carrion. Allen was becoming calloused towards his marriage. He had seen men, after the war, who viewed cruel things with a dispassionate detachment. Had he become one of these? If so, it was not of his doing.

Now to him, there was a balm. Fiona was a candle in the dark tomb of despair that often smothered Allen. Her cheery countenance and understanding heart cast a flame of warmth and he was drawn to her light.

"Fiona, you're quiet. Is it time to part?" Allen fumbled for his pocket watch and read its face. "It's seven o'clock. I guess I'd better go." He stood and looked down on the lass who sat still while the gray morning light was being flushed out like a quail from its briar bush by more dominant pink strains.

Fiona gazed up thoughtfully and stretched forth her hand. Her voice was as soft as the new morning. "Go, Allen. I'll be here tomorrow, when the rosy light is dawning." Then she smiled sleepily, her youthful cheeks glimmering with the daybreak.

Allen's hand reached down of its own accord and squeezed Fiona's. Surprised, he released it and stepped back. The warmth of it was a shock to his own cold and calloused one, but more so was the naturalness of the gesture. Allen left her there on the park bench, her eyes trailing after him, unsure where his loyalties suddenly lay.

*　　　　　*　　　　　*　　　　　*

Ridge Top
Franklin, Tenn.
Feb. 23, 1889

My dearest Annie,

It has seemed so long since I last saw you, but you are ever in my thoughts. Are you well? How is Berea? Is it all you hoped for in this new year?

I am well besides a few sniffles. I did fall off my horse, Johnnycakes, but it was my own fault. I know better than to take him down by the river in such mud. My lower half will serve as a reminder for some time.

I have a tutor now. He is a professor of the romantic lan - guages. Monsieur must be handsomely paid to subject himself to my French, but I did surprise him with my mathematical astuteness. (Chalk one up for The Bee?) Also, my geography is improving immensely. I can find Tennessee on the world globe very easily now.

I am sad to say that my father is still determined to bring order to the learning institutions of the South. I do not truly know to what lengths he will go, but I do know what it will mean. I send prayers upward on his behalf.

Write me, Annie, when time permits. You are my best friend ever.

With love,
Nellie Mason

Chapter Fifteen

My dearest Annie,
I most sincerely wish that you
May have many friends and who,
No matter what you are passing through,
Will stick as good strong glue.
Well, Annie, this is from your best friend.
Della E. Walker

Spring had breathed life into the region around Berea. Little green leaves unrolled their softness to face the gentle breezes of a new season. Even the trees' tawny brown bark glowed with a resilience that had outlasted winter.

Though the clouds blocked the sun and a blue sky above, the air was clear, and Cynthia noticed how well sound carried upon it. An excited squirrel chattered and scolded her for walking beneath his tree. Cynthia laughed at the noisemaker and found her own voice was carried down the path ahead so that a few students standing on the downswell turned to look up at her figure cutting across the walkway.

Cynthia had been visiting down in the little town of Berea. When she had first come in the fall of 1888, she had been shy and overwhelmed, and she had stuck close to the brick structures. Through the middle of the school term, Cynthia had been too busy with study. But now...well, these were the final days of the 1888-89 school year, and Cynthia had time to peruse the town between exams. And it gave her a happy feeling, one which generated a hominess. Berea was a gripping place to come to, but soothing as well. The very birds seemed to twitter a peacefulness to Cynthia–like a lullaby.

It was an unusual sight that met Cynthia's eyes, this town of Berea. Unlike Warsaw, the layout of the town held a mixture of homes. Some resembled little wooden saltboxes, nestled amid the sloping streets. Beside these, a more ornate house might dwell. Any of these would sport a garden and the customary "little building" out back. Some had wooden slat fences and a few even had carriage houses.

But the most unusual thing about the arrangement was the families on each side of the streets. Some were black and some were white, dwelling in close proximity to one another. There was no segregation here. It still surprised Cynthia, when she looked about. Back home in Warsaw, each race had its sections and boundaries. Kentucky had been a border state with pro-slavery loyalties, so Berea could be likened to the eye within the tornado.

Cynthia's musings were brought to a complete halt when Theodore Sileman broke into her range of vision. A sense of dread assailed her, but she recovered quickly enough to adopt a polite smile at his greeting.

"Why, Miss Ross, how pleasant to see you. Are you on an outing by yourself?" Theo was immediately offering his outmoded suit-clad arm while he made his inquiry. Theo Sileman was a nice fellow, but Cynthia considered him stuffy and immature. If he had yet touched a razor to his chin she would be surprised. But more jolting was his fashion sense. He wore atrocious shiny suits and wingtips, for goodness sake!

Cynthia peered over her shoulder in pretense. "It appears I am, Mr. Sileman." Why did it seem that her table was laden with all the "fruitcakes"?

But as a social gesture, Cynthia took the proffered arm and forced another dry smile to make up for her uncharitable thoughts. "Actually," Cynthia spoke, "I was returning from visiting the Crawfords on Center Street."

"He's a reverend, isn't he? Are you interested in Theology by chance? I find it a fascinating subject for discussion." Theo was excited now, his eyes popping open, like kernels over a fire.

Cynthia shook her head to stem the flow of enthusiasm which poured from him. *Daddy would skin me alive if I disre - spected religion by debating it as if it were common politics.* "Oh, no," she assured him, "I just went to see baby number fifteen. Did you know they had that many children?"

Theo stiffened, his keg of joy suddenly drained. "No, I didn't, but then I don't concern myself with progeny."

Amusement tickled Cynthia, light as a butterfly's wing. It thread itself breezily through her words. "Oh, I see. Well, perhaps, Theo, your calling will be for the priesthood."

The prim young man looked away from Cynthia and changed the subject. His voice was notched noticeably higher. "If you haven't observed, things are shifting here in Berea. There's been pressure put on the school by the state."

"What kind of pressure?" Cynthia asked, frowning.

"The kind that influential big-wigs in their gilded threads put on the state legislature by day, and then on choice inhabitants by night, decked out in white sheets. Know what I mean?"

"But," Cynthia faltered, "that's surely over with, here anyhow. This is 1889, on the threshold of a new decade and nearly a new century even. Really!"

"But it's true, Miss Ross. Things haven't changed. Haven't you noticed the faculty's ratio? And the boarding system? Most of it is segregated, revealing people's true feelings."

"Theo." Cynthia was unruffled, giving him a patient look like one addressing a child. "There's not nearly enough black educators. That's what I'm trying to change by becoming a teacher. And off campus, whites tend to room with whites and blacks with blacks simply because it's practical and comfortable. It doesn't mean they don't like each other. In our Ladies Hall, we have three rooms on my floor with girls mixed. See?"

Now Theo returned Cynthia's condescending stare. "Don't be naïve, Miss Ross. Men's hearts don't change in decades or in centuries. Are you familiar with the Dudley family on Broadway Street?"

Cynthia nodded, while a cold ribbon of air crept across

the back of her neck to settle on her shoulders.

"Well, Miles Dudley's father, Oliver, bought several acres of land on the Brushy Fork Creek but the white neighbors didn't regard that too highly. So the Ku Klux Klan lynched him over it and took care of that little quandary."

"Theodore Sileman, that happened seventeen years ago!" Cynthia accused him, "You're just courting trouble, talking about such perfidious business!"

Now Theo smiled. He turned toward her and stood with his polished wingtips toe to toe with Cynthia's laced boots. Gazing down, his dark eyes radiated his infatuation. "You know, Annie, I'd rather court you." He had traded his sober speech for enamored emotions.

Cynthia spooked, like a nervous filly. She hastily removed her engaged arm from his. She sputtered like a cat with a hairball. Oh, to say something graceful! "Why...why, Theo!" Somewhere a bell rang on campus. Cynthia exhaled a noisy breath. *Rescued! But, Oh my!* "Sounds like it's time to get to class. See you, Theo." In a rush, Cynthia fled from Mr. Sileman with only his gaze accompanying her.

*   *   *   *

The clock's hum was actually audible within the classroom. Cynthia swallowed and flexed her fingers beneath her desk. Having the last name Ross meant waiting while The Bee went down his alphabetical chart and called each student to his desk to receive their exam grade. This was it, her last grade, and she would possess a teacher's certificate.

Please, let me have an A, Lord. Cynthia could hardly stand the thought that Mr. Beeson would offer his advice to her in front of the class like he was doing to the students that had received low test scores.

When her turn came, Mr. Beeson's eyes followed her as she approached. He handed her the paper containing her class grade, along with the exam. Cynthia's eyes tore over its contents to see in black "Passed". Her math exam held a 93% at the top.

Quickly, her smile faded like a frosted daisy in December under Mr. Beeson's glare, his chalky pale complexion resembling an icicle. "You have passed, Miss Ross, but math is not one of your strong points, naturally being the weaker gender. Next year, Mr. Hathaway will be the instructor. Too bad you won't be here. With him you might have better grasped the fundamental properties of mathematics, seeing he's the flexible sort." He smirked, his tone spiked with acid. He turned his attention to the next paper as he virtually ignored her in his dismissal.

As she left the classroom, Cynthia was disturbed. What had Mr. Beeson meant by his comments? *Maybe he doesn't like blacks or women in particular. Or maybe more specifically, just me!* Did Mr. Beeson really think that because Mr. Hathaway was black, he would be partial to black students? Theo could have very well been right about racism creeping in.

Cynthia's walk lagged as another thought struck her, dismay clouding her face as her brows knit together in consternation. What if racism really was concealed right here within Berea, the paragon college whose constitution read: "...an influence strictly Christian, and as such, opposed to sectarianism, slaveholding, caste, and every other wrong institution or practice." It would be uprooting Rev. Fee's creed, all he worked and stood for. But then as she thought of that mighty champion, she felt herself relax. Whatever it was, Rev. Fee would set it to right. *He's the Moses-man, remember?*

*   *   *   *

Another school year was coming to an end. This always gave John G. Fee a dose of encouragement, a sentiment of hope that his dream was alive yet.

So why did he feel heavy-hearted, as if the flowers of joy had not borne fresh shoots this spring?

I'm getting older, mused Rev. Fee, *that is most of my problem.* But he did not fool himself. Sitting at his rough-grained desk, he observed the room. The familiar surroundings always brought comfort to him. His wife's picture on the desk

143

gazed at him from its oval frame. Matilda's smile revealed her faithfulness. The world globe across the room was a trusted friend as well, exhibiting the continent of North America only a visible sea-length away from Africa. There on a bench were the old primers he had tutored from at Camp Nelson. Dust now gathered upon their covers. And lastly, a small embroidered sampler, done by the past hand of one of his dearest friends, similar in heart and mind to that of John. It was Miss Fair who had stitched the alphabet and the Lord's words there: "Well done, thou good and faithful servant". Beneath a little green Tree of Life was situated a blue river of water meandering with the words, stitched in tiny crosses: "Enter thou into the joy of thy Lord."

How that piece of work strengthened him! He often studied it, finding in each little letter of thread the courage those hands had possessed. And now, Rev. Fee needed that courage as beforetimes, when he had battled to raise a small school where men could learn regardless of lineage. It had been a hostile region (a wilderness) but along with help from others, especially J.A.R. Rogers, they had persevered. They had fought the good fight against irate landowners, pro-slavery opposition, Klansmen, mobs, lynching, rocks, and fires. Physical conflict had come in all forms.

So now, why did he tremble with an intuition that plagued a niche of his heart? Why were unseen forces worse than those known? Because "a chain is only as strong as its weakest link" and somewhere there lurked an unsound coupling that would sever all that John G. Fee had worked for these past years.

It would come from the area, Kentucky landowners, those unreconciled individuals who still "waged" the War of Separation; only now not with northern foes, but here at home, with their black brethren. Down the ranks it would skip, like a spoiled child who had a lollipop in her grasp. The state government would adhere to its constituents' demands and pressure would be applied to the college. Its president, board members, and faculty, resorting downward to even the students, would suffer from the impact of "darkness in high places". It seemed that invisible discriminating foe would never be defeated. *In Heaven,* John Fee sighed, *where the former things are passed away.*

A knock brought Rev. Fee out of his reverie. "Come in," he called, rousing himself. J.A.R Rogers, colleague and confidante, ducked in the door. "John, you want some dinner? I'm on my way to retrieve some. I could bring you a plate."

Fee felt a surge of appreciation toward his loyal friend. They had stood together and shouldered their vision for thirty-one years now. John nodded and spoke, "I could indeed use some sustenance, Jars. And a double portion of your optimism."

Board member and teacher, J.A.R. Rogers, took a chair and settled on it. He knew Fee like a brother. "You're bothered by the heresay floating around here, huh?"

Rev. Fee nodded and held Roger's gaze. "And you?"

Rogers shrugged. "We've wrestled with Jericho before. No use shouting until we hear the trumpets blast, John. It may not ever culminate, this talk."

"Precisely, Jars. Whatever comes, the Lord can handle. But I fear...after all this time if we should lose and all our progress drains down the well...I'm not sure I could recover from it." John's face bore his deep anxiety.

Rogers smoothed his hand across the desktop, his own face grim. "We'll weather it, John." His features softened. "It's been a glorious thirty-something years, hasn't it? Remember old Clay and his staunch views contrary to ours? We carried on despite having to part ways, and through all our financial difficulties and Reconstruction. We've outlasted the KKK too, and the state's contrariness."

John G. Fee smiled. "Yes, we've been through the wilderness together. You're right, Jars, we've had a glorious stretch of years."

"Come on now, John. Let's go eat our meat with 'gladness and singleness of heart.'" J.A.R. Rogers stood, tucking his chair under the scarred desk. "It'll do us both good. We'll add in a piece of pie for good measure."

The Rev. rose and the lines on his face, revealing his uneasiness, had softened. "You know," Fee smiled, as he reached for his coat on the halltree behind him, " I've called you Jars for many years and yet I'm quite certain you never knew the connotation of it."

Rogers followed Fee out the door, brows raised in question. "I assumed you simply used my initials J.A.R. for that nickname. Am I wrong?"

Fee chuckled as the men strode toward the Dining Hall. "No, you're right but what I have always thought is how fitting those initials are."

"Say how?" Rogers was uncertain as to where John was leading him.

"Well, in Prophet Elijah's time, we know the widow woman sustained him. Her cruse of oil never failed. That, my dear friend, is how I think of you, an unfailing vessel, a jar of faithful oil, always there to uphold and sustain me."

Rogers acknowledged the esteem just given him with a slight nod of his head. After working together for thirty-one years, who needed words to communicate? The gratuity was wholly reciprocated. The two men continued walking, a rapport within their silence, an invisible bond between them.

Chapter Sixteen

Miss Annie Ross,
God made the flower and thorn to grow together;
Let us not separate them but with you
May the roses be many and the thorns be few.
Rosa L. Haynes.
Berea, Ky, March 1888

Allen's work shift was over. It had been another warm day and he loosed the top button on his shirt and headed for the river. Allen hoped to be alone, because he craved solitude. His tired shoulders and tense muscles contributed to his ever-present gloominess. His visage was darkened, as though a shade had been pulled over his eyes. Of all things, he was losing his job. It was something that twisted his insides with a cold fire, engulfing him in a stifling depression. It led Allen to count his mounting losses.

First he had lost his land. *I left it behind, because I ran away like some cowardly whelp.* His thoughts spewed his bitterness upon the plains of his mind. *I've lost Lucy. She's moved on without me, adjusting her life to avoid conflict with the past, while my battles continue to rage.* If she only knew about the struggles a man had to carry with him. They couldn't be abandoned like some stray cat.

Allen, reaching the end of his walk, stood staring at the Ohio River. Across the muddy expanse lay the soil of Indiana. Warsaw was situated along this western stretch before the water turned north and ridged Ohio. Here, on some days, the river's tang roamed from its mainstay and cloaked Warsaw with its pungency. Allen often forgot that he lived close to water, except when this occurred. Now he seated himself on the springy moist ground and watched the languid flow of the current. He felt as spiritless as the old river looked.

Here it is spring, a time for renewal, and I am no more alive than a sapless tree. Allen looked to the sky. Where was God, up there in that gray mass swirling overhead? Raindrops threatened, but Allen welcomed them. At least something was allowed to weep.

When had Allen lost God? Where was the flame his candle once had? The face of his treasured friend and comrade in the army, Bucky, swam before him. Bucky had told Allen about his candle in the eighteenth Psalm; how the Lord would enlighten his darkness. And indeed, in Allen's youth, he had felt that strength and favor upon him.

But he had not tended to it, that vernal flame, and it had gone out. He had not warded off the poisonous vapors that lay in the abyss of his heart. Eroded by neglect, time and age had become a pickax that had further chipped away at it.

Then there were the kids. He could hardly recall when he had last spent time with them. It was as if he was no longer a father and they were no longer his offspring. *How could one's family just ebb their way out of your life?* Allen wondered. Apparently his children did not need him: Willie was married, Cynthia off at school, and Henry nearly grown–looking to work on some fancy steamship in Cincinnati. And the three youngest, well, they had their schoolwork and hobbies that didn't include him. Sure, little Dee came out to his shop every now and then, but they hardly conversed about much. They had no common things together. *Another failing of mine*, Allen lamented.

For a long while, he sat there, nursing all the injury he had amassed and hoarded. The bulk of it had been forced upon him but, if he was honest with himself, much of it was self-inflicted.

Fueled by his despair, he dug up several stones buried in the mud and flung them into the river. One by one, they dropped out of sight, sinking into the brown flow. Allen wished his troubles would just plunge beneath a swelling tide and leave him free to travel on downstream.

Whoa! Allen reined in his thoughts. There could be a way to "travel on" but he would still carry a stone's weight. The

148

sawmill had offered for him to relocate, but he hadn't even considered it. Allen had had enough of moving but now…maybe a fresh start was what he needed.

Within his conscience, an inner voice jabbed sharply for attention. Where were his meetings with Fiona going? It seemed innocent enough, talking in the park, and yet if it was, why did he feel uneasy about it? *It's disloyal to Lucy and you know it. It's not right and nothing good can come of it.* Allen stood swiftly, giving his knees no time to protest. He brushed off his pants, feeling where the ground's moisture had soaked through. But Allen gave it no heed as he watched the Ohio flow away from him. His mind had heftier things to ponder.

Was that the answer he sought? That he should move the family away, launch a fresh course, and break his tenacious ties with Fiona? Allen needed to think on this some more. Abruptly, he turned and left the river behind. He did his best thinking at the pub. With renewed purpose, Allen headed in that direction.

*   *   *   *

Allen had thought if he picked a more public place, their talk would go smoother. It would rule out any loud outbursts on Lucy's part, but they never went anywhere together anymore, not even church. Here it would have to be, on the porch and on a Sunday evening. It was as social as he could get.

Being Sunday, the boys were off at various neighbors and Henry with his friends at the youth gathering down at the church. Lucy sat on the porch, appearing relaxed, except for her eyes, which studied the maple tree beside the walk, when they weren't cutting him wary looks.

Allen leaned on the porch railing, pretending to survey the neighbor's lawn. Lucy was situated in the creaky pine rocker, disguising her suspicion as to why Allen would be on the porch within her presence.

"Well, there's truth to the rumors of the sawmill closing down." Allen got right to the point.

Lucy's foot ceased pushing the rocker. Its protesting

149

hushed, and Lucy looked fully at Allen for the first time since he had come out to the porch. Only her thoughts broke the silence. *My name. He never says my name anymore. Is it because he can't say it without any affection?* Slowly she brought her mind around to focus on his words. *The sawmill is closing down?*

Allen shifted to look at her. His hands straddled the railing with a firm grip. The pressure made the wood wince. Allen willed Lucy to answer, his nerves taut.

"I wasn't aware of the rumor but you say the mill is really closing?" She looked suddenly anxious, as the meaning began to soak inward.

Allen nodded curtly and waited for her barrage of questions. When none were forthcoming, he grew impatient. He straightened and faced away from her, to see Homer Johnson across the street wave at them. He merely tipped his chin in greeting, hoping the man would go back inside. Once he did, Allen cast a sideways glance at Lucy. Still she was quiet.

Allen's irritation surfaced as he spoke roughly, "I've decided it would be best to relocate and work at the mill's sister plant, in Loveland. That's Ohio, if you didn't know. We'll probably sell some of the furniture and ship the rest by rail. We need to be there before September, so there's some time to make arrangements." He turned to find Lucy's dark eyes on the back of his head. "You gonna say anything?" he demanded.

Lucy felt a cruel pinch to the ridge of her brow and her lips felt tightly drawn against her teeth. It seemed she had no control over it, these cruel sensations. No more than she did over the painful thudding in her chest. "It sounds like...it's all been decided."

"I need a job, don't I? You wouldn't want to support the family, would you?" It rose between them, like a challenge.

Lucy snapped, "If that's what it takes. I'm not exactly thinking I want to move." In her mind, moving was not even a possibility.

"Yeah, well, there's probably always an opening with the temperance union," Allen said dryly. "Although I doubt the pay's real plush." He settled on the railing, allowing one leg to support his weight while the other dangled loosely. Allen rested one arm against the porch beam, a nonchalant stance considering the heat wave that surged between them.

Lucy swallowed the bitter bile in her mouth. It felt like it seeped downward from there, into her veins. The wrist resting in her lap bore evidence of her agitation with sharp angry throbs. Lucy tore her eyes from her hand to find Allen studying the wooden ceiling. Her voice could have made a dog wince; so sharply it rent the distance between them. "That's real funny but at least it would be an honest job, instead of one that causes drinking binges. And you might as well realize right now, I'm not leaving my home."

"Really?" Allen's tone refused to match Lucy's. "If we're going to discuss this, you better lower your voice."

"Why?" Lucy shot back, "You don't want anyone in the neighborhood to hear that you go drinking, but it's alright if they see you doing it?"

Allen's arm dropped heavily to his side, and he planted both feet on the floorboards. "My job doesn't send me to the bar." His voice coldly filled the space of the porch, while inside his heated thoughts silently vented, *you do.*

Lucy minded the way his eyes bore into her own. "Huh. So what is your reason?"

Across the street, neighbor Johnson was back at it again, messing around in his lawn, sending frequent glances their way. Allen's head grew painful with an increasingly angry pressure. "I said lower your voice, Lucy." His expression stanched any further words from her.

Pain pricked her heart. *Where is the man I married? Is there one shred of him left in this stranger before me?* She should refuse to back down, but icy fingers like that of a death knell clutched at her being. Lucy felt uncertainty creep over her heart. Allen's glare held all the chill of an arctic wave. What gain could she make by refusing? Holding her ground had yielded no victories thus far. It seemed her marriage hung by a pendulum by which time might run out.

In a rush, frightening thoughts slashed through her mind, and she faced the recent loneliness that had inhabited her world. What if Allen found another who could occupy her place in his life? It would be a bleak future destined for her, she had no doubt.

Lucy looked away from Allen. She could not bring herself to meet his intense gaze that disguised nothing. *Why did Allen look so darkly at her, as if hate had cordoned off any warmth in his heart?*

Lucy felt vulnerable, exposed by her own weakness. Her heart lay proffered and open, but Allen would not attempt in any manner to relieve its rent condition.

Finding her voice, Lucy's words were an undertone. "You tell the children." No longer able to face the enmity between them, she stood and went into the darkened house. Outside on the porch, the rocker reverberated from her vacancy of it. Allen did not move from the railing as the shadows fell, and the children returned home.

Yes, Lucy was well versed in defeat. After all, she had been a man's slave, but it had made her no coward. While she stood on this side of the sunset, no one could ever force her to believe that, save only for an angel of the Lord. And Allen…well, whether he acknowledged it or not, he still stood on this side with her, and he would be the first made to reckon with it.

*   *   *   *

April 18, 1889

Dear Sis Annie,

Hope you're doing fine. Just wanted to let you in on a few things. It wouldn't be nice to let them pile up and not share. (Ha!)

First, the sawmill is closing. I will lose my job and Dad too. There is another mill in Loveland, Ohio that Dad can work at so he is all for moving there. Mama isn't very happy, but she's starting to sort some things. I think she is waiting on you to come home this summer to help.

I'm not a bit sad for myself. I was ready to quit anyhow and go to work on a steamship line in Cincinnati. Ever since I cut my finger off at the mill, I hated the place. You remember how the foreman treated me and all.

Cousin Henry Allen is glad too. He thinks it is all Providential. He has saved his money for Berea and is ready to start school in the fall.

We will be glad to see you on summer break, as things are rather heavy here at home without you. Let us know when to meet you at the train station.

Love, your brother,
Henry

Chapter Seventeen

Miss Annie,
Remember me when this you see
Though in this world I may not be,
But if the grave shall be my bed,
Remember me when I am dead.
Nell

How the children of Israel ever found their way out of the Wilderness was more than Lucy could fathom. Here she was, trying to navigate around Warsaw, Kentucky, and it was rigorous enough. Then Lucy remembered they had the cloud of smoke by day and the pillar of fire by night. All she had was the river's smell and the whistle of the factories for guidance amid all the new structures and brick stories laid out like a jumbled maze. How had she ever escaped slavery from Clover Hill plantation in Madison County? But of course, she'd had Mama.

It wasn't really that Warsaw was so huge, but it was expanding rapidly. There were new streets being dug and homes springing up daily. It was large enough to have what the white folks called the "colored section" divided into two areas, and Lucy did not know everybody. It seemed so many folks were on the move, migrating north from their home grounds of enslavement or the scraps of land they sharecropped for their old masters or the carpetbag Yankees.

Lucy had to chide herself over that. Those words were like those years, in the past now, and must be let go. Narciss would scold her and say that life was too short to hold on to any bitterness. She often quoted "let bygones be bygones". *Remember the hairs on your head are all numbered, Lucy, and you aren't Methuselah.* This was sobering.

Thinking of Narciss, Lucy made her way toward the

155

older part of town. She lived in the business district where her husband Henry Wallace owned a storefront, which sold food and the usual sundry items. Above and behind the store, the couple lived very comfortably, along with their daughter Elizabeth.

It wasn't hard to get there from home but Lucy had detoured by walking to the riverbank and then onward to the mill to take Henry his forgotten lunch pail. She did not look for Allen. They had arrived at a silent truce. He recognized she would move to Loveland and cause him no trouble. And Allen would do his part and take care of the details of finding them a suitable home. At one time, Lucy wanted to remind him, she had been happy with a shack, but no more. She would expect something more lavish, maybe nicer than their moderate home here. *As if it could make up for the strife between them!* This is the way it became when a marriage's main artery had been ruptured. Lucy was learning that negligence was a potent blood thinner in love's vein.

Lucy turned in at Wallace's Supply Store, and slipped past Henry Wallace and his customer, Ben Reid, with a brief wave, heading to the back of the store and into their private quarters.

Narciss was adding wood to the cookstove when she turned and smiled her surprise. "Lucy! If you hadn't come, I'd have come to see you!" She pushed back the blue-speckled granite kettle to the hottest part of the blackened stove and grabbed two cups.

Lucy took off her wraps and laid them over the closest chair. She felt warmed just to be in Narciss' kitchen with her. How could she tell her she would be leaving? How would she ever survive being unable to visit with her sister? The weight of it hung like one of old Cissie's voodoo charms around her neck.

Narciss was full of smiles and spoke pleasantly on every little token of interest she could unearth. She settled Lucy and herself in the living room with tea and butter cookies. Lucy felt the tug of envy pull at her heart. Henry Wallace loved his wife and showed her in a hundred little ways. Narciss' happiness was evident and Lucy knew she deserved it. But oh…where had her own gone? Was she no longer entitled to it?

"Lucy." Narciss set her cup down on the side table and leaned forward in her chair. "I've got some wonderful news to tell you." Her shining face made Lucy's sober one appear more despondent. Funny Narciss seemed unmindful of her misery. Usually she was as sensitive to Lucy's moods as a butterfly's wing to the air currents.

Narciss' words tumbled on out, "Henry has found a good opportunity for Elizabeth and Charley after they're married. One of Henry's cousins wrote that there is a need for a grocery store in Lockland, Ohio. Lizzie and Charley can open a store and run it, kind of an extension of ours. Charley thinks he would like that kind of work." She waited expectantly for Lucy's response.

Prodding herself to life, Lucy attempted a suitable reaction. "Well. That's good news for you and Henry." She had trouble swallowing.

Narciss leaned over and took Lucy's hand in hers. "I know, Lucy, about you moving. Allen told Henry. I thought if you knew Elizabeth and Charley would be close, you would feel better. Lockland isn't too far from Loveland. In a year's time, they'll be married and join you."

If Narciss thought this was an immense consolation to Lucy, she was mistaken. Lucy frowned at her sister's enthusiasm. She was too drained to share any of it. *I know you're try - ing to comfort me, Narciss, but it's like washing without water–totally senseless!*

Narciss continued, "Lucy, I know this isn't easy for you, but you remember what Mama taught us? She always said 'shore up, girls' and take what life hands you. You're never truly alone, not when you have the Lord close by your side."

Lucy pulled a hankie from her dress pocket and swiped her leaking eyes. "I didn't come here for a sermon, Narciss. I came to tell you about the move before Lottie Wetzel does. But it appears I could have saved the trip. I know there's church there now, up from Tate's Creek and Richmond. Other family is moving north, too, besides your Lizzie. I'm not wanting to go, but I'll make out. You don't have to lecture me." *I love you, sister, and I'm going to miss your wisdom.*

"Yes, Lucy, you're right. If anyone needs a lecture, it's me. You've always been the strong one of the family, and if anyone can adjust, it's you." Narciss looked fondly at her older sister. *Oh, Lucy, we're just like a horse! Just when our gait gets going good, we throw a shoe!*

Lucy wanted to return the favor, but she felt ungraciously dry as day-old bread. "Narciss, you'll take Cynthia in, while she teaches, won't you? If she gets a school close by here?"

"Of course, sister. She's like my own girl. She'll want to help with the wedding plans, and we'll help her with her schooling." Narciss stood and patted Lucy's shoulder, like she had suddenly become the eldest. "I'm going to heat soup and you stay for dinner, Lucy."

As Narciss went out to the kitchen to put on a pot of soup for their lunch, Lucy pulled herself together. She would have to "shore up", meaning she must change her outlook and look out for herself. And as Narciss had reminded her, she had no other choice, being she was her mother's daughter.

*   *   *   *

Cynthia arrived home from school, expecting the household to be the way she had left it, but it was in total chaos. Mama and Daddy looked haggard, as if they had been run through a wash wringer. There were bags under Mama's eyes as if she never slept and her face was thin. Daddy wore a dusting of new gray in his hair like he had messed around with flour in a bakery. Both were short with words and smiles. It was not the homecoming Cynthia expected.

"Henry," Cynthia demanded of her brother when she caught him alone. "Why didn't you tell me about things? I've seen funeral parlors with more life than what's going on here. What did you mean by saying things were 'heavy' around home? They're downright ponderous! How did you boys stand

158

it?"

Henry held up his hands in a defenseless gesture and shrugged. He didn't want to tell his sister he had spent a lot of time daydreaming or just away from home and hadn't noticed how unraveled things had really become. She would shame him with a guilt trip.

For two weeks after Cynthia's homecoming, she visited her Aunt Narciss and Cousin Elizabeth and heard about the wedding's progress. Cynthia got reacquainted with Charley Mitchell, Elizabeth's fiancé. She spent a day with Brother Willie's family. Cousin Henry Allen Laine dropped by with his exciting news, that in the fall, he would be going to Berea. Friends and neighbors paid calls amid the jumbled up mess of boxes, trunks, and crates all over the house.

When the happy reunions were over with, Cynthia settled down to help Mama pack. It was a tedious procedure. Lucy held up a box of linens she had pulled out of the china cupboard and sighed. "What do I do with these? Maybe you'll want them, Cynthia."

Cynthia wasn't interested in the yellowed tablecloths, cheap doilies or wrinkled linen napkins. "Mama, I think we should just give those things away. They're in bad shape now. By the time I need them, they'll crumble to dust. Besides, we can always sew new ones."

Lucy frowned at her daughter. She was becoming like all the younger generation who didn't know hardship from hindsight. *Sew new ones?* "'Waste not, want not' they say. You apparently never had to live through lean times or a war, have you?" Lucy's face held a bitter expression Cynthia had never seen before on her mother. She was immediately contrite.

"You're right, Mama, I haven't. I'm sorry. We'll just use them to tuck around these dishes. That will pack it all nicely."

Then there was the furniture to choose among. "All the bedroom furniture is going. The washstand was Mama's. See that rough gray box under the edge of the bed? Pull that out, Cynthia. Let's get rid of that old thing! Why your father keeps

159

that ridiculous box is beyond me."

"What is it, Mama? I don't remember seeing it before." Cynthia tugged the gray weathered wooden box from beneath the bed.

"Oh, it was in the attic all these years. We cleaned that out before you got home and your daddy put it under there for safekeeping. Humph! Ugly old thing!"

"Well, shouldn't we ask Daddy first, before we just pitch it?"

Lucy glared at her daughter. "And then what? We'll just be overloading the wagon with that useless thing! Because, of course, your daddy won't part with it."

"Mama, it seems wrong to throw it out if Daddy wants it. What's so special about it?" Cynthia was curious and surprised over Mama's callous treatment of the object.

"Oh, I can't tell you that! But your father thinks it's from a good friend back in Kentucky. A crazy man named Lee Jake Worth, who lived all alone in the woods. He loaned your daddy a gun before the Klan came that night." Lucy seemed void of emotion as she pulled open drawers and emptied them, all the while talking indifferently like she had never been related to the incident or happenings she described. "We were ready to leave for Warsaw and your daddy comes lugging that thing home. I asked, 'Where did you get that thing?' He told me from Lee Jake. It was a going away present. 'What's it for?' I asked him. Your daddy said Lee Jake Worth thought it might help your daddy out, until he could get a job." Lucy snorted.

"How's that?" Cynthia's curiosity rose several degrees.

"Oh it's a shoe shining box. A man puts his foot on top and there inside are the brushes, polish, rags and such for cleaning shoes up real nice. I told your daddy he should just heave it. If we were moving north so he could shine some white man's shoes, we better just stay put and fight the Klan." Lucy stopped talking and sat down hard on the floor, clothes in piles around her. Her face looked pale, like she had seen a ghost when she had dredged up the past.

"Mama, you all right?" Cynthia was concerned, but she

160

did not move. Could it be that Mama was exaggerating such a small thing?

Lucy looked away, then down at the collection of things around her, shoes, pants, work shirts, folded dresses and a shawl. "I suppose you better just leave it. Your daddy would take it along if he had to carry it on his back all the way." Mama sounded defeated, her voice empty and forlorn.

Cynthia rose and sat on a crate of toiletries from Mama's bureau. "What's going on between you and Daddy?"

Lucy avoided her gaze by slipping her dresses in a trunk. "Nothing, Cynthia. We're both just tired with the move and all." She didn't sound convincing even to herself.

Cynthia slid to her knees and helped pack her father's pants into the trunk. "Mama, I'm not a little girl anymore. You sent me away to get educated you know."

Lucy's head cocked and her brows rose inquiringly. Cynthia flushed. "Oh, Mama, I don't mean anything by that. I studied the three R's only, 'rithmetic, reading and writing! What I meant is I'm growing up. I felt the tension at Christmas. I can see you and daddy are not happy."

Not happy? That was one way to put to words the feelings existing between them. "Well, Cynthia, if you're so grown up, you know to respect your parents by staying out of our business." To soften her words, Lucy reached out her hand to touch Cynthia's shoulder. She should be glad her girl cared.

She studied her daughter's face where so much innocence and pure beauty was contained. Would it one day vanish, stolen away by life's hardships? "Cynthia, I think you needn't worry. Dad and I are facing one of those marriage mountains. You will probably come up against it sometime in your life when you marry. It's when one of you wants to fly over the mountain and the other one wants to go around it, but what we both have to do is climb it. We're just feeling a little too old and tired to try, but we'll get it figured out. You don't fret. All couples face it at one time or another. It's life."

Lucy gathered up some clothing to give to the church's charity barrel. She chatted about Cynthia's studies, about Rev.

Fee, and Cousin Henry's good fortune to be done with the mill and ready to attend Berea. It seemed to calm her, and Cynthia let her trepidation slacken as they finished and went to start supper. If there were such mountains in matrimony, Cynthia would stick to the plains and her future plans.

*   *   *   *

Allen felt like some sideshow charlatan, crouched down in the alley. He regretted it had come to this, hiding to meet with Fiona, like a man might do if he were cheating on his wife. *Ouch!* Allen's shoulders hunkered down in reproach. These thoughts were like ulcers deep within his stomach. His legs had fallen asleep. He rose slightly to perch on a rickety broken-down crate for relief. Pulling out his pocket watch, Allen knew he would have to leave soon if Fiona didn't show up.

Then there, around the brick building, Fiona's bright head bobbed and she hurried towards him. On this dark morning, it looked like she had brought the sunshine with her. She laughed to see him amid the trash in such a place, like it was some joke they shared between them to meet here.

"Allen, have you waited long? I'm sorry. Mrs. Ferguson couldn't make up her mind on which cut of meat she wanted for supper tonight, and I could not leave. Poor scatterbrain, she is. Tell me, how are you?" Fiona's lilting voice was music to his ears, but in a moment he would stop the symphony and halt the composition. No more beautiful scores would be played.

"Fiona," Allen paused, his eyes memorizing her face. He drew a shaky breath. "I have something hard to say to you, but it must be said. I can't meet you anymore. I'm leaving Warsaw." After all the practice Allen had given this little recital, the words had turned blunt and rolled out as though they were attached to ready wheels. Fiona's stricken face attested to the fact. She looked like she had been run right over.

Allen understood. He felt as if a meat cleaver had

162

chopped clean through him. "I'm sorry, Fiona. But it has to be this way." He stood now, his legs weak as if they owned none of his life's blood. Allen watched her swallow hard as she lifted her apron's hem and wrung it in her fingers.

"Well." Fiona spoke in a small voice. "I don't know what to say, Allen. This seems all very sudden."

Allen looked away from her. Fiona's pain was obvious. But Allen had never made any declarations of love to her. They were simply friends–good ones. His unhappiness vented itself as anger, his words coming out roughly. "I told you we shouldn't be friends, right from the beginning. It doesn't work. It never has and it never will."

Fiona raised her eyes from her apron. They were pooled with unshed tears. "Never is a long time, Allen. Don't say 'never.'" She shook her head to clear her vision. Two tiny tracks of moisture followed the bridge of her nose. "You warned me, but we're friends nevertheless. Our color didn't make it impossible, so you are wrong." She swiped at her face.

Allen sighed and looked down at the dirty pathway of alley they stood in. "The mill's closing, Fiona, and we're moving to Loveland, Ohio, so I can keep my job. We have to say good-bye."

Fiona was quiet for so long he finally looked at her. Allen steeled himself for her pleading, but that was not her way. Instead she stepped forward and wrapped her arms around him in a tight hug. Then as quickly, she retreated. "You have been a good friend, Allen Ross. What would I have done without your company? May God go with you and the saints of Ireland guard you in their care." She looked wan, like a little lost waif as she fled the alley.

Allen felt cursed. Fiona's haunting sadness tore at him. He wanted to rage at God for allowing this to happen but the overcast sky stopped him short. It was darkened as if the sun did not want to rise. Was it really God's fault or Allen's? The truth was apparent, even to an infidel.

In disgust, Allen clenched his teeth as he pulled out his pocket watch and peered at it. Fiona's wish for God to be with him was the most ludicrous thing of the morning. And Allen's watch hands were the only thing laughing–he was late.

Chapter Eighteen

Dear Annie,
They are never alone
That are accompanied
With noble thoughts.
Your friend,
A. Y. Merchant
Berea, Ky 5-29-1888

On Friday, Cynthia was up with the dawn. The day promised to be a warm one, but the sky was clear. She was thankful there was no rain in sight. Before long, the family had stirred and ploughed into the task of moving their belongings. Cynthia planted herself on the wagon to supervise the loading of it. She didn't trust her brothers to manage this job. She wanted the wagon bed stacked uniformly with boxes, so as to get as much on as possible. They had only contracted two wagons and everything must fit. She knew the way the boys did things: Bang, Crash, and Dump.

Henry, John, and James soon complained about Cynthia's "picky" method, and the fact she thought she was in charge. "You boys don't know a thing about efficiency!" Cynthia told them.

"And that's what you went away to school to learn?" Henry demanded. "We might as well have saved the tuition."

"Yeah, Annie, you already knew how to be bossy!" John threw in.

Cynthia glowered at them. She took the boxes from their loaded arms and deposited each one in a certain spot according to how Mama had marked them. The boys knew positively nothing about order and housekeeping.

Lucy came out on the porch for a break. She smiled, her

165

hands on her hips. "Good job, children. It sure helped the wagons were brought over last evening. We'll have them all loaded and ready to roll tomorrow morning."

"What's this 'we'?" Henry whispered to James. John was scowling. Dee was out of breath, "Are we done yet?"

Lucy came down the steps to the street where the wagon was and studied it. She pointed to a barrel situated among the crates. "I once rode on a thing like that into Camp Nelson. I've half a mind to try it again."

"Mama," Cynthia admonished, "Surely not! Everyone will stare at us!"

Lucy's eyes twinkled. "Well in that case, Cynthia...maybe you would like to give it a try? You would probably attract a lot less attention than me."

Cynthia was horrified. Her brothers laughed. Dee was excited. "Come on, Cynthia, try it! It'd be fun!"

"No, thanks. We'll be stared at plenty as it is."

"Alright, let's finish up this wagon and eat some dinner. Then we'll wait on Dad for the heavy furniture this evening. We'll hope for no rain tonight, and then tomorrow the freight fellows will come hitch up and pull it to the station." Cynthia noticed her mother felt more lighthearted over the move since they had been surprised by Brother Willie's news that his family would accompany them to Loveland.

*   *   *   *

Fiona had slipped behind a protective elm tree and watched the scene before her. Even though she had never been to Allen's home, she knew immediately that the family loading the wagon was his. She squeezed herself up against the rough bark and rested her cheek against it. The canopy of shade above blocked the summer sun and helped cool her warm head. But the greater of the warmth came from the fact she was spying.

Fiona could not quite reason why she had felt the need to just once see where Allen lived. Maybe it was a tangible connection she could add to her scanty memories. So here she was,

166

watching Allen's family load their belongings on a wagon in preparation to move, and the sight of them caused a pain in her ribs.

A young boy, his arms full, staggered to the edge of the curb and heaved his box onto the bed of the wagon. A girl, his sister no doubt, bent down and spoke to him. Fiona could not hear their words, but seeing the spunky youngster put his hands on his hips told Fiona he was sassing the girl.

Two older boys came out of the house, their arms piled full. The oldest closely resembled Allen, so that Fiona caught her breath. He was slighter of frame than Allen, but she felt like she was getting a personal glimpse into the past of the man she loved.

Now, a woman with another son in tow, came out of the house. She wore a cotton print dress of blue with an apron wrapped around her middle. She approached the wagon and children. Fiona knew this was Lucy. Immediately, Fiona felt an enmity toward her. She was very pretty, despite her age, and Fiona wondered jealously why Allen had distanced himself from her. The woman looked pleasant enough, but Fiona knew looks were deceiving. Allen must have a good reason for the disunity between himself and his wife. None of that mattered now though, because she was in his life.

Allen made Fiona feel like a prized emerald among lesser stones. Before she had met him, Fiona must always give to others: her time, her hands, and her ears. Allen was the first person to give these things to *her,* along with attention and concern. All she wanted now was his heart.

Fiona had seen enough. She turned and stole away, pretending to blend in, going from tree to shrub or hedge until she had put some distance between herself and Allen's home.

No, she mustn't be discouraged after seeing his family. He had told her the breach between them seemed irreparable, which gave her hope. Fiona's temptation to worry was strong, but she would overcome it. She was adept at doing that. And she would not abandon her plans. She would find a way to remain in Allen's life. Weren't her people a mixed heritage of

Celtics and Vikings? There was no more stalwart combination, of this Fiona was certain.

*   *   *   *

On Saturday, Allen felt little cheer. His impatience mounted as the morning wore on while he waited to be underway to the train station. Allen carefully kept his back turned away from the house to avoid any sentimental displays, but he needn't have worried. Lucy went through the house silently one last time, then came out looking almost pleasant. Allen was puzzled over her behavior, but guessed she was satisfied with things, especially since Willie and Laura Belle were moving too. Many family members, up out of Kentucky, had moved to Ohio and their church, like the Nile River, had steadily stretched its tributaries northward.

The two men who had been contracted to move the wagons and load the train for them arrived. They each brought a team, harnessed, and shortly had them hitched to the wagons. In the last minutes, Cynthia and Lucy were still adding things, a hatbox here and a bucket there.

Henry and the three youngest boys, antsy with excitement, had already started out on foot to the train station. Allen hankered to join them but knew he had to take care of business first. He felt his shirt pocket for their tickets and paperwork, satisfied he had everything. The house would soon be occupied by a new family, Henry Wallace having helped in the sale of it. Things could not have progressed any better, Allen told himself. He should feel pleased with the way things had turned out.

*   *   *   *

John Hannon poked his friend, Simon. "You about ready? We need to be there in twenty minutes."

"Sure," Simon spoke, stuffing his late breakfast biscuit into his mouth while he adjusted the harness on Mr. Dixon's livery horses. He swallowed the crumbly mess and said, "When do

168

you think these old nags are going to the glue factory? Mr. Dixon should really think about updating his stock."

John paused as he studied the team Simon now led out of the barn. They were definitely aged but still capable of labor. "Oh, I don't know, Simon. They've probably got enough strength to pull for a few years yet."

Simon snorted, "Mr. Dixon probably started out his livery with these behemoth boys. That makes them twenty years old or more. Here fellow, pray tell. Let me get a good look at your molars." The horse closest to Simon took offense and drew its lips back to nip him. "Playful old nag, aren't you?"

John gathered that the horses weren't real impressed with Simon. Sometimes John wasn't either, but he had needed his help to bring the two teams to a man named Allen Ross, to haul his freight to the train station by 9:10 A.M. He had never met the man, but he knew he was black from Mr. Hopkins, the grocer. Mr. Ross was also a member of the Mt. Zion Predestinarian Baptist Church, like John was, but strangely he hadn't seen him there and didn't remember him. Mr. Hopkins said he was a nice fellow and would pay cash. Anymore, John didn't know all the black residents in Warsaw. So many came and went. John and his parents had only been there in the river town for two years themselves.

When they arrived at the house, John spoke to Mr. Ross, the owner, and got his instructions. After he shook Allen's hand, he led his team to the wagon full of furniture. He noticed Simon had already hitched his team to the other wagon and was helping a girl throw one more item up on the colossal stack of household goods. *It figures,* John observed wryly. *Even moving freight, Simon could be clever with the ladies.*

Once all was ready and secured, John strode ahead to speak with Simon, who was still engaged in conversation with the girl. He tapped him on the shoulder. Simon turned around, annoyed at the interruption. "What?"

"Time to head out. I'll follow you." John looked past Simon to the young woman. She was even more appealing close up. Why did his friend always seem to profit on these jobs? And why, in pitiful plagues, did John keep asking for his help?

Deciding not to be outdone, John stepped forward to shake her hand. Focused on the becoming face, he clearly forgot about the protruding wagon tongue behind the horses. His shins caught against it, and he pitched forward, to land on his hands and knees at her feet. John hastily up-righted himself, dusting his hands off briskly, and settling his hat on straight. He couldn't shake her hand, not now with his own all dirty. Besides, his face was flushed a sweltering red.

The girl stepped back, concern on her face. "You all right?"

"Oh, he's all right, aren't you, John? My ol' pal here is used to such mishaps. That's what hauling freight is all about. That and building muscle." Simon slapped John on the back, like he was some clumsy adolescent without a trace of wit or brawn.

A Bible verse rang through John's mind: "For if they fall, the one will lift up his fellow: but woe to him that is alone when he falleth; for he hath not another to help him." John figured Simon must have missed out on this scripture during Sunday school, because his friendship was like mercury, it rose and fell according to the benefits it brought him. And now, clearly Simon's degrees read cold toward John where the girl was concerned. *Fine, I won't count on Simon's "helping hand"!* John's embarrassment forbade him to look directly at the girl. Instead, he turned to his "friend", Simon, and said sourly, "Let's go."

The womenfolk climbed up on the load of household goods and settled down between the boxes, hidden from view. The mother laughed good-naturedly as she had picked her way aboard. But John did not glance at the daughter. He was glad they were on Simon's load. John looked behind the wagon after he had guided the horses forward. Oddly, the man, Allen Ross, trailed behind, trudging along with his head down. He gave the appearance of one who was overburdened–a forlorn figure–even though there wasn't an ounce of baggage in his hands.

"It looks like home, Mama, except much nicer. What do you think?" Cynthia had emptied out the last box of china into its cupboard, and she stood back to admire it, along with the whole room.

Lucy smiled, "Yes, it is nicer, and it already feels like home to me. I think I'm going to like it here." *Yes, I believe so. A new start, family near, and no bars in sight!* Lucy paused and took in the picture Cynthia made in her faded wine-colored dress. One elbow had worn thin and a row of bottom ruffles hung limp. The dress was on its way out, having grown a little snug as well, but oh, how Lucy wanted to stop time and hold Cynthia close. Her youth and innocence radiated from her like steam from boiling water. Her daughter had grown up and now planned to teach school back in Warsaw. Where had time gone?

Lucy bent to the task of cleaning up empty crates and boxes to obscure the moisture that had sprung to her eyes. "I only regret that we'll be farther apart, Cynthia."

Cynthia took her mother's cue and began cleaning up the living room also. "Oh well, Mama, I'm only just a train ride away. Wouldn't it have been nicer for you to arrive at Camp Nelson aboard a train rather than bumping along in a wagon? I sure got a taste of that on the ride to the depot. I'm just glad no one could see us crushed in there, among all our stuff."

Lucy was amused. Wagon rides had been special to her at Cynthia's age. In those days, all she ever had for transportation were her own two feet. "I think someone was very aware you were hiding there in the wagon."

Cynthia's face shot upward to peer at her mother. "Who, Mama?" She looked alarmed, like maybe some of her town friends had seen her.

"That boy driving. He was turned around so often on the seat, I was sure we would be going back the way we came."

"Oh, him." Cynthia shrugged. "He thought his boots were lined with gold instead of manure."

Lucy smiled at Cynthia's disinterest. "The other fellow, was he just as bad?"

Cynthia smiled. She thought he had looked familiar, but she wasn't sure where she had seen him before. "Oh, Mama. He was good looking to the fifth degree, but I sure hoped he could drive better than he walked!"

Lucy recalled hearing how the young man had tripped over the wagon tongue and went face down. Poor boy! She carried her collection of empty boxes and called to her three sons who were out in the yard, "Boys, here's more for you to carry out back. Come and get 'em!"

The boys didn't think she was funny, but they obediently carted away the borrowed crates to be taken back to the train station.

Lucy paused and took stock of things. Allen was not around, having gone to secure his job. The boys had adjusted and already made friends in town, which was not far away. Next week, Willie's were to join them, living close by. Niece Elizabeth's wedding was to follow, and Cynthia would hopefully be teaching, while son Henry went to Cincinnati.

Lucy went into her new kitchen and sat down. She couldn't help the sigh that escaped, overflowing with sentiments. She longed for an interlude, for the hour hand to pause in its daily constant counting, and let her gather up these weeks and suspend them for a span. She was older now; in her youth she would not have thought to ever hinder time. But even Motherhood held no seniority with that Master of Minutes.

Lucy shook herself. She was no mathematician, but in whatever manner memories were calculated, she would tally them up the best she was able, to be reflected upon later. Lucy was well versed in the knowledge that the Lord gave, and that ultimately, He took away, too. That fact needed little ciphering skill or schooling. Lucy would try to be content and make the most of now. Her mama would have, and it was all that was promised to her.

Chapter Nineteen

Miss Annie Ross,
Think of me early, think of me late,
Think of me as a friend and an old schoolmate.
Ever your friend,
A.L. Davis
Mt Sterling, Ky 3-16-1888

Cynthia let her fingers glide over the beautiful creamy white fabric piled in a little mound on the bed before her. From the window, the fragrant air of summer's splendor breezed in. The roses on the side porch lent their perfume to the current threading its way into the room. Animated birdsong trilled out long vivacious notes that created cheerful visions only summertime can give. The harmony of it all struck Cynthia so that she nearly thought being a bride might not be so bad.

Cousin Elizabeth sat beside the fabric and pulled some of it into her lap to admire. Her face glowed. Cynthia could hardly blame her. She peered over the dress pattern Aunt Narciss planned to use. "Lizzie, it's so lovely. And white silk! Mama wore navy at her wedding because it was so serviceable. I wonder if Mama will let me wear white, if I ever marry."

Elizabeth's eyes widened. "Oh, Cynthia! Aunt Lucy won't be that mean, will she? A girl only marries once in her life. You just need to latch on to a rich fellow who'll buy you the silk or satin."

"No, thanks. Besides, even if I was interested, where would I meet one of those?" Cynthia settled herself on the bed beside her cousin. She studied the pattern closer. "You're lucky your mama has a sewing machine. Imagine sewing this by hand!"

"Oh, I'd sew every single stitch myself if it meant marrying Charley!" Elizabeth assured her.

Cynthia wrinkled up her nose at Elizabeth. "Silk? You're crazy, girl! How can any one man be worth that?"

Elizabeth giggled, "You'll see someday, Cynthia. Anyhow, it's a good thing we live in 1889, not 1789, or I'd be doing just that. Do you think they had thimbles back then?"

Cynthia shrugged. "Who knows? Maybe there wasn't even true love back then because no one wanted to sew silk by hand. Maybe–"

"Oh, hush you!" Elizabeth tossed a pillow at her cousin. Just then, her mother appeared in the doorway.

"You girls look like you're enjoying yourselves."

"Oh, we are, Mama." Elizabeth agreed. "We have so much to catch up on, especially before Cynthia has to go teach school in a month."

"If I get a school," Cynthia cautioned. "If not, I'll have Lizzie bored to death, and she'll rush Charley to the altar."

"Rush that young man?" Aunt Narciss was grinning. She was amused by Charley's timetable. He seemed in no hurry to embrace matrimony. The couple's wedding date had been shifted forward several times to a future date. The family tossed little jokes around about it, though not usually in Elizabeth's presence.

"Mama!" Elizabeth cried, "Surely you're not poking fun at Charley?"

Aunt Narciss winked at Cynthia. "Lizzie, you know your mama! 'Course not, I'm just tickling your toes a little. We all think Charley's peachy sweet!"

Elizabeth's feathers unruffled, and she turned to Cynthia. "Let's go bake a cake for Mt. Zion's picnic. There's going to be an auction for them on Saturday evening and the money goes to Brother Davis and his family for their fire."

"Sure," Cynthia said as she scooted off the bed. Both girls folded the wedding material neatly and lay it in its box. They trailed behind Aunt Narciss, towards the kitchen.

Cynthia was happy to be staying with her Aunt Narciss and Uncle Henry Wallace. At times, she greatly missed her family, but the year away from home at Berea had helped her

174

deal with the homesickness. It was strange to be here in Warsaw, Kentucky, while the rest of the family were living seventy miles north in Loveland, Ohio. How wonderful to have so many close relatives that it felt like home away from home.

Cynthia had applied to two school districts that needed black teachers. She had no interest in marriage yet, the only other diverging path open to a young woman of color. She wanted to prove herself by applying what she had learned and perhaps affect lives, just as Rev. Fee and her teachers had done for her. It was a gift she yearned to return to others.

Cynthia eagerly visited the post office each day, although it was still too soon to expect an envelope. She cautioned herself to exercise some patience while she waited. Cousin Elizabeth helped her out in that area. There were countless things to do and people to visit, Elizabeth claimed, and she toted Cynthia along for all of it. "Come on, Cynthia," she would urge, "No sense sitting around waiting on the mail."

Cynthia would let herself be towed toward town on another errand, protesting slightly, "Give me a chance to catch my breath, will you, Lizzie?"

"Your breath? Oh, Annie! You're such a granny!" Under *her* breath, Elizabeth would mutter, "You're going to make the perfect old schoolmarm."

"Alright, Cynthia, wait until you hear my great idea for the funraiser!" Elizabeth whispered as she tiptoed to peer out the kitchen door. Her parents were both in the store.

Cynthia was immediately suspicious. "Elizabeth! I know you're up to something!"

Elizabeth clapped her hands together in pleasure. "Why do you think it's called a funraiser? You're supposed to raise some fun while doing it!"

Cynthia shook her head. "Cousin, it's spelled f-u-n-d. Don't forget the "d". Your spelling needs some brushing up on."

"Pshaw! Act your age, Annie, which is under eighty!

175

Now listen here. You remember how sweet Solomon Jenkins is on you, right?"

Cynthia made a face at Elizabeth. "Liz, I don't like where this is leading. That was ages ago, when we were kids. Please spare me whatever plan you've concocted."

"Cynthia, this is one of my last times to act merry before I marry! Charley will expect a mature, sober woman after we're married. I plan to have a tiny bit of fun before I don the coat of respectability befitting a married matron." Elizabeth was pleased with the joke she was about to reveal to Cynthia.

Cynthia perched on the table's edge. "Alright, Lizzie, what's going through that mind of yours?"

"You'll see." Elizabeth poked the fire in the cookstove until the coals glowed. She fed in a little kindling, followed by a larger hunk of wood, listening to the crackling it emitted. "Alright. Fire's good. Get out that mixing bowl, Cynthia, and the cocoa. We're going to make a cake that will snag the suspenders right off Solomon Jenkins! We all know he adores peppermints, so the outside of the cake will look like a beautiful peppermint delicacy, but inside we'll have a few of our own bakers' secrets!"

Elizabeth laughed so heartily that it was contagious and Cynthia joined in, but she still felt the need to caution her cousin. "I'm not sure this is such a good idea. It sounds...well, do you think it might be kind of mean?"

"Oh, Annie! We all know that Sol is such a know-it-all. Just once he won't know that the cake he bought isn't what he thinks it is. It won't hurt that fancy-pants any. If he gets wind you made it, he'll go after it like a piranha. Then after he tries it, he'll be too gentlemanly to mention it, but he'll think you're an awful baker, and drop his plans of escorting you to the preacher's. Great, huh?"

At Cynthia's disbelieving look, Elizabeth fussed, "Don't tell me you don't remember how much he hounded you before you left for Berea?"

"Yes, I remember, but...do you really think he's going to run away because of some botched-up baking? Besides, think of the money he'll spend on the cake. If it's worthless, it would be shameful to do that to him," Cynthia insisted.

"Cynthia, all the money goes for a good cause, it should be given anyway as a donation to the Davis family. And we won't make the cake worthless, just a little unusual."

Cynthia was running out of arguments. "So what's the 'unusual' ingredients you want to use?"

"Well," Elizabeth considered. She looked around the kitchen and spotted a jar of pickled beets on the counter. Her eyes glittered. "What do you say to a chocolate beet cake, full of that hearty root veggie that tastes so like Mother Earth?"

Cynthia raised her brows. "Lizzie, those beets are pickled!"

"Great! That's classic. You know, like in literature? It is a type of symbolism. Sol Jenkins will be showing off his daddy's money, and he'll find himself in a pickle–the red kind, not the green. And literally, he'll get a chocolate peppermint pickled beet cake, one of a kind, JUST LIKE HIM! More symbolism!" Elizabeth was extremely proud of herself.

Cynthia rolled her eyes and reluctantly joined Elizabeth, adding flour and cocoa with some sugar into the mixing bowl. She found the salt and soda, while Elizabeth fetched a dollop of lard. "Where's those eggs at?" she murmured as she searched the kitchen. Aunt Narciss happened in and Elizabeth asked about them. Aunt Narciss frowned and checked the pantry. She came back carrying a wire basket full of brown eggs. "Your papa puts everything in the strangest places. He had these on the top shelf. How are we supposed to find them there?" She shook her head. "It smells good, girls. Did you check your fire?"

"I'll check it," Cynthia offered. When Aunt Narciss left for the store, Elizabeth opened the jar of pickled beets. The girls added the beet chunks to the batter, along with a little juice for good measure. They poured it into two round cake pans. After it was safely in the oven, Elizabeth planned the finishing touches on the cake.

"We'll ice it, using a little beet juice for coloring, so it's pink. Then I'll get some of Daddy's store peppermints and crush them, for the top. Sol will adore it."

"Just a minute, Lizzie. There's one flaw in your plan. If I make the cake, and he bids on it and gets it, then I'll have to eat it with him on Sunday's picnic! First, I don't want to eat it with Sol, and second, what will your folks say if they try the cake?" Cynthia was more worried about this scheme as time passed.

Elizabeth got serious. "You're right. Well, partly right. I mean, I'll probably be eating with Charley and his family because I'm making another cake for him to bid on and so–"

"So the whole thing is going to fall on my shoulders? No, sir, I'm not going to go for that." Cynthia's voice had risen in tone.

"Cynthia, don't get so much air in your balloon! It will all be worth it to send Sol packing and get his goat! Tell you what, I'll finish the cake so you can wash your hands of the finished confection. How's that?" Elizabeth spoke convincingly, a smile on her face to put Cynthia at ease. "Really, no one is going to find out it isn't totally peppermint. My parents probably won't try it, they're always too busy with the affairs of serving and cleaning up. Since you don't want to marry, you need to do something to deter Mr. Jenkins or he'll continue to be your shadow. This will take care of it, and no one will be the wiser!"

Just then Uncle Henry walked in. "You're right about that, Lizzie. I'm no wiser! Where did your mother put the camphor oils? Mrs. Feldman is in need of a bottle and of course, it isn't where I keep it! Organization, my foot!" he muttered.

Elizabeth quickly recovered when she realized her father hadn't overheard her. She trotted into the pantry and pulled down a box. "Here, Daddy, I'll get more of this out on the shelves tonight. I think Mama puts it between the liver pills and blood tonic."

Uncle Henry snorted as he took the bottle. "Thanks, Liz. You're a doll baby."

Elizabeth beamed. Cynthia scowled at her. "Save your sweet stuff for Charley. If anyone finds out the cake is a joke, it will be raining on *your* umbrella, got it?" But she had to admit, if Sol suspected she had made the cake, he would bid on it. And he did like peppermint. She would "get his goat" for all the times he had harassed her.

Elizabeth poked Cynthia and put on a pouty face. "If only you were more fun-loving!"

"You mean if only I were as daft as you and would just go blithely along with your schemes." Cynthia told her.

Elizabeth grinned, "You went away to school, Annie, and got too smart!"

Cynthia took the kitchen towel and coiled it up tightly, then flicked it at her cousin. A sharp snap followed, but Elizabeth jumped out of Cynthia's reach, laughing at her. Cynthia was sure the customers would hear them up front in the store.

"I hope your beets burn!" Cynthia said, her own laughter choking her words.

Elizabeth shook her head and playfully snatched Cynthia's towel. "Dear girl, let me tell you something. Sol is going to be falling on his knees before you to eat that cake! And better that than at the altar!"

*   *   *   *

The Mt. Zion Predestinarian Baptist church grounds were teeming with parishioners after the supper hour. The evening was proving mild; the humidity had abated for a spell. The sunshine enthused the members with its golden glow and seemed to make the change in their pockets feel like pieces of that bright orb. It jingled in anticipation of the auction to come. Rarely was anything as exciting as bidding money and watching it exchange hands. The prize was the good deed done by buying a cake as all the money collected went to the Paul Davis family for the damage their chimney had caused when it caught fire. And sharing that cake with its baker was an added incentive, especially if it was a pretty girl or beloved wife. Of course, no man wanted to shirk his duty.

When the auction began, the congregation had crowded

around the minister. He stood on a podium and held up each cake for the audience to observe. His voice cracked honestly on the high notes for he was no auctioneer but that added to the festivities as far as the crowd was concerned. And Preacher C. H. Hughes had a great sense of humor, especially over his own shortcomings.

The little children had taken the front rows because of their short stature. They accumulated until they all were gathered on the lawn before the podium. Little Thea Wise told Jolene Wilson her mama made the best cake, but Jolene ignored her. She also ignored her brother, Tommy, and his cohorts who threw grass clippings at all the girls. She was impatient to watch the auction get under way.

To the right, the young men congregated, grinning. John Hannon was there without his folks, but he had strict orders from his daddy to bid on Mama's cake. Dad and Mama were at the Davis' with a clean-up crew. His father would do the masonry work on the new chimney when it was ready. John planned to help.

To the left of the preacher's stand, the young ladies stood giggling and whispering, their youthful cheeks flushed pink with excitement. Maryanne Jones hoped Simon would bid on her cake, June Rose was wondering whether she had forgotten to add the sugar, and Cynthia fretted over Elizabeth's little prank. Elizabeth, all smiles, was confident that Charley would do his part with the bidding.

Behind the young people stood the married members, husbands fixed to please their wives by showing their devotion through their pocketbooks, and wives proud to show off their baking abilities to one another.

As the bidding commenced, John tried to remember what his dad had told him. Mama's cake was a red velvet, frosted pink. John watched as cake by cake disappeared until his friend, Simon, jogged his shoulder, saying, "What are you waiting on?" John just shrugged.

Simon pulled out his money. "I'm bidding on Miss Ross' cake. She's sweeter than sugar, I'm telling ya."

Good for you, John thought, feeling irritated and wanting to brush away Simon like an annoying fly.

Simon continued, "I'm sure Sol Jenkins is after her cake, too. I overheard him ask her cousin, Elizabeth Wallace, which one it was. He's so arrogant. Do you think I have a chance against Mr. Big Bucks?" Simon sounded worried.

John opened his mouth to reply, when he noticed that Preacher Hughes was holding up a pink cake. He had missed out on its description but how many pink cakes were there? It was mama's favorite color. John raised his number, "28", and hoped for the best. For some reason, Simon bid as well and three other young men, including Sol Jenkins. John pursed his lips. *What were the fellows doing? Trying to run up the price? Some joke!* Maybe they thought since it was pink that one of the girls had made it. Or maybe they knew what an excellent baker his mama was.

John bid it up to sixty-five cents. He certainly hoped his dad wouldn't choke on that figure. Everyone dropped out except Sol. He ran it to seventy cents. John gave up, shaking his head, and let Sol have it. Disgusted, John prepared to leave. He would just donate the money to the fund and hope Dad understood. Mama, too. As he turned to go, Sol shouldered his way over to John. "Here, John, take this." He thrust a nickel into John's palm. "I want you to have the cake. Here's the extra I ran you up on. Sorry about that, friend." Then he rushed back up to the front where his cohorts were and resumed watching.

Confounded, John stared at the coin and shook his head. He made his way through the crowd and bid farewell to a few members. He stopped by the ladies' booth to pay his bill, glad to have gotten Mama's cake and hopefully satisfied his father. John went towards home.

Cynthia was tired of the auction. She had worn Elizabeth's smaller boots, and her feet were protesting. Elizabeth had insisted she wear them, claiming they were so "stylish". Well, modern or not, by the time she had them all laced up, her patience was melting away like an ice cube in the summer heat. When she discovered they were too tight, she refused to take them off, after all the trouble they were to get on. She dabbed her upper lip with her hankie, anxiously watching each cake as it was held aloft by Preacher Hughes. Her stomach churned, and she was jittery. As the sale wound down, Cynthia saw her cake on the table, making its way towards the auctioneer. She had seen enough. She went to the "little-building-out-back" and wasted time, hoping the sale would be over when she returned. She wanted to avoid Sol's jubilant face.

Elizabeth met her on her way back from the hill. "Did it go alright?" Cynthia asked her cousin.

Elizabeth assured Cynthia it had, but declined to mention that there had been two pink cakes. The Rev. Hughes had not been very distinct in their descriptions. Maybe Sol had gotten the cake, and maybe not. She wasn't sure which would upset Cynthia more, so she remained quiet. "I think Charley's ready to go," she said.

As the girls went towards the buggy, Cynthia spoke. "Well, Lizzie, once tomorrow is over, Sol Jenkins will forget all about me since he'll believe I poisoned him, and you'll have had your 'single-girl' fun!" Her tone sounded sour.

Elizabeth didn't answer but gave Cynthia her good bonnet to don, and they climbed up in the buggy. Cynthia sat on Elizabeth's lap since it was only a two-seater, all the while dreaming of unlacing the "stylish" boots upon her aching feet, which her dress hem had covered anyhow. Bedtime had never seemed so inviting.

*   *   *   *

The meetinghouse had been full, bench-to-bench. The members of the Mt. Zion Predestinarian Baptist church had been privileged to listen to the gospel and were renewed for the week ahead. They visited among each other as the men assembled the tables under the old shade trees on the church grounds, while the women set out the dinner. There was fried chicken and ham, sliced beef and tongue, baked beans, potato salad, and hardboiled eggs. Pickles (and pickled beets), biscuits, corn-bread, and stewed apples filled the tables. For dessert, each man would go collect the cake he had bid on and eat it with the baker and family. There was a host of excitement that wove its way through the tree leaves overhead and among the grasses as if magically surrounding the church-goers.

Snippets of conversation flitted about like birdsong. Between the young men, the ribbing was contagious. *"I got the best deal of any of you, boys! Mine's a chocolate supreme cake."*

"Too bad the gal you're going to eat it with ain't as good of a bargain."

The men heaved tables into place. *"Joe, get over here and help! If you don't work, you don't eat, the Good Book says so."*

"Aw, it's Sunday! Leave me be!"

"That table isn't level, George. You're wanting all the food to slide right off the table into your lap, aren't you?"

The women chatted happily. *"I know Salome has six children. Two were twins, but what's their names? I can't remember for the life of me!"*

"Lenora, tell me your recipe for molasses bread!"

"Where's Beatrice? She was supposed to be in charge of the coffee making! Don't tell me she's 'outback' again!"

The meal was similar in fashion, enjoyed with gusto and good visiting. Afterward, the men sought out the church's overhang where they retrieved the cake they had bid on. In charge was Miss Lottie Wetzel, who asked, "What was your number?" in an orderly fashion, just like at the post office.

John Hannon had shared with his parents how success-ful he had been on Saturday. Now cheerfully, he went to Miss Wetzel and told her, "Number 28". She handed him his mama's cake, a pink creation with small pieces of peppermint crushed on top. Mama sure was a good baker, and John heartily antici-pated the red velvet dessert. He took it carefully towards the tables.

As dessert time approached, Cynthia stormed to herself how dumb of an idea it had been to go along with Elizabeth. Could she bear Sol Jenkins for the twenty minutes it took to eat the cake? Should she woof it down in five minutes, and hope Sol found both it and her disgusting enough to politely excuse himself? What if he actually retched in front of her? "The way to a man's heart is through his stomach", right? Surely it could work in reverse, couldn't it?

Cynthia was full of these questions as she spied Sol up beneath the overhang. It looked like he was arguing with Miss Lottie Wetzel. *Was there some problem?* She should go see, but her feet felt glued to the grass. She was too nervous to find out.

Sol looked impatiently at Miss Wetzel. "This isn't the right cake!" He pointed at the imposter. "I bid on a peppermint cake by Miss Ross."

"Well, Mr. Jenkins, your number is on it. Number ten, right? See here, it says–"

"I know what it says, but I bought a peppermint cake, not a red velvet." Sol interrupted her. "There's been a mix-up."

Miss Lottie was flustered, "But Mr. Jenkins, how could that be? What can possibly be done now?"

"Whose is this?" Sol demanded, casting a withering glance at the offending sweet.

Miss Lottie peered at her register and checked numbers again. "Its baker was Mrs. Hannon."

Sol's mouth fell open. The postmistress continued, "I don't know how to remedy it, Mr. Jenkins, but I can assure you it will be delicious. Betty is an exceptional cook."

Sol's mind whirled like a windmill. His wide eyes rose until his brows met his hairline. Betty Hannon was John's mother. He remembered when he thought he and John were bidding on Cynthia's cake and then found out that, although the cake was pink, it wasn't peppermint, nor was it Cynthia's, as Elizabeth had let slip.

Miss Wetzel began to apologize, but Sol grabbed the cake. "I'll take it. I think I can fix this little predicament."

Determined, Sol set off at a march for John Hannon. *I'd better not be too late,* he fumed.

Betty Hannon shook her head. "Yes, John, I'm certain it's not my cake. This has peppermints on top and mine didn't. Whose name is on the bottom?"

Both mother and son peered under the plate. *C. Ross.* Betty smiled, John gulped. "There's been a mix-up. I'll just run this cake to the family and see if I can locate yours, Mama." John set off at a clip. *I hope I'm not too late!*

Cynthia rose from her bench. Her mind had been busy thinking about Elizabeth's silly prank. Had they really thought this trick on Sol would send him packing? She could stand it no longer. Clasping her shaky hands together tightly, she went towards where Sol stood under the awning with Miss Lottie. She would head him off. Maybe the whole congregation would miss them eating together. She would simply lead him around to the side of the church, away from the majority of tables, yet still in plain view. If they ate while standing up, it would hasten the duration of their shared company.

Taking longer strides then customary, Cynthia concentrated on what she would say to Solomon. In her flustered state, she failed to notice the figure approaching at an equally rapid pace. Cynthia cast a glance over her shoulder to see where Elizabeth was. In that instant–*Smack!* She encountered a solid surface. Stunned, she bounded backwards, her mouth falling open in disbelief. She had rushed headlong into the young man who had moved their things by wagon to the depot.

In his upraised and outstretched arm, he balanced a pink cake. The aftershock of the collision forced his arm to waver, and the cake slipped over the edge of the plate. John Hannon fumbled as he strove to right the lurching cake. In a series of wild motions, he flailed about, too slow to catch the swiftly plummeting confection. Down John went with the cake. It fell–*splat*–only a few feet from Cynthia's shoetops, just out of

185

reach from John's outstretched arms.

Cynthia bit her lower lip as she viewed the cake's destruction with John Hannon rising from the ground, a stricken look on his face. The silence behind them bore testimony that, indeed, the whole congregation had taken notice of the debacle. Sol Jenkins arrived, winded, coming to a stop by braking on the balls of his feet, a pink cake clutched to his chest.

In the silence that ensued, Cynthia looked from the cake to John, then Sol, and back again to the exploded cake of red beets upon the church's grounds. Grass stuck up through the pink frosting and the two layers were severed.

John strove to apologize, while Sol spit out his indignation over the muddled blunder. Cynthia laughed when the realization dawned upon her that she would have no need to subject herself to the beet cake or to Sol's company. Her mirth bewildered both young men.

All three spoke in unison, but their words trailed off. Cynthia was the first to speak again. "Well, gentlemen, I guess my cake is inedible. I'll have to apologize for not eating with you, Sol."

Sol looked at the cake in his arms. Suddenly, he smirked. "Well, there's this one yet. How about it? Shall we try it out?"

John spoke, "That's right, Sol, I owe you for this. I'm sorry. Just go ahead and keep that one there."

Sol raised his brows. "Yes, you do. That was seventy cents you just heaved on the ground."

Cynthia gasped. *Mercy!* That was an awful lot of money for just a cake. *Especially one made with pickled beets!* Suddenly Cynthia felt a burst of honest declarations upon her tongue. "Sol, I'm sorry. I can't have dessert with you. I'm just not interested at all, and it's unfair to you. Thank you for bidding on my cake. I know the Davis family will appreciate the donation you've given."

Sol's brows drew together in a bothersome formation, and his disgruntled expression was not lost on Cynthia or John. "Fine," he snapped, "there's other cards in the deck. Here," he shoved the pink cake he held into John's hands. "Go eat this with your mama." He strode away.

The hum of the people behind them had resumed so that John and Cynthia were less self-conscious. Looking at one another, they laughed. Cynthia spoke, "Are you always going to be falling at my feet?"

John smiled shyly, "If that's what it takes, I guess I could manage it." He didn't know where he had unearthed that bit of bravery in which to reply.

Cynthia was flustered. "Oh, I didn't mean that like it sounded. I meant…oh, well." She looked away, embarrassed.

John swallowed and took a chance on his fleeting courage. "Would you…Miss Ross, would you like to join my family and have a piece of my mama's dessert?"

Cynthia had recovered. "That would be very nice." They turned to seek out the Hannons, when Cynthia paused. "You know, you rescued me, Mr. Hannon."

John grinned, "Miss Ross, besides falling on my face, that's the next best thing I know how to do." He offered Cynthia his free arm. And Cynthia carried the cake!

*   *   *   *

Warsaw, Kentucky
July 23, 1889

Dear Nellie,

Bonjour! *I have thought of you many times in the past months and hope you are well.*

Thank you for your last letter. How are your studies going at this time? I have completed my schooling at Berea, and miss it very much. The girls there will forever be in my memo - ry, just as you will, and the teachers were outstanding educators (minus the Bee).

I have hopes of attaining a school to teach in the fall. It will be a dream come true. I will write whether I get it or not.

187

Please write and tell me of your future plans. Has your papa relented in his stand against Berea? My prayers are with you.

Your amie,
Annie Ross

P.S. I remembered the French you taught me!

Chapter Twenty

As I walked by myself, and talked to myself,
A sweet voice said to me—care not for thyself,
Think not of thyself. Then others will care for thee.
Samuel Hannon

It was an unladylike squeal, more akin to a frisky piglet or startled colt, but Cynthia gave air to her exclamation of delight with no thought to her repute. The post office's customers politely ignored her, given her age. Miss Lottie Wetzel, in her efficient manner, overlooked the improper outburst and asked, "Cynthia, dear, did it come?"

"Oh, yes, Miss Wetzel. They need a teacher in the Napoleon district! I'm so excited. I need to go tell Elizabeth. Thank you!" Cynthia called back over her shoulder as she hurried out of the post office. She checked the street hastily, hopping over horse droppings as she progressed up the main fare. To her amazement, there was John Hannon, driving a rig. He pulled up in front of her, reining the horses in to a stop.

"Good news, Miss Ross?" he questioned, his smile matching hers. He indicated to the envelope she was holding.

"Yes, Mr. Hannon. I've received a teaching position in the Napoleon district, starting the first of September."

"Great! Just what you've been hoping for. Will you be staying at the Wallace's or boarding closer to the school?" John tried to look casual as he awaited her answer by studying the horses' harness.

"I plan to stay at Aunt Narciss and Uncle Henry's. They'll be lonely since Lizzie will be married and gone by then." Cynthia paused, then added, "Probably I'll be busy helping in the store in the evenings after I prepare my lessons."

There. She didn't like it the way her heart seemed to beat out some strange and unfamiliar tempo when she came into contact with John W. Hannon. If he was asking about her, she must deter any interest. She was going to teach school and wouldn't allow herself to get stretched in two directions. Cynthia wanted to dedicate her whole self to her work.

"I see," John mused for a moment. He wasn't so dense he hadn't caught her meaning. "But you'll come to church on Sundays, right?"

Cynthia registered surprise. Then slightly abashed, she said, "Of course."

John Hannon smiled widely, "That's good news. I, too, have my work all week, and I wouldn't want to neglect my studies with Reverend Hughes. But on Sunday, well, there's a day full of opportunity, for both the Spirit and the flesh."

Cynthia wasn't so dull she didn't perceive *his* meaning. Though her tightly held composure rivaled John's tight hold on the horses, her amusement leaked out before she could rein it in. "You're right, Mr. Hannon, and since we both understand one another, I'm sure we'll be able to follow our callings."

John grinned, "Exactly. As the Lord leads, Miss Ross." He tipped his hat and pulled away, light-hearted. Cynthia was puzzled as to how the sunshine could be any more golden than it had been ten minutes earlier, but it was. She hurried home to the grocery where she could share her exciting prospects with Lizzie.

*   *   *   *

Warsaw Independent September 19, 1889

County Superintendent Chas. F. Burkhardt and the two examiners, Misses Emma Perry and Fannie Lindsay examined the following and granted certificates to teach in Gallatin Co., viz: Thos. G. Fletcher, Glencoe, 1st class; Miss B. McCann, Warsaw, 1st class; Bennett

*Graham, Warsaw, Ky, 2nd class. Miss Mayme
Stucy, Long Run, Ind. 3rd class. Miss C. Ross,
colored, Loveland, Ohio, will teach the colored
school in the Napoleon district and was granted
a third class certificate.*

*   *   *   *

Henry Allen Laine had little time to waste on leisurely
pursuits. He had arrived at Berea where his youthful mind and
muscles were to be worked. Henry had sweated before, having
labored most of his life but never before had he worked for his
own benefit. He had helped his daddy pay off the farm, which
had delayed his book learning. It was not a proud thing Henry
shared around, the fact it had taken him until he was eighteen
years old to achieve an eighth grade education. And even that
was from a former slave in an old cabin, who taught him all he
knew, all that the Webster's Blueback Speller contained. But it
wasn't from a lack of desire. No, Henry had plenty of fuel for
an academic fire.

Henry thought back to nearly a year ago when he had
wanted to enjoy himself a little before putting his shoulder to
the educational plow. That image had faded with the reality that
the pursuit of an education held a hearty appetite like that of a
hungry creature. The only way to sate its craving was to gulp
down his book learning as fast as that beast "knowledge" chal-
lenged him. It was a demanding test of merit, this taxing new
mode of life, but Henry Allen Laine hadn't been born black for
nothing. Being a son of former slaves produced its own mettle.

To attend Berea, Henry took any odd job around the
school he could. When Henry wasn't digesting a new theory or
pronouncing Latin words for biology, he was shoveling coal for
the furnaces or splitting wood for the kitchens. He could dance
a broom across the hallways as easily as spit-shining the classroom doorknobs. One duty supported another in the trestle
framework of his life; Henry must work to learn and learn to

191

find work, the kind he desired anyhow.

* * * *

"Henry Allen Laine! Yoohoo! There you are!"

"You sure do get around!"

"Just where are you rushing off to now? A cyclone hasn't got anything over on you, Sugar." A trio of girls appeared in his path. *Groan!* The girls hammered at him until he was forced to address them. Henry sighed. He had overspent his time in the library and was in a hurry to reach the campus kitchens. He would heave a few trays around and then load the bread shelves before math class.

It was perplexing to him how he had once scouted out girls in earnest, but to no avail. He had never even made one's acquaintance back home. But here at Berea, the female population had suddenly deemed themselves planets to his sun. Unfortunately, he now had no time for socializing; he was imbibed by the spirits of pedagogy and enlightenment.

"Sorry, girls, you've caught me at a bad time." Henry strove to disengage himself from the social band that encircled him. *What a problem to have!*

Clara Dewey smiled sweetly, "Now, Henry A., you can't keep running off from us. We'll think you're scared! Tell us, are you really so busy?"

"Yeah, Mr. Laine. How can any one person keep up such a schedule?" Eulalia Perkins chided. Her head was encased in a pleasing bow that matched her trimmed dress.

Yes, really, how was he doing it? Henry had no answer, for he wasn't sure himself how he was able to carry on. But for now…Henry smiled to appease the girls and lifted his hands helplessly. "I'm sorry, really, but duty calls. I've got to get to mathematics. You girls are patient and kind. Hopefully, I'll see you around." Henry spun on his heel and headed for the kitchens. As he hurried away, a small prayer stole upward from his scattered mind (or heart). Henry Allen Laine asked his wise, all-knowing Father for strength of character, moral integrity, and more than a little peace in the female department.

*   *   *   *

Charley Mitchell swallowed and his Adam's apple bobbed repeatedly. Funny how a man could feel clearly out of place at his own wedding. He wiped the nervous perspiration from his upper lip with the sleeve of his coat. This action earned him a glare from his grandmamma in the first row, but Charley was more concerned over the oddity of his cold feet in the heat of August.

Yes, Charley Mitchell had made it to the altar. He was standing before a man of God, ready to promise himself and vow to support, cherish, and love–well, to love Elizabeth Wallace–a woman as near to perfection as the Lord had made. *So what was the big scary deal, Charley?* It was indeed a leap of faith but sweet Elizabeth had enough of that for both of them. Charley stood a little taller and faced Preacher Hughes.

The bride was beautiful (in her machine-sewed silk), the day perfectly flawless, and the Wallaces thoroughly relieved. The young couple were showered with congratulations, tears, and rice. Henry Wallace had bought a fifty pound bag just for this occasion. The refreshments were simple and the gifts modest, but the joy was lavish.

Cynthia also had a new dress, a surprise Mama had brought along with her when they had arrived for the wedding. It was holly green, Mama's favorite color, and she had spared no skill on its making. Cynthia, herself, felt like a bride in it. Daddy teased her he would have to relegate himself to watchdog status to guard over her, in case some young fellow took a notion. "Ha, ha, Daddy," Cynthia told her father dryly.

But when John Hannon adroitly introduced himself to her parents, Cynthia masked her surprise and neatly avoided her mother's eyes. She had this strange sensation like that of an ocean wave which rolls in treasures from its depths and casts them upon the sands. Cynthia reckoned she would be presented with the "opportunity", as John put it, to decide which were

193

jewels and which was dross. It was disconcerting to Cynthia. Unconsciously, she moved closer to Allen and tucked her hand beneath his arm.

John, ever sensitive, noticed Cynthia's stance. It told him a few things, none of which were all that pleasing. He politely made small talk about his father having worked at the sawmill also, and then bade them farewell, avoiding any regard to the Ross' daughter. Unaware to both of the young people, John's insightful behavior had earned him a gold star near the cloud with silver lining.

When the day ended, Charley and Elizabeth were ready to depart in a hired surrey decorated with streamers. The couple were mobbed with kisses and hugs and wished well. Elizabeth clung to Narciss and then her daddy. She turned to Cynthia, who was like a sister, and held her close. Both girls laughed at the sudden teardrops in their eyes. There were really no words to say. After all the time they had spent together, they knew the other's thoughts. Cynthia waved goodbye at them until her arm ached. Henry Wallace carried his grain sack of rice around, urging the guests to "take some on home now", while Narciss sought out Lucy. Quietly the two siblings went into the privacy of Mt. Zion's sanctuary and amid sisterly comfort, they held each other and cried over the tangled peculiarities of life.

*   *   *   *

Ridge Top
Franklin, Tennessee
September 2, 1889

Dearest Annie,

How are you, my friend? I miss you and your cheery smile. You must write and tell me if you received the position you wanted. If not, please don't despair. You will make a perfect teacher, Annie.

As for me, I am just myself. You can see my handwriting has only improved slightly, but you will be glad to know I mastered geometry. Who said it was only a manly pursuit? I've told you about Monsieur, but did I tell you that the old coot has a young fils, *a son? Tres magnifique! He has come to visit his* le pere *and made my acquaintance. I am doubly devoted now to being* (connaissent bien en francais) *well versed in French!*

I sincerely hope I do not become too unladylike, but I have found my suffragist side. My father does not appreciate this new aspect of me, but Monsieur's son, Jean-Claude, approves of women who speak their mind. In France, women are regarded more equally than here in Tennessee. Papa could put that in his pipe and smoke it, but unfortunately, he raises his own "tobacco" here on Ridge Top, and it has to always agree with him (in all ways).

Dear Annie, write when time affords. You are often present in my thoughts.

> *Your friend ever,*
> *Nellie Mason*

*   *   *   *

Cynthia's brother, Henry Ross, breathed deeply of the river's smell. It was a heady perfume to him, just as the magnificent steamboat, *The Virginia*, was gorgeous to his sight. Henry knew he had found his calling. Being hired on as part of the crew, maybe not in the initial capacity he had hoped for, was still something he had only dreamed of.

It hadn't taken much convincing for his father to agree to it. Allen Ross had thought it over for a moment, and then told his son, "Go ahead, Henry. You're a man now, and one of us might as well live out our dream." What an odd thing for his dad to say, but Henry didn't question it. Older people always referred back to their youth like they should, could, or might have done things different. He was just elated he was allowed. Since Dad and Mama's house was just outside of town, there was a little ground with it. That had been a surprise to Mama, but it had pleased Daddy to own some land, and he planned to work it. Henry felt he had narrowly escaped that drudgery. Poor

John and James!

Here Henry was, aboard *The Virginia*, a packet line steamer on the Pittsburgh–Cincinnati line. The ship was fairly new and followed a schedule of leaving Pomeroy, Ohio, and going every Wednesday up to Pittsburgh, Pennsylvania, and then came back to its starting point. On Monday mornings, the steamer headed down to Cincinnati.

Henry would have a new home aboard the ship, but he would learn to live in Pomeroy on his days off. There was a hotel where he had secured a room. His wages were nothing to brag about yet, but he was certain he could work his way up. That brought about the remembrance of last week, when he had been hired. A thread of heat wound its way up Henry's neck at the thought of the past interview. Maybe he had a future aboard *The Virginia*, and maybe he didn't.

Upon his arrival, he had waited two days to speak with the General Manager, Jason Henderson. That meeting might not have happened if he hadn't nearly plowed the guy over, in his search of the captain. Mr. Henderson agreed to talk with him but had to round up the Assistant Manager Carl Thayer. Why it took two of them, Henry wasn't sure, but he would go along with just about anything to get a job aboard the ship.

The two men interviewed him in the hold, not especially clean or quiet. He felt he had to shout to be heard. In an informal quiz, the well-dressed men asked him questions like:

A. M. Carl Thayer: "Name and age?"

H. R.: "Henry Ross. Age eighteen, sir."

A. M. Thayer: "Place of birth?"

H. R.: "Garrard County, Kentucky, sir."

G. M. Henderson: "Have you ever been in trouble with the Law? Is there any warrant out for your arrest?"

H. R.: "No, sir."

A. M. Thayer: "Let's take a look at you."

From there, things got uncomfortable. Assistant Manager Thayer motioned for Henry to open his mouth. "Let me see your teeth."

Henry gave him a quizzical look. "My teeth?"

"This is a routine examination. We can tell a lot about your health. Haven't you ever checked out a horse's teeth?" The two men were enjoying this little "interview".

Henry made to protest, but the look Thayer gave him silenced it. The expression made it clear he should comply if he wanted the job. Henry opened his mouth.

"Uh-huh. Let's see your hands. What are you afraid of? This isn't the auction block."

Henry hesitated, then held them out, palms up. The manager, Jason, took a look and frowned. "What's wrong with that one?"

Henry swallowed the bile that had accumulated in the back of his throat. Things didn't seem routine to him, but then he couldn't be sure. He wasn't familiar with interviews. *But, auction block?*

Henderson looked at Thayer and shook his head. The assistant manager spoke, "Looks like your hand is abnormal. Where's your finger? That would impair your work. I don't think we can use you."

Stunned, Henry found his voice. "My hand is as good as the other one. I worked at the sawmill and never had a problem."

"Well, this isn't a sawmill. It's a first class passenger transport. People won't want a disfigured darkie handling their luggage."

Henry sputtered, "It's hardly noticeable. It's just one finger."

"Forget it. A purser is a prestige position. You're not the kind of material we're looking for."

In Henry's desperation, he overlooked the insult. "Well, I can shovel coal and feed boilers faster than the next man. I've lifted nearly double my own weight in sawn logs at the mill."

Jason Henderson paused. His sour look never faltered as he flipped his hand over in a motion of dismissal. Carl Thayer shrugged, "If we need you, we'll be in touch."

Henry knew it was the ultimate brush-off. He wasn't sure which emotion abused him worst, his disappointment or

197

his disgust. He turned to go. Henry's core substance contained too much of his daddy, Allen, to beg, but he had sorely wanted this job. He left the hold and broke out into the sunlight, when he heard his name.

"Ross, you know your numbers, as in counting?"

Henry leveled a look at Thayer. "Yes, I can figure. I can also read and write." A surge of sarcasm swept the words out of his mouth, which became lost upon the breeze.

Thayer accepted this and added a warning. "You can report to the engine room, tomorrow. We need a boiler man, but if you don't work out, we'll drop you in Pittsburgh. We don't hire uppity nigras." A taint of southern inflection accompanied the words.

Henry perked up. "Yes, sir. I'll do my best, sir." As he went up on deck, Henry was elated. He was an employee on an exquisite riverboat. He chose to ignore the stinging inquisition the job had been yoked to. White men like that were the real true definition of "uppity" and that was according to Mr. Webster.

*   *   *   *

Lucy loved her little home. It was a comfortable, modest dwelling, and she had the best of both worlds—close enough to see town and yet in the country, where it was quiet and green. Allen often walked around the acreage, mentally planning what he would plant next spring. He was itching to fall plow as soon as he could borrow the equipment.

Sometimes, in a rare moment, Lucy would spy Allen out the window, pausing to study his landscape. She would see the man standing there who had soldiered and farmed and sawed wood. It appeared he had quit his drinking. Lucy marveled over his ability to thwart his past vice, but it just proved his strength.

In a fantasy dream of her doing, Lucy would picture him turning towards the house and smiling at her in the window, maybe waving lovingly. Their relationship *had* improved, Allen even said her name with unclenched teeth. Lucy was hopeful.

Allen felt a small stirring of something good when he surveyed the ground around their new home. Here was a speck in Ohio where God's Hand was still visible. It gave Allen some prospects he could anticipate, some assurance of maybe a new life, where he could gain control of its course. Or trust God to.

Lucy had retreated in her war of harassment. Well, to be fair, maybe that was a strong word for her past attentions. Maybe it was because he no longer went to those establishments she despised. Lucy had never realized he had only gone to the pub for the atmosphere, as a place to get away. One glass could last him for hours, there had not been the money to buy more. It just proved how much she really knew or trusted him.

Sometimes Allen dreamed of Lucy like she had been before the Klan had targeted them in Garrard County, beautiful and pleasant. Then worry had not hounded her being. This was before her sunny disposition had been slowly gnawed away by the vicious teeth of fear. Now in his mind, he pictured Fiona in Lucy's place, with hair glowing like a sunset. Allen would cover his eyes with his hands to erase the image and squeeze away the painful pressure lodged there.

For a man who had always lived by his principles, this ensuing havoc within his soul made life a series of complicated skirmishes he must battle through. And he was daunted by the casualties that would most certainly occur. Could he sustain the injury, but more importantly, could he endure that which was sure to come upon the rest of the "troop"? It was a cost he wasn't sure he wanted to count.

Chapter Twenty-One

Miss Ross,
May your life burst forth into
Pure reality, scattering rays of
Sunshine all around you.
Your friend,
Elgetha Braun, Berea, Ky, 6-20-88

Warsaw. Kentucky
September 8, 1889

Dear Friend Nellie,

I was so happy to hear from you. You sound like "exciting" things have come your way. Am I correct to assume that? You must keep me posted on these new intriguing events (especially Monsieur's son!).

I have some exciting news of my own. I have a school to teach! It is such a nice place. There are several classes in the brick building, all grade school level. I've received a second grade classroom and am getting used to my students. So far they are all very good and interested in learning, except the wheel - wright's boy, Cecil. He may be the very one who defines a new word, a cross between whirlpool and whirlwind. What do you think of a "whirlswirl"? He is a fury on legs, to put it mildly. And yes, I have a teacher's pet (not of my own choice) named Lulu Mae. I'm learning about the kind of patience we were taught in Sunday school.

But all is well and going better than expected. I miss my folks who are living in Loveland, Ohio, but plan to go home for Christmas. Write soon, when you can.

Love, your amie,
Annie Ross

*　　　*　　　*　　　*

Sam Hannon watched his son lay another brick in place and expertly scrape the gray mortar away from the edge. He swiped the trowel over the sandwiched forms and looked up into his father's face. "What? Am I doing something wrong?" John questioned.

"Nope, son. Just admiring your work. You could probably take over this job for me," Sam replied, carting a flat tray of bricks closer to John's work.

John made a face. He hoped Dad wasn't going to start telling him how old he was becoming and all that rubbish. His father could still outwork him and probably out-lift him as well. John jumped up to help his dad with his load.

Rebuilding the Davis' chimney had been enjoyable for John and since that time, there had been several more job offers for the Hannons to do masonry work. John enjoyed laying brick or stone, and Dad was grateful for the help. They worked well together.

"So, tell me, son, how are the Wallaces getting along?"

John paused with his trowel. "Fine, I guess. Why?"

"Oh, just wondered. You were there last Sunday, weren't you?" Sam Hannon was mixing up the mortar. It looked like he was operating a butter churn.

"Well, Dad, I never saw or spoke to them, except at church. They looked well." John bent down to level a brick. "Are you worried over them or something?"

"No, I just thought you might have some news about them. Since you walked their niece home after church." Sam kept churning away innocently.

John scowled at the tool in his hand, sparing his father the brunt of his crossness. He knew what Dad was asking–*how are things between you and Miss Ross?*

Dismally, there were no particulars to tell, no details to even embellish upon. Besides making Simon, Sol, and a few other fellows envious, he had no news to report. It wasn't even

202

worth losing his friends over.

Miss Ross was cordial and kind, but he was aware he didn't set her heart a-flutter. She kept a polite distance. Of course, physically, he would expect and admire that, but mentally–well, he still stood on the first rung of the ladder with her. He hardly knew any of her thoughts, not even her favorite foods or best color. It was frustrating.

John looked over to where his dad was working. "We're on a first name basis."

Sam stopped his arms in motion and asked, "You call them Henry and Narciss?"

"Dad." John turned his back on his father and heard Sam's hearty laugh follow him.

"Son, cheer up. They didn't build the transcontinental railroad in one month you know."

"No, but they did go wooden tie by tie. And then they put down the rails–"

"John, you don't have to tell me about it. I built those rails, remember? But guess what? None of that distance matters, none of those miles of ties or rails does any good, unless you have pounded a spike. And it takes a lot more of those than wood or rails. Do you see what I'm saying?"

John sat back on his heels. He wiped the sweat off his face with his handkerchief. "Pound a spike? What's that referring to?"

"It means," Sam sat down beside John for a break. He, too, swiped the sun's condensation from his face with his sleeve and passed John the water pail. While John took a glug of the water, Sam continued, "that you may be judging how far along your relationship with Miss Ross is coming or going by false milestones. The spikes being driven down may be things she will come to appreciate, but sometimes it takes quite a few points to sway a woman. And be assured the Lord already knows the outcome."

"I know, Dad. I want to pray for the Lord's will. I guess I'm just impatient. All Cynthia wants to talk on is the weather. She is holding me at an arm's length pretty strongly." John looked discouraged.

"Well, son, don't despair. God will have His way, and you'll be the better for it. You know, your mama held me farther away than an arm's length." He chuckled. "More like a pole's length and then some. But, as I said, God had His way. Just trust Him to lead you."

John accepted his dad's words as he took another drink and started back to work. "I really think I've found my calling working with Reverend Hughes. But then at times, I seem to doubt the way things are moving or not moving. Then I feel like an utter failure." John mulled on his life and shook his head.

Sam Hannon smiled at his son. He handed him the fresh bucket of mortar. "You're not alone. Why, I imagine old Moses felt that way. Probably even Samuel or Elijah and David too. Just do what you know to do and keep pounding those spikes. Before you know it, you're laying miles of sturdy track. And hopefully, you'll reach the end of that line faithfully."

*   *   *   *

Cynthia watched the hands of the clock move into place. "Alright, children, you may go. Have a good weekend!"

A multitude of voices raised in farewell until the tin ceiling panels fluttered. "Bye" and "Bye, Miss Ross" filled the classroom, along with their steady footfalls as they departed this Friday afternoon.

Cynthia only smiled and waved. She was so terribly glad it was Friday! One month in the classroom, and she already felt like a true teacher. She loved each one of her little charges, but she loved sending them home, too. Their ability to learn new things astounded her. Every morning they read a Psalm aloud and then the lisping voices would sing out different songs she would assign. It was probably the sweetest moment of the day.

But, for some reason, this afternoon, Cynthia had a slight headache and longed to be home. Uncle Henry was coming for her, and she needed to be ready. Swiping off the chalkboard in quick motions, Cynthia erased the day's work. She stacked a few books and screwed on an inkwell's lid.

Seeing everything in order, she put her workbooks in her leather knapsack and got her shawl ready. Footsteps were approaching the classroom and Cynthia crossed to the doorway. Astonishment was stamped on her face. "Why, Mr. Hannon! I'm... well, surprised to see you."

John stood in the doorway, filling it up, so that Cynthia stepped back. "Where's Uncle Henry?"

"He needed some supplies at Grote's Market and thought the trips could be combined. The school's only another mile or so farther." John also fell back, but more from Cynthia's expression than from the close proximity in which they stood.

"But why didn't he come?" Cynthia looked around behind John, like her uncle might suddenly manifest himself.

John had the distinct feeling Cynthia wasn't as delighted about the arrangement as he had been. "Your uncle came to the livery to rent a wagon. He wanted to fetch some supplies and to come get you. I was there, turning in my outfit, since I'd hauled some paper for Mr. Davenport's presses. I offered to come instead and your uncle accepted. I thought maybe you wouldn't mind," John explained as he circled his hatbrim around and around in his hands.

Cynthia's eyes seemed to dart everywhere but towards him, like she was some trapped animal before her captor. John swallowed, feeling like a slighted little boy. He settled his hat back on his head. Disappointment seeped through him at her lack of enthusiasm, but it was his own fault. *Why had he assumed she would be thrilled to ride with him?*

Cynthia was torn. *Why had her uncle agreed to this? Some guardian he was!* Cynthia didn't want to admit that her uncle knew nothing about the chain around her heart. *Why, Uncle Henry had never had to guard his feelings!* Men simply wore their hearts on their sleeves. They had little pride in that area. She musn't learn to like John W. Hannon!

She was a teacher and her first lesson was avoiding masculine company at all lengths. Sooner or later, they got to a girl, either nauseating her or pulling her into love's snare.

Cynthia realized John was patiently waiting on her. She took a deep breath and nodded at his serious face. "I'm ready, Mr. Hannon." She moved forward, clutching her bag, but he didn't budge. Cynthia looked up expectantly.

John took the knapsack of books out of her tense grasp and spoke, "It's John, remember, Teacher?"

Cynthia flushed, "Of course. Even a teacher needs reminders."

"That and a little practice." His slightly roguish look rattled Cynthia as he moved to escort her towards the parked wagon. The horses pawed and tossed their heads. Cynthia knew how they felt. She was just as eager to be off. She climbed aboard before John could assist her and told herself to relax. It wasn't like John was some untrustworthy hoodwink who would swindle Uncle Henry. He had been paid to pick up the goods, as well as her. He was just doing his job. *Think up a safe topic of conversation, Cynthia.*

"Beautiful weather we've been having. When do you think it will rain?"

John gave Cynthia a weak smile. "If not tonight, maybe one of these days. We always have to just wait and see. And then wait some more," John said, finishing with a sigh.

*　　　*　　　*　　　*

Henry Allen Laine lay stretched out on his bed. He could not help dwelling on how abruptly his life had changed. He had gone from farm work to the sawmill to being jobless. And now, he had made it to Berea, his family obligations fulfilled. His life's path stretched out before him, much like his feet, which hung off the edge of the bed.

Henry was nestled in a little room situated on the first floor where "maintenance" was located. At first he had rebuffed the idea of being cut off from the rest of the male students. Henry had fully intended to enjoy his education, in all respects, socializing and joining in the repasts. He hadn't been ready to commit himself so fully until... well, until he got here. The studies were intriguing to him. He was a moth, consumed by the heat of the flame, where the drawing power of the light could not be dodged or resisted.

His favorite subjects were literary: reading, writing, spelling, and English. He would pore over a dictionary, absorbing new words for his stories that yet resided within his head.

Miss Dyerson, the literature teacher, encouraged Henry to try writing a journal. He had considered that for "sissies", but she coaxed Henry to start a few entries. "You know, Mr. Laine, some of the greatest men in history have kept a journal. Since you love the way words flow...well, shouldn't you attempt to record life as you see it?" Miss Dyerson had adjusted her spectacles as she peered over the rims at him.

Henry had swallowed. "Well, Miss Dyerson, I could give it a try." *How will I ever find time?*

But now, in the quiet of his lone room, all his work finished for the day, Henry sat at the little desk, where his legs struggled to rest beneath it and picked up a nibbed pen and unscrewed his inkwell. On a white sheaf of paper he wrote:

Berea, Kentucky
October 15, 1889
I am convinced I will be a scholar of the janitorial arts before long. The trade of fire starter is one I've nearly mastered. The craft of cleaning is now second nature. My friends are water, wood, and coal. Someday I will graduate, upward and onward to studies beyond this. I will write for the school paper, instead of for myself in this lowly journal. Because, Berea is for all men, black and white, lazy or lively, janitor or playboy.
My Kind of Man
The kind of man for me is one,
Who seeks no praise for what he's done;
Who labors not for man's applause,
But gets his share of praise because,

207

With an honest heart for right strives he,
And that's the kind of man for me.

Henry let the ink dry and blew out his lamp. He had given it an effort and even tackled a poem. The words had slipped right out of his head into his moving hand, like those two members of his body shared a special affinity with the other. Henry would copy it and send it to Cynthia Anne. She might enjoy it. Then Henry Allen fell into an effortless sleep, a peace upon him.

         *   *   *   *

Rev. Fee settled himself across from Henry Fairchild, the president of Berea College for nearly two decades. Just gazing upon his trusted friend usually brought about a generous comfort, but now, no warm responsive look was returned. Henry Fairchild lay in the pathos of death and no amount of cajoling or encouragement would revive him.

In earlier times, Rev. Fee, along with J.A.R. Rogers, both board members of the college, had combined their strength and skills with Henry Fairchild's to create Berea. Their three minds had possessed the fervor of justness, and a religion based on moral truths. Their dreams had materialized and when Henry Fairchild left this world, he should have no regrets that he had slacked in his labors.

John Fee followed the irregular rhythm of Henry's breathing. Funny how they should say he was on his deathbed because Henry was ready to leave his sojourn here. Everyone knew that going "home" meant "life", just not as mortals knew it. There was Life ahead for Henry Fairchild. John Fee was almost envious, yet he had never coveted his friends or enemies.

"You're going on to a higher clime, my dear friend. How faithfully you've served us all, both your white and black brethren. Your fight is over and you've earned your repose, although I suspect you'll find some work to do up there in the higher regions." John's chuckle floated above the still form, until he let it trail off. It was an intrusion in the still room where sobriety resided. A clock chimed, another encroachment, and Rev. Fee knew it would not be long. This would be the last time he would feel the existing presence of his close ally. He rose and gazed once more at the face that would be absent from hereafter. John backed away and slowly withdrew from the sick room. With heavy steps, he left the house after saying his condolences. What remained ahead for his beloved Berean Experiment only Providence knew, and John was content that he could not see into the future.

Rev. John Fee promised himself that, while he had the fortitude and health, he would uphold the school's mission, whether bulwarks or fortress barred his path. If it came down to the struggle he feared would ensue, he would carry on even if he were a lone warrior, because his Berean Experiment was the pinnacle and essence of constitutionality for Americans. Future generations must build on the school's paradigm and unfurl liberty and justice for all its inhabitants. How could the nation survive peacefully, if it did not accept the present reality that lay before it at this very hour in time? Only a greater One than he knew the answer.

Chapter Twenty-Two

Miss Ross,
Think of me in the hours of leisure,
Think of me in the hour of care,
Think of me in the hour of pleasure,
Spare me one thought in the hour of prayer.
Respectfully,
A. R. Cobb
Berea, Ky, 6-12-1888

The school terms at Berea glided through the seasons as busy days tend to do. Calendar pages turned like fall leaves and sailed upon the wind, sent "whither it goest." Two new years had fleetingly graced Time and created history; the years 1890 and 1891 came like guests before hastening onward. Now arrived, 1892 made no promises to linger but for the present, and carried with her the woes of the previous year.

Rev. Fee sat at his desk, cluttered by paperwork: admission slips, permission forms, textbook orders. None of it commanded his attention. His thoughts stole back to the death of Henry Fairchild. He still mourned him as though a brother. The man had possessed all the principles John held dear, tightly within his palm. Henry had overseen the college with a princely nature, tossing out fair and wise precepts like abundant confetti. He could have descended from the great Solomon of old.

The college had replaced Fairchild with William Stewart. Rev. Fee was satisfied with this choice. The disturbing influence of the racial policy across the nation had even touched Berea. Public opinion was beginning to sway the irreproachable school.

Unfortunately, Will Stewart had made a few enemies on

the Board and several trustees were unhappy with him. Rev. Fee had had to pull some weight to calm the animosity that had developed. He urged President Stewart to relax and retreat with his opinions in tow. No sense stirring up coals when "the house" was warm enough.

Rev. Fee was sure another man would be "up to bat" because of these differences. And then he feared the games rules would change. John sighed and stood up from his desk and stretched. It was long past the noon hour. Perhaps the head cook had some leftovers in the warming oven. Anymore, it seemed he lost track of time, and Cook learned to set something back for him. He blamed it on his age and Cook's respect for her elders.

On his walk, Rev. Fee thought about the success the college had enjoyed under President Fairchild. The school's goal had always been to maintain an equal ratio of black and white students. The year Henry died, the college had a total enrollment of 334 students, in which 177 were Negro and 157 were white. In previous years, as well, the ratios were similar. He could recall Henry stating firmly, "Negroes are to have, and ought to have, the same civil and political rights as white men, and the sooner and more thoroughly both classes adapt themselves to this idea, the better for all...". The war had changed things forever and the nation must conform its old presumptions to suit a new age. When a boat took on water, its occupants didn't just sit still. They bailed water or bailed out. This was reality.

Yes, John concluded as he reached the kitchens, it was time for the people of this country to face reality.

*   *   *   *

J. A. R. Rogers found Rev. Fee eating his lunch under a cypress tree, perched on a rock. His suit pants were showing wear, hiked up to reveal skinny legs. His dark socks had faded to a washed out gray. It made Rogers feel like things were more doleful than he realized. Jars approached him, trying to soften his expression so the grim words he spoke were a gentler bom-

212

bardment.

"John, they've ousted President Stewart and have nominated William Frost in his place. The contention was too strong for the trustees, neither party will reconcile their differences. They've submitted a petition and are calling a board meeting tonight." Jars let that soak in before he continued, "You'll be there?"

John Fee sighed. He set his plate down in the grass. His appetite had faded. "Yes, I'll be there."

Rogers placed a hand on Rev. Fee's shoulder. "I'm sorry, John."

"No more than I, Jars." John suddenly looked older than his years.

Rogers paused, then added, "We must remember we may have no need to worry. Things tend to appear more immense than they are at times."

"Well, usually that is so, but not where the black man is concerned. But we have fought many opponents. I suppose one more will not unnerve us."

"No," Jars agreed. "Well, I'll see you this evening, John."

After Rogers had left, John went back to his little office. But he could not concentrate on his work. A melody of a hymn his dear wife Matilda often hummed came to mind. Taking up his pen, he filled it with ink and wrote:

> Watchman, tell me does the morning,
> Of fair Zion's glory dawn?
> Have the signs that mark his coming,
> Yet upon thy pathway shone?
>
> Pilgrim, yes! Arise, look 'round thee,
> Light is breaking in the skies;
> Gird thy bridal robes around thee,
> Morning dawns, arise, arise.

> Watchman, see! The light is beaming
> Brighter still upon the way;
> Signs through all the earth are gleaming,
> Omens of the coming day.

From these treasured words, John took heart. He knew that there were many watchmen who saw the coming light and observed the omens. And when the jubal trumpet sounded, the struggle would go to the righteous. Although, John was forced to consider, it may not occur in this present world.

*   *   *   *

This was one of the hardest things John W. Hannon was about to do. He stood perspiring before the congregation of Mt. Zion–seventy or more people–to whom he was going to preach the Gospel. Had he not been prepared for this moment, this wonderful opportunity to spread the Lord's message? But somehow this wasn't how he had envisioned it. In his little dreams, he stood tall and confident. There had been no "butterflies" or "puppy dog tails" romping within the confines of his stomach. There had also been no sweaty hands or pumping heartbeat to distract him.

This was his first time sermon, a small part following up Rev. C. H. Hughes. It was only ten minutes and just an introduction for a fledgling minister. All week John had thought on the words he would want to proclaim. Rev. Hughes had said he would speak on dedicating our lives to the Lord.

Now John surveyed the congregation and his nervousness threatened to swallow him. Cynthia had told him to pretend he was a teacher and the congregation was small children whom he needed to instruct, just like she did every day. She thought her advice would help calm him. John told her he would have to pretend to be Adam since Widow Rutherford was nearly as ancient, if he wanted to be *her* teacher. Besides, he was only twenty-three. He felt that many of the members knew their Bible better than he did.

His mama had said, "John, go ahead and look at the faces on the bench. You know each one by heart. Think on their individual hurts and sorrows. Think on each one's joys, like a brother towards them. You'll reach each one that way with sincerity and humbleness, the best virtues a preacher can have."

So John concentrated on the faces staring up at him, from little Thea Wise to Deacon Philip to the Widow Rutherford. When Rev. Hughes motioned for him to step forward, he stood before the small wooden podium and let it mask his jumping heart.

"My fellow brethren and sisters, today we have heard an inspiring message." A few "amens" rang out. "We have listened to the Words from our God, put here in this book," John lifted his Bible, "for the meditation of man. In the first Psalm, it tells us a man's delight is in the law and in it doth he meditate both day and night.

"I want to add to Reverend Hughes words on dedicating our lives wholly unto the Lord. We can give our all to do this every single day of our life, and no, it would not be good enough. Brothers and sisters, the angels look down and say, 'You're falling short' and it would be so. But not because we're sluggards, but because, of our own selves, we can not do it. Yet we don't need to despair. It takes God's help to continue on, to fulfill the duty of man, as put here by our Lord's commandments.

"We may feel it's a hard lot, we may feel it's a hard row to hoe or a stubborn mule to drive along, but by God's grace, we can persevere.

"And then, brothers and sisters, then comes a time of refreshening. In the Bible, if we look in Judges, we see Samson, a mighty and valiant man, who needed refreshment in the physical sense. He had battled the Philistines and was thirsty, so he called on the Lord, 'Thou hast given this great deliverance into the hand of thy servant; and now shall I die of thirst?' and we know the Lord carved out a little hollow in the jawbone that Samson used to slay his enemies and 'water came thereout; and when he had drunk, his spirit came again, and he revived.'

215

There will be this time for us, too."

The congregation offered their affirmations as John continued, "That Living Water the Lord told people of, the water that will forever refresh us, spiritually and physically, is free for us to partake of. Fear not, to labor on little flock. Fear not to walk in this land, brothers and sisters, because we know there is a time of refreshing for each one of us at the end, one that will be worth it all and will forever slake our thirst."

The congregation was encouraged and shared it. Words of "praise the Lord" and "amen" swelled the air, cascading down like a gentle rain shower. John wiped his face with his handkerchief and dared to look up and out over the benches. Cynthia offered him a special sweet smile while Mama shone like a beacon. John stole a look to the rows where the old folks were situated. Widow Rutherford was sound asleep but she offered a ceremonial snore.

*   *   *   *

Cynthia's finger followed the words across the page, willing Jimmy to say each one correctly. At the end of the page, the little boy pronounced the last word and broke into a grin. Only then did Cynthia realize she had her toes curled up tensely. She exhaled.

"Wonderful, Jimmy! You did much better. See, practicing is the key to success. You may run on out to recess now."

The youngster hurried out of the classroom with a happy countenance. Cynthia was pleased with his progress. She had kept him in on recess to read to her since the little boy's attention span never seemed to be able to finish his lesson with all the classroom distractions. Even the clock ticking seemed to sidetrack the boy. And he was behind for his grade level.

Cynthia watched out the window as her class enjoyed their free time. She felt wistful over the school year coming to a close. Her teaching year had been interesting and fun, just like the previous one had been. It now being the spring of 1892, she would soon part company with this class and prepare for another. Or maybe not. She wasn't sure where her relationship with John Hannon was going. Although she thought she had bound her heart up tightly, the cord had unraveled, leaving her susceptible to Cupid's dart. She was no longer sure what she wanted her future to hold.

Remembering her previous weekend at home, John had walked her to the store after church and had dinner with them. Rev. Hughes and his family had been there and old Widow Rutherford, too. It had been a nice table full and would have been nicer if June Rose Hughes hadn't considered it *too* full and scrunched close to John. Cynthia wanted to think John was just being a gentleman, but he didn't look like he minded it too much. Cynthia recalled how the dinner had went:

Rev. Hughes congratulated John on the end of his studies and his brief introduction behind the pulpit. He claimed he had nothing more to offer John. Cynthia noticed June Rose beaming at John and patting his arm. *Except his daughter,* Cynthia mused.

"Wonderful, young man. You'll be a great preacher," Old Widow Rutherford said, her tone blaring across the table. The poor woman was nearly deaf. "I remember you playing fox and geese in the empty lot next to my house. You were always the loudest, if I remember correctly. Yes, the makings of a preacher!"

John stared at the older woman, his brows raised. The Widow Rutherford went on eating voraciously, unaware she had passed on anything except a compliment. Cynthia ducked her head to hide her amusement but when she peered up, John's gaze was leveled on her. He sported a mischievous grin before June Rose stole his attention with some insipid story. Cynthia concentrated on her meal.

"What will you do now, John? Any more schooling?" Uncle Henry questioned, accepting a loaded plate of pork from Aunt Narciss.

"Well, sir, I'm not sure yet. I'll probably hope to be ordained a full minister in the future, but I'll keep helping Dad with chimney work and freighting, until I feel directed to do something else."

Cynthia took a drink and over her glass, her eyes met John's. Quickly she averted them.

"How is teaching school going for you, Cynthia Anne?" Rev. Hughes asked as he wiped his chin with his napkin.

"Fine, Reverend. I'm enjoying it very much. It is amazing how much children's little minds can absorb. They are an encouragement to me." Cynthia smiled and glanced around the table. By accident, her gaze met June Rose's. That was a mistake.

"My, Cynthia Anne, how you do it is a wonder to me! I never could handle so many children, but it must be your calling. Some of us teach our own little ones, and some of us teach other's little ones. I wish I had it in me to be a schoolteacher, but I probably will be called on to be a wife." She looked as pretty as her namesake and sounded so sweet, Cynthia nearly choked on the sugar content.

Widow Rutherford stopped eating long enough to scowl. "Not much ambition on the girl's part, Reverend. When I was her age, I had more important things on my mind."

Rev. Hughes smiled conciliatory. "Indeed. But I always say there is no higher calling ordained by God for the dear sisters. We all hope to fulfill God's will for our lives, whatever it might be." He turned to Uncle Henry. "Tell me, how's business? Have you got any more willow bark or feverfew in yet? I've found it helps Theresa's headaches, if I can get her to drink the tea I make for her."

Theresa Hughes waved a hand at her husband. "Now Reverend Hughes, these fine folks don't need to hear all about that. You know I try–"

"Pie? Is there pie on the table?" Old Widow Rutherford started to grope around the tabletop, her hands searching for dessert. Her sense of sight was direct kin to that of her hearing.

Cynthia shook herself back to the present when the antiquated brass bell rang, ending recess. The children came streaming in. She must get ready for an afternoon of noun and verb sentence dissection. Cynthia lamented if only John Hannon's mind were as easy to read and examine.

*   *   *   *

Henry Ross' shift was nearly up. He heaved another shovel full of coal into the burning mass of flames and heat and shut the heavy boiler lid. Once latched, he pulled off the heavy work gloves where his hands sweated pockets of water. The gloves had been sweaty when he had put them on and they would remain so for the next shift, a fellow by the name of Tom.

The heat in the engine room was like a hot summer day in the South to a Yankee. Henry's shirt stuck to his ribs and back like he had doused himself in a pool. He wiped the sweat from his eyes, gritty and blurred. It was hard work and many a man quit after a few days. Boiler men were always being replaced, Tom had said. In fact, the day Henry had walked on board, the fellow before him hadn't shown up for duty. It happened all the time, Tom added.

Henry could see why. It was nasty work for little pay. That's why the majority of workers were black. A bitter thought surfaced–black men would take any job available. Because he also knew that only black men could bear the work, since they had lived through slavery.

Although there were a few white men that had shifts too, along with Henry. Most were crusty, grumpy old codgers with thick barrel-chests. A few were stout Irish, resembling prize-fighters. Henry was the only young fellow with a slight build among them.

Tom had probed him. "How's a babe like you gonna keep up? You're nothing but a sapling. You got to have muscle on them bones to do this job." Tom had flexed arms the size of the smoke stacks on the ship. He continued, "Why ain't you one of those porter-purser fellows upstairs? You got the light skin for it. They hire them up there and send us coal black ones down here." He laughed like it was some big joke.

Henry found nothing funny about it. Tom treated him

219

well, but was a little strange. Something had happened to him while he had been a slave, some injury, and now Tom would laugh for little reason or else he would just up and cry.

Tom came on duty, taking the sweaty gloves from Henry and asking, "You thinkin' your turn's done for, boy?" He also liked to tease.

Henry nodded wearily. "Sure am, Tom. Ready to get out of this hothouse."

Tom clapped him on the shoulder. "Well, then be gone and gets some rest for them bones of yours. You've lasted a week, longer than I'd have guessed you'd make it."

"Thanks for your confidence," Henry told the older man. Tom started laughing in reply, and Henry wasted no time in leaving the hold. He trooped up the stairs to the deck and was amazed to see it was dark out, just like the engine room. It was easy to see how a man could become disoriented about time down there. Henry understood how a miner must feel. But ahead of him lay rest and relief. He had completed a ten-hour shift, for the previous six days, sleeping in a minuscule bunk on board, and now had two days off in Pomeroy. Henry looked forward to his bed at the hotel.

Walking beneath the stars cleared his head and the fresh air soothed his lungs in his chest. He went straight to the hotel and entered by a side door. He was conspicuously filthy.

A bellboy came hurrying towards him. "You supposed to be here, sir?" He looked Henry up and down.

"Yes, I am. I'm a paying customer and have a room on 4C." Henry pulled out his room key and dangled it in front of the boy's nose. "Shouldn't you be home and in bed?"

The boy, probably twelve years old, scowled at Henry. "You can find your own room, I guess."

Henry smiled at the youngster, whose skin was a lot like his own. "Here," he pulled a penny out of his pocket and flipped it through the air at him. The boy caught it mid-air. Henry smiled. "I see that fancy uniform don't hinder you any."

"No, sir," the boy smiled back. "What's your name, sir?"

Henry told him, then asked, "Is there any way I could have a bath drawn?"

The boy looked skeptical. "I can see. But you're up on the fourth floor. That's a lot of water totin'."

Henry nodded. "What's your name?"

"Daniel, sir."

"Tell you what, Daniel. You find a way to get me a bath for room 4C, and I'll make it worth your while."

"Really? No foolin'?" Daniel looked hopeful.

"Yes, really. Promise. Now I'll go on up. I'm tuckered out." Henry left the boy, hoping he would do all he could for some warm water and a tub.

He unlocked his door and went in. The room was fairly simple and very plain. A washtub would hardly fit between the bed and dresser but Henry would manage.

Soon Daniel came up the stairs, lugging a huge metal tub. It clanged wildly against the railing, and Henry wondered how many complaints management would receive. Daniel was puffing when he brought it into the room. Two more trips brought four buckets of hot water, and Daniel pointed to a narrow door at the end of the hall.

"There's the water closet. You can add cold water iffen you need it."

"Thank you, Daniel. Here's your reward. I'm going to enjoy this." Henry gave the boy a dime. Daniel's face lit up.

"Anything you need, Mr. Ross, you let me know. I'm always around here."

Henry agreed he would and closed the door. As soon as he had the tub filled, he sank into the warm water. And then, Henry, very promptly, fell asleep.

When Henry recovered, he slept for twelve hours before he saw daylight. The first thing to speak to him was his stomach. The incessant growlings led him to rise and dress for the day.

Hurriedly, he filled the pails with his left-over bathwater. Opening his door, he took two of the buckets and stepped into the hallway. He placed them on the floor and went back for the remaining two pails. Once all four were in the hall, he debated whether he could handle all of them and make it to the water closet at the end without spilling any of the dirty water. He was worried if he didn't get the pails and the tub back where they belonged, he might be charged extra. On his meager pay, that would hurt.

From behind him came a soft "umm-hmm", a gentle clearing of a throat. Henry turned around quickly. A room maid stood studying the sight of the four pails with Henry.

"Sir, you making off with those pails somewhere?" she asked him.

Henry pointed to the water closet at the end of the hall. "Just to there. I was emptying out the tub and going to get it back downstairs. They don't charge extra for the use, do they?"

The maid shrugged, "They've been known to. 'Course, they don't allow it on the colored floor. But here, that's my job. I'll take care of it for you." She reached for a pail. "You can just go on."

Henry refused, stopping her. "I'll empty it. They're pretty heavy. But I would let you take the tub back. Maybe before anyone notices."

The girl smiled. "Oh, they've noticed alright, but only the cook. And me. I wondered where my buckets got to. How did you get all these?" She gestured to the four filled pails lined up in the hallway.

Henry looked around, hoping "management" didn't appear. "Some boy helped me out. I really needed the bath. I tipped him good."

The maid nodded, her sprightly face looking like she knew a secret. "I'm sure you did." She reached for the pail again. "Go ahead and attend to your business. This is all part of my job."

"Well then," Henry said, bending over and grasping two pails in each hand, careful the water didn't slosh out, "I'll just help you with your job." He carried them down the hall to the small bathroom for guests and poured it in the sink. It left a black residue.

"Sorry about that. It's coal dust." Henry saw the look on the maid's face. She quickly covered her surprise.

"No, problem, sir. I'll clean the sink when you're done."

Henry soon had the tub emptied and rinsed and left it with the girl. She thanked him for toting all the water.

"That's alright. Can I ask your name?" Henry was thinking that, besides the bellboy, Daniel, he might be making his first friend in Pomeroy.

"It's Sallie." They stood there smiling at each other until Sallie spoke. "You had better go get yourself some lunch downstairs. You're too late for breakfast."

"Me? What about you?" Henry was feeling in high spirits. He had a job on a steamer, his own hotel room secured and maybe a new friend, a very pretty one at that.

"You're a paying customer, I'm hired help. There's a big difference between the two. Besides, I've already eaten and I know you haven't, for a fact."

Henry drew in a breath and rose to his full height. "You know that, huh, for a fact?" He pictured her in the dining room, aware of his absence.

"Sure, who wouldn't? Your stomach has been fussing ever since I found you in this here hallway." Sallie pulled a dust cloth from her apron pocket and waved it at him. "See you around."

"Yeah, see you." Henry watched her disappear into the room next to his. His ego had been deflated but that it didn't affect his stomach any. Henry went on downstairs.

Chapter Twenty-Three

Dear Annie,
You would have been married a long time ago
And perhaps living happy, but you had such a
sheepish beau, he wouldn't ask your pappy!
Dear old girl, my most ardent wish is that you may be
As happy as generally falls to we poor creatures' lot
and get a beau next time— Who'll ask your pappy!
Unknown

Henry Allen Laine wrote like his pen was on fire. And in a way, it was. An inferno from the poets and scribes of the earlier times seemed to have infused their strains from the scholarly harp upon him. Each string pulled released a flow of melodious words from Henry Allen's being. It felt like he was making music and Henry's hand rushed to capture it all. Often his journal entries were sporadic and resembled a literary grave-yard of jumbled thoughts, rhyming lines and stanzas, and Henry scribbled it down to make sense of the symphony inside him.

Miss Dyerson glanced at the entries on the sheaves of paper Henry Allen presented her. She smiled her praise at the young man. "Henry, will you let me read through your work and offer you an honest critique? Unless, of course, you're not serious about writing."

"Not serious?" Henry Allen looked puzzled.

"Yes. Honest criticism is never pleasant but is essential to any writer. You can accept my advice that's offered or not. But I would like to look over your work regardless."

Henry nodded. "Miss Dyerson, it will be fine for you to read over it and let me know where I need improvement." He paused and felt a shyness steal over him. "I really enjoy writing.

225

It...it uplifts me somehow."

Miss Dyerson nodded. She knew. Writing from the heart was a calliope of whistled words powered by the steam of creativity and imagination, which resulted in sweet tunes of satisfaction. "I understand."

After she had finished her day's classes and was alone, Miss Jane Dyerson settled at her desk with a cup of tea and Henry Allen's work. Being a black woman at a college was prestigious, at least for her family, who had all been born slaves. Not much was open for black females in the 1880's and 90's, so Jane Dyerson was blessed to be at Berea. The love of her life was the pursuit of education; her "baby" the student body.

Focusing on the page before her, Jane Dyerson read Henry Allen's poem:

"Gwine Back":
"What's the trouble Uncle? May be
I could help you if I knew."
"I can't go–somebody's robbed me,
Purse am gone and money too!"
"Lost your money? Where'd you started?"
"Back ter ol' Kentucky whar
De ol' 'oman an de chil'n,
Side by side are buried dar!

I could fin' dey graves dis morn'n,
Under dat big elm tree,
On de knoll behin' de orchard,
An' a place wus lef' foh me!
Ain't bin dar since mars Jeems sol' me,
Got behin' an' couldn't pay.
Las' I saw dem all dey's cryin'
Forty years ago today!

Miss Dyerson read on through the stanzas telling how the poor old black man remembered his home and family and being sold away. Then how he had saved all his money for twenty years to go back to Kentucky. Folks at the train station, where his money had been stolen, began to pool their money to buy him the fare to return home. She finished the poem:

With uncovered heads, and silent,
Stood the crowd, that sympathy,
Which lies dormant in each bosom,
Started tears in every eye;
But the silence soon was broken
By the coming of the train,
Each, to his thoughts returning,
Thundered on his way again!

"Thundered on" much wiser, better,
Through each heart the feeling ran
That to scatter human kindness,
Is the noblest work of man.

Jane Dyerson paused and removed her glasses. She rested her head in her palm and behind closed eyelids let the scene replay in her mind. The poem had stirred up the humanity whose habitat was within the heart.

So many new young black writers would not write in the slave dialect, considering it distasteful or condescending. But what was truer to life for her people than this piece where the language bore testimony to the greed and immorality of the masters that had oppressed and kept them in darkness?

When Henry Allen had written this, he had captured the perfect plight of so many individuals who had saved and suffered loss, only to lose again. Yet, the act of kindness at the end helped rescue the scene from despair. The beauty of it touched Jane.

She turned the page. Here Henry Allen had written a brief account of his day in colorful terms and tongue twisters like "Berea's baker's brandished balky buns with burnt bottoms". His teacher smiled at his passion for words. Retrieving her glasses, Miss Dyerson examined his next poem:

"Those Good Old Days"
That good old day has almost passed,
When any honest man,
With brains, could rise from poverty,
And lead our nation's van;
That good old day is almost passed
No more to come again,
When those who climb to honor's heights,
Were plain Log-cabin men.

. . .
. . .

We would not have that old day back
With its grand and chivalrous men;
We do want back that sentiment,
That ruled our country then;
When offices of public trust
Could not be bought or sold,
And brains, and push, and honesty
Could wield more power than gold!

Miss Dyerson smiled. Indeed Henry Allen had a large reservoir within him. She would take his writings home and peruse them later. As she pushed back her chair and gathered her things together, she thought on the poem of office-holding. It was true that President Frost now resided on the college's board, pleasing many. He seemed to be efficient and smart. In Jane's opinion, maybe *too* smart for them all. He spoke the right words to stifle any uneasiness but something didn't quite measure up. She wondered if his direction for the College was the same as the one the founders had laid, specifically Rev. Fee. She guessed time would tell, and for now, she reminded herself, it was only her job to teach literature.

*   *   *   *

Cynthia doodled on her paperwork, making bold sweep-

228

ing lines with her name, stopping just before she wrote "Ross". She hesitated. Would she always write that last name? And did she want to? And "Ross" was a very nice name, after all.

Her musing was interrupted this Saturday afternoon by Uncle Henry with a visitor in tow. Cynthia was used to that, but usually it was an older Mr. or Mrs. he brought into the kitchen. Not John W. Hannon.

Cynthia bolted upright in her chair. She dropped her pen and covered her scrawled name with her hand. John shot her a smile as Uncle Henry said, "Cynthia, John here wanted to visit with you a spell. You done with your lessons?"

"Yes," Cynthia squirmed in her chair as she pointed to the seat across the table from her. She hastily gathered up her lesson sheets and graded papers. John handed her a few, peering at the names.

"Georgie, huh? Needs a little more practice on his hand-writing it looks like."

Cynthia laughed. "Yes, along with about fifteen others. You did well deciphering that one." She stashed the homework papers and carefully executed lesson plans into her knapsack. "I don't usually see you until Sunday."

"I know, but I wanted to talk to you about something that doesn't include a table full of people. Although Widow Rutherford is deaf." John raised his eyes from the table causing Cynthia's to dive towards it.

John continued, "This summer I'm going to hope to be ordained. I'll need to finish a complete sermon under trial and then one for the Predestinarian circle of ministers. If that goes well, they will decide if I have what it takes to become a minister or not."

Cynthia nodded, her relief giving leave to an expelled breath. "Sounds daunting but really, John, for you, it ought to be like eating cake." She laughed, but John's face didn't change its serious lines. "What's wrong? Are you nervous about it?" Cynthia sobered and patted the back of his hand, which lay upon the tabletop.

Quickly, John caught her hand up in his. "Yes, but not

near as nervous as asking you what you intend to do next fall."

"Why, John, I suppose teach. What else would I do?" Cynthia was puzzled. "I'll be around to see you ordained. I'll be there to offer you moral support, alright?" She smiled understandingly, while she disengaged her hand from his.

John shook his head. "You probably love teaching. You probably wouldn't consider leaving that to keep house or raise little ones." A glumness settled over his features. Suddenly the whole world seemed a little dim.

Cynthia shook herself and leaned over the table. She gave him a direct look, one void of pleasure. "John Hannon, you are spending too much time in June Rose's company. And," she frowned, "No one's to say I can't do or have both. I'm not pushing fifty yet, you know."

John swallowed. "Cynthia, but would you...would you quit teaching if I asked you to share my life?" John had rested his elbows on the table and peered at her anxiously.

Cynthia leaned back in her chair. She felt as if someone had pounced on her lungs, dispelling all available air. "Are you serious?"

John scowled. "Of course I'm serious. I'm not asking you to a barbeque, woman. I'm asking you to–"

"Share *your* life?" Cynthia broke in.

"Yes. If you need some time..." John looked hopeful.

Cynthia was quiet. When she did answer, there was a vigor to her words. "I'm not sure I want to 'share your life", especially that of a minister with you. I've never pictured myself being a parson's wife. I'm not cut out for it."

"I think you are, Cynthia. You're...well, you're compassionate, kind, and sweet." John put up an argument. "I can't think of anyone better–"

"Except Miss June Rose." Cynthia stood now, shoving her chair in. "I think John, you're 'barking up the wrong tree', as they say."

John sprung up from his chair. "Cynthia, what could I do to persuade you that–"

"Nothing, John, that you shouldn't already know. If

you're going to be a preacher, you've got a lot to learn. People can't be swayed with reasons and objectives. It takes faith in a man to believe his words, just like the Lord's."

John drew himself up to his full height. He asked, "And you're telling me you don't have faith in me?"

"No, I do. Lots of it, but you're heart must be on vacation. I'm going to wait until you say the right words, then I'll decide."

John was clearly confused. "The right words?"

Cynthia's voice took on a higher note. "I thought a man asked a woman to marry him and said 'I love you'. Maybe you were raised on a different planet?"

"Why, Cynthia, I meant that. I thought that's what I was asking," John sputtered.

Cynthia nodded. "Well, to me that sounds a little better than 'sharing your life', which sounds a lot like its all about you. I guess that means you care about me?"

John's jaw tightened. "Yes, Cynthia, how can you doubt? I'm in love with you. I want to marry you and for you to be my wife."

Cynthia smiled slowly and her stiff stance dissolved. She held out her hands to John. He clasped them within his own. "There you go. You're learning, John. Always use your heart on these matters."

John smiled, "See why I need you? And Cynthia, as for Miss June Rose," he paused and drew Cynthia close, whispering, "A rose's beauty and scent fade shortly, but the thorns...well, they always remain."

Narciss looked at Henry, her smile triumphant. "See?" she whispered, "What did I tell you?"

"Guess you were right, honey." Henry rubbed his scratchy chin. "I sure wouldn't have put my money on it though."

Narciss laughed softly. They were behind the storeroom curtains, where a small boxy room with swinging doors led into their kitchen. It was the perfect place for eavesdropping. And

231

while "chaperoning", they had been privy to the couple's conversation.

"We should be ashamed." Henry told his wife. Narciss nodded but couldn't contain the grin that appeared. "How often do us old folks get to witness young love? Even the angels would steal peeks on such going-ons, don't you think?"

*   *   *   *

The meeting had adjourned. John G. Fee sat still in his chair while the others filed out. Jars, also, sat motionless until the room emptied. The two men listened to the clock chime on campus and to a mockingbird outside the window, pretending to be something other than what it was. Spring had arrived, and with her, everything new. But that was only meant for nature, John noted, not policy or convictions or the Gospel.

"Jars, I have a bad feeling over the future of Berea under our new president. Frost has said he is in accordance with the college's creed but personally, I fear he is not. You heard the ring in his voice when he mentioned the usual 'separate but equal' garbage that Southerners spout. He agrees with that sentiment, or I'm off my oats."

J. A. R. Rogers nodded. "It struck me odd, too, the way things were worded. I felt like putting on the brakes. The wagon wheels have begun rolling, haven't they?"

"Yes," Rev. Fee tapped his knee in thought. "Well, one must fight fire with fire and with a few well-turned furrows of sod to halt the advancing inferno. I suppose we'll end up rolling up our shirtsleeves on this one."

Jars laughed, "I have no doubt. But we'll try, and we'll try our hardest, because John, there is no way we're letting Berea go up in smoke."

*   *   *   *

Lucy read Cynthia's letter and clasped it to her chest. Her girl, her only daughter, engaged! And at the bottom of the

232

letter, a tiny postscript in Cynthia Anne's fancy writing that said, *"P.S.: Mama, is this alright with you?"*

That dear girl! Lucy wandered outside to see the boys doing yard work. It was nearly summer and school was winding down. Soon the boys would be at home, and Lucy would have company during the days. And Cynthia would come home for a visit.

Allen was trimming a branch off an old apple tree in the side yard that a storm had recently broke loose. Lucy took the letter and went out to him. She paused as the branch crashed to the ground. Allen let the saw dangle from his hand while he mopped the sweat from his face with his handkerchief. He looked at her expectantly.

"A letter from Cynthia. Do you want to read it now or later?" Lucy let it flutter in the breeze.

"Now's a good time as any." Allen said and took the letter. Lucy sat on an upturned bucket, balancing herself by lodging her skirted ankles against it. She watched Allen while he read, wondering how he would feel about the news.

"Hmm." Allen pulled his eyes from the paper to Lucy. He handed it back and studied the saw blade. "Hard to believe it's time for that, already."

Lucy stood. "I guess we'll hear more about it when she gets home this summer. The Hannons are nice people."

"Uh-huh." That was all Allen offered as he reached down and dragged the branch back towards the fencerow.

Lucy guessed Allen was bereft of sentiment where his children were concerned. He didn't mind letting Henry go to Cincinnati, saying it was time to be a man. He didn't seem to care that their daughter would soon be another's responsibility. Why, he hardly worried over James, John, or Dee either. Maybe he thought they should be men too. Lucy felt like the sole parent. Parents were meant to worry over their children because they cared. Allen was not interested. Analyzing his brooding expressions, Lucy wondered if Allen should see a doctor. They had no need to secure a physician as of yet, but she had heard

233

that a Dr. Haarlamert or Dr. Smith would see them. They were one of the few in the area who would accept a "colored" patient.

Lucy should just ask Allen what was wrong. But she feared it was the mind sickness, one like Jake Lee Worth had, a somber depression caused by the war, where they always "had a tick under their collar". That was how Allen behaved. He only seemed to enjoy being out on their ground when he got home from the mill, otherwise he was lifeless and dull. Allen answered her in mild tones but it was like his mind was far away, with only his body present. And although his anger was vacant, she was afraid he would become stirred up if she asked. It was better for him to be despondent than angry, she reasoned. At least for the family's sake.

Could she live this way with a man who was like a silent creature within their home? Just what did Allen need to shake him out of the slump he wallowed in? Obviously more than what Lucy had to offer.

It seemed that she did not have the answer or the remedy. Yes, Lucy reasoned, if this was all Allen could offer her for now, she would accept it. Their marriage was a commitment of time and effort, tears and blood. Who was she to ask for more?

*   *   *   *

May 11, 1892

Dear Mama,

I hope the family is doing good. I miss you all but my job is going fine and I love The Virginia. *She's one sleek ship. It's amazing that I help keep her going. I haven't been seasick even once.*

This will come as a surprise, Mama, but I'm a married man now. In the hotel where I'm staying, I met the sweetest girl and we got yoked up. The best part is that she's a maid there, and we got us a discount on a bigger room–management's wedding gift to us. She's really good at her job and can stay there working while I'm on a run. Her little brother,

234

Daniel, works there, too. You would love them both. I'll try to bring Sallie home whenever I can take time off. Give Dad my greeting. Love to all of you,

Henry

Chapter Twenty-Four

Miss Ross,
Life, death and immortality,
These three—the first—the Road,
The second—the Gate,
May you walk safely the first,
Pass triumphantly the second,
And rest forever in the third.
Your friend,
Mr. Cuth Taylor
Berea, Ky, 5-5-1888

Cynthia would not wear white after all. Allen offered it to his daughter, one last gift he could give her. After quiet reflection, Cynthia said, "Daddy, I think I'll wear the green dress that Mama made me for Lizzie's wedding. I've only worn it twice and really, it's absolutely perfect."

Lucy went alone to her bedroom and relinquished the emotional hot tears of bittersweet motherhood. Cynthia wanted to wear the dress she had made for her! Lucy felt loved and honored. And then, there remained the ghostly memory of the distant past, in which a young girl dreamed of wearing a beautiful green dress to welcome home a soldier in blue.

Lucy insisted though on adding a few touches to the dress. She bought faux pearls and using leftover material, fashioned a train over the bustle on the back of the dress. Then she bought a piece of beautifully tatted lace and made a small collar. Satisfied, she presented it to Cynthia.

"Oh, Mama, how gorgeous! But it's too much! I never dreamed of such a dress." Cynthia draped it over her frame, and Lucy smiled, pleased and proud as a mother hen who had hatched a charming chick.

Then in the usual sequence of time, August of 1893 arrived, serenaded by the crickets who chirped for all their worth and the returning horseflies, who were eager to join the warm melee. The grapes hung deep purple and the sunsets were masterpieces from the Maker's Hand. Fireflies woke up the evening and the doves cooed goodnight to their young. School children lamented the end of their free season–commencing without a certain teacher–all this when John W. Hannon wed Cynthia Anne Ross.

Mt. Zion Predestinarian Baptist church once more witnessed the union of two of its congregation. The Warsaw church welcomed the gathering with the ladies pitching in to provide for a meal. Aunt Narciss organized the details until Lucy and Allen arrived. Betty Hannon was glad to help as well and the affair went smoothly.

Later, when all the fanfare was over and Uncle Henry's rice shook out of every tendril of hair and nook and cranny of clothing, Cynthia sat beside John as the sun descended with a glorious display. The Ohio River had stilled and the twilight deepened.

"This little cabin is the perfect place for a honeymoon." Cynthia leaned back in the chair situated on the porch of the cabin. John sat beside her, taking in the view of the sunset and his new wife. "It was nice of the Reids to offer it."

"Three days of solitude!" John sighed.

Cynthia pulled their wedding certificate from the small Bible on her lap. She read it over and smiled. "I wish we could have spent more time with our families but whew! The day was big enough."

John agreed, "Too bad your brother, Henry, couldn't make it."

"Yes," Cynthia said, "He wrote saying he couldn't take off from his job and he really prizes that job. Besides, he's a married man now and has responsibilities. Surprise of all surprises!"

John laughed, "You're all keeping your parents busy. What next?"

Cynthia dismissed the tense thoughts of her parents and their strained relationship. She didn't want to spoil a perfect evening. Instead, she crossed her ankles in her fancy green wedding dress, and took John's hand. "Wasn't my cousin, Henry Allen Laine, proud of his teacher's certificate? He's reached a mountain milestone and plans to keep on scaling upward. Henry Allen wants to continue at Berea and take all the classes offered. I'm glad for him. He's always wanted to get an education. We all admire Mr. Booker T. Washington and Mr. George Carver and the Tuskegee Institute. I think Henry Allen could go on to be a man like both of them, don't you?"

"Sure. He's dedicated enough. What about me? What great things do you predict for my future?" John propped his feet up on the porch railing, nonchalantly.

"Well, it looks like you've already achieved the best thing in your life." Cynthia smiled. "You married me."

John leaned over sideways on his chair towards her. The wooden frame squeaked in protest as it rested on two legs. "You don't say!" He looked at her. "Can you prove it?"

Cynthia playfully shoved him upright. "I told you we should have skipped the pageantry and you could have married us right here."

John pretended to ponder this. "Yeah, wow! I could have married myself, but then, what would you have done?"

"Oh, you!" Cynthia fluttered her hand at him. "But I guess we wouldn't have missed being with our families for anything."

"No," John slapped at a mosquito on his arm. He straightened in his seat. "Which brings us to our future. Are we decided on this move to Lockland?"

Cynthia squeezed her hands together around the Bible in her lap. She thought about the invitation that had come from Charley and Elizabeth Mitchell. Cousin Lizzie had begged them to come to Lockland where they lived and now operated a grocery store. Charley could use the help, and they could house near one another on Mulberry Street. Besides, in Lizzie's letter, her voice could be heard through the lines on the paper. *"You just should come, Annie. It would be so fun and make life merry, wouldn't it, to be together again?"*

John had helped enough at the grocery in Warsaw where he hauled goods for Mr. Hopkins to know he could do that for a living. Further schooling was not an option and now that he had been ordained, he was more than excited when Lizzie wrote saying that the Traveling Zion Predestinarian Baptist Church there in Lockland under his uncle Rev. Charlie Merritt could use another minister. Things seemed to be opening up for a reason.

Cynthia pondered all this before turning to John. "I suppose it will be a good thing. It will give us an income and the opportunity to use your training."

John spoke softly, "I think I've always wanted to work in the Lord's vineyard. I appreciate your sacrifice for me."

Cynthia squeezed her husband's hand. "That's what a 'help meet' means, right?"

"Do you ever feel cheated, being born a woman?" John was interested.

Cynthia made a face at him. "Are these the kinds of conversation we're going to have as we grow older?"

"Why? Isn't this fun? Besides, I'm curious. Do you feel cheated?"

Cynthia shook her head. "If I were a man, you would be the one being cheated!" She gave him a mischievous wink.

John grabbed her arm. "I didn't realize you were so saucy. Maybe I should reconsider what I've gotten myself into. But before I do that, I'm still waiting on your answer."

"John! I gave you one, but if you must know, I'm perfectly happy. I've went to Berea and taught school. Now I'm ready to support you mentally like I hope you'll support me in the material sense."

"Material?" John swatted a mosquito away from Cynthia's nose. "Define that, Mrs. Hannon."

"Well, you know me. I like to set out quite a spread on the table, and I'm not used to walking, so I'll want a carriage,

240

and let's see...I never wear the same dress within a month's time..."

"You got the wrong man. Maybe you meant to marry Solomon Jenkins instead?" John teased back.

"I wonder if those pickled beets did something to me? Like maybe affected my sense of reasoning. Can vinegar intoxicate a person?"

"Cynthia, you didn't actually eat any of that cake, if I remember right. So you chose me fully in possession of all your faculties. Guess you're stuck now."

Cynthia smiled, her eyes twinkling like the evening's fireflies. "And, Mr. Hannon, there is nowhere else I would rather be stuck, or with anyone else, for that matter." The sunset, in harmony, cloaked them with its radiant agreement.

*   *   *   *

The three days of honeymooning had gone the way of the Ohio as it rushed inevitably to meet the Mississippi. John and Cynthia stayed temporarily with Sam and Betty Hannon until plans were finalized for their move to Lockland, Ohio, where Cousin Elizabeth Wallace Mitchell and husband, Charley, lived. Betty was full of motherly advice, accented with concerned last-minute instructions.

Sam, very gently, squeezed his wife's form. "Betty, I believe Eve was fashioned from one of Adam's ribs."

"So?" Betty gave him a perturbed look, because if she knew Sam, he was going to admonish her and probably be right in doing so.

"Well, from that rib she became his 'help meet', remember? Not his mama. She was someone perfectly fashioned to help Adam handle his duties. So starting out, right from the beginning, he had a wife. Not a mama, see?"

"Sam Hannon, I follow your logic, which scares the apron right off me! I just hope it's because I've lived with you so long, not because we think alike!" Betty huffed at him, her way of agreeing, and left off the motherly cajoling.

Cynthia shot an amused look at her new in-laws, but she also smiled her gratitude. She was not born yesterday in the cabbage patch–she was twenty-five years old and a Berean graduate!

Cynthia's parents had left for Loveland but not before they all had a good visit. While Cynthia and Lucy caught up on news in Narciss' kitchen, Allen and John talked as they unloaded crates of supplies and stocked shelves for Henry Wallace.

Seeing Allen was quiet, John opened the conversation. "You're probably itching to get back to your ground. Those weeds don't rest, do they?"

"No." Allen shifted the bag of flour from his shoulder to the wood-planked floor. "We finished the wheat before your wedding, and there will be a little corn to husk come fall. Besides that, there's the garden Lucy has. It'll need weeding."

"I remember weeding my mama's garden. Seemed endless under the hot sun to me. John, James, and Dee probably think so, too. They help you in the field much?" John asked.

"They don't have a choice, come harvest. 'Course, Lucy spoils them. She takes care of most the gardening so that 'it's done right'."

John decided to sidestep the irritation he heard in his father-in-law's voice. "We'll be a lot closer now, living in Lockland. That makes us only ten miles apart. Maybe I could help you out in the fall, if you need an extra hand."

Allen turned to look at his son-in-law. "That would be appreciated." He stacked two more crates on their ends, and they worked in silence, reloading the wagon. After they started for the train depot, Allen surprised John by saying, "So, how's it feel to be a minister? I never would have thought my girl would marry one." He shook his head.

"Are you disappointed?" John asked good-naturedly.

"Oh, no. Cynthia's done well for herself." The older man let a smile slip. "You're so young, that I wonder how it must feel to know you're accountable to the Lord all the rest of your life?"

242

"Well, sir, aren't we all?" John caught the look Allen's profile flashed. "I mean, we all have to answer to the Lord, and do what's right and our best at it." John didn't like how his voice trailed off weakly, but neither did he want to anger Cynthia's father.

Allen sounded cynical. "I guess if the Lord takes an interest."

John had the feeling his feet were sinking into swampy ground. "You know, sir, we all go through times of doubt but it doesn't take much to rectify that if we just open up His Book. It erases all doubts, I think."

Allen was quiet for the next quarter mile. He finally cast a cursory glance at John. "So, tell me about your ordination. I missed your trial sermon before the ministers."

John had noticed, but he filled in the details for his new dad-in-law. "It was one of the biggest days of my life, I'll tell you. Except for marrying Cynthia," John hurridly interjected. Allen smiled. "Anyhow, I stood up before the congregation and tried to ignore all those eyes looking at me. I don't know if it was by chance or not, but the panel of ministers from other districts were seated in clumps of two or three." John sighed. "You probably knew some of them. There was the Elder Dennis Arnold. You would know him from here, but he travels around some. And, of course, Reverend Hughes. There were also a few elders from Waco and Richmond, Kentucky. You know the Reverends Robert Covington and Leroy Estill?"

Allen nodded. He had made one's acquaintance and knew the other by visual observance. "So you had to preach before these ministers? Showed them your stuff, huh?"

John flushed. "Well, sir, I guess the Lord's anyhow. If God's Spirit doesn't move a preacher, I think it's evident."

"You got that right. I've set through some pretty boring sermons where I know the Holy Spirit wasn't awake either." Allen thought this was funny, but John wasn't amused.

John continued on, "There was my uncle, Charlie Merritt, from Lockland. Have you met him?"

"I have. I helped Lizzie and Charley settle in their home

and store and met the man. How's he related to you?" Allen, who usually possessed no inclination to study the family tree, was curious.

"My mama's brother. Mama was a Merritt. But you know how our histories are. They seem to be intertwined and connected in all manner of ways because of the slavery years.

"Most of our family started out as Clarks. John Clark owned Mama's people. Story goes he loaned out some of his slaves to a neighbor man by the name of Will Royston. When John Clark died, his children wanted their daddy's property back, but Royston hadn't thought about that. By this time, they had increased in number. Things got a little sticky then. But I guess the Clark girls, and there were a passel of them, got back a lot of the slaves. One daughter, Nancy, then sold hers to a George Merritt. And that was Mama's mother. Her and Uncle Charlie took the Merritt name since that's all they ever knew."

Allen shook his head. The family connections were like a spider's web–fragile and yet of a tough fiber; delicate when the master's hand moved and tore the web asunder, and yet strong because the families would cling to one another and trace each other if possible, following each thread.

It disgusted Allen, the way their lives had been tossed about like manure on a pitchfork, no thought as to where it would all land.

John sensed the agitation that seemed to lock up any lightheartedness in his father-in-law. He changed the conversation. "Cynthia's schooling will be a big help in the store. She's good with numbers. Did you get to talk to Henry Allen at our wedding?"

Allen nodded as he steered the horses to a tie post at the depot. He set the brake and spoke. "He's nearly ready for another teacher's certificate, another class higher. Also writes for the school newspaper."

John smiled as he leaped over the wheel hub. "He's going places. He'll be a real credit to the family."

Allen agreed, "It's about time for a little recognition and achievement. The Dark Ages ended long ago."

*   *   *   *

Settling in her new home was as easy as drawing breath for Cynthia Anne Hannon. If one stood on the curb where a rather uneven sidewalk had been laid and gazed at the house on Mulberry Street, an observant person might have said, "The porch foundation is cracked and it all slopes a little to the left. The front two windows were definitely installed without a modern level, and perhaps a child stacked the bricks for the chimney."

And then, maybe if one were being kind, they might add, "But it has that quaint weather-beaten look of the houses in Cape Cod–a real oceanic appearance." Only this was Ohio and no salt air had washed the paintless wood. But it did not matter to Cynthia Anne. Her heart was full of love for her and John's very first home, and besides, Cousin Lizzie's looked worse! Her's was a decrepit yellow (where there remained paint), and Cynthia's had harbored gray. Only one house stood between them, and it, of course, tried to put their's to shame.

The interior needed a good cleaning. Elizabeth helped Cynthia tackle the work and they laid rag rugs and hung curtains, which hid a multitude of imperfections. Cynthia had a cookstove and new dishes from her wedding. Mama had sewed linens from her supply and Cynthia felt she lacked very little.

John destroyed the wasp nests that dotted the eaves and porch and studied the chimney. "I'll redo that thing after awhile," he told his wife. He knew a thing or two about masonry, thanks to his father.

As a typical young couple in the beginning of their life together, they made friends of their neighbors and met the congregation of the Traveling Zion Predestinarian Baptist Church. John's uncle, Rev. Merritt, was not a lot older than John himself in actual years, so the two men were easily in accord with one another.

It seemed nearly every evening after the store closed at seven o'clock, the two young Mitchell or Hannon couples were at one another's to eat or visit. During the day, Charley Mitchell or John ran the store. On certain days, Lizzie or Cynthia helped out. On Friday and Saturday, they both came down to the store as it was busier and often one of the men was gone to retrieve supplies.

When at home, the two women met for a mid-morning chat, and then at noon, devised a lunch for their menfolk, which they took to the grocery. At three o'clock, the two cousins helped each other with small jobs, like taking down laundry or preparing ahead the supper meal. Then they would part company until evening, when all four of the young people would sit on the porch or gather in chairs in the backyard.

The only small drawback was the house nestled between them. An older widower, Mr. Chester Burroughs, lived there and tended his flawless property with zeal. He enjoyed his two young neighbor girls much more than they enjoyed him. His advice and suggestions soon grew rather tedious as the cousins politely tried to act interested and appreciative. Comments on how much paint saves and flowers add to property value were offered. Suggestions on how earlier bedtimes would fight digestive diseases or camphor in the eardrum helps eliminate wax buildup was given. It was also good for rheumatism.

Lizzie called him "Chester, the Pester" or some form of that. "I tell you, Annie, if The Pester gives me any more recipes for bowel complaints or headache powders, I'll scream."

"Well, we could use his powder ideas, since he's the initiator of our headaches. Besides, John reminded me to remember Colossians, "Put on therefore, as the elect of God, holy and beloved, bowels of mercies, kindness...', you know."

Elizabeth narrowed her eyes and covered her ears. "No more about bowels! And sure! John can say that, he's a preacher. Where is he when The Pest is offering medicinal advice I won't need until I'm fifty? You know that I wasn't born with one-third an ounce of patience! Promise me when he corners me out in the yard, you'll rescue me."

"Rescue you? Like how, Lizzie?" Cynthia questioned.

"Fall down and sprain your ankle or get stuck in the

privy or something!" E l i z a b e t h 's animated hands gestured wildly.

Cynthia laughed, "Sure, cousin, I'm here for you. I'll wreck my health so The Pest concentrates on me and leaves you alone."

"Thanks, Annie. And don't worry. His antidotes will either kill you or cure you, and meanwhile you'll be taking Colossians to new heights. Or should I say depths? John will be so proud of you!" Elizabeth smiled sweetly at Cynthia. Cynthia swatted at her.

Chapter Twenty-Five

Miss Ross,
Shall we ever meet again ?
When you look over your album
In days to come,
One half of we — is your friend
And schoolmate,
J. H. Wingo,
Berea, Ky, 6-18-1888

Henry Allen Laine wasn't as nervous as he thought he would be sitting up on the erected platform stage. He could look down on the seated crowd and see row upon row, stretching across the campus.

Today was Decoration Day, a day to remember the soldiers who had traded their lives for the present freedoms. Everywhere patriotic banners had been hung to wave a welcome to the congregating people, with patriotic bunting and streamers decorating the stage. All were in finery for the occasion, the women clothed in white and the men in suits.

And it was more than just remembering the war and those men who had sacrificed the ultimate; it was another year passed in the mending of the nation. Hurts still pulsed on both sides and in Kentucky, Henry Allen could sense it more so. The division within the state certainly echoed that of the nation, and old resentments and anger still smoldered upon the grudging embers.

Assembled up on the stage with Henry Allen, was the President of Berea, William Frost, and Rev. John Fee. The mayor of Berea and the town trustees were present, along with the constables and volunteer firemen. A band was stationed on the left to play after the ceremony, which would include a few speeches.

Henry ran the program through his mind. Rev. Fee would draw the minds of the crowd together with a leading prayer and speak for a few minutes. President Frost would deliver a fifteen-minute address on Berea and what the day meant to the college. Then Henry Allen would be invited to recite the poem he had written especially for the celebration. Miss Dyerson had declared that, of all her students, she felt Henry Allen could write the poem for the day's remembrance and capture the essence of its meaning better than anyone.

"You have a gift, Henry Allen, a talent that you must use." That had silenced his protests and led his mind to study and accept the challenge of putting the significance of Decoration Day into words.

After his recitation of the poem, the Ladies' Home Auxiliary would present a wreath for the doors of Berea's Main Hall. Then the crowd would disperse and travel to the nearby cemetery to place, upon the soldiers' stones, small flags or miniature wreaths that the Ladies had made for the blue and gray alike while the band accompanied them.

Reverend Fee called them together with a hymn, "The Christian's Journey" and a prayer. Then he offered a few remarks. "Fellow Kentuckians and dear brothers and sisters in Christ, we gather today to commemorate those dear deceased members of the human race who offered their utmost, their most sacred lives, to restore peace and ensure freedom to all. They answered the trumpet of old, the cry in the breast of the oppressed, and with willing hearts, they stepped up to the charge and delivered a liberty that is essential in any civilized government.

"And knowing how the spirits have gone on before us, we take up the charge they laid down when they embraced eternal sleep. We carry on the banner against the present battle of hatred and racism. 'Love your brother and neighbor as yourself' is our calling and battle cry today. And I might add, we can all be soldiers of the cross."

Rev. Fee sat down and President Frost stood up. His string tie situated under his cravat was untied and hung askew. A wisp of hair stood at attention before the top hat on his head, and his cheeks glowed like two red crabapples. His appearance was one of eagerness. "Thank you, Reverend Fee for your remarks. In the spirit of the occasion, I wish to reinstate the great College of Berea's maxim, the mandate of the most Holy, as Reverend Fee has refreshed our memory. Nowhere are brothers more loyal than in Kentucky. We support one another and uphold each other, regardless of past differences. We will continue our walk here at Berea with an integrated education for all!" President Frost raised his hand, tightly fisted, for emphasis and accidently knocked his top hat forward, covering one eye. The front rows tittered.

Straightening his towering black silk headgear, President Frost cleared his throat and continued, "So to all those who long for an education, those who have been denied the basic fundamentals of an individual's liberties, step forward! Berea is here for you. Color is no barrier and poverty or wealth no determinate here on this wholesome campus. Plain folk, Appalachian folk, send your people from mountain crags and hollow deeps. We are your school!"

The applause was hearty, allowing those seated to shift slightly and unrudely in relief. Next, up to the front, stood a black student. He was impeccably dressed and handsome to the eyes. Curiosity sparked a number of low murmurs that rippled through the crowd. Who was this young black man? Was he really the chosen student to deliver the dedication poem, out of the entire student body?

Henry Allen was suddenly flanked by Miss Dyerson, who announced, "I want to present to you a poet and writer, whose ability is undoubted. He is the Recording Secretary for the *Berea College Reporter*. Today he is a fresh new and 'au courant' writer, tomorrow a distinguished scribe. Introducing Mr. Henry Allen Laine."

Henry Allen turned slightly to his teacher and if her eyes weren't touched by the glare of the sun, they certainly would

251

have been blinded by Henry Allen's deep brown ones, shining with gratitude.

Henry turned to the rows of chairs dotted with people and began.

Thirty Years of Peace

Time rapid rolls to many here,
　It seems but yesterday,
Since horrid war's grim crash and roar
　The very mountains sway–
When sunny South with scattered wreck
　Was strewn from shore to shore,
And blackened chimneys marked the sites
　Where cities stood before.

When Negro slaves (by Christian men)
　Were landed on our shore,
Peace fled and base contentions rose,
　Increasing more and more,–
Like subterranean fires, that
　For years unheeded burn,
When suddenly in wrath burst forth
　And mountains overturn!

So the fierce fires of smothered hate
　Grew more and more intense,
Until the South rose up in arms
　To fight for the defense
Of that the greatest of all sins,
　The sale of blood and tears;
Their failure freed the Southern slaves
　And answered prayers of years.

God bless our heroes all today!
　Who through Death's valley rode,
And on the flaming battle field

Their love of country showed.
Who bade farewell to home and friends
    To rescue Uncle Sam,
When Lincoln called they answered back
    "Ay, Father Abraham!"

From every mountain, hill and dale,
    In eager haste they pour,
And many a fireside plunged in gloom,
    Was brightened nevermore.
All honor heroes great and small
    Who bravely wore the blue!
Our country's peace, and strength, and hope
    We owe it all to you!

As time rolls on and I look back
    And see what has been done,
In thirty years to reunite
    And make our people one,
My heart in gratitude goes out,
    As I look 'round and see,
Where once the vilest hatred reigned,
    Now peace and harmony.

All honor to our unknown dead
    Who fell amid the fray,–
Whose bodies lie beneath some plain,
    Or hillside far away.
On bloody fields they face no more
    The blazing cannon's mouth,
But from their ranks celestial watch,
    The progress of the South.

O'er forty-five progressive states
    These honored colors wave,
The North and South united firm,
    And not a single slave!

The slaver's whip, the clanking chain
Have long since passed away,
And white or black no matter now
A man's a man today!

When Henry ended, he swallowed in an effort to moisten his throat. He said, "Thank you" and took an offered seat
near the back of the stage. It seemed the very air had stilled and
Henry had a rush of emotion surge through him. Had they liked
his poem or not? And then, his eyes glued to the wooden boards
beneath his feet wavered, and Henry feared he would faint. His
vision tunneled into a dark ring, and Henry lowered his head in
an attempt to fight off the woozy feeling. Then somewhere
before him, he heard clapping, more fervent and clamorous by
the seconds that pealed away from the clock. Henry felt a rush
swell through him, and he released a breath. Inhaling, he lifted
his head to view the many citizens, standing before their chairs,
commending him with an ovation. Hands fluttered like white
doves, a testimony to the merit of his work. Black hands pulsed
the air, like a rapid heart, generating the beating blood of so
many kinful souls.

Miss Dyerson just smiled and adjusted her spectacles, a
matriarch of wisdom. Henry knew he would remember this day
for a long, long time.

＊   ＊   ＊   ＊

The men all sat around the pinewood table in silence
until the voice queried again, "Who is in agreement?"

The group was hesitant to speak with John G. Fee present. Even if their opinions differed, their respect stood as a
forceful nominative, staunching any voice of opposition.

"Well, gentlemen, it was just a suggestion. There's no
need to upset the batter bowl." William Frost nervously slicked
down his eminent cowlick. He attempted a shrug like the issue
mattered little. Only his darting eyes revealed his apprehension.

John Fee knew otherwise. "You propose to direct our attentions towards the poor whites in the Appalachian regions. It is a good quest but not for our school. We have a commitment to our area, and our endeavour is to turn no one away. But…there are many schools that take white students and only one here that enrolls black ones. Our obligation is that the racial masses learn in harmony with one another and break down barriers existing between the two. There is no reason Appalachian whites couldn't find an entry into education through other facilities."

President William Frost frowned, "That is all true but there is none that will make that leap and reach out and persuade. These people need urging. I can only think how much talent is going to waste within those mountains. Their culture is distinct and unique. The effect on society could one day be momentous."

"William," John Fee spoke sharply, "We have a problem here that has been going on since 1619 when the first African was brought to these shores. It is ongoing and the War did nothing to solve it. I feel it is up to us to work to ensure that race relations can and should be mended. 'For ye have the poor always with you' I believe our Lord said. We cannot confuse our mission here at Berea or we will be stretched too thin to do one or the other any good."

Jars interjected before Will Frost could speak. "We want all to be able to partake of an education, but Berea's root function was to aid our black brethren with this goal. There is nowhere else they can go."

President Frost commented, "The Tuskegee Institute in Alabama is an excellent–"

"Indeed. But who wants to go south? Lots of the people are working their way up out of that direction." Jars replied.

A board member, Jonathon Stokes, spoke, "I think what President Frost is trying to say is that there is a warning along with this from the state of Kentucky. The legislature, backed by some influential landowners, want to see 'separate but equal' policies put into practice, starting with education. A lot of southerners still balk at Berea's ideals. The public and social pressure is becoming more distinct. Berea is becoming a very unpopular tare within the wheat."

"Horse feathers! It's always been that way. When has Berea ever ridden an even keel upon the oceans of unrest? It all boils down to wealth and politics. I refuse to bow to such base influences!" Rev. Fee felt like he had delivered a sermon. Now he curled his hands in his lap and took a deep breath.

Will Frost looked coldly around the room. "We'll adjourn for now. But each one must think heavily on this matter and weigh the future of Berea within his mind."

Rev. Fee's eyes sought J.A.R. Rogers. The steely resolve there was unmistakable. Jars gave a slight incline of his head. The match had been struck.

*   *   *   *

Fiona O'Hugh possessed many devices but deceit was not among them. She had realized her great need for stability and happiness in this new country. These two blessings had been absent nearly all her life and Fiona made the decision she would seek this at any cost. She had not thought it would be found on two legs, but good fortune came in all forms. Indeed, the gold lay on the streets of America, but it was rarely yellow and shiny.

Fiona congratulated herself on arriving safely in Loveland, Ohio. It had not been hard to find, as the train station listed all its stops north. A kind gentleman had pointed the town out to her, as her reading skills were very rudimentary.

Once in Loveland, she found a modest boardinghouse and using her saved wages, which were becoming pitifully depleted on each step of her journey, Fiona secured a room for a week.

Then she set about to find employment. A small shop, located on the main thoroughfare, had a "Help Wanted" sign in the window. After inquiring within, Fiona walked away a happy woman. She was definitely being blessed by the saints. It had been a good idea to follow Allen after all, she concluded.

Although the work was not Fiona's first choice, she was determined to get along well with her new job. She would sew ribbons on felt or feathers on straw if it meant achieving her dream–persuading Allen to make a new life, with her included.

Loveland was small enough that Fiona had no trouble locating the sawmill. After work, she followed discreetly behind Allen to the edge of town. There her trailing of him was cut short. He might notice her behind him on the open road. But no matter. It was not yet time. Fiona intended to plan the perfect meeting. There would be another day to orchestrate a harmonious reunion.

* * * *

Allen's thoughts strayed often to his new son-in-law and his daughter, Cynthia. She was his only girl and he wondered if he could have given her away better equipped for her new life. They had bought her a used cookstove, and it had been nice enough. He reasoned that was a good gift, but he hadn't given her anything personal. Allen had barely hugged her goodbye, feeling stiff and awkward at the train station.

Allen made up his mind to get Cynthia a gift and ship it to her as a surprise. His girl had a rough life ahead of her, being a preacher's wife. She would make many sacrifices of her time and her husband, during her married life. But what could he get for her? He thought of the last time he had seen her. It was after the wedding, and she had been standing beside her stylish cousin, Elizabeth. Suddenly, Allen knew. It would be something not easily affordable on a workingman or a preacher's salary. But something women seemed to adore.

The little bell tinkled behind Allen as he entered the millinery. Everywhere hats were displayed on little stands. The whole colorful array reminded him of an exploded peacock on the 4th of July. Black, navy, peach, white, yellow, green, and scarlet–the hats were of every color imaginable. Rick-a-rack decorated the brims or crowns in the forms of ribbons, feathers, sequins, buttons, or jewels. Some had fake flowers or slight veils or bows. The ones with little birds on them nearly made Allen choke. He looked around nervously, being an intruder in feminine territory.

A white woman appeared from around a row of fake heads perched with hats. She took in his appearance swiftly. Allen had the urge to seek the door, but he squared his shoulders and stepped forward to meet the woman.

She smiled, "Can I help you?"

Allen had not been sure she would wait on him. Sometimes he received a brusque reception and was unwelcome in the white shops. He never knew quite what to expect.

"I need a hat for my daughter, one I can ship to her. I was looking for something fine but simple."

The woman nodded and went over to a plain looking hat of cream. "This would suit any ensemble she wears and usually flatters any face shape, yet it's quality enough to wear to church."

Allen looked at the headgear and agreed. "Maybe it should have a little...um...a tiny bit of..."

"Ornamentation?" The white lady smiled. "Of course. What girl doesn't love a little bit of frippery?" She pulled out a tray of stones and buttons. "We can keep it toned down by sticking to a few cream-colored ribbons. Maybe she would like a rosette? How old is your daughter?"

Allen had been staring wide-eyed at all the "ornamentation" but quickly looked up. "She's twenty-five now."

"Alright. Is she a working woman?"

"No. No, she's married, a preacher's wife. She was a teacher and a Berean graduate." Allen hadn't realized how much pride he felt in Cynthia until he spoke those words.

The lady smiled. "She sounds special. I'll make her a hat she'll love. I have ideas already. Just one thing more. Do you know her head size?"

Allen looked vacant. He wondered how to acquire that. He didn't want to include Lucy in on the gift. It was from him to his daughter. Then an idea struck him. He would measure Lucy's old hat. Surely Cynthia and her mother had similar measurements.

Allen spoke, "I don't know right now, but I'll get it for you. Do you want payment now?"

"No." The white woman showed him a card. "Do you read?" Allen nodded. "Here's my name, Miss Annaliese Gillian." She gave him the little card. "When you come back, I'll show you the hat. We'll make it the right size and then you can pay."

Allen was grateful to the proprietor for her help and kindness. If only more white women were like her, the world would be a little easier to navigate. Allen thanked her and promised to bring Cynthia's head size soon. As he left, Allen felt like whistling. This little endeavor had given him a light feeling and driven away some of the weighty gloom from his encumbered mind.

Allen handed the paper to Miss Gillian. She took it and read the numbers on it. "Good. We'll have it ready next week. And for an extra fee, I have hatboxes, too. It would be just the thing for shipping it to your daughter."

"Great." Allen was enthusiastic. He had found Lucy's hat on a shelf and measured it the best he could. He noticed that her black velvet hat wasn't in very good shape. It caused a twinge of guilt, but only for the length of a heartbeat. Allen gave Lucy money for groceries and such. If she needed a new hat, she could easily go buy one. Lucy knew he wouldn't care, or he wouldn't trust her with his paycheck.

Now, he told Miss Gillian he would be back next week to pay for it. After he thanked her, he left the shop behind with the tone of the bell tinkling in his ears.

Miss Gillian carried the measurement to the back of her store. There, working on a stool, sat her new girl. Miss Gillian was pleased with her. Not only was she industrious and clever with a needle, but she had a magnificent head of hair in which Annaliese had taken to using to model her hats for her customers. All the hats looked beautiful atop such interesting tangerine curls, upswept in braids or a full bun.

Fiona looked up, "Miss Annaliese, another customer?"

Her employer shook her head. "Just that black man who ordered a hat for his daughter. Here's the head measurement."

Fiona took it and pinned it to the cream-colored band on the new hat. "It's real nice of you to let him pay when he picks it up. Most don't seem to trust the black people."

Annaliese Gillian shrugged. "He wears working men's clothes. A man who works pays his bills. At least I believe he will. Anyhow, how are you coming on Mrs. McCasland's monstrosity?"

Fiona eyed the creation in front of her. She could probably roost a chicken on the thing and still have room for the henhouse. "Oh, it's coming. What would you like to see over here? I put on the little ferns, but between these rosettes and feathers, there's blank space."

"Oh! Mercy forbid there would be an empty spot on the headpiece of the banker's wife!" Annaliese put a hand to her throat in mock horror.

Fiona laughed. "Maybe if her bill is as big as her hat, she'll tone it down a bit next time."

Now it was Miss Gillian's turn to chuckle. "Fabulous, Fiona! We'll see what we can do about that!"

Chapter Twenty-Six

Dear Cousin,
When on this page,
You chance to look,
Just think of me —
Close the book.
                    J.S. Laine

As always, the two cousins were in harmony with one another. What one had, she shared. It was no different when Elizabeth and Cynthia were suddenly both blessed like Rachel of old. The only difference came that Lizzie spent her mornings facedown in a chamber pot until noon, and Cynthia did not. She breezed through her first trimester.

Charley Mitchell took to visiting the Hannons for breakfast, so Lizzie wouldn't have to cook or smell food. After the men left for the grocery, Cynthia would go next door and straighten up the house, open windows, and empty Elizabeth's sick bucket. She would lend a sympathetic ear to her cousin's declarations of being on her deathbed when actually she was full of "life".

Cynthia would try to soothe Lizzie. "It's only for a little while. Things will get better."

Lizzie would choke, "So why aren't you sick?"

Why indeed? Cynthia tried to ease her cousin's annoyance. "Do you want me to ask The Pest what he recommends for morning sickness?"

Elizabeth rushed to grab the enamel pot and answered Cynthia soundly. Moaning, Lizzie told her cousin, "That's what I think of your humor!"

After three and a half months, Elizabeth could finally smile once again. She was a lot thinner, but time would take care of that. Cynthia was glad to turn Elizabeth's household duties back over to her.

And then, the two cousins literally had their hands (and arms) full. Elizabeth's baby, impatient to the core, arrived first. Narciss came to stay with her daughter for two weeks to help. As soon as Cynthia's baby took its cue from its cousin, it too, brought Lucy to Lockland. Allen and the boys were to fend for themselves for a few weeks.

For the four women and the two new members of the family, it was a joyful time of togetherness that could not be replaced by any other bliss. Many years later, Lucy would pull the memories out from within her mind's treasure box and like a jewel, admire its shiny facets.

Cynthia, holding the tiny babe wrapped in the blanket her mother had sewed for it, said, "Mama, her name is Scarlett."

Lucy was surprised at the choice of name. She tucked the quilted flannel around the small face. "What's it mean to you?"

Cynthia smiled, "We named her Scarlett because there's a lot of good things that share that color. John said the virtuous woman's household was clothed in scarlet. And the Lord's sanctuary had fine linens of blue, purple, and scarlet. It's a royal color. Besides, think of our hearts and life's blood sharing that color. Grandma Angelina, you and I, and now Baby Scarlett. We all have the very same blood running through us. Isn't it amazing?"

Lucy's face was all tenderness as she gazed at the wee brown face that squeezed its eyes shut and wailed. "Yes, it is. God is good to us."

*   *   *   *

John Hannon's preaching was not affected too badly by becoming a papa, except for the loss of sleep, which occasionally derailed his train of thought. He found an easy entry into the pulpit. Uncle Rev. Merritt took the main text and John followed up after him and closed the meeting. It was a satisfactory arrangement. The congregation of Traveling Zion

Predestinarian Baptist Church was pleased with their two ministers. There was no Widow Rutherford to gauge the level of boredom he inflicted upon the flock, but there was Rita Henshaw. The miniscule baby girl took to squalling five minutes into closing, and John usually had to make the announcements at the top of his lungs. John suffered from many sore throats until his vocal cords had strengthened.

*   *   *   *

Allen enjoyed the solitude while Lucy was gone at Cynthia's. He let John and James, who were nearly men now, go on a camping trip. It was time they had a little freedom. Both worked faithfully and John was courting a girl. James had finished school and was practicing a trade. Allen was proud of them. They were sturdy, good young men, capable and self-confident. When Allen was their age, he had done much more and worked harder than their muscles could attest to, but he had been a lost ship upon the sea, whose sails took him whichever way the wind blew. He had floated alone and had no anchor or mainstay. But he had been a slave–another man's property.

Until Camp Nelson and the Army. And Lucy. Allen wanted to let those tender feelings within his heart romanticize the past, but it was no use. Now was the present and Camp Nelson was long gone. Lucy had changed. She no longer saw him as the one to trust and be in charge of their family.

And Allen was no longer the same man. He would always be ashamed of leaving Garrard County and letting Lucy run them away from the fight. And him a former soldier, no less. She had ruined the way he saw himself, and the depressed image of an intimidated man stuck fast in his mind like barnacles to a ship's hull.

Allen blamed Lucy for his sour outlook. What worth was he as a man if he couldn't stand up for his rights? It was as if he had never been a soldier and held a measure of dignity.

After work, Allen brushed himself off and tried to look presentable on his way to the milliner's. He was excited to see the handiwork Miss Gillian had made for him and get the gift ready to send to Cynthia. He felt his pocket to ensure the money was safely there.

Entering the shop, Miss Gillian came forward, carrying a wooden form of a head and on it was the cream-colored creation. Allen was pleased. It looked regal and fine, something Cynthia might have chosen herself.

"It's perfect, Miss Gillian. My daughter will love it." Allen pulled his money out of his pocket.

Annaliese smiled. "Good. Shall I add a hatbox to the bill?"

Allen said, "Yes. And could I add a little extra for you to pack it for me as well?" He looked hopefully at the proprietress.

"Of course. I'll make out your bill and send my girl in the back out to help you assemble it for shipping."

Allen paid the bill after Miss Gillian had tallied it. She gave him his change and disappeared in the back of the store. Allen waited on her helper. She arrived, carrying a floral octagon-shaped box. "Here you are, sir."

Allen's eyes shot to the flaming hair and he asked incredulously, "Fiona?"

Fiona's white countenance mirrored his reaction. She looked like she was seeing an apparition from the dead. "Allen?"

Allen recovered enough to step toward her and lower his voice. "What are you doing here, Fiona?"

"I could ask you the same, but I know, since I made the hat." She reached out for his arm. "You are well?"

Allen nodded. He heard Miss Gillian in the rear of the store and was mindful of appearances. He moved to the counter and laid the hat down carefully. Fiona followed, setting the hatbox down, too, and retrieving brown paper. She began to crumple it, whispering, "I had no idea it was *you* getting the hat."

Allen placed the hat in the box. "I had no idea you were in Loveland."

Fiona's head peered around to see if Miss Gillian was

near. "It seemed the place to come. An appropriate name, I think." She smiled into Allen's eyes with her own very blue ones.

Allen stepped back, his mind turning cartwheels. He was confused over this sudden discovery. "Fiona, I'm not sure about...things. About you being here–"

"No need to gall yourself, Allen." Fiona took another peek to locate her employer. "Meet me at that huge willow tree, at the edge of town at ten o'clock tonight. We'll talk."

Miss Gillian arrived to study the job they were doing. She tucked another piece of paper along a side and covered the hat with a loose layer. Closing the lid, she told Allen, "I'll secure it with twine cord and you can take it." She turned to smile at Fiona. "This is my hired girl. She had a large hand in designing your daughter's hat. She does fine work, yes?"

Allen nodded, avoiding Fiona's gaze which was locked upon him. "Yes. She's very talented." When he looked over at the Irish beauty, her smiling eyes suppressed all raging doubts.

*   *   *   *

A grown man who avoids his own sound judgment, deserved to tumble from his perch, no matter how precarious it had been. How easy it became to cast his moral conscience away, like flinging bread upon the ground for the birds. Like idols of pleasure, his fleshly nature gobbled it up greedily, relieved to have finally been fed.

Meeting Fiona beneath the willow tree had been Allen's demise. With Lucy gone, they had time to talk without fear of detection. After several meetings, Allen realized he needed Fiona in his life. What he did not see was that they were two needy people. She erased the inferior feelings and inadequacy that chained him down. Fiona made him feel free and whole. He had not felt so carefree in years.

Fiona told him, "We must be blessed by the saints of Ireland. Things are working out for both of us. We belong together. Your wife has six children to look out for her, and I have no one who cares for me on this whole earth. Except you, Allen."

Allen struggled with his conscience at quiet moments. Sometimes it was like a hard fought wrestling match. He watched his sons for an answer. They seemed content and lived their lives independently of him. They did not need him, not even the youngest. Little Dee played at all the interesting games that kept boys busy, unmindful of his father.

By the time Lucy returned, Allen had abandoned his inner struggles. The die was cast. The decision brought relief to his disruptive mind. Lucy was self-sufficient. She had traveled and taken care of Cynthia. She had raised the boys up without trouble or much help from him. Allen was sure she could manage without him. His only decision lay in whether to tell her goodbye or just quietly walk away.

Lucy noticed the change in Allen. He was nearly cheerful, even in her presence. Lucy wondered if it had anything to do with her being gone. Had he missed her or had he been relieved she was absent in his life? She was soon to find out the truth.

On the Wednesday after she returned, she had filled Allen in on Baby Scarlett. Allen had listened and seemed genuinely interested. Lucy followed him down to the barn where he paused to look at her. "Lucy, why don't you sit down on those bales there. I need to explain something to you."

Lucy felt alarm race along the nerves of her spine. She had never liked to be asked to "sit down". It usually meant a rock was about to be dropped on your head. She would rather face it fully, on two stable feet. "Allen, you can just go ahead and tell me. I'm not made of sugar."

Allen frowned at her. He didn't like her defensive stance. "Well, I've done a lot of thinking while you were gone. And I think I need to go away for awhile, to get things worked out."

Lucy felt the blow clear to the souls of her feet. Distressed, she sank onto the hay bales. "What things?"

Allen put his hands on his hips. "Things like how I can become my own man again."

"Your own man? What's keeping you from that now?" Lucy was bewildered.

"You are." Allen looked away. "I have no self-respect anymore. We aren't good for each other."

Lucy felt her heart hammering. "Not good for each other? I know we're having some problems but nothing time won't–"

"Lucy. You need to face it. We no longer love each other. We don't see eye to eye. I need to leave, to give us each a little space."

No longer love each other? "Allen, I don't need space. That's all we have between us. I need you to stop changing." Lucy stood up, her cheeks warm, stained with color.

"All you used to want was for me *to* change. To leave Garrard County, to high-tail it out of there like some coward. Well, you got what you wanted. And I lost what *I* needed."

Lucy worked to keep her voice from cracking. "Which was?"

Allen shot back, "My self-respect. I should have stayed in Garrard County and fought back."

"You would have lost your life. You think you could have bested the Klan? You're crazy! You're only one man. We made the best decision we could." Lucy's vocal cords quivered with a mixture of anger and fear.

"What's this 'we'? You made the choice and you nagged me like a she-goat that's fence-bound. You didn't have a speck of trust in me to care for the family. Admit it!" Allen kicked at the barn wall.

Lucy's eyes widened in surprise. "It had nothing to do with trust. Think about the children. How would I have raised them in Garrard County by myself?"

"See. You didn't trust me to protect us. You had no faith whatsoever in me. Just so sure I'd get killed. Well, listen to this. I'm a whole lot smarter than any white Klan, and I'd have nailed their hide to the wall." Allen's fists curled in anger.

Lucy knew he wanted to strike something in his agitated state. It had just better not be her. Yet she also knew how he felt. She wanted to slug some sense into him. The words burst out of her. "You're as crazy as Jake Lee Worth! Maybe you should just go live alone with your self-respect. Better yet, go back to Garrard County and fight the Klan. End your misery and mine!"

Allen's cold gaze cut like a bone saw through Lucy's ribs. It punctured her heart. In an agonized state, Lucy reached the house. She burst into their room and locked the door. Throwing herself across the bed like a distraught youth, Lucy bawled. She was no longer young and so much more than just distraught. Her torn heart was bleeding itself to death.

The morning that she saw his things gone and his bedside unslept in, Lucy counted herself a widow. From that day forth, she would be for all purposes, a woman whose husband had entered the grave. And Lucy hoped for an eternity he stayed there, where hope was absent, for this horrible thing he had done to her.

She put on her worn black velvet hat and went down to the train station. The irritated ticket man grudgingly gave Lucy the information she sought. "Yeah, I sold him some tickets."

Lucy raised her brows, "Tickets?"

"Yeah." The station worker chomped down on the end of his cigar. "Two tickets. He pulled out of here with some white woman. Maybe his employer or something, on the two-thirty bound for Cinci. That's all I know."

He did not realize the blow he had given her. Mechanically, she thanked him and walked to a wooden bench and collapsed. *Two tickets–a white woman?* It couldn't be. The man *had* to be wrong. Lucy stuffed the confusion and disbelief in a mental lockbox within her brain.

She went to the bank, then the sawmill. Allen had taken care of business at both places. The banker told her Allen would continue to care for the balance on the house, although there might be a change of address. He gave her an odd look. Lucy left hurriedly and went to the mill. The foreman told her Allen had given his notice of departure abruptly, just last week.

On the walk home, Lucy organized her immediate future in ten minutes. She went into her room and pooled her money from under the mattress. Then she waited on her sons to come home from work and school. Once they were all together in the living room, Lucy told the three boys, "Mama has some sad news." She took a deep breath and groped for the right words. "Daddy has left for awhile. He's been sick and I'm sure the doctor would have told him to go rest. So that's where he's gone, to Cincinnati, to feel better.

"We are also going on a little trip. If you can arrange for a few days off, boys, we'll go to Lockland, and you can all see your baby niece, Scarlett. Won't that be a fun change for us?"

The boys took in the red-rimmed eyes of their mother, along with her fake smile. "Fun" seemed the wrong word for their mother to use in her present state, but the boys did want to see John and Cynthia and the baby.

"Sure, Mama," John said. "We'd love to go. I'll see if I can get off."

James nodded, "Yes, Mama. Sounds great. Mr. Lowe will probably be agreeable." He paused, then asked, "Dad will let us know how he's getting along, won't he?"

Lucy swallowed and strove to keep her composure. "I'm sure we'll know something at some point. Meanwhile, your father could use your prayers."

Dee piped up, "I'm going to make a present for Baby Scarlett." He ran from the room like it was on fire.

Lucy watched him go, aware that he showed little concern over his daddy's departure, but then, he thought he was coming back.

The horrible reality would catch Lucy at any lone moment, and she would wash her vision with enough tears to start another Great Flood. Only hers was different from God's purging flood. Lucy had no consolation–no promise or rainbow–at the end.

Henry Allen Laine stretched out beneath the tree beside the creek and rested his head in his hands. Shadows flitted across his face as the tree's limbs swayed gently by a breeze. It ruffled the leaves, shooting shafts of light into Henry's eyes. He closed them and reveled in the beauty of Kentucky. How glad he was to be here and be a part of the land and the ongoing social change. It was, after all, the home of Berea.

Henry Allen smiled. It was a funny thing to smile when a person was all alone. But what else could he do when life seemed as good as milk and honey? He wasn't the shouting type. But he did write. A few lines skipped across his mind, and he pressed them into his memory. When he got back to his room, he would release them on paper.

He heard a holler, followed by a few shrieks, on the river. Two canoes, loaded with students, paddled by and waved at him. Henry Allen sat up and waved back. He hadn't done much relaxing for awhile. This afternoon, he had come down to the river to rest. All his social problems had dissolved since he had no social life. The girls soon tired of his busy schedule and had lost interest. Well, it suited him fine. He wasn't keen on the serious thought of adorning his finger with any ring of commitment. Berea was all he needed, for now.

A small frown crossed his face when he thought of Rev. Fee. He had not been his usual happy self. Henry enjoyed visiting with the wise older man. He spoke on some problems with Berea's Board, and Henry Allen was curious. He had noticed the influx of white students and that the black numbers were declining. But Henry Allen wasn't worried. Wasn't Berea's motto "God has made of one blood all peoples of the earth"?

He was accomplishing many things at the college. Being on the school's newspaper as Recording Secretary and submitting some of his work was thrilling for him. As he lay there, he worked on the verses that came into his mind. When he left the riverbank, he would copy down the lines he had reworked. Before long, Henry Allen would finish with Berea and be an actual educator for his people. He would explore the openings available to him or create his own. That was something to think about. There were some great men to follow–Booker T. Washington, W.E.B. Du Bois, and George W. Carver. These men embodied the spirit of change through education that required no meager amount of courage.

Henry Allen wanted to achieve all he could and emulate their valuable service to society and bring integration to Kentucky. He leaned back and closed his eyes to enjoy his state's appealing weather.

A Kentuckian's Appeal

On history's page an honored place,
    You hold, beloved Kentucky;
Shall mob-rule blot with disgrace,
    Kentucky, O Kentucky?
The good with shame astonished stands,
    While bold law-breakers form in bands,
To raise against thee bloody hands,
    In treason, O Kentucky!

Thou art the garden spot of earth
    Kentucky, great Kentucky;
And we, permitted to be born
    On thy good soil are lucky.
Dame Nature Bluegrass carpets spread
    Where feet of the loveliest women tread;
'Tis here she rears the thoroughbred,
    Both man and beast, Kentucky.

But where's thy patriot spirit brave,
    Kentucky, O Kentucky?
Gone? Hast thou become a slave
    To lawless men, Kentucky?
Shall the home of Lincoln, Marshall, Clay,
    Its blood-bought glory cast away,

Thy valor won in a darker day,
   Kentucky, O Kentucky?

To spare the rod will ruin the child,
   Kentucky, O Kentucky;
You've dealt with mob-law far too mild,
   In years gone by, Kentucky!
Too long thy coroner's verdicts read:
   "Death caused by unknown hands" has spread,
Contempt for law. Anarchists dread
   Thy courts no more Kentucky!

If thou would rise up in thy might,
   Kentucky, great Kentucky,
And punish criminals, black or white,
   By honest law, Kentucky,
Then capital with longing eye,
   Distrusting thee now passing by,
Would soon return and lift on high
   Its banner bright, Kentucky!

Chapter Twenty-Seven

Dear Annie,
Work for the night is coming,
When you can work no more.
C. W. R.
Mt. Sterling, Ky

Cynthia stretched out the full length of the bed. Sunlight tickled the bed covers, and the curtains shed the glory of a new day. She snuggled down deeper within the quilt, thankful for the last three hours of uninterrupted sleep. John lay beside her deep in slumber. His faint snores were a testimony that he was catching up on his rest as well. The baby had been awfully fitful last night. She had cried for hours, and Cynthia had rocked her endlessly in an attempt to soothe her to sleep. Maybe it was her stomach that hurt her. Scarlett wouldn't eat and curled up her little legs, as if in pain. But she was quiet now, probably tuckered out.

Cynthia rose. It was Saturday, and the Mitchells had the morning covered at the store. The couples rotated the early Saturdays every other week. Cynthia was relieved they had this one off since Scarlett had been so fussy.

After putting coffee on, Cynthia washed and dressed. She crept into the baby's room and saw her bundled up like a small cocoon. Cynthia couldn't resist going over to the crib to observe her lying so peacefully. She was such a beautiful baby.

This morning she looked like an angel. Her hands were curled together, as if in prayer, but to Cynthia something seemed odd. She put a hand to the tiny forehead. It was cold. Concerned, Cynthia felt her hands. They were like spring water to the touch. Swiftly, Cynthia unwrapped her, bewildered as to how the baby could be so cold when she was securely folded within her flannel quilt.

Baby Scarlett did not wake as her mother pulled the covers off her. She lay still in repose, estranged from the warmth of her name.

Cynthia gathered her in her arms, gently shaking the small frame, and then bent her head down to the little face and chest. "Nooo...oh, John! John!"

*   *   *   *

Lucy boarded the train with her boys once more, for the short distance to her daughter's. She could have walked it easily in her stuporous state, uncaring whether it was ten miles or if she got blisters. But she had her boys to think of.

Lucy told herself to be strong for Cynthia and John's sake. The funeral was a hushed, quick affair. There was none of the animated visiting that usually occurred if the deceased had lived a full life.

When the tiny coffin was lowered in the gaping hole, Rev. Charlie Merritt said all the proper things, but Lucy barely heard. She was relieved and grateful though that Cynthia could cry, as she was held between John and Elizabeth. She felt devoid of comfort, and she wasn't sure she could support her daughter. What an awful mental decline she was experiencing since Allen had left her!

When she had done all she could for her daughter, Lucy and the boys went home. She had to carry on with life, whether she wanted to or not.

*   *   *   *

The clock hands swept onward, mimicking little resolute soldiers marching across a battlefield. When Lucy observed her appearance in the mirror, which she rarely did unless necessary, she could tell there had been a passage of time. But within her heart, time had stalled when Allen had left.

Outwardly, Lucy had "shored up" and adjusted. She lived for her sons, following a household routine to keep some

274

balance in their lives. Lucy began to face the decision of whether to sell the little farm and move into town. The boys had day jobs and the ground had served its usefulness. Often Lucy surveyed the properties in town, wondering which house would be suitable.

Through the passage of years, Lucy had been spared the embarrassing explanations to her children. They had accepted what she had told them and remained silent on the subject of their daddy. She only surmised, that with age, they had figured it out for themselves the way things were. Her children were sharp ones, born free. They hadn't been ushered into slavery beneath a boll in the cotton field.

It was May of 1899, the year that stood before a new century. Lucy was putting a lot of stock in the new age before her. Maybe the lingering sadness would dissipate like a pre-dawn mist, because now she was a grandmother once more. Henry and Sallie in Pomeroy, Ohio, had Chauncey. She had only gotten to see the little fellow a few times as Henry was still working on his beloved riverboat. Lucy had hoped Allen would return home as the years passed, if only to see his grandchildren. She often lamented that Allen had walked away from so much more than just her and the children.

Yet there were more exciting things to come. In the fall, John and Cynthia wanted to move to Loveland. It gave her hope that things might start to heal for her; that things might be scaling upward toward some plateau of happiness.

*   *   *   *

Ridge Top, in Franklin, Tennessee, was once more humming like a hive, similar to its former days when the plantation buzzed with activity. This was how Emmitt Mason liked things. He only regretted the absence of manpower on the place and the fine crops the many acres had produced in its glory days. He relished the memories when his people had controlled those with dark skins that glistened with sweat under a baking sun. The plantation, at its peak, had been a magnificent operation. That was almost fifty years ago, a long time, but not to Emmitt Mason's antebellum mind.

Now the bustling activity came from this designated headquarters for Mason's prominent organization. High-ranking men from the War, influential landowners, and even several senators came and went on the grounds between scheduled meetings. And Emmitt Mason controlled it all.

Behind a massive cherry desk that would dwarf most men, Mason sat on a throne-like chair of equally impressive stature. Emmitt, himself, was of Paul Bunyun proportions, his wealth and bearing casting him as a figure of incredible size. He stood a solid six feet and three inches and carried two hundred and thirty pounds effortlessly. Emmitt was a considerable intimidator for a sixty-eight year old man. This was how he liked it.

The organization had made progress through countless meetings. Job bosses had arranged their networks of contacts stretching throughout the area far into the North. The northern territory was one they had longed to confront, to conform the Yankees' civilization to the Society's standards of supremacy. And now with one forceful strike, they would demolish the demographical areas in question, and achieve the desired results of white supremacy over the land. He could nearly envision his name printed in future history books as the man who had rid the United States of their mistakable blemish, of the lazy populace that thought they were equals.

"Mr. Mason," an agent rapped on the door, pulling Emmitt from his fanciful visions.

"Come in," he ordered. Entering was the Colonel Martin Reese. Mason offered him a chair and cigar. "What's the news?"

After lighting up, the Colonel gave his report. "All three of your riverboats have booked agents on them, as well as their supplies for carrying out orders. It's all been arranged and their codes have been established. The operation is on schedule."

"Grand. We're going to rock those Yankees like a steamer whose boiler blows." Mason was grinning.

"Well, sir, quite literally." The Colonel felt a superstitious tug that caused a fine line of worry on his brow. "Let's hope it's all on land though, like planned."

Emmitt laughed at the Colonel's sudden display of weakness. "I can hardly wait to invade the North. 'If at first you don't succeed–try, try again.' This has been decades in coming. *The Virginia* and *The Queen City* have taken on the explosives?"

"Yes, sir, Mr. Mason. They're full with a double cargo load, and both captains were paid to let matters rest. We'll bypass inspections with a few minor erratic departure times for one run. We've good foils in place." The Colonel blew a smoke ring. "Once the job is done, things will be so close on schedule, no one will suspect the steamers' involvement."

"Well done, Colonel Reese. There will be an extra reward for your efforts."

Once everyone had been seen and dismissed, Emmitt Mason studied the map on the wall of his study. Strategic spots were marked in red. These circled towns, where the majority of the inhabitants belonged back in their southern homeland, would learn their place the hard way. He relished the thought of blowing up entire neighborhood hovels and outcroppings of rubbish. It was a brilliant plan.

Gazing at the silver statue on his desk, Emmitt Mason reveled in the feel of raw empowerment. He had had the figure specially made in honor of his secret assembly. Its creation greatly pleased him. Sunlight reflected off the cast of a hooded man, decked in sovereign robes, grotesquely brandishing a burning cross.

Nellie Mason tried pleading. "Please, Papa, I've been really studious and done nothing but learn. My grades are perfect and I've completed every college course available. Monsieur will be there as a constant chaperone. Please, may I accompany Jean-Claude to France? I do so want to see Paris and the school where they teach."

Papa Mason looked bored. He stared out the window.

"Nellie, you can not go to France. I don't trust Frenchmen. Especially not where my daughter is concerned. How would I know you would come back safely?"

"Well, Papa, I would. You can trust *me*. I'm plenty old enough to find my way home if it should become necessary. There's only one Atlantic Ocean and one North America."

Emmitt Mason gave his daughter a hard look. "I know my geography a little better than you ever will. My answer is no. When that popinjay gets serious about you, he can ask to court you proper."

"Papa," Nellie's pale cheeks were touched with coral streaks of color. "He has tried, but *you* haven't taken him seriously. He is due back in Paris in four weeks to prepare for his teaching position. Time is running out."

Emmitt reached for his ever-present cigars. He lit one and after a long drag on it, he spoke, "You're too good for some Frenchie. What's wrong with good Southern Anglo-Saxon stock? You don't know what's best for you. You're a female and therefore subject to unreasonable whims. Am I correct?"

Nellie bit her tongue and spoke passionately, "Papa, I love Jean-Claude. I can't let him go."

"What do you know about love?" Emmitt looked sternly at his daughter.

Nellie's eyes flashed. *That's right! I've learned nothing of it from you, that's for sure!* "Papa, please understand. I am nearly thirty! An old maid! You don't want me to be a spinster for the rest of my days, do you? What would your colleagues think?"

"They would probably congratulate me on keeping you in possession of a good aristocratic name and thwarting any foolish matches that would ultimately end in ruin. Now, let the matter drop, Nellie. I have your welfare in mind. Trust me. You can go to your room now." Emmitt was clearly through with the discussion. He pulled out a folder and sorted the papers in a dismissal of her.

Nellie knew when to stop pushing her papa. She moved to the door. The map on the wall caught her attention. "Papa, what are all those red circles on those towns for?"

Mason looked up at her briefly. "Never mind, Nellie. It doesn't concern you. Just a little work of my organization. You would hardly understand the strategy of it all anyhow."

Nellie turned her back on her domineering father. She went to her room and locked the door. Pulling out a carpetbag, she began to fill it. She would be traveling light. Nellie paused as she held up a picture of her father down at the horse stables. Then hastily she tucked it in her bag. She would soon be a citizen of another country. Maybe someday, when she was old, she would want to remember her papa with a smile.

*   *   *   *

As evening drew on and darkness stole over Ridge Top, Emmitt Mason felt the past draw him in like the miasma of the bayou country. It both softened his heart with sentimental vapors and simultaneously curdled his senses into an angry haze that only good Tennessee whisky could lift.

Nellie was all he had besides his White Knights of the Loyal Brotherhood. Each year, she grew farther away from him. He supposed she took after the nature of the family before her, although she never knew any of them.

Long ago, he had left behind his father's people–the Altons. Ashamed of his own father's policies where his Negroes were concerned, Emmitt had borne all he could until he was a man and could leave Allcorn Hill in Madison County, Kentucky. Behind him, he left a full brother named Thad and two half-siblings, William and Leticia. Their mother was a slave on Allcorn Hill's plantation. Disgusted at his father, Emmitt never forgave him for his breach of devotion to his and Thad's mother. His hatred of blacks grew intensely and he would not, in any manner, claim kinship to two black slaves. It enraged him how his full and half-brothers, Thad and William–born only three days apart–were treated equally. The youngest, his half-sister Leticia, was a spoiled brat.

When his mama died, Emmitt left Allcorn Hill and went

to Ridge Top in Tennessee, where his mother's family resided. He dropped the name he was born with–Alton–and adopted his mother's maiden name–Mason. He wanted no connection to his father's disgrace at Allcorn Hill.

Now he engineered a powerful leadership of the KKK. His White Knights of the Loyal Brotherhood had evened the score where people like his father had transgressed. They spread their justice of terror throughout the countryside, teaching blacks that they would always be an inferior race and should have remained slaves. If hate was the motivator, well, that was fine. It harnessed a power that was tough enough to fight through any obstruction–be it the blood of families or just wisps of sentimental memories that lingered on when day faded.

*　　　*　　　*　　　*

Henry Ross let his eyes adjust for a few seconds to the dim interior of the hold. He pushed a cart on wheels into the storage area and took a shovel from against the wall. Filling the cart, he made several trips to the boiler room.

Tom had come on duty and told Henry he could go, if he wanted. "Gotcha covered, Sap!"

Henry smiled, wiping the coal grime off his face with an equally sooty sleeve. At one time, Henry had taken offence at Tom's nickname for him. But the older man had confided to Henry that he had lost his two boys, and Henry reminded him of them. "You're like they was. Full of vigor and vim, life running like sap through a tree. 'Course, it be true you're nothing but a sapling yet. But you'll grow."

Henry *had* grown and filled out. Sallie could cook like a gourmet angel, if she had the provisions, but he worked hard and sweated off any extra pounds between her cooking. Of course, his feed on the ship wasn't bad either.

"Well, Tom, I'll take off, but let me get you one more load before I go."

Tom didn't argue. The loads were hard on an old man. "Well, that would be fine, Sap. But you need to get some off the back pile, under the loft area. The boss man said it's the old stuff and it'll burn hotter. He wants to mix 'em."

"Sure. I'll do that." Henry pushed the cart to an unused area in the hold. He didn't know why they needed this older coal, but it was true it burned a little hotter. Must be *The Virginia* needed to make good time.

As he dug his last shovelful, he struck something solid. Peering closer, he saw wooden crates stacked beneath the coal. Wrapped bundles were stowed inside. On the wood, a stamp was burned into the slats reading, "W. K. L. B." That was encircled by a helmet and knife, around which a noose was tied, the White Knights of the Loyal Brotherhood. Perplexed, Henry peered at the contents. For some reason, it was put here and hidden under the coal. It must be something of importance. Maybe the Captain had taken it on and it was none of his business.

Suddenly, voices filtered through the hold's dim and dank interior and floated towards Henry. They were around the corner of the built-in sectionals the hold contained. Henry thought if it were a few other boiler men, he might could just ask them about the crates.

Laying the shovel across his load, he started for the voices. The words "explosives" and "nigger populations" struck him like sharp water which slapped against the hull. He froze.

A low chuckle floated towards him, growing closer. "...easier to unload at night. The boat will be here, docked in Pomeroy, until tomorrow morning. We're going to do the unloading, can't trust the darkie crew to handle it."

The other agreed, "One of them might just light up, and we'll all go to Kingdom Come. Hey, did the Captain promise to pull out early?"

"Yeah. We'll be headed for Pennsylvania. Norris' men will work eastward after that. The Knights have the districts coded."

"Brilliant plan. This ought to strike a little fear. Lynching only gets 'em one by one, but dynamite–that's a whole different matter."

The voices came around the wood partition and Henry

looked for a place to hide, but there was nowhere he could conceal himself. Quickly he reached for his shovel and scooped a load of coal into it in an attempt to look busy. Two men appeared and stared at Henry in shocked surprise to discover someone else in the hold with them.

Henry did what his people had done for centuries. He adopted the usual survival mode and pretended ignorance. With a lackadaisical grin, Henry said, "Afternoon, sirs. How ya doin'?" He was smiling and bobbing like they were old acquaintances.

The men's rough looks were not lost on Henry. "What are you doing down here?"

Henry raised his brows in innocence. "Why, sir, I work down here. Hauling coal for the boilers."

One of the men stepped closer and inspected his loaded cart. Then he noticed the edge of the crates exposed within the pile of coal. "What's that?"

"Not sure, sir. I just struck it, but seein' my load's full, I was ready to move on. They need this in the boiler room. Just not sure what that is, but probably somethin' that's been here a long time and got coal dumped on it. You never know down here. Likely the Captain done forgot about it." Henry babbled on, trying to appear dumb to the men.

The two men were silent. Henry didn't like the way they stared at him. Even in the dark area, he could see their eyes were callously cold in their hardened faces.

"You hear us talking, boy?" The one asked.

"No, sir, I sure didn't. I was busy doing my job." Henry was sweating profusely.

The other man came closer. He stood nearly on top of Henry. "Well, boy, we didn't hear you if you were so "busy". Why's that, I wonder?"

Henry swallowed. "Not sure, sir, but you can see I got a full load here. I'd best get it on back to the fellows. They're waiting, I'm sure."

The two white men didn't move. Henry felt a lingering chill as if his fate was before a jury, and there was no other considered verdict but "guilty".

The men silently reached a mute decision, and stood aside. Henry grasped his huge cart. "Thank you, sirs. I'll get this to the boiler room, and we'll keep the ship going strong. Yes, sirs! Thank you, sirs."

Henry could not steer the load away quick enough. He felt their stares like a dagger in the back. He pushed it into the heated room and dumped the mass of coal into a pile for the other men, trying to defuse his uneasiness. It was his lunchtime, but he felt too shaken to eat. Besides, he was off duty, and he wanted to leave the ship as quickly as possible with those men aboard. Henry went up on deck into the fresh air. He breathed deeply, trying to force the worry away. What he had heard below deck had frightened him. It sounded suspicious and illegal. But what could he do about it? Who could he tell? No one would believe a black man, anyway. At least not the police. If it were something foul directed at black people, most law enforcement looked the other way.

Henry signed out on the ship's log sheet and turned to go. He wanted to be home with Sallie more than anything. Assistant Manager Carl Thayer appeared from around the port side. He approached Henry. "Ross, management wants you to stay on duty until tonight's shift is over. We need extra help while we're docked here. Report to my office in fifteen minutes for orders. Oh, grab your lunch. You won't eat until quitting time tonight."

Henry attempted to moisten his lips. He spoke, "Sir, my wife will be worried."

Carl Thayer gave him a disdainful look. "She'll survive. She wants you to keep your job, doesn't she?" He looked smug. "Isn't she used to you roaming the streets late at night after your shift?"

Henry clamped his mouth shut. Whatever Thayer was insinuating, Henry wasn't quite sure, but he felt like wiping the man's smirk off his face and with a little more than just an eraser.

Turning, he went to the boat's kitchen to get his dinner. Henry was forced to consider that maybe working on the steamer wasn't worth all the drivel he had to endure.

It was eleven-thirty when Henry was dismissed. He had stowed luggage on board and unloaded the cargo from Pittsburg. Tired, he bid Tom goodnight. Tom was puzzled as to why Henry had to work overtime while they were docked in Pomeroy. Feeling sympathetic, he told Henry, "Go on home to Sallie and get your rest, Sap."

"Sure will, Tom," Henry went above deck and prepared to write in his correct departure time on the worksheet beside the Captain's quarters. He remembered he needed to erase the time he had written in at noon. Reaching for the pencil, he felt a pressure in his side. Someone stood up against him, and the tension pushed deeper into his ribs.

A low voice whispered, "We're going to take a little trip to the hold. Get moving."

Henry paused and considered making a run for it, but the sharpness beneath his ribs increased until he felt it nick his flesh. Another dark figure emerged from the darkness surrounding the boat and stood close upon him, blocking any escape. As if reading his mind, the two flanked him and hurried him towards the steps he had just ascended five minutes earlier.

Down into the ship they shoved Henry until they were in the recesses of the coal room. Activity was quiet in the boiler room, and Henry could hear the water slap the hull below the portholes.

One of the men spoke, a sardonic grin decipherable even in the darkness. "We thought we'd help you get off the ship. The gangplank's been blocked so you have no choice but to swim."

Henry recognized their voices as the two men who had found him in the hold earlier. His thoughts went to Sallie and Chauncey and he wondered if she had come to check on him. "What do you guys want?"

"Want? We don't want anything from you. We're here to help you get to shore." The unhumorous laughter was wry with sinister tones.

Henry swallowed hard, but refused to panic. "I don't need any help. My family is waiting on me, and if I don't show up, they'll go to the authorities."

Henry's bluff didn't work. "Really? What authorities? You think they're going to believe some low-down nigra?"

The man held his knife up in front of Henry's face. "It's too bad you happened to be in the wrong place at the wrong time. You know a little too much, boy."

Henry had backed away from the glinting knife, which glimmered a sharp silver in the moonlight. His back struck the wood framework of the old coal chute. "Listen, I don't know a thing. Nothing at all. I don't know anything about those boxes."

"Is that so?" The man shoved the knife until its point strained against Henry's shirt and skin beneath. "You're a dirty liar, just like the rest." Then, just as quickly, he pulled his knife back and swiped his suit coat front aside, revealing an embroidered emblem sewn to his shirt. "See this?"

Henry could not make out much of the patch in the darkness, only where the moonlight shone through the porthole. But in the center, there was no mistaking the white letters of the White Knights, part of the Ku Klux Klan. It matched the brands that were stamped on those crates covered with coal.

Now Henry considered his options. Should he attack the two men by flailing at them and hope the blade didn't make contact, or should he try to reason his way out of the ordeal? The knife was a wicked deterrent. "I'm not lying. I don't know anything. Just let me go, and I'll get out of your sight. I'll never say a word about any of this or step a foot on this boat again."

"You're right about that, nigra." One man reached for a shovel that was leaning against the hold's frame, and charged Henry, swinging it towards his head. Henry attempted to ward it off, while the other klansman used his knife to accomplish its mission, connecting with tissue and blood.

Henry slumped over, slipping forward on the cold damp flooring of the hold. The men stripped him and opened the porthole window. Struggling, they hoisted him up and shoved him through the window. Henry was by no means a lightweight.

A significant splash indicated the men had disposed of him. Using Henry's trousers, they cleaned the knife blade and began filling the pants with coal. Then they tossed it, too, out the porthole window. Straightening their clothes, they moved towards the stairs.

"Good work for a night," the one commented.

The other Knight replied, " Our work is just beginning. We've got that shipment to unload in two hours. Let's go get a drink. I think these two Loyal Brothers deserve one." He clapped the other on the back.

Quietly hidden beneath the stairs, Tom listened for their footfalls to fade. He was shaking from the horror of what had just occurred. He hurried up the steps, propelled by fear.

Because of the distance and the dim light, Tom did not know who had just been murdered, but he knew what the "White Knights" meant. He also knew what "shipment" those men were talking about because he had secretly come across the crates on his shift.

Later, he had sneaked to the pile and investigated. He knew what dynamite looked like. Tom had been a slave in Texas, and they had used the stuff to carve out traces through the rough country.

Tom had little time left. He knew the dynamite would be used for a villainous act, if the KKK were involved. Determined to do something, he hurried up the steps to fetch a bucket and rope.

Once again in the hold, he tied the rope to the bucket's handle and slipped it out the hold's porthole. He tried to erase the memory of the body being shoved out the very same opening.

The bucket made a splash when it hit water. Tom was glad for his strong muscles as he pulled the rope back and forth to let the river's water fill it, then heaved it up to the window and lifted it inside.

Carrying the bucket of water, Tom hurried to the coal

pile. Using the offending shovel, he worked until the crates were exposed. Then taking the bucket, he poured its contents through the slats into the crates. Over and over for an hour, Tom worked tirelessly. Satisfied, he re-covered the area and taking the bucket and rope, he hid it beneath a tarpaulin on deck. He scanned the area to see if he had been noticed, but all he could hear was the raucous laughter from the saloon area.

He crept to his sleeping quarters and joined the other men in their slumber, satisfied with his "night's work".

Chapter Twenty-Eight

Dear Annie,
May your life be like the day, more beautiful in the evening,
like the summer aglow with promise; and like the autumn
rich with the golden shearer, where good works and
deeds have ripened in the field.
These are the wishes of your friend,
Sallie B. Kincaid
Berea, Ky 5-5-1888

The telegram met Lucy at the door. She took it from the postman like it was a live virus. Although Lucy had never received a telegram, she had no excitement over its arrival. Only something very important warranted such a delivery and to Lucy, there were few vital matters in this life that contained such gravity.

MAMA STOP PLEASE COME QUICKLY
STOP HENRY GONE STOP SALLIE

Lucy groaned and sank into her old rocker. *No, Lord, don't let it be!* She could not handle one more loss. *I can't, Lord, I can't! Surely you can see that!*

But, by evening, Lucy was packed and on her way. She gave instructions to her boys not to forget to feed the chickens and to keep the windows closed when it rained.

Lucy arrived to have a tearful Sallie collapse on her. "Now, Sallie," Lucy said soothingly, "Tell me what's happened."

"That's just it, Mama Lucy. I don't know what's happened. Henry never came home." Sallie hiccupped and her tears began afresh. "Why would he leave me and Chauncey?"

Lucy sat in the nearest chair and let her bewilderment overwhelm her. *Yes, indeed, why would he? I'm certainly the wrong one to ask, child!* Lucy removed her hat and motioned for Sallie to follow her to the kitchen. "Where's Chauncey?"

"He's at the neighbor's," Sallie said. Lucy gave her the teapot with instructions to fill it, while she got the tea ready. "Let's have a cup of tea and you can tell me just when it all happened."

Sallie immediately launched into the details without waiting on the hot water. She finished with, "Oh, Mama Lucy! I've never given Henry a reason to want to leave me! Do you think he's just like his daddy?" Sallie clapped a hand over her mouth. "Oh, Mama! I'm sorry!"

Lucy pressed her lips together and pulled the whistling kettle away from the heat. When she turned to her daughter-in-law, she gave her a gentle look. "Sallie, we may not know what's going on, but what we do know is that Henry loves you very much. I'll go to the boatyard tomorrow. We'll find out something." Lucy was resolved that the men at the dock would not deter her. A worried mother who had forged her own freedom from the days of slavery would get to the bottom of this enigma.

Lucy waited until the steamer came in on Wednesday in Pomeroy. She arrived early and demanded to see the Captain. Instead, an impatient assistant manager met her. "What do you want?" His arrogance matched the stench of the surrounding water. She would not let his attitude unnerve her.

"My son, Henry Ross, has worked on this riverboat for years. A week ago, he never came home. I want to talk to the management about his disappearance."

"So talk." Carl Thayer cut her a glance before resuming his scan over the log book in his hand.

"When was he last seen here? What day and shift?" Lucy asked.

Thayer gave her a scornful look. "How would I know? Go ask his wife. We have plenty of boiler men and most of them are a shiftless lot. Just walk off and never show up again. Like your son."

Lucy's expression hardened. "My son's worked on this boat for years. I know he never just 'walked off'."

Carl Thayer spoke scathingly, "I don't have time for games." He flipped through the book he held and shoved it at her. "See here. Ross signed out at noon, May 30th. Wherever he went or whatever he did, I don't know. All I do know is I had to hire another worker to replace him."

It was apparent by the darkness in Mr. Thayer's eyes that he felt no fondness or sympathy for his "workers".

Lucy hesitated. She peered at the writing on the page; it was Henry's handwriting. The sight of it triggered a smothering sensation in her throat. Carl Thayer turned his back on Lucy and stalked off. She stood for a moment more, until the vertigo in her stomach settled. Her next course was to go to the police station. She turned and caught sight of a black man, hunkered down beside the stairs. Being discovered, he bolted away, down into the dark recesses of the ship.

Lucy paused and wondered about the man. Did he know something about Henry's disappearance? She started for the hold when *The Virginia's* Captain intercepted her.

"You can't go down there. Ship policy. What are you wanting?"

"My son, Henry Ross, worked down there. Now he's disappeared. I wanted to ask around." Lucy let the words leave her mouth while her mind darted in several directions like a captured hare.

The captain's lips were straight as the funnel stacks on his ship. "I'm afraid not." His firm expression made Lucy's decision.

"But my son is *missing*. He was last known here on this ship."

"I'm sorry." The captain was less brusque than his assistant manager but just as brief. "Men are always failing to show up for duty." He shrugged and gestured toward the gangplank.

Lucy left and headed for the police department. Her

reception here was similar. The officer behind the desk handed her a form. "Fill this out. Answer all the questions. We'll get to it." He yawned.

Lucy stood before the desk, sure her expression conveyed her disbelief. A man was missing and no one cared! And it was all because he was black. She took the inkwell and pen and wrote quickly, then hurried back to the desk. "My son–"

"I know, we get lots of reports on missing people. We'll get to it, like I told ya." He reached for the paper in her hand.

"But this is urgent. He's just disappeared, for no reason–"

"Yeah, I know. They all do. I wish you people had your own colored police force. You know how much time we spend looking for so-called 'lost' darkies? And there they lay, in some alley, drunk as a skunk." He shook his head, disgusted.

Lucy opened her mouth even as her argument died within her. It was no use. She turned on her heel, shutting the door behind her forcefully. Standing on the top step in the sunshine, Lucy drew the new summer air into her lungs to dispel the panic rising within her.

There was no one or nowhere to go for help. It reminded her of slavery days where there had been no shore or haven of safety–until Camp Nelson. And they had had to run to it. She would keep looking for Henry until she found him. Her mind raced ahead to her next course of action. She must talk to someone in the boiler room of the hold. They should know something. Somebody–somewhere–knew what had happened to Henry.

$$*\qquad*\qquad*\qquad*$$

Berea was divorcing herself from her vows. Her genesis was an unraveling book, where pages, loosely sheaved, fell away from a broken binding. Rev. Fee and his trusted ambassadors worked tirelessly against the uprising that was occurring in Kentucky.

It was not a new movement, but rather the old time-worn adage where the European continent's superiority to the "native" continents was distinctly apparent, especially when viewed from the length of the nose, in the gravitational direction of downward.

The college's founders fought hard but Kentucky's wall of prejudice was of stones set in mortar and a pickax did little to dismantle it.

When President Frost swung Berea's emphasis from interracial education to helping breach sectional lines within the state, monetary contributions increased the school's treasury dramatically. In this vein, President Frost felt he had proceeded in the right direction. He was puzzled as to the co-founders' irritation over this obvious good piece of fortune.

At the monthly board meeting, Rev. Fee stood before the members. Sadly, his aged appearance had diminished many of the members' opinion of him. His worn and faded clothing projected, in their simplicity, an "old-fashioned" ideal that linked the trustees' admiration to superfluous vanity.

But John Fee's sturdy bedrock remained unmoved in mind and spirit. "Gentlemen, I fear we are betraying our creed and being unfaithful to the original design of the college. Much more is being done to bring in white students than black. Our black brethren know and feel this. It is pure betrayal, I say." He swung his gaze to William Frost.

"It is true we now have a full purse, but what matter is money if the college's unadulterated principles become polluted? We have a solid foundation to build on and we must not construct our edifices out of rotted lumber or the pithy boards of neglect. Our own pockets must remain empty in the course to aid a humanity that most needs our help."

President Will Frost moistened his lips. He did not rise to his feet but disdainfully directed his words across the room towards the reverend. "Times change and so must the institutions dedicated to nourishing them. Needs change as well. The Appalachian whites were ripe towards the charitable instruction we offered." He straightened his cuffs on his shirt. "You know, Reverend Fee, public opinion is a dictator and dictators subsequently hold the purse strings. Kentucky is very unpleased to see white and black students intermingling. Men and women of separate races actually keeping company with one another...it seems very unnatural to the majority of Kentucky's Southerners."

Rev. Fee drew in a hasty breath and struggled to maintain a calm. "I'm sure it seemed "very unnatural" to the Jews under Paul that the Gentiles be converted. Yet where would we be if Paul and the apostles disobeyed God?" He studied his shirt buttons and then spoke quietly, so that the room of men had to strain to catch his words.

"The tendency now in Berea is to run down to a mere white school. Berea College will then be no different than thousands of other schools in the South. Ichabod will be written upon the face of Berea College: the glory is departed.

"Do not each of you feel a moral obligation to help and aid our black brethren after the travesty this country has wreaked upon that race?"

There was only silence stuffed into the corners of the room. A few shifted uncomfortably in their chairs. J.A.R. Rogers sighed. How easily a stirred conscience was waxed over when it wanted to appease the popular sentiments of its peers!

Rev. Fee took his seat. But as he sat he spoke again. "Gentlemen, I appeal unto you one final time. You must make a choice." He looked around the room, all friends and colleagues before him. New faces–youthful faces–unschooled in the ways of dedication and devotion. What a sad new era dominated these "narrow scenes of night"!

Sadly, John G. Fee finished his plea, "The early stalwarts of Berea would rise from their graves as Rachael of old and weep because their cherished design is not being carried out." His head hung. "Just as I am."

The somber meeting ended. William Frost paused in the doorway and looked back. Rev. Fee sat, a morose figure, still now as the breeze that had died beyond the windows. J.A.R. Rogers remained also, a statue affixed to his chair with stony face. A dismal scene, but as William Frost's eyes narrowed, he felt pity for the two old men who blindly refused to see the coming signs of the times.

*   *   *   *

Henry Allen Laine had graduated with full honors. He was a man whose future stretched before him with promise. Excited about the prospects opening up to him, Henry Allen wrote to his family after his commencement, telling of the many offers for teaching positions he had received. He was eager to pass on the knowledge he had secured at Berea.

In his letter to Cousin Cynthia Ross Hannon, he wrote: *"Oh, Annie, the wonderous days of Berea have become like a fire burned out. Not by lack of care by those devoted guardians of the school, but by a society who cannot reconcile itself to change. A paradox that the school board is confused over.*

I've seen the disappointment of those members who try hard to be a dam of protection against the rising waters unleashed by Kentucky's pro-southern forces. Forces that want to reinvent another slavery for us. Why are whites threatened so severely when we make advancements? Especially since we are considered socially and mentally inferior to them. Could a little schooling, in their minds, change that belief? Fear strikes a match in their heart and the fiery hatred burns! Will this world ever make any scholarly sense?

Now, I've also sounded as despairing as my classmates over Berea's change of course in its policies, but I will send you a poem I wrote that tells my friends to keep being strong and will tell my students in the face of adversity to hold fast and push ahead towards brighter days. I'll end with:

> *Being black is not a curse,*
> *Poor attitudes are much worse!*
> *Love from your cousin,*
> *Henry Allen Laine*

PUSH

Don't fret and whimper your life away,
   And growl about no chance,
For the poor man to edge thru the frenzied crowd,
   Or up in the world advance.
Tho' the fight grows hot for power and place,
   Just join in the maddening rush;
Keep a level head, an open eye,
   And—Push!

The world may try hard to crowd you back,
   And elbow you out of the race;
But press right on, keep your temper and smile,
   With your eye on a higher place;
Be firm, and true, and honest through,
   Don't beat about the bush;
Be frank, and fair; treat all men square,
   And—Push!

Oh! don't, over small things, worry and fret,
   And hasten your health's decline;
You'll soon, at best, be laid to rest,
   Under the drooping pine!
For the old folks' sake, learn a warm handshake,
   Win lass' and lad's best wish;
Have faith in God, in Man, in Self,
   And—Push!

*   *   *   *

Lucy pressed a gloved hand to her lips. *Give me strength, one more time, Lord, for what lies ahead!* She put her hand to the door's knob and then hesitated. How strange to see her fingers encased in fine gray gloves, so unlike her usual wardrobe that accompanied her outings. But since staying with Sallie in Pomeroy, she felt like she should be dressed up for vis-

296

iting. And here–of all places–required gloves! *What if she must shake the mortician's hand?*

The door to the morgue opened silently, too quiet, in Lucy's opinion. She stepped into the small room, designed for the business aspects of death, and wrinkled her nose at the smells which permeated the air. She would not believe she might find her son in this place, it was simply too disturbing of an idea. She had always adhered to "no news is good news". But the lot had fallen on her to find out if the report was true. For Sallie and Chauncey's sake, and for her own as well, she supposed.

"Yes?" The voice floated across the small area, nearly ghostlike. Lucy shook herself. This was getting creepy and, she, of all people, was not into spooks. Gathering her courage, Lucy said, "I've come to identify a body brought in yesterday. The report was given to us about its...arrival."

The man, in a gray suit encompassed over by a white apron, nodded. The air about him was grave, much as was expected of a mortician, Lucy noted. A surging memory flickered within her mind's eye. He had the same look the surgeons had worn during the War. It was one of having seen humanity through a narrow periscope of suffering that others could only wonder about.

"This way, ma'am." He showed no sign he saw her black skin as he opened the small partial door to admit her past the office, towards the back room.

Lucy unquestionably followed the somber man, all the while sure in her most hopeful heart, it would not be Henry lying there on some table. Henry could swim, he would not have drowned, as appearances had given.

Lucy pictured the worker who stood at Sallie's door yesterday, clutching his hat to his chest, telling them that he worked at the barge yard where a body turned up, floating in the water. "You'uns need to go to the morgue and identify it, ma'am." He looked at Lucy since Sallie had sunk to the sofa, weeping. "Word got around that you're looking for your man. We wanted to let you know about this." His sorry look conveyed more than his words said.

Lucy found her voice, which had deserted her seconds earlier. "Thank you for coming. We'll check into it."

Now focusing on the reality before her, Lucy stepped into a wide room where several tables were arranged in a symmetrical pattern. Three bundles lay atop a trio of tables, covered like mummies in white sheets. Ice-filled trays, which melted beneath the white forms, created a steady *drip-drip* sound in the room as it flowed into a bucket on the floor via a thin tube. The room felt cold to Lucy, more from its sterile appearance than its temperature. The blinds were pulled, and Lucy let her eyes adjust to the filtered light of the room.

"Over here, ma'am. This was the one brought in yesterday, found floating in the barge yard."

Lucy stepped closer to the table, but not before the past, like an intruder upon any given moment, reared its head through the decades to trample her. First–the smell, distinguishable as Death. She would know it anywhere–had known it intimately in the past. Those years were when death ran rampant, like a thieving gnome. It had been no stranger to each new sunrise. Images of the War and Camp Nelson's sick quarters pulsed through Lucy's mind. She saw a gray, rotten barn where dirty straw and sick people littered its earthen floor like refuse, and the space was rank with death's perfume. Beautiful Miss Fair lay there, waiting for the Dark Angel to cover her with his robes.

"Ma'am? Can you do this?" the inquiring eyes searched hers, his spectacles magnifying their seriousness.

Lucy snapped to the present. Steeling herself, she sounded gruff. "Of course," she answered as she tucked away any vestiges of a soft heart and looked on the scene with sterile eyes, matching the man and the room, and the somber silent figures adorned in their white shrouds.

The mortician pulled the sheet back, efficient and professional. There a face, strangely arrayed in the most unnatural hue met her sight. The eyes were closed, and the face was tinged with a pallor belonging to that of a plaster cast. Being Death's claim, it was all swollen wildly as if to burst. Lucy was froze by the horror of it.

"He is actually preserved quite well. Do you see any resemblance to your son?" The matter-of-fact voice continued, "I can show you his teeth, if it would help."

Lucy ignored this as the fascinating horror drew a further examination out of her. "Why is the head shaped funny here?"

"The victim has suffered a blow to the head. Blunt trauma."

"I see." But Lucy did not really see. She simply looked on, freezing her emotions within the confines of her heart.

"How did he die? Drowning?" Lucy asked carefully.

"Obviously yes, but not the cause. He bears a hole in the torso, a stab wound likely."

Again Lucy said, "I see." Quietness reigned within the room for a minute's time, except for the constant drip of water. A dart of a thought shot through Lucy. She could walk out of here and tell Sallie that she was not sure about the body. Spare Sallie the pain of a funeral and destined widowhood. But at length, Sallie would suffer worse at the Hand of Uncertainty, a sometimes far worse master. Lucy looked at the tables where the ice melted and the clear water droplets fell. "They say water is the source of life."

"Yes, ma'am." The mortician answered calmly. He did not hurry her as he patiently pushed his glasses up on the bridge of his nose.

After many seconds, Lucy collected her thoughts as if they were a bundle of letters held together gingerly by a ribbon. She looked for the face of her once beloved son in the vestiges of the lifeless corpse before her. "Can I see his right hand, please?"

The mortician nodded and exposed a hand. It contained only three fingers beside the thumb, the middle finger missing. Lucy drew in a breath at the proven finality before her. She asked tentatively, "Do you believe, sir, that once life leaves the body, the soul ascends to somewhere higher, a more beautiful place?"

"Well, ma'am, I am scientifically-minded, but...anything is possible."

Lucy held out a gloved hand and the mortician shook it gently. "I thank you for your time and your honesty. I appreciate the care of my son's remains."

"No need, ma'am, to thank me. I propose you arrange burial here and soon. Coroner Scott will see to it that he is buried in an uncostly manner. One can always be moved to another location at a later time."

Lucy nodded. She went through the motions of paying and stepped out of the building. A shudder tore through her. The enigma was solved in the physical sense, and yet a myriad of questions still remained.

Lucy had held herself together. The formality in which the mortician had conducted his business had composed her, kept her innermost feelings in ice, like those corpses in death.

But now, away from the man and building, her defences crumpled and broke loose from its moorings. *Why, Lord, oh why me?* Her battered heart wailed. *Why must I be the one to have to see such things? No mother should have to see her baby like that.* Of course Sallie must be spared such a thing. She was young and unfamiliar with the twisted cruel perversions existing in this life.

But the revulsion of it bore down upon Lucy's mind like a whirlwind intent on destruction. Lucy drew a sharp ragged breath. An escaped sob attempted to be a shield and buckler against such a force.

Child of mine, whence hast thou forgotten me? Lucy closed her eyes and concentrated on the voice that suddenly resounded through her being. *Thy son is in the Hand of his Maker, no more to suffer the afflictions meted out to man. The mottled and marred shell left behind is only a form that once contained his radiant soul.*

Lucy quieted herself. The ghastliness faded. The truth shone and stretched across her mind like the clear light of early dawn. Of course it was not Henry who lay upon that table in the morgue. His spirit had gone on to a place where "God shall wipe away all tears from their eyes; and there shall be no more death, neither sorrow, nor crying, neither shall there be any more pain; for the former things are passed away."

Henry would not have to be subject to any more evils. He would not have to be called "nigger" or "boy" anymore. He had been a fine man in every sense, faithful in his work and to his family. Henry had fulfilled his place and design. Lucy found a peace in his accomplishments–ones that marked a man's life as having lived well.

Excerpt from the **Pomeroy Democrat** *June 7, 1899:*

Floater Found

The dead body of a colored man was found in the river up at the boatyard this morning by Charlie Bowen.

He had been in the water several days and had an ugly looking spot in the top of his head where he had evidently been hit with some instrument.

He was dressed only in a shirt and drawers and had evidently been slugged while in bed and thrown into the river.

His face and head where covered with blood and the middle finger of one hand was missing.

The remains were viewed by Coroner Scott and taken, in charge by Undertaker Biggs.

*   *   *   *

Floater Found

A floater was found this (Wednesday) morning at the head of the barges at the Pomeroy boat yard. The corpse was that of a colored man and had a hole in his head and breast.

He was dressed in shirt and drawers–no pants. Coroner Scott buried the remains in the paupers portion of Beech Grove Cemetery.

Chapter Twenty-Nine

"Ichabod has been written upon the face of Berea College; the glory is departed."
John G. Fee

Matilda Fee's voice was soft, caressing, as it murmured a chapter in Timothy from her Bible. It was a genteel voice, sweetly tinted with the mellowness given to Southern women. She paused to study her husband who lay motionless upon the bed. The chamber had been converted into a sickroom and had become a dreaded but necessary haven for Matilda.

She searched for stirring limbs or any eye movements from her husband's bedside, but there was only labored breathing. The doctor had diagnosed it as bleeding on the brain, but Matilda would say the Lord had called upon John G. Fee, and He was ready to conduct him home.

She was not sure if her tone could reach John anymore, if he knew the Words of Life were there to usher him into his newly prepared future. "'For I am now ready to be offered, and the time of my departure is at hand. I have fought a good fight, I have finished my course, I have kept the faith. Henceforth there is laid up for me a crown of righteousness, which the Lord, the righteous judge, shall give me at that day: and not to me only, but unto all them also that love his appearing.'"

Now Matilda paused as John's hands rose slightly. Did he see or hear something that she could not, maybe some presence from a realm that existed beyond any human perception?

She could not know that John felt alive, vibrant in his form. His mind was clearer than it had been for days. He was in his prime and exercised the aura the Lord had given him in his youth.

For John was again existing in the days of 1855 when he had begun his "good fight".

John let his eyes fall to the Honorable Cassius M. Clay's silk cravat. His neatly trimmed beard did not interrupt the sheen of the expensive material or the tasteful gold and diamond stick - pin situated there. "My dear sir, I fully appreciate your offer. Your six hundred acres, I'm sure, is prime ground. I understand your desire to have a settled church here, and I would greatly enjoy serving as its pastor. But you see, I have never given myself over to any bargain with a man such as this. I am a ser - vant of the Most High and must first go where duty calls and in whatever form, within the Providence of God."

Cassius Clay wielded his silver knobbed cane with kid - skin gloves that kept his white-clenched knuckles from view. "My dear Reverend Fee, you know there is none other I would be so inclined to consider to pastor a church here, on my prop - erty." He sighed. "But I know you are like Gibraltar, unmoving. I will go on now. Mayhap you will change your mind?" He studied the reverend, brows raised as if to force an affirmative answer.

John G. Fee stuck out his hand. "We will strike hands as faithful friends, Cassius, for today and tomorrow."

The Honorable Clay sighed and shook hands with his old-time friend, Fee. He looked up to notice H. Rawlings loiter - ing about. He was a rough sort of fellow, uncouth and coarse, who often came to meetings to linger about and make wise - cracks. But Clay never overlooked a political ally when they were a registered voter. "Ho there, Rawlings! You must per - suade our friend Fee here to consider my proposal as church pastor. I have only had a smattering of luck."

Hank Rawlings eyed the two men; one a dandy and the other a religious zealot. He stretched to his full height and took his time replying. Tobacco juice welled up in his cheek and he took a practiced aim toward the perimeter of dust near the two men's feet, imagining them as bull's-eyes. He swiped his red-flannelled arm against his mouth and grinned. He was in fine company, here in the arbor where John Fee held services for the mismatched lot of Kentuckians who assembled. Rawlings him - self was no believer, at least not as of yet. He came for the grub, *which the fine ladies set out after services.*

Abruptly, Rawlings' southern twang filled the air. "Use your noggin, preacher." Cassius Clay strode off in disgust.

Rev. Fee regarded the words of Rawlings with interest. "Speak on, man."

"I said you need to use your noggin, preacher. Clay's offering you a free home, on a good piece of ground. You gonna wait on God to speak, then you might be waiting 'til you're face to Face. Be a little too late then, preacher."

Rev. Fee silently studied Hank Rawlings. Then a slow smile tipped one side of his face. "Thank you for having my interests at heart. I'll consider your advice."

Rawlings turned carelessly and ambled away. Calling over his shoulder, he bequeathed more wisdom. "Surveyor is here, preacher. Could get you all fixed up."

"Rawlings!"

Hank paused and turned to face John Fee. "Yes, preacher?"

"You go and mark me off a spot."

*   *   *   *

John Fee rode his borrowed horse to the edge of Clay's land. Here was the plot surveyed for him and his family. The land was located at an extreme edge of Clay's six hundred acres.

John studied the piece of ground and his eyes fed his brain disappointment. No human habitation was visible. At the base of one acre of hillside, the ground was cleared as though a giant broom had swept the hill clean with vicious strokes. All around dense brush and undergrowth grew thick like moss on rocks. Waist high and sharp, bramble bushes were a lace upon the ground's rough shoulders. John's eyes popped. A mildewed, moldy pond adorned the plot. Noisy peepers and belching bull - frogs assaulted the air. Was this the spot that Providence had selected while he fulfilled his post of duty?

Voices drifted over the frogs' cadence to reach John's ears. He nudged his horse toward the sound, around the base of the rough hill to see two figures sitting on a fallen tree trunk amid the mottled ground.

"Howdy, preacher," Rawlings called out. The man beside him was clearly amused. Hank gestured a hand out over the land. "Nice little 'rosy' here, don't you think?"

John sat stiffly in the saddle. It took considerable restraint to calmly face Rawlings and his buddy. Honesty prevailed. "Well now. I think this is actually a dreary spot in which to bring a family, truth be told."

Silence reigned for a few moments. A bird's lone cry rose to mingle with frog-song. Then silence again, heavy like wet wood. Rawling's sarcastic twang broke the noiselessness, as he quoted, "'...prisons would palaces prove, if Jesus would dwell with me there.'"

John was familiar with the hymn in his little black hymnbook. Amazed that Rawlings would be able to quote this concept, much less think it, Fee sat quietly astride his mare.

Horse hooves beat the dusty ground and around the hillside rode a man. He tethered his beast on the fallen tree, beside which Hank and his cohort had settled.

He offered greeting and said, "Reverend Fee, the surveyor sent me out. Thought maybe you had a little work of which I could get started on." He held out his hand. "Stanton Thompson, sir."

John was aware of Hank and friend's smirk. "Very well, Mr. Thompson. Thank you. Take your axe and drive a stake by that little hickory and we will build a house there." He felt momentarily better, only to have his ambitions squelched when he realized that there was no fresh source of water.

"Mr. Thompson, halt there, please. I see an absence of water hereabout." Rev. Fee stroked his beard, discouraged. What of this predicament?

Silence again lay heavy on the air. And again, a familiar twangy drawl, in a grave tone, spoke aloud another goad. "Moses smote the rock and the waters gushed out."

John G. Fee narrowed his eyes at the heretic. Rawling's gray eyes gazed back, their light steady with mirth.

"Thompson!" Fee gestured wildly to his right where a little scrubby dogwood stood alone. "There yonder! Dig a well beside that tree."

Although swathed in unconsciousness, John recalled that the well was dug and water issued forth. A home was built and soon following, a schoolhouse, which doubled as a church. Berea had sprung from the dayspring on high, not to cease—a cruse that refused to go empty, much like John's ministry.

In John's comatose state, his hand moved across paper, writing to his beloved wife, telling her about the exciting events that were occurring.

Dear Matilda,
    Along with my deepest regards for your care and that of our family, I write to say we will soon be together. A house has been built on a piece of property that the Honorable Cassius M. Clay has donated for our use and that of the Most High. I hope you will find it suitable. I am most urgent for us to be reunited. Will send instructions presently. My fondest hopes are sent to you by post **until we meet again**
                    Bound through Christ,
                    Yours devotedly,
                    John

A small utterance, an exclamation, came from John's lips, and they were the last words Matilda would hear on this Earth from her husband of half a century. She rose unsteadily, causing the Bible on her lap to slip to the floor. She hastened to his side and clutched the fluttering hands, but John had slipped away. His garbled words had faded only into the passage of time now called the past.

Matilda squeezed the hands that had handled the affairs of the Gospel for many long years. Her tears descended upon John's peaceful form. She must tell the children and alert the world that it had just lost a paragon of true Biblical love, a mountain of wisdom, a warrior for righteousness, and a brother to all. *Until we meet again.*

The viewing line at the funeral stretched mightily like the Kentucky River through her native state. Mourners, black and white, rich and poor, came to pay their respects and homage to a beloved figure who had forced the progressive issue of "brotherly love", lending the precept a spirited vitality.

The hushed lull as the coffin was lowered into the gaping hole of brown earth conveyed the sorrow of this final act being done for the newly departed. The preacher's words filled in the spaces, but for Henry Allen Laine, his mind sought his own words to offer towards the great man they now laid to rest. He composed the lines as they took turns shoveling in the dirt that would blanket the body. The clods of ground landing atop the wood sounded loud to the mourners but in time, it would gratefully hug the dust that God, in His mercy, had dedicated back to Himself.

Berea's Founder And His Work

In every age there rises up a man,
God-fearing, firm, embodiment of truth,
Called, not his will, but God's alone to do,
Like ancient Samuel, summoned in his youth.
Howe'er corrupt the world may seem to grow,
Or swallowed up the hearts of men in sin,
Tho' doubts and error cast their blighting shades
Lo! Here and there Truth's light comes breaking in.

Falsehood and wrong may flourish for awhile,
Eternal Truth and Right forever stand,
Like beacon lights along some rocky shore,
To warn sea pilots of the wreck-strewn strand.
I've witnessed much so sublime, grand and good,

It stirred my soul; but the sublimest sight
Is to see a good man dare to stand alone,
Despised, and scorned, because he stands for right.

Aye, such a one I knew, a southern man,
Taught from his childhood no man had a right,
To membership in Man's great Brotherhood,
With rights full equal, save his face were white.
Reared in Kentucky 'mong his father's slaves,
With good Scotch-Irish coursing thru his veins,
With just enough of sturdy English mixed,
To give aggressive, strong, resourceful brains.

With tender heart, religious nature strong,
With firm convictions all men should be free,
To make of self all that is possible,
Such was Kentucky's hero, John G. Fee!
In early youth he gave his heart to God,
And placed his feet in that straight, narrow way,
That leads to Life Eternal and that Light
That shineth even to the Perfect Day.

His soul, heroic, scorned a life of ease,
But joined the ranks of that God-fearing few,
Who seek for Truth, content with nothing less,
And in God's grace, and knowledge daily grew.
He reads somewhere in the Good Book that God,
Created of one common blood all men,
If God made all of every shade and tongue,
He made the Negro, he's my brother, then.

Must I, because my brother, then, is black,
Deny to him, what for myself I claim—
Refinement, culture, bliss of happy home,
Full civil rights, and social rights the same?
These rights are due to every worthy man,
Who bears his full responsibility,

Of Public duty. Color should not count,
In boasted times of Christian Charity!

Is it man's color, or his character,
That's tested in God's balances above?
Is human hate the passport at the gate,
Or meekness, kindness, justice, faith and love?
The Negro simply claims to be a man,
No more, no less, with man's full rights implied,
God-given rights that bondage could not kill,
Nor will he aught with less be satisfied!

This good man saw the Negro's claim was just
And straight became his champion at the bar,
Public Opinion, drawing to himself,
Sharp criticism, near, and from afar.
But soon he found, what all wise men have found–
That words, mere words will never aught avail,
Unless supported by some worthy deed,
The bravest words must soon ignobly fail!

Ye Negro Leaders! Learn a lesson here,
Whose eloquence so charms the listening crowd,
Facts setting forth with wit and logic sound,
While answering plaudits, echo long and loud,
The man who something practical can do,
For the advancement of the human race,
To lesson pain, and happiness increase,
In human hearts will find a lasting place.

Our Christian hero, with unshaken faith,
In God's great love and simple justice saw,
That some men up and some forever down,
Illogical, contrary to God's law!
For lo! The treble curse that blights the land,
Is ignorance, and selfishness, and sin,
All evils that afflict the human race,

Traced back, we find, in that foul source begin!

His duty clear, he straight forsaking all,
Home, parents, friends, and childhood's happy
scenes,
And started out to preach impartial love,
Trusting in God for guidance and for means,
Like some frail bark that leaves the peaceful shore,
And ere her rigging drops from sight of land,
The rising storms arouse the threatening roar,
Of angry waves that dash on every hand.

So rose mob violence round the martyr, Fee,
And filled his strongest, bravest friends with fear.
But Providence provided some escape,
When personal harm and death itself seemed near!
But threats of mobs, nor sting of social scorn,
Nor the base failures of the cringing law,
Swerved him a hair-breadth to the right nor left,
Whenever he his duty clearly saw!

By Duty led to yonder dreary spot,
Where rugged hills and quarry low-lands meet,
A tangled thicket, full of stagnant pools,
For owls, and bats, and frogs, a safe retreat,
There built a church and next a village school,
To which he gave the fitting name Berea–
A Christian College in the reach of all,
Was started there upon its great career.

For forty years it placed in reach of all,
Christian instruction, turning none away,
Who sought for knowledge, culture, higher life,
The Cause of Christ promoting day by day,
How many youths, Berea, have reached success,
Their parts well acting in society,
Who trodden down by ruthless power of Fate,

Inspired to rise to honor and fame by thee?

Thy work was so beneficent and kind,
That Charity outstretched her generous hand,
To aid thy cause. And students white and black,
Flocked to thy halls from all parts of the land.
The mountains sent her sons and daughters down,
And sturdy youth came from the cultured North;
And youths and maidens "carved in ebony",
Swarmed to thy halls and proved an average worth.

And to Kentucky's honor be it said,
For thirty years she scorned to lay a straw,
To check thy progress, or embarrass thee,
By threat of base coercion, or by law!
And why she then, so quickly grew alarmed,
So frightened at the "social boogerboo",
Has puzzled me for, lo, these many days,
And doubtless, it has puzzled others too!

Much has been said and much more strong
believed,
Of plots, intrigues, and base ignoble schemes,
Laid hatched and brooded in those sacred halls,
To rob the Negro of his fondest dreams.
What e'er of truth, or falsehood of this charge,
Brought by both races, justly both complain,
One thing I know, the blacks were forced to go,
The whites, protesting, kindly bade remain.

Berea School-men, pleading innocence,
Say, why such haste to hurry plans along?
Ere that High Court the Day-law could decide
Your "jim crow" plans endorsed the Negro's wrong.
Almost three centuries this kindly race,
Thru hardships and thru troubles too, untold
Has come, rough ore thru hardship's furnace heat,

To shine forth yet, the Nation's purest gold!

Farewell Berea! The Negro looks to thee
For championship of equal rights no more;
Upon thy new found creed, the martyr, Fee,
Looks down, and weeps, from yonder better shore.
So long as in the Negro's feeling breast,
There beats a heart of love and loyalty,
Will Fee's great name, with Garrison's, Philips',
Stowe's,
Be ever held in grateful memory!

Henry Allen Laine's face softened. His pupils tried so hard to please him. As their teacher, he could not complain. Just now, Philip Baxter struggled to recite the Preamble of the Declaration of Independence, leaving out the valuable words of "the separate and equal station to which the Laws of Nature and of Nature's God entitle them". Yes, Teacher Laine had been a twelve-year-old boy once too. His desire to learn had made his studies easy but not everyone possessed the skill of memorization.

Philip finished and took his seat, a nervous glance shot towards his teacher where otherwise he was extremely interested in his scarred desktop.

Henry Allen waited patiently at the front of the room, with his well-disciplined class, until little master Baxter finally raised his eyes to his educator.

"Philip, how did you do?"

"I …I'm not sure, Mr. Laine." He looked painfully away. "I…I…Did I do alright?" His hopeful eyes waited on his teacher.

Henry Allen's detained smile spread slowly across his face. "Philip, you did admirably. But our founding fathers would want us to commit to memory the reasoning for our liberties. Practice this evening and you may recite it again

313

tomorrow."

Philip's expression hovered between relief and dismay over another recitation.

Henry Allen dismissed the class and watched his pupils file out of the room. He enjoyed teaching as much as learning. He felt a sadness to realize Berea was altering her course since the Day Law would soon control Kentucky's educational system. Any and all black schools would be exclusively black, and along with this went inferior textbooks and classroom helps. But not so with educators; Henry Allen would see to it that his students got the best education he could give them. Whatever the future held, Henry Allen hoped he would always be involved in education and that he might exercise it with a flowing pen of scholarly words.

Chapter Thirty

*"Walk in the light! Thy path shall be
Peaceful, serene, and bright;
For God, by grace, shall dwell in thee,
And God himself is Light."*

At the edge of the graveyard, a lone figure squatted at the foot of freshly mounded dirt. He had come to pay his respects and let his sorrow be visible, but in a secluded place where the only witnesses were the mourning doves who monotonously cried along with the bereaved.

After a brief stay, the figure, hunched in melancholy, made his way toward the entrance of the cemetery. His amble led him mistakenly into a woman, who likewise had her head down, unseeing, lost in her own thoughts.

Startled, Lucy looked up into a wrinkled face, lined with care and age. "Pardon me, sir," she exclaimed, clutching her reticule close to her chest.

The man was no less shocked and seemed unable to speak. Once his surprise evaporated, he managed to say, "Sorry, ma'am. I didn't see you."

"That's alright." Lucy relaxed at his polite words. "In a place like this, it may be a good sign. To see someone else, living, you know."

The man, a collection of sinew and muscle despite his age, rubbed his beefy arms. "That's right, a good thing, I reckon." He looked around at the unmarked mounds and the cheap wooden crosses of unpainted boards. "You got a loved one here, ma'am?" He hastened to add, "If you don't mind my asking." He cast dark looks around the cemetery.

"Well, yes. For now. My son is buried here, but we'll be taking him home before too long, I hope." Lucy carefully worded her next sentence. "You have someone here as well?"

315

"Just a friend, a good one. He...he was awful young to go on to Gloryland, you know. But...it shouldn't have happened, if I could have helped it."

Lucy felt a rush of sympathy for the older man who appeared to have a wedge of guilt upon him. "We often think if only we had done this or that, but it makes no difference in the end. Don't you think it's all in 'the handwriting on the wall', so to speak?"

The older man ceased rubbing his upper arms. He thought about Lucy's words. "Maybe."

Lucy continued, "I had to bury my son here. He worked on one of the boats on the river. He sure loved his job, but one day he never came home and then he was found floating in the river. His widow is having a hard time. And I'm struggling to make sense of it." Lucy shook her head. "It just isn't logical for Henry to have drowned."

The man's eyes grew large, and he began to glisten with an anxious sweat. He stammered, "Henry Ross was your son, ma'am?"

Lucy nodded. The old man swallowed hard and put his hands to his gray temples. "I just came here this eve to see him, ma'am. He was my friend on the boat. An awful good friend he was to me, too." He looked stricken.

Lucy also swallowed and blinked. "I don't understand what happened."

The dark skinned man let loose a rush of emotions, rearing free, like a runaway horse whose restraint had ended. "It shouldn't have happened! I should have stopped it. Poor Henry!" The old man's face crumpled.

Lucy could not stand for the old man to break down and cry. "Don't. It's alright. Whatever happened, you mustn't blame yourself. Henry wouldn't want it." She watched silently as he struggled to compose himself. "Who are you?"

"I'm Tom, ma'am. I was Henry's friend."

Lucy saw that the shadows had deepened and soon it would be dark. She spoke quickly, "Tom, if you can tell me what happened, it would ease my mind."

316

"Ease your mind?" Tom looked confused.

"Why, yes. I'd rather know what happened than to keep guessing," Lucy said. She felt a surge of hope and expectancy.

Tom looked her in the eyes and was silent. His own dark ones had a distant look, which troubled Lucy. What was Tom going to say?

Tom saw the tides of time adrift in Lucy's eyes. There in the brown pools was a harsh overseer who laughed over a woman and child's demise. Not just any slave woman and babe, but Tom's very own. How often Tom had wished he never knew the end. The torment had haunted him, more so because of the cruelty hedged about it. The hurt had no end, nor would it ever, and forgiveness eluded his heart. He would lay no such burden upon another soul.

"Your Henry was a sleepwalker, ma'am. Right? Did you know he was? I think he thought he was at home, he did. He just sleepwalked right off the boat. If only I could have woke up and saved him. Right off the boat he fell, and he just kept on sleeping. He worked so hard during his shift, ma'am. He was always so tired at night." Tom hung his head, remorse heavy upon his shoulders.

Lucy touched his arm, her surprise masked. "Mr. Tom, thank you. His widow and family will rest easier, knowing. It was a peaceful ending for such a good man." She strained for control.

Tom gripped her hand and squeezed it. "A real good man. You always have that comfort."

Lucy regretfully left the pauper's section of the cemetery and started homeward to Sallie's without having visited Henry's plot. She would repeat to the family what the boiler man had said. Pulling a handkerchief from her reticule, she covered her moist eyes. The others did not need to know what she had witnessed at the morgue. For them, Henry's end would be tranquil.

Old Tom, also, turned toward the entrance gate. He paused and leaned against the stone columns, watching Lucy's form disappear into the shadowy distance. His breath came

317

heavy with the force of a mental agony driven outward. The deep cavity that stored his anguish now leaked freely for all the unjust suffering in this world. The brutal loss of his friend pierced his being. Tom's shoulders shook convulsively as he slid to the ground, overcome with grief. The evening moon, new and pristine, began its ascent. It perched in silent sympathy to the greeting of old Tom's sobs.

*   *   *   *

Lucy patted the last of the dirt around the stem of the newly planted lilac tree. Leaning back on her bended knees to rest on her heels, she ignored the grimace her body gave her. *There!* This little tree was planted in front of her little house where she now lived in town. Lucy had always wanted a white lilac; it was a small piece of sentimentality. Lilacs were beautiful and fragrant but also hardy survivors. She had had lavender ones, but she wanted one with white blossoms representing a kind of peace. This is what she wanted to remind herself of, every time she gazed on it or smelled its scent. Lucy needed to admonish herself to strive to feel amicable with the world, with the past, and mainly with her God.

She went into the kitchen and pumped water on her hands, watching the crumbling dirt wash from her skin. Yes, water was indeed a refresher. Lucy took a metal cup and caught a stream of water in it. The cold drink was satisfying after her warm morning outside.

Lucy's eyes rose to the calendar hanging above the pump and enameled sink. She put her cup down on the counter and studied the page. Lindeman's Hardware proclaimed its excellent service and merchandise as an advertising stint while below the words were pictured a red rowboat on a blue pond. Lush greenery encircled the year–1904. Lucy's gaze was pinned to it. It said many things without speaking. Mainly it verbalized the fact that Lucy was now fifty-nine years old. She had been alone for nine years, a facaded widow, she called herself. Now she lived in town and had created a life for herself. When any worry or discontentment arose, Lucy strove to root herself in her blessings. She had learned, by 1904, that like her tender lilac, she could only grow positively in good soil.

There were many pleasant things in her life. She had her family close by, John and Cynthia with their three little girls, Esther, Ethel, and Nellie. John was now the minister of the Loveland Predestinarian Baptist Church, and Lucy enjoyed taking a large part in the affairs of the church. She was one of the older matrons and gave her advice on the social gatherings and fundraisers.

Loveland was a nice town, and she was glad they had settled there. Lucy's boys all had stable jobs and were on their own. She had a dear friend, Harriet Shearer, who had come to fill a void in her life. Harriet's friendship was prized more each passing year by Lucy as it vied to replace her missing Narciss.

The two women shared similar circumstances. Harriet had been a slave too, and came from Madison County, the location of Lucy's early years. She was the daughter of a white man who could sell her if he wished–a father who felt no affection or claim towards his own offspring. When slavery had ended, Harriet had come north to Loveland where other clans of relatives had emigrated.

Interestingly, Harriet had told Lucy that her mother had been named Margaret Ross. Lucy, always quick to recover, had smiled. "So maybe we're related, Harriet? Wouldn't that be something?" Later, Lucy took this piece of information and let herself think on it. Harriet could probably and very likely be related to Allen. If he were still with Lucy, how would he react? Would he search for a connection? It brought the reality of Allen's departure vivid once more, and Lucy felt the hurt and sadness again.

For nine years she had been on her own and managed well. Somehow, by a mysterious means, the farm had gotten paid, and she brought in the money she needed to live on. Of course the boys had helped. Lucy had no inkling where Allen might be or if he was still alive. Her anger at him had cooled, a lot like the plates of the Earth. The deep core, far beneath the surface, existed as a ball of heat, but it hardly ever reached the uppermost levels. This was how Lucy could move on and live each day, by ignoring the buried fire and hurt.

Why Allen would leave his children puzzled her. She mourned for the children having missed out on a father, and all the time that was forever lost. These disappointments in life, along with the loss of Rev. Fee, were something she worked hard to keep at bay.

When the news came that Berea was being dissolved from the school it was intended to be, Lucy could have wept. It was another setback for her people. Carl Day had pushed a law through Congress and it was warring through the courts to end any integration of schooling between blacks and whites. Across Kentucky, segregation was being finalized by destroying the one place where equality had existed.

Undaunted, black schools were springing up like clover among crabgrass to fill the demand for black education. Black citizens would not be denied an education, their ticket on the road to freedom.

John G. Fee's work had come to an end in the state of Kentucky. How irritating that something so precious was being discarded by the white folks. It reminded her of a big dog who possessed a juicy bone and saw the small dog with a scrap of hide. Unable to bear seeing the little fellow with anything at all, the big dog took it away, unmindful of the small dog's loss.

One Sunday in September, Lucy settled on the bench in church feeling tired and almost dispirited. How good to be in this sanctuary of God, close to Him, when she needed it most. Harriet Shearer arrived and scooted down the bench to sit beside Lucy. The two women exchanged warm smiles as the Rev. Charlie Price stood up in front and a deacon opened with a hymn.

"Walk In The Light" vibrated the walls of the church and Lucy closed her eyes as the words slipped out of her mouth effortlessly. When she sang these words, it seemed simple and easy to follow them. Rev. Charlie Price greeted the members and continued the thought with scripture from 1 John 1:5, "My beloved brethren and sisters, hear ye this! 'This is the message which we have heard of him, and declare unto you, that God is light, and in him is no darkness at all.

'If we say that we have fellowship with him, and walk in darkness, we lie, and do not the truth:

'But if we walk in the light, as he is in the light, we have fellowship one with another, and the blood of Jesus Christ his Son cleanseth us from all sin.'

"Why, brothers and sisters, do we want to walk in the light? Any little child here could tell you the answer to that! Because darkness is scary. It's a frightening thing to all of us, when we can't see our way. It's also not in accordance with God and His ways. His ways are truthful and we all know that the truth is light. Truth has no dark side, but lies are all dark. More importantly, this light we want to cling to and follow and be a part of gives us a fellowship, a connection to our Lord and each other. Where would we be without it? We would be lost and cast into an outer darkness where there would be no return."

Lucy let her eyes lift from Rev. Price to the windows where snatches of the sunny world lay. Strangely, her mind felt her heart beat out the words. *Oh, Lord, I need thy guidance like never before! The Lord is my shepherd; I shall not want...* No, Lucy had no reason to want what the Lord had not given her. *I know it's for my best. Maybe if Allen had stayed, something worse might have occurred. Something in which I could no longer walk in the light.*

Now John Hannon was speaking, following up the Rev. Price's words. Lucy admired her son-in-law as he stood up in front of the congregation. He was already an Elder in the church and at such a young age. He was so distinguished and calm, speaking with quiet authority. Lucy believed it was because he tried truthfully to be a servant of the Lord. "My dear fellow believers in the name of Christ, I greet you this morning in Christian love. It has been on my mind very much this little while about the affairs of the nation and our place in it as Christians. You're all aware of the Day Law and its impact on our beloved school of Berea. While this seems a huge turmoil to us, we must realize God has a plan. Just like the Hebrew children stuck in Egypt, God had a plan for their deliverance. Though we are no longer under the rule of slavery, we see that the story of the Israelites doesn't end there. No, we have more in the works for us. But, as in all things, it will be in God's good time, not our own.

"I like to think one day we will all commune together, if not in physical proximity, in a larger sense, where each of us is respected, no matter our color. Maybe someday men will attempt to look only upon the heart."

John paused and thumbed his Bible absently, thinking about his words. He looked up and his eyes locked on his wife, Cynthia. "It will probably be too much to hope for but maybe we can dream of it. The Bible tells us of many dreams and their fruition. We know only God can see our innermost heart but what if we all 'walked in the light' and just by looking at one another, we could tell what another's heart was full of by the aura we possessed? It's a fanciful thought, but one I do dream and hope can happen. The Lord's spirit cannot be hidden, and we read that we must let our light so shine before men, giving glory unto our Father."

Lucy's thoughts soared through her life and stopped where she was now. Her need for grace was apparent, since Lucy knew she burned with cinders of anger and bitterness toward Allen for leaving her. *Oh, Allen, I could almost forgive you, if only you hadn't left me for someone else...* Lucy swallowed painfully. It seemed nearly impossible to burst out of the cocoon of hidden hurt she had wrapped around her feelings towards Allen. *If this keeps me from the Light, what am I to do?* Lucy made a desperate plea.

Rev. Hannon smiled at the believers before him and read out of 2 John. "'Again, a new commandment I write unto you, which thing is true in him and in you; because the darkness is past, and the true light now shineth. He that saith he is in the light, and hateth his brother, is in darkness even now. He that loveth his brother abideth in the light, and there is none occasion of stumbling in him.'"

John spoke, "We hear it plainly. The instruction here comes from God's mouth and there can be no argument with it. Further on, we read 'Beloved, let us love one another; for love is of God; and every one that loveth is born of God, and knoweth God.

'He that loveth not knoweth not God; for God is love.

'In this was manifested the love of God toward us, because that God sent his only begotten Son into the world, that we might live through him.

'Herein is love, not that we loved God, but that he loved us, and sent his Son to be a propitiation for our sins.

'Beloved, if God so loved us, we ought also to love one another.'"

Lucy opened her eyes to the room. It seemed to glow brighter. A clear, sunshiny hue cast the members in a pleasant glow to Lucy's eyes. She blinked and looked at Harriet. She looked more vibrant to Lucy, her blue hat more cerulean and her pale dress a glowing white. Rev. John looked rich in his suit of black while the paneled wood shone like someone had taken lemon oil to it. Lucy smiled, not sure why she felt so alive and happy when earlier she had been feeling dismal. *What is this, Lord? Are you telling me something?* If so, Lucy heard nothing, only saw everything through a set of happy eyes, if there was such a thing. The world looked so beautiful to Lucy from where she sat. She wished she could cling to this brightness that suddenly surrounded her.

Lucy knew directly the future held hope, for herself and for her people. And for all people–God had made of one blood all peoples of the Earth. Whether the Day Law controlled the land, God still controlled the world, His realm beyond earth and sky. *Allen, I will work on forgiving you and wish you the best wherever you are. Lord, good men can turn bad and bad men can turn good, but your great and precious promises endure for - ever, thanks to your Son.*

John Hannon's vibrant voice encouraged Lucy as he spoke, "Let us now sing this new hymn that embodies the truths we wish to embrace. It's called 'Lift Every Voice And Sing'. A

Mr. James Weldon Johnson first wrote this as a poem and then his brother, Mr. John Rosamond Johnson set it to music. Our deacon will get us started. And while we sing, let us be full of hope and dreams for our young towards the future, because...we have no reason to be otherwise."

Lift every voice and sing,
'Til earth and heaven ring,
Ring with the harmonies of Liberty;
Let our rejoicing rise
High as the listening skies,
Let it resound loud as the rolling sea.
Sing a song full of the faith that the dark past
has taught us,
Sing a song full of the hope that the present has
brought us;
Facing the rising sun of our new day begun,
Let us march on 'til victory is won.

Stony the road we trod,
Bitter the chast'ning rod,
Felt in the days when hope unborn had died;
Yet with a steady beat,
Have not our weary feet
Come to the place for which our fathers sighed?
We have come over a way that with tears has
been watered,
We have come, treading our path through the
blood of the slaughtered,
Out from the gloomy past,
Til now we stand at last
Where the white gleam of our bright star is
cast.

God of our weary years,
God of our silent tears,
Thou who has brought us thus far on the way;

Thou who has by Thy might
Led us into the light,
Keep us forever in the path, we pray.
Lest our feet stray from places, our God, where
we met Thee,
Lest, our hearts drunk with the wine of the
world, we forget Thee;
Shadowed beneath Thy hand,
May we forever stand,
True to our God,
True to our native land.

Lucy let the melody ripple through her. It tickled an unexplainable ray of joy and lightness within her, a passionate urge to *do* and *be* good. Tomorrow Lucy would rise and face the sun of a new day. And she would walk in the offered light, *between two suns*.

RIG_{in}HT

Recognizing

Individual

Greatness

Historical

Testament

This concept embodies the concern over the historical bias in naming patterns and the contemporary artificial barriers limiting the expansion of ownership identity to public properties, and thus further imposing limitations upon those individuals belonging to groups that had traditionally been denied consideration. **RIGHT** seeks to re-evaluate the standards of heroism and societal acceptance of those who may have been deemed not to be valued or worthy of having their names adorn public facilities. **RIGHT** advocates a proactive effort in naming public properties that is more reflective of the diversity within the community and that acknowledges from a historical perspective the merit of greater inclusion with regards to race, gender, ethnic and national origin in expanding *ownership identity*.

Berea College on October 8th of 2009 honored the noted Madison County, KY educator, poet and Berea alumnus Henry Allen Laine. Mr. Laine attended Berea between the years 1889 to 1897. While at Berea he distinguished himself as a noted writer and poet and sharpened his skills as a member of Phi Delta Literary Society. We believe that Mr. Laine possessed the kind of character, notoriety and public service that in retrospect should have resulted in ownership identity during his life as well as in contemporary times. Mr. Laine wrote:

The kind of man for me is one,
Who seeks no praise for what he's done;
Who labors not for man's applause,
But gets his share of praise because,
With an honest heart for right strives he,
And that's the kind of man for me...

His poem "My Kind of Man" serves as a testament to the RIGHT model of greatness.

His book of poems titled **FOOT PRINTS** initially appeared in 1924 and is accessible on the internet at Kentuckiana Digital Library:
http://kdl.kyvl.org/cgi/t/text/textidx?c=kyetexts;cc=kyetexts;xc=1&idno=b0 2-000000017&view=toc

Henry Allen Laine was also inducted into the Kentucky Civil Rights Hall of Fame in 2003.

Henry Allen Laine

Henry Allen Laine posthumously, received the
John G. Fee Founder's Day Award on October 8, 2009.

To Bereans everywhere who will study and do the RIGHT thing.